"SHE COULD HAVE BEEN THE BLOND-HAIRED, BLUE-EYED SCANDINAVIAN GODDESS OF HIS DREAMS. IF HE THREW HER DOWN ON THE GRASSY KNOLL IN FRONT OF THE CATHEDRAL AT HIGH NOON, PUSHED HER TIGHT SKIRT UP OVER HER SUMPTUOUS HIPS, YANKED HER PRETTY PINK PANTIES DOWN TO HER HEELS. . . . IT WOULD BE OKAY . . . IF HE WERE A GANGSTER."

If Grover Mudd wanted to change that, he'd have to go up against a drug king named Dag Rankin. He could also deal with a ravishing moll called Roxanne who would do anything for her next opium dream. But either one could make him a dead man.

SAINT MUDD

A Novel of Gangsters and Saints

by

Steve Thayer

A SIGNET BOOK

SIGNET
Published by New American Library, a division of
Penguin Putnam Inc., 375 Hudson Street,
New York, New York 10014, U.S.A.
Penguin Books Ltd, 80 Strand,
London WC2R 0RL, England
Penguin Books Australia Ltd, Ringwood,
Victoria, Australia
Penguin Books Canada Ltd, 10 Alcorn Avenue,
Toronto, Ontario, Canada M4V 3B2
Penguin Books (N.Z.) Ltd, 182–190 Wairau Road,
Auckland 10, New Zealand

Penguin Books Ltd, Registered Offices:
Harmondsworth, Middlesex, England

Published by Signet, an imprint of New American Library, a division of Penguin
Putnam Inc. Previously published in a Viking edition. Originally published in
different form by Birchwood Page Publishing.

First Signet Printing, February 1994
15 14 13 12 11 10 9 8

 REGISTERED TRADEMARK—MARCA REGISTRADA

Printed in the United States of America

PUBLISHER'S NOTE
This is a work of fiction. Names, characters, places, and incidents either are
the product of the author's imagination or are used fictitiously, and any
resemblance to actual persons, living or dead, business establishments, events,
or locales is entirely coincidental.

For the late Ollie Bakken
and all those who grew up
with him on St. Paul's East Side

Saint Prologue

When the boy and his feebleminded twin brother started down the narrow passage that morning it seemed to be just another cave, no different from a score of other caves that ran under the cliffs, caves that were explored by every adventurous kid in the city. They would not have ventured in at all, except they were playing on the railroad tracks along the river and stole a lantern off a caboose. When the harbor patrolman chased them they scrambled up a bluff and hid in the thick brush between two trees. The boys got wet. Running under them was a stream of ice-cold water. In the steamy August heat it tasted heaven-sent. The harbor patrolman passed them by.

They followed the stream through the brush to a slit in the cliff and slithered through on their bellies. No pop bottles littered the entrance, no tin cans or coals from dead campfires. The mouth of the cave was so well disguised by nature it could only be found by accident.

The boy pushed the lantern in front of him, and his simple brother quietly crawled along behind. Often more of a shadow than a brother, he had been silently tagging along since the day he was born with the wrong number of chromosomes.

It was damp and cool. The sand was soft and gutted down the middle, as if a steamroller had preceded them. Suddenly, the ceiling expanded and rose to a capacious dome of unimagined height. The boy stood and held up the light. Before him was a magnificent lake, with water so clear he could count the pebbles on the bottom. "Wow!" he exclaimed, and his echo reverberated through the cavern like a roaring locomotive that shook the walls to the point of collapse.

At the shore of the lake was a beach of the finest, whitest sand he had ever seen. They jumped into the sand and tossed it into the air. The sugary grains snowed down upon their red heads.

His dumb brother spotted the wood crates first, stacked at the edge of the shore, like freight for a boat. The boy held up the lantern and read the writing stamped on the sides: ST. PAUL FRUIT CO. The lid of the top crate was loose, and he watched his brother wiggle his hand under a slat and snap it open. The crack of the wood shot through the cave. Then the boy with the silent grin held the fruit in his hand. It was round like a baseball, only bigger, wrapped in green paper like medicine from a drugstore. He tore away the wrapping. It was an ugly fruit, with the hard skin of a dead plant. He split the skin with his fingers and found a ball of black powder. He squeezed it. It broke to dust. He licked his fingers and his face soured.

The boy left his simpleminded brother to play with the black dusty fruit while he explored the edges with the hijacked lantern. He found strange writing on the walls, and a crude carving of a serpent among initials and dates from a time long ago. The light was not strong but the cave seemed endless, a cavernous museum of gloomy splendor. He did not know it, but they had unlocked the best-kept secret on the upper Mississippi. Then it was over. Splendor to horror.

The boy heard a guttural groan, a woeful gasp. He turned to see his brother hoisted through the blackness. His eyes were bulging, silently screaming for help. Blood spat out of his nose. His bones snapped like twigs, and he fell to the sand like a rag doll—the life squeezed out of his neck.

The boy dropped the lantern while his own cry for help bellowed mockingly through the deep chambers and came back to chase him. He jumped into the entrance shaft like an animal, on all fours, his hands clawing the sand, his knees tearing through his knickers. It was as dark as dark can get, and he was as frightened as a boy can be without losing consciousness. The passage was too shallow to stand in. He bruised his head on the soft stone. His naked shoulders scraped the walls. But he kept crawling. Crawled for his life; crawled through the dark, through the rock and over the sand. He bounced off stubby columns and rolled from wall to wall. He tore his filthy undershirt as he frantically felt his way along. He scraped his knuckles and jammed his fingers. *It* was after him. He could feel it on his heels. Its devil's breath shot over the back of his neck. Sand sprayed his face, clogged his nostrils, and bled through his mouth. He was choking. He saw a speck of light.

They had been told to stay away from the tracks, there were hoboes down there. Now his idiot brother was dead. God, the boy wanted to tell his brother how much he loved him, and he wanted to say he was sorry for the cruel tricks he and his friends had played on him, for all the days they had ditched him and left him behind. He raced through the passage in terror, sick in the belief that he had ditched his brother one last time.

The twilight was a full circle now, and the boy screamed a merciful prayer at the ray of sun as he shouted to be free. But it was not to be. The unholy force crushed his legs and gripped his ankles so hard they broke. He never stopped crawling, never stopped wailing, but from the moment he was caught he sank rapidly, dragged back through the sand away from the light, away from life, back into the abyss, where he joined his brother in death.

But, of all the Midwest cities, the one that I knew best was St. Paul, and it was a crook's haven. Every criminal of any importance in the 1930s made his home at one time or another in St. Paul. If you were looking for a guy you hadn't seen in a few months, you usually thought of two places—prison or St. Paul. If he wasn't locked up in one, he was probably hanging out in the other.

—**Alvin Karpis, Public Enemy #1**
The Alvin Karpis Story **(1971)**

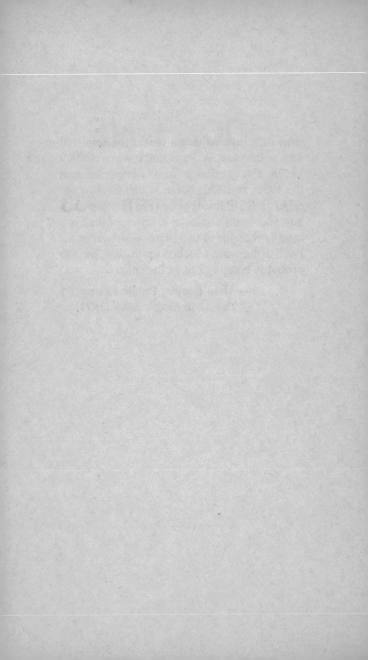

BOOK ONE

Summer Autumn 1933

Saint Grover

In St. Paul, gangsters can fuck in the street. The average, everyday, law-abiding citizen can't, but gangsters can. If you have a hankering for guns, laundered money, fast cars, faster women, moonshine, dope, prostitution, protection, gambling, and a theater of changing seasons, come to St. Paul, Minnesota. Nestled above and behind a sweep of high, white sandstone bluffs on the Mississippi River is a magical little city where you can fuck right in the street. You can take the blond-haired, blue-eyed Scandinavian goddess of your dreams, throw her down on the grassy knoll in front of the cathedral at high noon, push her tight skirt up over her sumptuous hips, yank her pretty pink panties down to her heels and slide right in there. And if a policeman should happen along while you're banging away and yell, "Hey, you can't do that out here in front of the cathedral," not to worry.

Between the moaning and groaning you just say, "It's okay, Officer. My name's Buggs Palooka. From Chicago. I used to be with Capone."

"Have you checked in at the Hollyhocks Club, Mr. Palooka?"

"Of course I have, I know the rules," you impatiently grunt out, thrusting deeper and deeper, barely able to breathe.

Three hundred feet below the cross atop the grand dome, St. Paul's finest avoids the creamy white legs kicking high in the air and paws through the trousers wrapped around your ankles until he finds your wallet.

"I got a wad of fins in there," you inform him, rising to ecstasy. "Take two, they're small."

The cop shoves ten bucks in his pocket.

Then, as the palms of your hands melt into her ass and your tongue becomes her tongue and you explode into orgasm at the sound of the church bells, John Law will say, "Thank you for visiting St. Paul, Mr. Palooka. Come again." That's what gangsters can do in St. Paul.

Grover Mudd turned away from the window, away from the massive parade passing through the streets below. He tossed his column for the next day on the desk and slouched down in his swivel chair. The dirty brown leather was cracked at the seat and back; the stuffing of the armrest was taped in. It was hot. His suspenders were sweating through his white shirt at the shoulders. His tie was off. The heat wave was into its sixth week; the crime wave was into its seventh year.

Grover worried he was becoming some kind of sex fiend, a middle-aged maniac. It seemed the older he got the more he thought about it. Did it have anything to do with love? He did not think so. Sex was easy enough to come by in this lecherous town, but love? A college boy's crush and a soldier's overwrought memory carried him into marriage, two children, a house, and a divorce, but not much love. The lousy bitch.

Grover jerked his hand to his mouth and coughed, coughed until his eyes watered. It was a hacking cough, with nails that tore deep in his chest. He wrote it off as a summer cold brought on by the heat. Earlier in the year he had written it off as a spring cold brought on by the rain. Grover had a lie for every season. He reached for his Lucky Strikes, lit up, and looked out at the newsroom. It was all but empty. What few workers were left behind hung out the upper windows, taking in the spectacle. Fuzzy Byron, nearly blind, was aiming a camera down at a crowd he probably couldn't even see. The rest of the staff, those who had escaped the

layoffs, were marching in the parade, dressed in white
with black trim to symbolize the *Frontier News*. Every
business in the city had locked its doors early that afternoon so employees could stomp through the downtown
streets behind the giant blue-eagle emblem of the National Recovery Administration.

From his closet-size corner Grover Mudd could see
the entire news-gathering operation, including Walt
Howard's comfortable office across the way. The editor
joked that Grover was supposed to keep an eye on him,
but Grover knew damn well who was keeping an eye
on who. He also knew that if the merger with the daily
across the street went through, "Grover's Corner"
would not be a part of it. Grover's office did not amount
to much: a partition half of plaster, half of glass; a
doorway with no door; a carved-up desk that must have
been built in because it was too big to get out; and a
file cabinet he was afraid to open. Back copies of the
St. Paul Frontier News were stacked on everything.
Crumpled typing paper carpeted the floor. The latest
edition of the *St. Paul North Star Press* was stuffed in
the wastebasket. He brought a new plant to work every
month to replace the one that died. It took up one
corner. Stormy told him the plants could live for years,
but they died. A dangerous-looking fan with a frayed
cord and rusty blades sat atop a stack of newspapers in
another corner, blowing the sultry air around.

Tacked to a wall of faded blue, peeling paint above
the desk were his paper memorabilia: bills he refused
to pay, WANTED posters, facts on crime, articles on
gangsters, his favorite name-calling letters, his favorite
death threats, and some excellent Walt Howard editorials. Hanging in the middle of this scrap was a Christmas card from Scott and Zelda. It was seven years old
and yellowing, the last one they sent him. Had Zelda
really cracked up? Was Scott a lush? Would he ever
see those beautiful fools again?

They grew up on the sidelines of St. Paul's finest

neighborhood, Summit Avenue, and went to school together at Saint Paul Academy before Francis Scott Key Fitzgerald was sent east for a better education. Rags-to-rags Mudd struggled through prep school and spent his three years at the University of Minnesota studying the fine points of Golden Gopher football and a touch of English. Grover played, Daddy paid. It wasn't that Grover was from the wrong side of the tracks; Grover Mudd *was* the tracks. His father spent a lifetime at the railroad to see that his boy got a decent education. And while Grover's friend Scott found in the East the success he wanted, he missed out on the once-in-a-lifetime experience he longed for, the best experience a writer can have. War.

But Grover Mudd was there. It was the one credential he held over the Great Fitzgerald—he had been to war, though his writings on the subject were prosaic and poorly received. He had to admit the literary world would be far better off if F. Scott Fitzgerald had been the St. Paul boy who saw France from the trenches. Then, too, Fitzgerald could have the dreams that came home with the experience.

Don't run, Grover

Grover blew smoke at the ceiling and breathed a sigh of relief. The dreams did not come anymore.

When Roxanne Schultz was nine years old her father was tarred and feathered and run out of the county over the rails, the atrocity committed because he was a German immigrant and a member of the Nonpartisan League who spoke out in favor of land reform and economic democracy for farmers. Socialism flirting with communism.

They were living in a small farmhouse near St. Cloud, Minnesota. The family was sitting down to dinner one evening when the screen door was torn from the hinges and five of their neighbors burst into the kitchen. Rox-

anne was knocked to the floor along with her potato
stew and glass of water. She heard her father screaming,
"One at a time. Try me one at a time."

The intruders were yelling stuff like "Goddamn
kaiser-lover" and "German scum." They did not know,
and did not care, that the man they were wrestling from
the house had a son serving in America's elite Rainbow
Division, a master sergeant in Minnesota's 151st Field
Artillery Regiment, which was fighting its way through
Europe one yard at a time.

Roxanne's mother grabbed her hand, pulled her to
her feet, and hurried her through the broken door.
Outside, her father had his hands tied behind his back,
with a rope around his neck by which he was being led,
sometimes dragged, down the dirt road that led to the
railroad tracks.

It was a hot and muggy summer night of the kind
when the sun burns until late and the mosquitoes are
thicker than dark. The sky was orange. Tears were
streaming down her mother's face. Roxanne did not
remember her own tears; she only remembered the
terror, repeating "Daddy" over and over again as they
ran down the road after him. They stayed a stone's
throw behind the sordid parade. In his broken English
her father kept shouting over his shoulder, "Go back
home. Take Roxy and go back home." But they never
went back to the farmhouse. They followed their man
to a clearing by the tracks where more men and a bucket
of hot tar were waiting for him.

Roxanne and her mother leaned against a tree and
cried for help. Her father was stripped naked, thrown
to the ground, and beaten. Between the kicking and
stomping he pleaded to the sky, "Bitte, Gott, nicht
vor meinen Frauen. Please, God, not in front of my
women."

Her mother held her close and tried to cover Roxanne's eyes but she witnessed everything. She saw two
men urinate on her father's head. She watched others

dip sticks into the potbelly bucket and coat his skin black. She stared bewildered as they sprinkled blood-stained feathers over his prostrate body. They laid a splintered railroad tie across his shoulders and strapped his arms to it. Then he was stood up and pushed through the thick foliage and over the sharp cinders to the tracks. To nine-year-old Roxanne he looked like the pictures on the Sunday school walls, his arms forming a cross, the blood and sweat trickling down his face, his sad eyes begging for help, knowing there was no help. Then Roxanne and her mother were off running again, carrying his clothes in their arms.

The St. Cloud dirt farmer was chased down the tracks with sticks thrashing his buttocks until they bled. This went on for a half-mile before he finally collapsed.

"We're across the line," one of the men declared. "Don't ever come back to Stearns County, sauerkraut." For their part the atrocity was over. They walked away.

Mother and daughter helped their man to the edge of a swampy lake and tried their best to clean him up. They dressed him in his underwear as he lay on the soggy bank, crying, blood running out of one nostril, snot out of the other. Large black flies buzzed about his wounds. It was the first time Roxanne had seen a grown man cry.

They made their way to St. Paul, where they were known as the Smiths, and they moved into a smoke-encrusted shack in a shantytown called Swede Hollow, a low-rent, no-rent, deep and narrow ravine that sat in the shadow of Hamm's Brewery, a mile-long slum for poverty-stricken immigrants, a filthy community where outhouses were built on stilts over Phalen Creek and people emptied themselves in the swift water that ran to the river. Her father, a broken man, never spoke out again, and he never saw his son return from the war. After several months in the hollow he hanged himself on the back porch. He was buried in a pauper's grave with the tar stains still on his body.

Roxanne's brother did come home, but he was forced to move to Arizona. Two years later he died, when the mustard gas ate through his lungs.

Grover Mudd wiped the perspiration from his receding hairline and shoved the large red engineer's handkerchief back in his pocket. Ninety-eight degrees was what he had heard last, five degrees cooler than the day before. The long sleeves of his shirt were rolled up over his elbows. Turning a deaf ear to the noisy parade outside, he picked up his column again and read.

O'CONNOR MUG ON NEW CITY HALL
by Grover Mudd

I stood in front of the Fourth Street entrance, dumbfounded. I could not believe it. But there it was, one of the best-kept secrets about our new St. Paul City Hall and Ramsey County Courthouse. Carved in stone above the doorway is the mug of the late Richard T. O'Connor, alias the Cardinal, onetime czar of St. Paul politics and co-founder of that curse known as the O'Connor System.

The four-foot-high placard is a portrait of civic responsibility cast in rosetta black granite. On the far right corner is a policeman with a whistle in his mouth guiding children across a street. Behind the policeman and to his left is unmistakably the profile of O'Connor. Oh, yes, they tried to make it look like a blind man, but we know it's the Cardinal, who was one of the Big Four in national Democratic party circles and a close friend of President Cleveland. It's all there, the hat, the cane, that big rear end, etched in stone for the next hundred years.

I immediately searched the building to see if I could find some remembrance of the Cardinal's older brother, John J. O'Connor, alias the Big Fellow. I studied the giant murals. I examined artwork cast in bronze on the elevator doors. I inspected knotholes in the rare woods. I even ran my fingers across the tiles in the lavatories. But, alas, there was not a likeness to be found of the old police chief, that local legend who patriotically left this world nine years ago, on the Fourth of July.

It hardly seems fair that King Richard got his mug engraved on our new City Hall, but not King John. After all, they were equally responsible for what our city is today. At the turn of the century the Big Fellow put out the word: St. Paul is a "safe city" for gangsters. Only three rules. Check in with Dapper Danny Hogan at his place on Wabasha Street. Spend money. And all crimes are to be committed outside the city limits. The Cardinal handled the political end of things. No Democrat held office without his say-so. Now if that's not fifty-fifty, what is?

And what of poor Dapper Danny, who stepped on the starter of his shiny new Chrysler one morning back in '28 and was blown to smithereens? Where's his memorial? If I were his family I'd be at the next City Council meeting demanding a monument.

Our only comfort is the fact that these three outstanding St. Paulites, O'Connor, O'Connor, and Hogan, are once again united. And as hot as it is here, it's a lot hotter where they are.

Grover laid his writing on the desk; if he wanted to read it again he knew where to find it. "Grover's Corner" appeared five times a week on the penultimate page, right next to "Sister Ruth's Kitchen," with her recipes and menus for a hungry world. The O'Connor System was still intact, but the rules of sanctuary were no longer obeyed, and there were no Cardinals or Big Fellows to enforce them. How many unsolved murders had there been since '25? How many robberies, shootouts, kidnappings, hit-and-runs? Grover had lost count, and he was one of the few keeping count. Now two children were missing.

St. Paul's pugnacious columnist pulled a bottle and glass from the top drawer of his desk. He poured himself a shot of Stearns County 13 and walked back to the window. The parade was going strong. The men who led the array, Governor Olson and Mayor Mahoney, had passed below two hours ago, but the waves of marching people still seemed endless. There were over four thousand firms taking part in St. Paul's show of support for the NRA. The Twin City Rapid Transit Company was the area's largest employer, and their line of clanging trolleys was strung out for three blocks and surrounded by thousands of transit workers. Clip-clopping after the streetcars were the retired Hamm's Beer trucks, pulled by four-horse hitches of huge Percherons with grizzly dappled coats, a nostalgic touch from the brewery, which had been booming since beer was made legal again back in April. Stepping lively around the horse manure behind the beer trucks was Otto's Little German Band. They were playing a hasty march, a song a young marine lieutenant had first heard in Europe years ago. The musical memory put a lump in Grover Mudd's throat and he looked away.

From his third-floor window he could look up to Kellogg Boulevard and see the newly completed and much touted St. Paul City Hall and Ramsey County Courthouse he so often lambasted in print. It stood tall over the Mississippi River, twenty stories high, and was molded in the latest architectural style, Art Deco. In one of his best columns he had suggested that bars be placed over the windows. That way, Grover wrote, when St. Paul's civic leaders gathered inside for the dedication ceremony, the doors could be padlocked, later to be sealed with cement. Sentenced to life in Art Deco. Forced to spend the rest of their years counting perpendicular and zigzag lines. He flicked his cigarette butt to the crowd below and downed his drink. "Best moonshine whiskey in America," he burped out, setting the rancid glass aside. "Homegrown."

Grover Mudd wanted to fall in love. Just like in the movies. Love at first sight. Rejection. Contempt. Competition. Struggle. Conquest. The happy ending. He shoved his hands into the deep pockets of his baggy brown trousers and searched the parade route for a woman who could fulfill his dreams. Fifty-five thousand workers marching down Robert Street from the Minnesota State Capitol, then up Fourth Street, squeezing by the *North Star Press* and the *Frontier News*. One hundred thousand spectators lining the curbs, leaning out windows, perched on rooftops. Not a bad turnout for a city of only 270,000. Somewhere in that sea of people had to be a near-perfect lady, a woman he would never tire of being with, a lovely, sensuous creature he could bring to climax night after night, month after month, year after year until death due to sex.

Actually, Grover had fallen in love on a number of occasions. Twelve-second affairs with all the passion, eroticism, and satisfaction a man and woman could hope for. Like this morning at the kidnapping trial. The verdict was read. Pandemonium followed. Everyone was on their feet shouting. He moved toward the aisle. She was in the back near the exit, on the arm of a Buggs Palooka type. She was blond—beautifully blond. Short blond hair with just a slight flip forward at the ends. A summer dress of lavender form-fit a curving figure. Her angel face was cheeky and fresh, her baby complexion the color of strawberry cream. Little makeup. A natural. She did not look his way, but he knew her eyes were blue. The Scandinavian goddess of his dreams. He was in love. He moved to get closer. If only their eyes could meet. If he could just say hello. The crowd was in his way. She walked out the door. His twelve seconds were up.

Grover reached behind him, grabbed an apple off the file cabinet and gave it an affectionate look before biting into it. He kept telling Stormy he loved her. And he really did, if only . . . A present. He had to buy the woman he loved a present. Something special this time. She was pestering him again about taking her out to a movie. Was there somewhere in America he could do that? New York? California? Chicago, perhaps? Certainly not St. Paul.

As Roxanne Schultz sat in the back row of the fanciful courtroom waiting for the jury to come in she could not help but dwell on the injustice her family had suffered. The law was for those who could afford it. Once again she found herself cheering for the bad guy.

The trial of Roger Touhy, charged with the kidnapping of William Hamm, Jr., was front-page news across the country. Although Touhy was the first alleged kidnapper tried under the new Lindbergh Law, St. Paul was carrying on as if he had killed the Lindbergh baby. In fact, Hamm was released unharmed after a hundred-thousand-dollar ransom was paid.

Roxanne could find no sympathy for the Hamm family and the still-missing money. She remembered countless nights in the hollow, sitting on the back porch, staring up the steep hill at the Hamm mansion and trying to count the numbers of rooms in the Victorian brownstone, dreaming of what life might be like behind the ornate windows. She could close her eyes and still see the thousand lights of Hamm's Brewery kindle the dark sky; she could see the trains that rumbled through the ravine disappear into the pink structure below the towering smokestacks. When the first snow came, a Christmas tree was placed in a bay window and the Hamm house became Santa's castle, the brewery his toy factory. But as she matured into womanhood and became increasingly aware of her plight, she thought the mansion ugly and a cruel joke—prosperity overlooking degradation.

Roxanne Schultz and gangster Dag Rankin were lucky to have gotten seats in the jam-packed courtroom. A stilted fan stood whirling behind the bench. The huge windows were open, letting the flies in. Light fixtures of bronze dangled from the lofty ceiling like frozen pendulums. Heavily armed guards stood watch over the trial from the solid oak balconies above her, as rumors of an escape attempt persisted.

To Roxanne, court proceedings were a childish game; the judge and his little hammer, the prosecutor and his big mouth. And sorriest of all were the reporters: pack rats with pencils, dressed in sloppy, ill-fitting suits, with silly-looking press cards sticking out of their cheap hats.

She opened her purse, dug out a compact, and checked her makeup. A natural beauty, she did not wear much. The flips in her blond hair were beginning to fall, but still she was glad she'd had it cut. The August humidity was murder. Yet even in the sweltering heat Roxanne Schultz looked resplendent. Nobody had to tell the girl from Swede Hollow what a living doll she'd turned out to be; she knew it. And if she had to spread her gorgeous legs for a few carefully chosen gangsters to enjoy the better things in life, then she'd spread her legs. Like for the homely and impotent jerk sitting next to her. He could never again get the damn thing up, not that it would do her any good if he could.

Roxanne smoothed a wrinkle from her lavender dress and watched as a marshal paraded twelve St. Paul citizens into the mahogany jury box. Her own courtroom appearances had not been so dramatic, except for the one time when she was seventeen. A fat judge with a billy-goat beard ordered her into his chambers before sentencing. He sat majestically behind his stately desk in his authoritative robe and explained to her, in strictly legal terms, how he could take a young, wayward girl of her grace and beauty into his home and educate her to the norms of St. Paul's high society, escort her through the doorways off Summit Avenue, harbor her until she was of legal age, when she would be well on her way down the path of righteousness. She went to him, hiked her skirt up, and placed a bare knee on the chair, between his legs. She ran her hands through his

greasy gray hair and pulled his head to her breast. He
gave her a weak squeeze. She tilted his chin back with
the tip of a finger, looked at the ancient red eyes and
the tobacco-stained teeth, spit in his face, ruptured his
balls, and had assault added to her theft charge.

The jury was seated. The room fell silent. The hot
sun could be heard shining through the windows. The
silence made the odor of perspiration more noticeable,
almost unbearable.

"Has the jury reached a verdict?"

"Yes, Your Honor, we have."

"Will the defendant rise."

A scrawny man with dark bushy hair stood at the
defense table. He had a cocky way about him; years
later his sour-looking face would be removed by
shotguns.

"Read the verdict."

"We, the members of the jury, find the defendant,
Roger Touhy—not guilty."

The courtroom exploded in shock and anger.
Amazed reporters lunged for the door. The judge made
pounding noises with his little hammer but was largely
ignored. Roxanne remained in her seat, amused by
the whole scene. Roger Touhy had found the law
affordable.

Dag Rankin reached down and took her arm. They
moved toward the aisle but found the exit blocked by
the passing parade. Touhy was handcuffed and pulled
along by federal officials who were trying to clear the
way. The press was shouting out questions. The authorities were yelling back answers.

"It's a disgrace."

"Only in St. Paul."

"He's still under arrest. He'll be returned to Chicago
to stand trial for the Factor kidnapping."

"I ain't never kidnapped no one," cried Touhy. "And
I didn't shoot Cock Robin either."

"Give us some room here," his lawyer begged.

They moved into the hallway with the flow of the crowd, and Dag Rankin, being no stranger to the federal courthouse, led Roxanne to a side stairwell. They watched Roger Touhy being shoved into the detention room. Holding on to Roxanne's arm, Rankin limped down eight flights of white marble stairs. They ducked out a side exit into the bright sun and skirted traffic to St. Peter Street.

The "not guilty" news had reached the sidewalk. A mob gathered at the front doors and in the sizzling heat grew more hostile by the minute. At Rice Park, across the way, a rope was strung from a tree, a hangman's noose tied at the end, with the public library serving as a backdrop.

The unruly throng of people surrounding the Richardsonian Romanesque-style Federal Courts Building with its spiring conical towers, dormer windows, and Syrian arches, reminded Roxanne of a scene from a movie, *A Connecticut Yankee in King Arthur's Court*, with Will Rogers ready to be burned at the stake; only, in St. Paul the sun had been blotted out a long time ago. She wondered if the indignant citizenry would be as upset if the kidnap victim had been a banker or a judge instead of the man who made their beer.

"A guy can get away with murder in this city," said Dag Rankin with a malevolent grin. "Why not kidnapping?" He was relaxed now, suddenly cool and confident in a hot, precarious town.

"What will happen to him now?" Roxanne wanted to know.

"If the feds can sneak him out of here they'll take him back to Chicago and probably convict him for kidnapping Jake Factor. The fool. If you're going to play the snatch game you've got to play it right. Him and his brothers are through." Rankin shaded his eyes from the sun and looked across the street. "There's a bar in that building over there. If they hang him I think we can still see it. What do you say, doll?"

"Is it air-cooled?" she asked.

"I think it is."

She slipped her arm through his. From under an umbrella station a traffic cop gave them a white-gloved signal and they crossed Sixth Street at St. Peter and entered the Hamm Office Building to share a cold beer.

As for Chicago gangster Roger Touhy, son of an Irish policeman, Windy City beer baron, and leader of the Terrible Touhys—he was indeed a kidnapper. But, for the first time in a long time, the people of St. Paul had done something right. Roger Touhy never kidnapped William Hamm, Jr.

———————

Grover Mudd stuck his head out the window and stared into the cloudless sky. He looked down the hill toward Lowertown. They were still coming—the Jacob Schmidt Brewing Company, Minnesota Mutual Life, the Ford Motor Company, Anderson Boot & Shoemaker, Yoerg Brewery, the Harding High School marching band, a feisty sandpaper company nicknamed 3M—hordes of them marching up the street through the heat to the big rally in Rice Park, where the politicians were waiting to speak.

Grover's body was changing and nothing he did could stop it. In two more Halloweens he would be forty years old. He looked older, felt older still. His black hair was thinning. His eyes were stony gray with creeping lines of red. He shaved every other day; shadows crisscrossed his face. He wore a scowl, seldom a smile. The rest of him was filling out, his waist, his hips; he felt it most in his thighs. His gait was slowing. He felt sluggish and forlorn. Gertrude Stein was right, Grover thought, they were a lost generation.

At the Great Northern Railway Company his father had been known as the librarian. In the engineer's cab of the locomotive there were always books to be found:

a dictionary, a classic, a best-seller he didn't care for. "Books," his daddy would tell him, "the most noble thing you could ever do is write a good book. Don't ever forget that, Grover."

"How about a column for the local yokel's newspaper, Daddy?"

Daddy never lived to hear the question. Daddy fell asleep at the throttle.

The Farmer-Labor party went strutting by, placards held high, their sweaty faces beaming with pride. For the first time their man was in the governor's office. Descendants of the Nonpartisan League, they broke Republican domination of state politics and left the Democrats fortressed in St. Paul's City Hall. The end of the parade was nowhere in sight, but Grover could sense the end of the O'Connor System. Floyd B. Olson was Minnesota's new governor. Franklin Roosevelt was in the White House. How long could this city hold out? The system was cracking and Grover Mudd would help bring it down, make Daddy up in heaven proud again.

Walt Howard was the key. Behind those wire-rimmed glasses was an editor with impeccable integrity, a newsman with a deep conscience who did not need glasses to see what was happening to his city. His writing on the crime wave was sharp. Only one thing was wrong with Walt Howard's editorials. They were on the editorial page.

"We don't cross the line, Mudd."

Why not? What does it matter to a dying newspaper? Any better way to rid the city of Public Enemy #1—apathy? What would it take to make Walt Howard cross the line? What would it take to turn this parade on City Hall?

Grover's eyes wandered along with his mind. It was a walk of fifteen minutes from the steps of the new City Hall to the steps of the Minnesota State Capitol. The same distance to the Cathedral of Saint Paul. St. Peter Street, which bounded City Hall on the west, led past

the cathedral, and Wabasha Street, which bounded City
Hall on the east, led to the capitol. Both streets ran
north from Kellogg Boulevard, which topped the river
bluffs. For the first few blocks, up to and past the baroque Federal Courts Building, the area was more than
respectable—the James J. Hill Public Library, Rice
Park, fashionable hotels, small shops and office buildings. Then around Seventh Street a strange thing happened. As St. Peter Street veered west and ran up the
hill past the cathedral, and Wabasha Street continued
straight and on up another hill to the capitol, the area
became a pit of depravity, a sanctum of sleaze. St. Peter
and Wabasha became Sodom and Gomorrah. The
closer the twin streets got to the seeds of Christianity
and democracy the more sacrilegious and illicit they
became—church and state overlooking debauchery.
What really gnawed at Grover was not the seedy little
neighborhood that blighted upper downtown, it was
those two architectural wonders that overlooked it all
that made him shake his head in disbelief. They made
the city the great paradox it was.

The Cathedral of Saint Paul. After twenty-five years
of construction its massive gray stone walls and green
oxidized-copper domes could be seen from every corner
of the city, and there still remained ten years of finishing
work. It was Archbishop John Ireland's dream come
true, though he died years before the first service could
be held. The church was modeled after Saint Peter's
Basilica and stood at the peak of the hill where Summit
Avenue began its reign. A touch of Rome in Minnesota.

Down the hill from the cathedral, across the valley
of lawlessness, and up a twin hill stood the Minnesota
State Capitol. Famed architect Cass Gilbert, the man
who designed the new United States Supreme Court
Building, saved his finest work for his adopted hometown. It was not as redoubtable as the one in the nation's capital but it was certainly as elegant, a structure
of white Georgia marble that left forty-seven other

states envious. Six statues of Greek gods were perched
above the main entrance and faced the city. They represented Bounty, Prudence, Wisdom, Courage, Truth,
and Integrity. And at the base of the dome, the charm
around its neck, was a gilded quadriga, four spirited
horses drawing a chariot of gold in which rode the figure
of Prosperity. A work of art attesting the triumph of
government.

Grover Mudd propped a foot on the windowsill and
marveled at the passing parade. Thousands and thousands of people endorsing in sweat and shoe leather the
New Deal, manifesting unabashed faith in Franklin De-
lano Roosevelt. Grover leaned across his knee, took
another bite of his apple, and stared incredulously at
this city built on seven hills, built over ancient Indian
graves. "St. Paul, Minnesota," he mumbled with his
mouth full, "the only city in America where gangsters
can fuck in the street."

Homer the Gnomer

While Roger Touhy was being transferred to Chicago to stand trial for the kidnapping he was guilty of, the real abductors of William Hamm, Jr., were enjoying ice cream cones a few miles down the river in South St. Paul, a smelly little cow town of stockyards and packing plants.

The two kidnappers were perched on a split-rail fence, and sprawled before them was a maze of pens, corrals, and chutes, miles of gray fencing erected to keep a quarter of a million animals in some kind of order. Midwestern farmers had shipped 100,000 hogs to South St. Paul to take advantage of the government's buying program. When these new porkers were added to the cattle and sheep the yards became hopelessly overcrowded. Yard workers ran along the overhead walkways, more confused than the livestock. Carpenters were busy building new pens. Power lines were haphazardly strung from pole to pole. Town children were hired to chase escaping pigs. The government ordered a four-day embargo, but the hogs kept coming. The sound of pig squeals, cow moos, and lamb cries was deafening. Flies swarmed over anything that breathed, and lunched on the dead. Some of the stock were bound for Swift & Company; others were bound to wear the Armour Star. None were bound to live much longer.

Alvin Karpis found the chaos between man and beast entertaining, as did his partner, Freddie Barker. Karpis brushed the crumbs from his hands and licked his fingers. "Reminds me of when I was a kid in Topeka," he said loudly. "Used to grease a pig every Halloween and chase after it, blindfolded, with a bunch of other kids." He was a short and slender man with an egg-shaped head and the beady black eyes of a comic-strip crook. His new tan suit was neatly pressed and it fit him well. He cocked his panama hat and turned his attention to the slaughterhouses along the river. "Can you imagine going to work every day at the same place for the rest of your life?"

"Nope."

"That's what they do here." He yelled to be heard over the noise. "They line up every morning and march into those buildings, just like sheep."

"So what?" Freddie Barker yelled back. "If we get caught they send us back to the pen, just like cattle." He was a short, stubby man, even shorter than his partner. A wide, red tie dangled from his chubby neck. His shirtsleeves were rolled up. Sweat was dripping from his dirty brown hair. The heat was bothering him. He gnashed his gold teeth together and took a swipe at the flies. "Just like cattle," he repeated, "every day for the rest of our lives."

"See that building over there?" Karpis asked, pointing.

"What about it?"

"That's Armour's."

"So what, we're gonna rob Swift's."

"Homer Van Meter worked there last summer, up on the top floor. Kill floor. He stunned 'em."

"Stunned who?"

"The cows."

"The cows thought Homer was stunning?"

"He had a sledgehammer with a big spike on the end of it and he hit the cows over the head."

Freddie Barker crunched down the last bit of his cone and winced. "Do you mean that jerk-off Van Meter sat up there with a sledgehammer and hit cows over the head for eight hours every day?"

"Twelve hours. After he stunned 'em they got picked up by the heels and got their throats cut."

"Be a great guy to have along on a bank job." Barker laughed, crumbs spitting out of his mouth. "Can't ya see him going down the windows with his sledgehammer, sapping tellers? What else he tell ya?"

"It operates on gravity," Karpis went on, shooing a fly off his sticky nose. "The head goes down one chute, rest of 'em goes down another. Cows, pigs, sheep keep dropping from floor to floor. Come out packaged at the bottom. You got ice cream on your pants. Ma's gonna kill ya."

Freddie Barker smeared the ice cream into his trousers and climbed down from the fence. "The flies are gonna kill me. Let's get going."

The notorious bandits kicked dust down the gravel road as trucks carrying more hogs sped past them. The brilliant summer sun beat down on the backs of their necks. Alvin Karpis flagged down the ice cream vendor again and bought another cone.

"Where the hell are they?" complained Barker. "I said ten o'clock. Did you hear me say ten o'clock?"

"Relax, Freddie, for thirty Gs they'll be here."

Karpis and Barker leaned against a Chevy coupé and waited.

They did their waiting just off the railroad tracks a block below Concord Street, which was the main street in South St. Paul and the only paved road that ran in and out of the seedy cow town. The river was the eastern border, and tall bluffs made for early sunsets to the west. Banks, stores, and a hundred other places of business that counted on the slaughter of animals for their livelihood were strung out along this main street. It was said that, after visiting St. Paul, the James Gang rode down Concord on their way to Northfield. Cole Younger and his two brothers came back Concord

Street on their way to the state penitentiary in
Stillwater.

The United States Post Office was on historic Concord Street.

Buried in the bluffs above South St. Paul was a cattle-
men's bar, and in that bar at a corner table sat three
phony musicians with banjo cases at their feet. It being
a weekday morning, they had the place to themselves
but for the bartender, who went about his opening
chores, spreading clean sawdust, unstacking chairs,
opening windows, plugging in the fan.

"Nothing like a cold one before work," said Homer
Van Meter, chugging a mug of beer. He was six feet
tall and skinny as a rail, 125 pounds and double-jointed
at almost every joint in his body. His stringy black hair
was cut high above his long, pointed ears and parted
down the middle. This, coupled with a sickly yellow
complexion brought on by years of confinement in the
Indiana State Prison, gave him the face of a gnome.
Some of his front teeth were missing, but of late he was
worried something else would soon be missing. Homer
Van Meter had syphilis. The word HOPE was tattooed
on his forearm.

Tommy Carroll, his head buried in a newspaper,
agreed with him and raised his glass in salute. He was
a quiet man, older than the others and not too bright,
but smart enough to keep his mouth shut and not show
it. In his youth the slender Carroll dreamed of being
the middleweight boxing champ, until one day his
dream broke along with his jaw. When he could no
longer chase dreams with his fist he chased them with
a machine gun. In the underworld he was a heavy-
weight.

"What you reading? Sports page?" Van Meter asked.

"No. *'Grover's Corner.'* "

"I read him."

"We were kids together on Grand Avenue. My pop worked with his at the railroad."

"Still see him?"

"Not in years."

Lester Gillis, alias George Nelson, slammed his hand on the table. Beer spit on their faces. "Well, call him up." He was a fruitcake of a gangster with a squatty little body and a baby face where whiskers refused to grow. The only thing bigger than his irascible ego was his mouth. Gillis leaned forward. "We can use the publicity." Then he lowered his voice and talked with a malicious passion. "All I need to be front-page news is a name. Like Machine Gun Kelly. He was just a penny-ante bootlegger until his wife gave him that name. That's what I want, a name that'll make kids wet their pants."

"How 'bout this?" Van Meter grinned. "Pester Lester."

"From now on it's Nelson," declared Gillis. "Machine Gun Nelson."

"No," said Van Meter, shaking his head, "the kids will get you mixed up with Machine Gun Kelly and they won't know when to wet their pants." Van Meter and Carroll guffawed loud and hard.

Gillis was on his feet. "When people hear Machine Gun Nelson they'll shit their pants." This time he brought both hands down on the table and splattered beer across the floor. The bartender glanced their way.

"Sit down," ordered Van Meter. "You'll queer this job before it even gets started. This heist is a plum. Better than the Sioux Falls job."

Gillis took his chair. "That's another thing," he said. "They didn't let us in on the Hamm snatch. How come they're letting us in on this?"

"This is a lot different," explained Van Meter. "Takes experts. We were one expert short so we brung you. Besides, we didn't let them in on the Sioux Falls job." Homer Van Meter found Lester Gillis exasperating, but he had an even stronger dislike for his new bosses. "There's a gang in the Michigan City pen that would make this Barker-Karpis gang look like bumbling Boy Scouts."

"You and your gang at Michigan City," chided Gillis. "If they were so hot they wouldn't be locked up."

Van Meter gulped down his beer and checked his watch. "Christ almighty," he said, "it's ten-fifteen."

Outside, the morning sky was filled to the brim with sun. The brightness stung the gangsters' eyes as they threw their banjo cases into the backseat of a blue-and-black Hudson four-door, an awesome machine in immaculate condition. Tommy Carroll slid into the backseat. Lester Gillis climbed behind the wheel.

"What do you think you're doing?" asked Van Meter.

"I'm driving."

"Like hell you are. I'm wheelman, you're shotgun."

"I'm Machine Gun Nelson and I'm driving." Gillis set his jaw and gripped the wheel.

And just when the squatty gangster was sure he was going to be the wheelman, the cold steel of Tommy Carroll's tommy gun froze the back of his neck. In a soft and steady voice he was told, "Slide over, Pester Lester, and don't queer this job."

Lester Gillis complied, and not only lost the privilege of driving that day, he lost the name he was born with.

"He's pouting," said Van Meter. "Look at that baby face, Tommy."

"I wouldn't talk," shot back Gillis. "Your puss looks like it went through a meat grinder."

Homer Van Meter laughed a laugh that could be heard down on Concord Street. "Baby Face Nelson," he roared as he pulled away from the curb and dropped into town.

Down below Concord Street Alvin Karpis and Freddie Barker were in no laughing mood. Karpis was lapping up his third ice cream cone when the Hudson bounced over the tracks, rolled by them, made a slow U-turn, and coasted to a stop.

"Mr. Karpis, Mr. Barker," said Homer Van Meter, leaning out the window, "meet Baby Face Nelson." Again he broke into belly laughs.

"Where've you guys been?" demanded Barker.

"Stopped in a bar up the street for a beer," Van Meter told him. "A Hamm's." He smiled, showing his missing teeth.

"Goddammit," screamed Freddie Barker, "we got less than a half-hour. Now shut up and listen to Alvin here."

Homer Van Meter dropped his skinny arms out the window and let his head hang over the door. "We're not gonna go over the plan again, are we, Freddie?"

"Damn right we are."

"We've only been watching these pigeons for a month," Van Meter muttered.

Karpis put a finger under Van Meter's chin and lifted his face. "We always go over the plan one more time. We're pros. Or would you like to go back to the pen for another ten years?"

For the first time that morning the smile was wiped off Van Meter's face. His eyes caught fire. He grabbed Karpis by the tie. "I ain't never going back to the pen."

"All right, then," said Alvin Karpis, pleased he had everyone's attention. "There'll be two runners from Swift's and two cops, gift-wrapped in a squad car. First they go down to the depot and lift a satchel of silver. From there it's up to the post office for a satchel of cash. Then they hike down to the bank. We hit 'em at the post office. Me, Homer, and"—he checked his words—"Nelson."

Van Meter's laugh was reborn.

Karpis continued. "The coupé will be stashed on the corner at Third. Tommy and Freddie will be in the Hudson a half-block south. The squad rolls north on

Concord and stops in front of the post office. The skinny
runner runs inside. Coppers pack thirty-eights in shoulder holsters. That's all. Soon as we see the skinny runner step out the door with the loot we hit 'em. Any
shots fired, any heat shows, Tommy and Freddie ride
up like cowboys after Indians. If everything's jake just
pick me up and we'll be on our way. Stick to the plan
and we should be back at the lake swimming in an hour
with a big fat payroll and not a shot fired. Questions?''

Homer Van Meter wet his cracked lips. "Do you
believe in reincarnation, Alvin?"

Creepy Alvin Karpis stuck his head in the window.
"Yes, I do. And I'm coming back rich. Let's go, boys."

The gangsters, clutching their musical instruments,
switched cars. The Hudson with its deadly combo
danced up to Concord Street and swung left. An even
deadlier trio squeezed into a Chevy coupé, sang up to
Concord Street, and pitched right.

———

On the same steamy morning when Alvin Karpis and
Homer Van Meter were staking out the post office in
South St. Paul, a few miles up the river a St. Paul
motorcycle cop was pulling his stake out of his favorite
speeder on a gravel bluff above Point Douglas Road
where warring Indians once kept a lookout.

Patrolman Emil Gunderson stuffed his meat back in
his pants, zipped up, and climbed out of the backseat
of a rusty Plymouth. He was a huge man, strong as an
ox and not much smarter. He pulled an expensive medal
of Saint Christopher from his sticky skin and swore,
something about sweaty women. "Now, Mrs. Johnson,
that's the third time this month I've caught you speeding. Next time I'm gonna give you a ticket. Understand?"

"Yes, Officer Gunderson. It's just that I love the way
you sneak up behind me."

"Yeah, you love everything I do behind you."

In Minnesota there was no such thing as a police school; brawn meant more than brains. In St. Paul it was best to be Irish—big, mean, and Irish. If you couldn't be Irish, Scandinavian would do. Others need not apply.

The best beat was downtown, Gunderson's old beat. In the clubs he could get free drinks, lay down a bet, or pop into a whorehouse for a quickie. All this while on duty. It was downtown that he became a police legend. Patrolman Emil Gunderson killed a man once. A railroad man who had traveled from the old land. He didn't kill him in the line of duty, just while on duty. His victim was a boy, really, a beautiful Catholic boy, twenty years old, with Saint Christopher, patron saint of travelers, dangling from his neck.

It was payday at the railroad. That meant trouble downtown. Railroad workers put in fourteen-, sixteen-, eighteen-hour days, and when they got paid, they got laid. In the depression, they had jobs and money. The clubs downtown lured them in where the whores preyed on them. Drinks were poured and fights were brewed. If they had any money when they left, there were midnight ruffians known as Chicago Star Cleaners who rolled them as they headed home.

Gunderson found the boy, still greasy but already drunk, on Wabasha Street in mid-afternoon, making a monkey out of *King Kong*. He'd smashed the display glass and ripped the big poster off the Strand Theater. Then he tore the big ape to shreds. He was holding Fay Wray in the palm of his hand and fondling her breasts when Gunderson arrived on the scene.

"Look at the mess here. What is this?"

"I had to save me beauty from the beast," the boy laughed out, and the crowd that had gathered to watch laughed along with him.

"Gotta take you in now."

"Up the old ass with ya, Jack. The best of the king's men in County Cork couldn't bring me to bay. The

King of Kong couldn't best me. Think I'm going to be
shackled off to the hoosegow by a gorilla from St.
Paul?"

But the King of England didn't have any men like
Emil Gunderson. "I don't use shackles," the King of
Brawn told the boy. With lightning quickness he snared
the drunken young fool in a headlock. Up Wabasha to
Kellogg Boulevard they marched, the boy doubled
over, his head clamped like a vice in Gunderson's muscular arms. They started for Steep Street, crowded sidewalks parting way. To those who worked downtown,
Gunderson's arrests were a common sight. But they
hadn't marched far when the pretty Catholic boy
stopped walking. Gunderson didn't notice, just dragged
him the rest of the way, into the station house and up
to the sergeant's desk.

"Okay, Emil, you can drop him now."

And that's where the boy's travels ended, on the
station-house floor. He was dead, his skull cracked in
two.

Gunderson ripped Saint Christopher from the boy's
neck and stuffed his body into a jail cell, where he wasn't
officially discovered until the next morning. The cause
of death was inconclusive, as was the subsequent investigation. But everyone on the force knew it was the
beast that killed the beauty, and Gunderson's reputation was made. Even among cops he was feared.

But now the giant Norwegian's arrest methods had
gotten him into trouble with a judge. The new assistant
police chief stuck him out in Battle Creek, patroling
the sticks. St. Sauver the Dickhead, Gunderson called
him. There was nothing worse than an honest mick.

Battle Creek was undeveloped woodland, beyond the
East Side, where the Chippewa and the Sioux once
killed each other before the white man arrived and
killed them both. Arrowheads could still be found in
the sandy cliffs. Gunderson walked to his motorcycle
and mounted it with the pride of a warrior mounting a

stallion. The city stretched out before him. He scouted
the seven hills. The sun made him squint. It was out
there somewhere. Mind-boggling riches. Prohibition
was on its last bootleg, but there was a new game in
town and he and the boys wanted to play. All they had
to do was find the stuff. No easy task.

Nina Clifford could be dead soon. Hell, one good
push down the stairs would do the old bat in. Then he
could take over her operation. Still, she was only on
the receiving end. The big cop stomped his bike into
gear. "Where are you, sweet dreams?"

There were so many places it could be stashed: the
big brick warehouses of Lowertown; a maze of boxcars
chasing the tracks; barges like football fields floating on
the Mississippi; ancient caves crawling under the cliffs.
He watched an airplane drop in on Holman Field.

What Emil Gunderson didn't see as he rode away on
this particular day was the sodden bodies of two Irish
boys as the current in the river dropped them off and
pushed their bobbing heads into a lake called Pig's Eye.

By the time Alvin Karpis took his position at the south
end of the post office his ice cream cone was soup, more
of it going down his arm than his throat. He threw it
to the curb and licked his fingers.

The post office was housed on the first floor of the
Exchange Building, another brownstone fortress designed to protect employees from months of winter. It
did that, but in the summer months it became a three-
story barbecue. Open windows begged for a breeze.
Telegraph wires ran out the upper windows to rooftop
antennas and pulled in the latest livestock prices. Pigeons used the roof to home in on grain that spilled
from the trucks. So many pigeons lined the rooftops of
Concord Street that poison was sprinkled in the feed
to control the pests. Pigeon shit spotted the sidewalks,
and dead birds rotted in the gutters.

At the north end of the building the vines that climbed the walls wilted in the heat. The grass out front was yellow and brown for lack of water. It was there Homer Van Meter rested his banjo case. He was still wondering why he'd tied up with this rinky-dink gang. They got lucky with Hamm. What they needed was a real leader, like his friend J.D. Was he still locked up? Van Meter made a mental note to find out. The heat was cramping his stomach and making the painless sores in his pants sticky.

At the foot of the stairs that led through the arched doorway, the newly named Baby Face Nelson was doing a poor job of looking inconspicuous, holding his banjo case like a football and pacing like he had to piss. A .45 revolver was stuffed under his shirt. He saw Van Meter shake his head in disgust. The temperature had reached 90°.

At ten-thirty a squad car rolled out of the sun. Traffic on Concord was light. The police car pulled to the curb and stopped a few feet from Nelson. A skinny Swift's messenger jumped from the car. He mumbled "Morning" to the gangster and darted up the stairs into the post office. A chubby messenger and one patrolman also got out of the car. The messenger clung to a satchel and wiped his brow. The other patrolman was left squirming behind the steering wheel, his sweat-stained shirt sticking to the seat.

The cop on the sidewalk talked about getting off duty early and taking his children to the state fair. The Swift's messenger complained about the humidity and the smell of manure emanating from the yards. They paid no attention to the trio of odd musicians until Nelson mounted the stairs, sprung open his case, and shouldered a machine gun.

"Not yet, Baby Face!" screamed Van Meter.

"Stick 'em up!" shouted Nelson. "We mean business."

Van Meter tore a shotgun from his case and stepped

forward. "Put that satchel down and get your hands in the air. Now."

Alvin Karpis popped open his banjo case and drew his own machine gun. He covered the squad car. The cop inside threw up his hands.

Nelson was everywhere, like a hoofer on a Hollywood sound stage. He did a two-step up the stairs, a leap to the sidewalk, a waltz around the police, with a chorus of outrageous orders. He grabbed passersby and lined them up against the car. "This is a stickup."

Homer Van Meter was sick. He had an eye on the post-office door. He kept his gun on the messenger and the cop. He wanted to kill Baby Face Nelson. Then came the dog, a St. Bernard. Nelson had collared its owner. The dog circled Van Meter, barking, saliva drooling from its jowls. He kicked at it. "Scram, pooch."

The skinny messenger stepped out the door, cash in hand.

"Put that satchel down and beat it," Van Meter ordered. He turned to the chubby one. "You too."

The Swift's messengers backed down the street, hands above their heads, leaving Van Meter facing the cop and kicking at the dog.

"This is a federal crime," the cop told him. "They got a new place for guys like you. It's called Alcatraz."

Homer Van Meter put the shotgun to the policeman's face.

Surprised by the blast Karpis took his attention off the patrolman behind the wheel. The cop drew his .38 and managed one shot. He missed. Alvin Karpis opened up on the car.

The Hudson screeched to a halt in the center of the street. Freddie Barker and Tommy Carroll jumped from the car, machine guns blazing.

Nelson was ecstatic. He drew his six-shooter and fired at fleeing citizens, missing every one of them. The Exchange Building was peppered. The pigeons were off and flying. Glass flew like bullets. A choir of screaming workers dodged the windows.

The Swift's messengers were never swifter. They sprinted down the street and dove for cover.

Freddie Barker cried, "Let's go!"

Homer Van Meter grabbed the satchel of silver and sprinted for the Chevy. Baby Face Nelson chased him. They raced away north.

Alvin Karpis nabbed the satchel of cash, leaped into the Hudson, and put the pedal to the metal. Freddie Barker clung to the car from the running board and sprayed one side of the street with his machine gun while Tommy Carroll raked the other side. The shooting spree went on for two blocks until a jolly truck driver hauling a load of hogs and singing "Sweet Adeline" saw Ma Barker's boys coming and threw his sweet ass across the seat of his cab. Bullets shattered the windshield. The truck jumped the curb and careened through the plate-glass window of a hardware store, overturning the trailer, freeing the load, and sending a hundred Minnesota porkers squealing up Concord Street.

Karpis slowed up and allowed his torpedo men to crawl inside. Picking up speed again, he threw on the siren.

Barker settled into the backseat. "Holy Toledo, that Homer Van Meter is a real asshole, ain't he?"

Karpis shook his head. "Those two gotta go."

"Better throw the smoke," said Barker looking out the back window. "Just in case."

The sparkling getaway car sped for St. Paul with a police siren wailing and thick black smoke belching out the rear. The elaborate escape plans were unnecessary. There was nobody chasing them.

South St. Paul was stunned, hit over the head with a sledgehammer. People were in gutters, under cars, crouched in doorways. Storefronts were shattered. When the echoes faded and the smoke cleared in front of the United States Post Office a wounded St. Bernard was yapping for help. On the sidewalk among the pigeon shit and the arriving flies was a cop with his head blown off. In the bullet-ridden squad car his partner was trying to keep his eye from falling out of its socket. The two messengers from Swift & Company were hiding under a cattle truck. An ice cream cone was melting over the curb. The pigs were running free. And the sheep were being led off to slaughter.

Saint Sauver

Like the Hamm kidnapping and the trial of Roger Touhy, the robbery and shooting in South St. Paul made national headlines. Details of the savagery splashed across the front pages of America. Not only had the Barker-Karpis gang murdered a local police officer, but, by robbing a United States post office, they triggered the ire of a young organization in Washington, a division of the Justice Department becoming known as the FBI. In September these men, led by a bulldog of a man named J. Edgar Hoover, sat down to a map and literally outlined the Midwest crime problem. Among an un-checked wave of violence was the kidnapping of an oil baron in Oklahoma City; the massacre of four lawmen at the Union Depot in Kansas City; a bank robbery in Mason City, Iowa, with a running gun battle; over twenty post-office robberies in the state of Wisconsin; and a bank heist in Sioux Falls, South Dakota, where more than a thousand people stood on the street and watched helplessly as women hostages were forced to stand on the running boards of the getaway car. After connecting the dots on the map the G-men found them-selves with an incongruous circle. At the center of that circle—St. Paul, Minnesota.

The Selby–Lake Line trolley clanged over the Lake Street Bridge, one of the many bridges that spanned the Mississippi River and connected Minneapolis to St. Paul. It squeaked to a halt at Cleveland Avenue and picked up a rumpled newspaperman. Then the banana-yellow streetcar, with a big Coca-Cola bottle cap pasted to its nose, continued its long run through the Twin Cities. It was a hot, hazy ten-thirty A.M.

Grover Mudd loved to sleep late. In his previous life he was a possum, hanging from a tree branch by his tail, looking at the world upside down. In his next life he was going to be a bear, crawl into a cave come winter and sleep until spring.

Grover lost his car in the divorce: a Studebaker Dictator, cream-tan in color, with an air-curved chromium grille and teardrop lamplights floating over wide, round fenders. Inside, a Philco custom-built radio turned a ride into a rolling melody. The machine was a treasure. In court his ex-wife sarcastically referred to it as "the other woman." Waxing the Dictator on Saturdays and cruising the lakes alone on sunny Sunday afternoons was an affair he could not break off. In ways he felt worse about losing the car than he did about losing his children. There was never a chance for them, but he was counting on those wheels. When the judge took the little Dictator away Grover wanted to kill. The lousy bitch did not even drive.

He left his coat at home. His only hat had been sitting on a closet shelf for months. A loud tie was draped untied over his off-white shirt. His trousers were badly wrinkled at the lap. Grover dropped a nickel in the fare box, slid into a window seat near the rear, and hung his head out the electric car, like a boy going for a ride in the country. The heat wave had continued past Labor Day. Steam rising from the bricks hit his face and left him longing for a day at beautiful Como Park. As the trolley rolled along he closed his eyes and saw himself lying on the park's grassy lakeshore in front of the promenade enjoying a summerfest concert with Stormy at his side. An innocent smile illuminated her pretty face. Her arm was wrapped around his. Her head was on his shoulder. People were staring at them. Grover opened his eyes.

The trolley stopped at Dale Street and the colored people boarded. They made their way to the back of the car. Grover avoided their eyes. Nobody sat next to him. The bell rang and they were moving on the rails again, along a tree-lined street with narrow front lawns that were yellow and brown with the dog days of the hottest summer on record.

The streetcar entered the dark tunnel that ran under Cathedral Hill. It was cool and dank and smelled of fresh dirt and sour wine. A bottle broke under the steel wheels. A tin can ricocheted off the wall and did a jig beside the track. The sojourn underground felt good. Then it was over. The trolley emerged into the vile heat again, into that part of town that never slept.

Downtown streets were being torn up and widened. Clouds of dust drifted by. To avoid the inevitable traffic mess at Seven Corners, Grover jumped off the clanger at Pleasant Avenue and hiked down Tenth to St. Peter Street where he stood across the street from the ruins of the old State Capitol and waited for the traffic signal to change. He glanced down Tenth to Wabasha Street. The Green Lantern Saloon was on the corner, behind a cigar-store front. For ten years it had been the place where the underworld checked in, and Dapper Danny Hogan had been the man to see. Soon after Hogan's explosive demise the Hollyhocks Club down by the river became the place where gangsters checked in, and Dag Rankin became the man to see. But Wabasha Street remained famous for its speakeasies, a garish array of cigar stores, cafés, bakeries, and barbershops with a grimy saloon in every one of them. Backroom joints built to burn. They had live entertainment, dancing, food, and booze. And they had gambling, the second-largest money-making operation in the city of St. Paul. Around town punchboards alone took in fifteen million dollars a year. Other millions were gobbled up by slot machines, roulette wheels, and blackjack.

The walkway was congested and Grover soon found himself waiting shoulder to shoulder with a sweaty crowd. Cars lined the curbs. Parking downtown was expensive. Open lots charged 15 cents a day, or $2.50 for a monthly sticker. Garages were twice that. The sun reflected off the windshields and stung his eyes. A big Buick overheated. A truck hit it from behind. A radiator burst. Steam poured into the crowd. The light changed. Grover scaled the fenders and started down St. Peter Street.

In his daily column he once wrote how Indian Chief Wabasha would be thrilled to see what an exciting stretch his namesake street turned out to be. But Grover doubted Saint Peter would feel the same way. The bawdyhouses lined St. Peter Street, the number-one money-making business in St. Paul. For every speakeasy on Wabasha there were three whorehouses on St. Peter. They were hidden in hotels behind Victorian façades of brick and iron with large neon signs fastened to the false fronts. The Gladstone Hotel, the Bradford, the Arcade, the Palace Hotel—those and a score more competed for sex on St. Peter Street. Girls that did not qualify for the houses plied their trade at the curb.

The signal at Exchange Street was stuck. Grover squeezed through the stalled traffic. He walked in the shade to avoid the sun. Most of the buildings were tall and shared by a variety of tenants, turning the sidewalk into a tunnel of advertising. From the cafés came the smell of fried foods and from the bakeries the aroma of fresh pastry, but in the morning heat the scents were wasted and cruel. At the Salvation Army next to the Carleton Hotel a breadline was jerking forward, and people, poor as sin, stood in the shadow of the depression staring at their shoes.

At Ninth and St. Peter traffic was at its worst. Exhaust

fumes hung in the air. Grover stopped and rubbed his eyes. The smell of hot tar burned his nose. He cleared his throat and spit in a trash can. He looked around for something to drink. Mother Merrill's Café was not open yet. To his right was Assumption Church, where the German Catholics prayed, an old church with celestial twin towers that seemed born with the skyline. Across the way the lots were vacant. A young couple smiled down at him from a billboard, with two mugs of Hamm's beer in their hands. Grover wanted to crawl into the painting, drink the beer, and have sex with the girl. Then he saw who was standing below it. In a church made of gravel on a street made of sin was the Big Holy Spook. Grover hated him.

He was a street preacher, a colored goliath with the strongest vocal cords in town. His arms snapped through the air like mammoth black snakes. Sweat rolled over his fat cheeks and ran down his stallion neck, where pulsating veins looked ready to burst. His monstrous red tongue spit out visions of the apocalypse like a machine gun spitting out bullets, vicious eardrum-piercing threats about the wrath of God descending on the city. Back when he had the dreams, Grover once dreamt the Big Holy Spook was beating him to death inside some forbidden dwelling. The preacher poked his fat black finger through the noisy traffic and screamed his loudest. "Sinner! Your soul will burn in the eternal blazes of hell. The time has come."

Grover Mudd was already on fire. He walked a block down and crossed Ninth Street at Wabasha.

As it had over much of the country, Hollywood fever swept over St. Paul. Two square blocks downtown offered every star from James Cagney to Claudette Colbert. So, along with the speakeasies, the air-cooled movie houses decorated Wabasha Street. Gaudy marquees hung low over the walk and overdramatic posters jumped out at Grover as he browsed by. At the Lyceum Theater the Barrymore family could be seen in *Rasputin and the Empress*. At the Strand Theater Spencer Tracy and Fay Wray were starring in *Shanghai Madness*. Squeezed in the middle of this row of silver screens was Grover's favorite specialty shop, stacked with Coke, candy, and Flavo-Korn popcorn. He bought a cold soda and downed it in front of the legitimate and respectable Saint Francis Hotel, which housed the less than respectable Royal Cigar Store, owned and operated by Dutch Otto. Behind his cigar store was a racehorse syndicate that operated with help from the police. A wire service from a national betting organization was fed to the store over a phone line from Minneapolis. Gamblers crowded in early because they could place bets on races at various tracks around the country. It was rumored Dutch Otto took in ten grand a day.

Grover Mudd crossed the street and hurried to work. He couldn't afford to look too sanctimonious as he marched down Speakeasy Row. At one time or another he drank in all of them.

He bounded down sloping Fourth Street and up the crumbling brick stairs of the Frontier Building. He wrenched open the door and jumped into a waiting elevator. It got stuck between floors two and three. He pressed the alarm button, then sat in the corner.

As an example of their in-depth reporting, the *North Star Press* had conducted a survey of downtown office buildings to see who had the fastest and the slowest elevators. Of course they found that the Frontier Building had the slowest, and jokes were made about stories being stuck in the elevator. It wasn't the fact that the *North Star* printed such tripe that pissed Grover off as much as the fact that it was true. He extended his leg and slammed his foot against the alarm button. The squeezy heat intensified. He felt his pockets for a smoke. There were none. He opened his shirt front and stared at the trapdoor on the ceiling.

Grover Mudd would wake in the morning and clear his throat and lungs of the phlegm that had coagulated in the night. With some coffee and a doughnut in his stomach, and a shot of whiskey to get him started, he'd be off feeling pretty good. But, as the hands chased around the clock, his wounds would catch up with him. His throat would puff, his lungs would swell, his eyes would turn red and water. By nightfall his chest was an abyss of cough. Stormy understood. His ex-wife never did. Eat right, she would tell him, see a different doctor. The doctors only gave him pills and syrups and whispered wishfully of outlawed narcotics. He closed his ears to them and sought relief in divorce court and outlawed whiskey.

From overhead came the vacuum sound of sliding doors and the flat echo of footsteps on a ladder, slower than usual. The trapdoor above jerked open and Fuzzy Byron's balding gray head bobbed through the hole in the ceiling. "I thought it was you, Grover. More murder."

"Fuzzy, what are you doing up there?"

"Silas got laid off," Fuzzy told him, showing faint yellow teeth patched between a sickly, prickly beard. "It's a bit fuzzy up here but he showed me what to do."

"Where's the murder?"

"Pig's Eye Lake. They found those Kendrigan twins." Fuzzy was an old man, well into his sixties. The spectacles, precariously balanced on his permanently inflamed nose, were thicker than Coke bottles and did about as much good. If he did not die in total darkness he would die in a fuzzy world. And a curious intellect came with the crusty messenger, a genuine sage among drunkards. When he was sober, which was only by day, he spoke with a Bohemian wit, never mentioning his past or his problems. When he was sozzled he spoke only of himself, often with a bitter tongue, spinning outrageous yarns about artistic genius and phantom paintings. He was ugly, oafish, and incorrigible, but there was something about the old wino Grover could not help but love. Fuzzy hung a bulky Brownie from the ceiling. "Mr. Howard said for you to take this camera and go on down there."

"Me? What's wrong with Hermanson, or Roth?"

"Hermanson and Roth got laid off. Roth took the Chevy and said he's not returning it until he's paid. Take the Desoto. It's in the garage. Here's the keys. Catch the camera." Fuzzy dropped them into Grover's hands. "Now, standard operating procedure involves some stomping. So push the lobby button, Grover, and kiss the wall. I'm going to stomp." The trapdoor closed and the elevator bounced downward a foot at a time before it began a quick descent with a cry from above. "Wheee . . ."

Grover's workday had begun.

At the same time as Grover Mudd was fighting his way out of the Frontier News elevator, Roxanne Schultz was fighting for a shot at sexual bliss. On satin sheets in the master bedroom of the Hollyhocks Club, Dag Rankin made love to her with his fingers. Lately, it was not as much lovemaking as it was an exercise in futility. When her futile attempt to make him hard was over, his futile attempt to bring her to climax began.

It had been a long night: The club was open till dawn. She was the lady of the house and she stayed sociable until the last guest departed. Then she bathed in cool, scented water and readied for bed. She pulled the black shades against the fierce morning sun and turned the ceiling fan on low. Rankin came to her after counting the night's take.

Roxanne was never totally naked with a man. She found them more attracted to partial nudity and she needed the security of that piece of clothing clinging to her body. This morning it was a nightgown of light, white silk. No panties. Rankin pulled the straps below her breasts and worked the hem up to her belly. He sucked on her nipples before backing off to hover between her legs. From there the lovemaking was always the same, the only way it could be. She took his limpness in her hand and pushed the head in her slit and stroked herself with it, but it was only a prelude to his fingers.

In their early days she would go down on him, but he was scarred and deformed and when he refused to return the favor it became an unspoken understanding that she would do it no more.

He had long fingers, crooked and rough, but she waited for them eagerly. He brushed her hairs and she felt the first sensation. Then he crossed his middle finger with his index finger and slipped them inside her. Her legs spread even wider, her hips swelled with excitement. She ran her hands under her thighs and spent the first minutes in swaying relaxation. He kissed her mouth hard, licked her neck, sucked a nipple, all the time stroking her. She put a hand to his mouth and gently nudged him away, wanting only the rhythm of his fingers. She whispered orders to him. "Slow, slow, slower." Then it was "Fast, faster, slow now, slow." And he would obey, and he would wait.

Roxanne put her mind in a euphoric state and tried to take the trip without the opium. Her body always took on the tingle of womanly pleasure, and she knew it could happen if he only allowed her the time. It took time. Sometimes she couldn't even do it to herself, but Rankin did it to her often in those early days before he owned her. But time was on the lam, his arm was weakening, the strokes were uneven, his fingers became cold and insensitive, physical, not sensual. She could feel his frustration, his impatience. It became difficult to concentrate on the faint spasms of delight she was feeling. Again the elusive climax was slipping away. Tears welled up in her eyes. She held them back. She put her hands to her grimaced face and thrust her hips violently, savagely into his fingers, knowing it was not going to happen. Then he withdrew his hand and was through playing with her. The golden hair on her head was wet with perspiration. Sweat trickled down her red face to her lips, where the salty taste rinsed away the spite she wanted to spit at him.

He pulled a sheet over them and curled up to her, kissed her cheek. It was a kiss of perverse satisfaction. She knew he did not want it to happen. He wanted her to feel the same frustration he felt. He would allow her only one source of pleasure. The same as his. Nina Clifford's.

It was during a weak moment in the opium den, before she smoked the magic, that she told St. Paul's first lady of the evening everything: about life in the hollow and the death of her father, about the violent, painful night she lost her virginity. Roxanne confessed that her most sensual feelings came from a man's fingers. The penis itself only brought her hostility and physical discomfort.

Nina Clifford, a seasoned authority on the ways of women, told Roxanne that, with the right man, she would one day feel the joy a woman should feel, but Dag Rankin was not the right man. She also concluded that Roxanne's climax could only be brought about with loving fingers, that she would never accept the real part of a man because the first time she saw the male organ it was humiliating her father. The second time it was humiliating her.

Rankin was asleep. Roxanne rolled away and stared at the streaks of morning sky seeping through the shades. Perhaps the time had come to get out. She dreamed of California, of palm trees and movie stars. Except for Jean Harlow, she believed she was as pretty as any of them. But there was her mother. And there was Dag Rankin, growing more powerful and more reckless with every passing day. Although Roxanne tried her best not to hear things, she suspected him capable of the most sensational crimes.

Grover Mudd cruised past the cliffs and caves of Battle Creek Park, slowed through the construction, then drove another mile into the sticks. He swung the Desoto off Point Douglas Road, bounced over the railroad tracks, and wheeled down a dry mud path that ran through the bog to Pig's Eye Lake, a Mississippi River backwater. The pathway was narrow and the deep ruts in it could only handle one car at a time. The trees grew at sharp angles. Branches slapped the Desoto as it rumbled along. Up ahead was a highway patrolman. Grover had forgotten his press card. But the cop didn't ask, just directed him right with a pointing finger.

He steered out of the ruts and parked in knee-high weeds next to the police cars. Grover climbed out and batted the gnats away from his eyes. Grasshoppers leaped in front of him. The shoreline was swathed in deep summer green, but the lake was low. Swampy edges were drying up leaving cattails and reeds to wither and die. Bloated carp lay rotting in the morning sun. A putrid smell was flushing out of the new sewage-disposal plant on the island.

The police stood near the stagnant water on the mosquito-infested shore. Two of them were in uniform, including the giant patrolman Emil Gunderson, who Grover recognized immediately. Five other cops were in plainclothes. One of them was taking pictures. Another was taking notes. A fat detective was enjoying a beer. The others were trying to keep the bugs away.

Assistant Chief Gil St. Sauver, newly appointed, was the man in charge. He looked professional even in the middle of a heat wave, standing in a dark brown suit with a matching homburg, his necktie pulled tight and proper. He greeted Grover indifferently, if not bitterly. "Grover Mudd, the only guy I know who can find a drink being served before breakfast." They didn't shake hands.

"Morning, St. Sauver. What's America's highest-

ranking traffic cop doing down here? Someone speeding?"

Grover had known Gil St. Sauver for years, watched
him rise through the ranks, mostly traffic divisions.
Grover believed St. Sauver to be one of the few sincerely honest men in the upper ranks, which was probably why he had spent his career in traffic. But Grover
did not like him, or any other cop. To reporters, cops
were as bad as crooks: dangerous, unpredictable, and
habitual liars.

The distrust was mutual. Police believed reporters,
contemptible liars one and all, would rather nail a cop
than a crook. Gil St. Sauver ran a soiled hanky across
his brow. "Take a look," he said.

The police stepped aside. Two small bodies lay at
their feet. They were children. Grover Mudd had seen
this kind of death before. He felt the old ache stir in
his back. He shook it off, and his reporter's eye gathered
the facts. They were stretched out on their backs and
hog-tied at the ankles, their arms at their sides. Their
feet were still in the water, and small waves made a
slurping sound as they lapped over the heels. One of
them was missing his shoes. Their knickers were on
straight, belts pulled tight. The once-red hair on their
Irish heads was coated with sludge. Their eyes were
swollen closed. Leeches sucked on their necks.

"The only thing connecting their heads to their shoulders is the skin," St. Sauver told him. "If you pulled
real hard they'd probably come off. One of them is
mongoloid, though it's impossible to tell which one right
now. Looks like they've been in the water for a week,
maybe two. The one with no shoes has broken legs.
Really smashed. You can flop his feet around just like
his head. Somebody, or something, broke these kids
like matchsticks. The only thing I can figure out is that
gorilla from Omaha arrived early."

"This is no gangland murder. This is sick."

"Brilliant observation, Mudd. I couldn't agree more."

"Then who's the gangster?"

"What gangster?"

"The gangster from Omaha?"

"No gangster, Mudd. A gorilla. A big monkey with long arms and a hairy beer belly. Got a face like yours. There's something wrong with his dick so the Omaha Zoo pawned him off on Como Zoo. Christ, the mayor is sending half the force down to the depot to meet him. The only reason I mention it is because this reminds me of that Poe tale, 'The Murders in the Rue Morgue.' It's hard to believe anything human did this."

"Any leads?"

"The harbor patrolman says he chased a couple of kids away from the tracks below the cliffs on the day they disappeared, but he couldn't tell us what they looked like. He chases kids every day."

A steamboat sounded its deep-toned whistle as it rounded the bend in the muddy river and steered for the Lower Landing. Boxcars smashed together in the train yard. Across the lake a great blue heron circled the trees above its nesting ground before gracefully nestling in. Grover took a swipe at the flies and thought of his own children sleeping in the sun on the banks of Cross Lake during a northern vacation trip. He pulled a small notebook and a stubby pencil from his hip pocket. "Who found them?"

"Gunderson over there. Says he came down here to take a leak, or something to that end." St. Sauver slapped at his face hard. "Damn mosquitoes are killing me."

"Has the *North Star* been here yet?"

"They were here and gone. Where have you been, stuck in your elevator again? Where's your camera? Don't you want a picture of this? It looks like something the *Frontier News* would slap on the front page—boost circulation, increase advertising, save your dying asses." Gil St. Sauver turned to the fat detective with the beer. "Finish up here, Crumbs, then run them down to Doc Bjorkland and see what he has to say. And get rid of the suds before Mudd here starts taking pictures."

"Ah, c'mon, Gil," cried the cop they called Crumbs, "it's hotter than hell out here."

Grover and St. Sauver walked back to the cars. "So you're the new assistant police chief. I can see you command the full respect of your men. I heard you got a new office, too. Overlooking Nina's house."

"If it's the last thing I do before I retire, I'll fix Nina's ass. You can quote me on that."

Grover looked over his shoulder. "How did you get stuck with Emil Gunderson?"

"Judge Parks said if he dragged one more prisoner into his courtroom with the snot beat out of him he'd throw him in jail. So they turned him over to me. My luck. I stuck the dumb ox out here to patrol the sticks. Wouldn't surprise me if he murdered those kids."

St. Sauver grabbed a copy of the *Frontier News* from the front seat of his squad car while Grover pulled the camera out of the Desoto. He checked the sun, then aimed the Brownie at the cops standing over the bodies, making sure to keep his distance. Crumbs downed his beer and pitched the bottle into the lake. Gunderson pulled out his dick and aimed another piss at a tree.

"No close-ups, Mudd?"

"You seem uncharacteristically riled today, St. Sauver."

"You don't think two murdered children riles me?"

Grover waited for Gunderson to zip up; then he snapped a picture and advanced the film. "I think it was about seven years ago, wasn't it? Two cops, ambushed while on duty at Laurel and St. Albans. The car with the killers sped off. You never solved that crime. Two of your own. And over the next eighteen months there were twelve more murders went unsolved. It's been seven years now and dead bodies are turning up around town about once a month. Last month it was a cop in South St. Paul, this month it's a couple of boys in Pig's Eye."

"Last night I picked your paper out of the trash can, flipped to the back and found 'Grover's Corner.' " He showed him the article. " 'New Police Promotions Big Joke,' by Grover Mudd. I've got a nice family. Do you think they enjoy reading this stuff? Do you have fun writing it?"

"How long have you been a cop in this city?"

"Twenty-one years."

"And how many police chiefs have you served under, not counting O'Connor?"

"Twenty-four."

"Including your father."

"Watch it, Mudd."

"About one a year. And now we have another one. The real gut-buster is that all these police chiefs can't be fired, they're only required to take a step down. We've got more ex–police chiefs than most towns have police." Grover moved away and looked for a better angle.

"That's only one of the problems, Mudd. Why don't you tell the few readers you have left the real problems?"

"And what are the real problems?"

"The real problem is that in the midst of a crime wave the Ramsey County prosecutor's office has only one investigator. That's like trying to combat this heat wave with one fan. The real problem, newspaperman, is a law that prevents police from confiscating guns unless we can prove they were intended to be used in a criminal act. That includes machine guns, handguns, and sawed-off shotguns. Did you know, if a doctor treats a man for a gunshot wound he doesn't have to report it? Not in this state. Why don't you write about that? And another thing, scoop, you've got a real mean type-writer when it comes to chewing up city officials, but what about gangsters? Why is it we never see their names in 'Grover's Corner,' until they're good and dead? What's the matter, big shot, don't you know what they look like? They look a lot like you. Better dressed."

"Gangsters aren't the cause, they're the result. It's hard to have an underworld without an overworld."

"You're a two-bit rumormonger for a dying newspaper. Stillwater prison rag has more credibility."

Grover laughed. "This two-bit rumormonger heard a great rumor the other day. Gil St. Sauver is going to run for public safety commissioner next spring. Comment?"

"Things are going to change in this town."

"Yeah. We've heard it twenty-four times in the last twenty-one years."

"Go to hell, Mudd."

"You're the second person to tell me that today." Grover walked back to the car and threw the camera in the window. He climbed behind the wheel and gunned the engine, whipped a U-turn, swerved back into the ruts, and bounced out of the bog.

Assistant Chief St. Sauver smashed a mosquito between his palms.

Saint Steff

Special Agent Steff Koslowski walked out of the Federal Building in Sioux Falls with his new marching orders: Go to St. Paul. The sun beat down on South Dakota like no place he had ever been before. The wind was constant, and the fine dirt it swirled filthied his face and irritated his nostrils. At night thunderstorms rolled in and muddied the streets. At dawn the sun and wind were back. By noon the dust was back. God, how he longed for the old Polish neighborhood, where a cool clean breeze blew in off the lake and children sold nectar on the streetcorner. Sure, Chicago had its share of bad weather, but in Chicago a guy could bellyache about it, get up a good head of steam and blame it on somebody. He tossed his coat in the black Ford and rolled up his sleeves. Nobody bellyached in South Dakota. They made brilliant observations:

"Kinda windy."

"Gonna be bad don't get some rain soon."

"Too much rain ruin the fields."

His Illinois education had not prepared his ears for this three-week onslaught of platitudes followed by bromides, spoken in some of the most insipid voices imaginable. He cursed the bank robbers who'd brought him here.

Steff reached across the front seat and grabbed a screwdriver from the doorless glove compartment. He popped open the hood of the car and looked around for help. Downtown Sioux Falls was a joke. The Federal

Building was the tallest thing in town. Three stories.

Across the street a forlorn farmer was propping up a drugstore with his elbow. He had a sunburned crew cut on top of a red, pocked face. His bib overalls were grimy gray and the T-shirt he was wearing might have been white once. Steff waved him over.

"Gonna be a windy one," the farmer announced.

"You bet," said Steff. "Going to be bad if we don't get some rain."

"Too much rain ruin the fields."

"You bet," agreed Steff. It was too bad he was leaving, having mastered their native tongue. "I want you to take this screwdriver and stick it in the carburetor like so." He demonstrated the procedure. "Car won't start without it." He handed the screwdriver to the farmer.

"Your car?"

"No. Government car."

"Government man?"

"Yes, I am. Department of Justice. Investigation bureau."

"J. Edgar Hoover?"

"My boss." The little dictator. Steff crawled into the car and pulled a second screwdriver from the glove compartment. He wished the dog-faced director were with him now, trying to start a five-year-old Ford with a pair of screwdrivers so he could chase down gangsters in their new Chryslers and Terraplanes with twelve-cylinder engines, steel windows, and detailed road maps of every back road in America. The gangsters shot their way into the twentieth century while law enforcement wallowed aimlessly in the nineteenth. Teamwork, J. Edgar told them, teamwork will get the job done every time. What a team, Special Agent Steff Koslowski and a nameless Sioux Falls farmer. He jammed the screwdriver in the ignition and stomped on the starter. The engine burped. He pumped the gas. The engine turned over, burped again, then caught.

"Started right up," the farmer said as Steff collected the tools and closed the hood.

"Teamwork."

"Pardon?"

"Nothing," answered Steff hopelessly. "Appreciate your help."

"Welcome." The farmer turned his head to the sky and walked away. "'Nother windy one," he muttered.

Steff stood at the door of the Ford and looked at the Federal Building for what he hoped would be the last time. Like most of the buildings in Sioux Falls it was constructed of Sioux quartzite and had a pinkish tone to it. The density of the rock that resulted from cementation and compaction made it virtually erosion-proof. To prove it, townspeople would proudly point to the everlasting falls that had been flowing over the quartzite for ten thousand years. That meant when Chicago was lost forever, when Lake Michigan had swallowed the waterfront and fires erased the great ethnic neighborhoods and the wind claimed the last of the streets, pinkish Sioux Falls, South Dakota, would still be standing, celebrating its ten-thousandth birthday. The thought of it soured Steff's stomach. He jumped behind the wheel, curbed a U-turn, and drove up to Minnesota Street, where he headed out of town.

Steff Koslowski came from a police family. His grandfather still walked a beat, and his father, now in private practice, had been a Department of Justice investigator and a member of the famous "Untouchables" who rid Chicago of Al Capone and other gangs. Besides training under his own elders, Steff had studied at the University of Chicago School of Police Administration and the Police School of Northwestern University. By the time he was twenty-two years old he knew more about police methods than even his father did. He was an electrical wizard, but they scoffed at his ideas. He was one of the few men in the world who could operate the lie-detector machine, but the machine was not trusted. When

J. Edgar Hoover launched his recruiting drive for a federal police force that would break new ground against crime the precocious detective from Chicago was ready to be plucked. He was then twenty-five years old.

Mr. Hoover had men like Steff Koslowski in mind when he wrote the book on qualifications. A Hoover man must come from a good family and have an outstanding scholastic record with a degree in law or accounting. A Hoover man must be physically fit and respectably handsome, like fair-haired, square-jawed Steff Koslowski, with his six-foot frame and well-trimmed poundage. He must dress in a professional manner. He should be single, his only love the Department of Justice. He must be a team player. This so J. Edgar Hoover and his team of Steff Koslowskis could chase down the conniving, coldhearted, glorified scum that threatened the American way.

Steff drove past Firehouse Number One and prayed the brakes would hold as Minnesota Street began its precipitous drop.

He had been with the bureau two disappointing years now. He had yet to fire his gun, he had not captured anybody on the Most Wanted List, and if the federal bureau was modernizing he did not feel a part of it. Then he was ordered from Chicago to Sioux Falls to investigate a bank robbery.

Steff decided to make a suggestion. Surely Director Hoover was open to suggestions. He worked on the letter for a week. When he was satisfied with its simplicity and clarity he mailed it to the director in Washington. The letter basically suggested that his unique skills were being wasted. The reply came two weeks later: Go to St. Paul.

At the foot of the hill was the Minnehaha County Courthouse with a four-sided clock carved into its tower. Steff noted the time. It would be six hours to St. Paul. The street bottomed out. He put his foot to the gas, leaned back, and began to ascend the pernicious Minnesota Hill. Facing a forty-five-degree angle and slowly inching his way up the only mountain in Sioux Falls, Steff found himself once again gazing at Saint Joseph's Cathedral. The big beautiful church seemed out of place in South Dakota, but he found it comforting. He admired the mystic watch it kept over the town. As Steff neared the crest, it finally struck him: Saint Joseph's Cathedral belonged in Chicago. It was homesickness he felt whenever he saw it. He tried to put the gas pedal through the floor. The car chugged upward, while far below the raging falls of the Big Sioux River flowed over the quartzite and roared past the John Morrell Packing Plant.

At the top of the hill, where the state penitentiary stood, the old Ford leveled off with a cough from the carburetor, and Special Agent Steff Koslowski left Sioux Falls behind. He headed into no-man's-land where the pavement surrendered to the dust. What road he could find was his. He rested his wrist on the wheel and bounced east, past decaying barns and farm homes that were home only to the wind. The clouds of dirt he raised made the mirrors useless, but it did not matter; he knew what was back there. Dust. Dust, where cornfields were supposed to be knee-high by the Fourth of July. Dust, where golden rows of wheat were supposed to grow. Everywhere he looked, amber waves of dust.

Steff Koslowski also knew what wasn't back there: three of the men who stuck up the bank in Sioux Falls. They were in on the post-office robbery and shooting in South St. Paul. As Tin Lizzie sputtered along he placed a rap sheet over the steering wheel and read.

HOMER VAN METER—AGE 32—INDIANA PAROLEE—
ARMED ROBBERY—MURDER—GRAND THEFT AUTO—
VIOLATION OF THE DYER ACT—ARMED AND
DANGEROUS—POSSIBLE MENTAL DISORDER—
DESCRIPTION—:

He skipped over that and stacked a second sheet on top.

LESTER GILLIS—ALIAS GEORGE NELSON—AKA BABY
FACE—AGE 31—ESCAPEE ILLINOIS STATE PEN AT
JOLIET—ARMED ROBBERY—GRAND THEFT AUTO—
VIOLATION OF THE DYER ACT—ARMED AND
DANGEROUS—POSSIBLE MENTAL DISORDER—
DESCRIPTION—

Steff picked up the third rap sheet.

TOMMY CARROLL—AGE 38—RECENTLY RELEASED BY
ST PAUL POLICE—ARMED ROBBERY—GRAND THEFT
AUTO—VIOLATION OF THE DYER ACT—MACHINE
GUN EXPERT.

It was the Dyer Act that made it a federal crime to drive a stolen vehicle across a state line, and that the FBI used to chase gangsters local police could not apprehend. Still, Steff thought it strange he was being transferred just to pursue three suspects. Perhaps there was more to the move than he originally thought.

A note was attached to the rap sheets.

STOLEN VEHICLE RECOVERED IN ST PAUL
—CONTACT ASST CHIEF ST SAUVER ST PAUL PD.

And there was a memo out of Washington:

SHARE NO INFORMATION WITH ST PAUL POLICE.

Steff set the papers aside. He knew his talk with the assistant chief would be brief, his cooperation with that police department nonexistent.

He was almost two hours out of Sioux Falls and near the town of Pipestone, Minnesota, when the teapot sounded under the hood. The car lost power and jerked from side to side before choking to a halt. Steff was shocked. Steam rose in front of him the way smoke signals once rose from the Black Hills. He scrambled out of the car and tore open the hood. The engine spit

rusty water in six different directions. A minute later it
was dead. Stuck.

Steff looked around. He was near a road that led to
an Indian reservation. Already the dust bowl was behind him. A hot wind circled the Minnesota prairie and
fashioned waves of ever-changing colors. Shades of
brown and orange gave way to gold and yellow. Wild
sunflowers peeked out of the tall grass, and purple blossoms sprinkled the horizon. Pocket gophers scampered
across the road, slipped through the thistles, and were
lost in the silverleaf and honeysuckle. Storm clouds
powwowed in the western sky. Not a caring soul in sight.

Three weeks of Dakota anguish and prairie heat did
to Steff's temper what Minnesota Hill had done to Uncle
Sam's Ford. He wanted to climb onto the roof and shout
obscenities into the wind. He was fed up with small
towns and small-town ways, with rubes and Republi-
cans. He was sick of having dirt literally kicked in his
face every day. But he was a professional. A G-man.
He could take it. Steff bit his lower lip and vowed to
pursue Homer Van Meter and his slimy gang wherever
the filthy road led. He wrestled his coat and papers
from the car and grabbed his gun.

From where he stood Steff could see the prairie open
up to quarries of red stone, pipestone the color of blood.
The Indians believed the stone was sacred, coated with
the blood of their ancestors. Standing in this vestige of
the Great Sioux Nation, he thought of old Tom Mix
movies, the reckless cowboy riding the plains on his
horse, Tony, with a six-shooter on his hip and a Win-
chester over his shoulder, felling the wild and woolly
buffalo, bringing the savage red man to his knees. Steff
prayed the savage red man could help him get to St.
Paul.

Special Agent Steff Koslowski stuffed the gun in his
pants, slung the coat over his shoulder, and mumbled
to himself as he started down the road to the Indian

spiritual quarries. "Go to Chicago, Homer. Please go to Chicago."

———————————

About the time Steff Koslowski was seeking help from not-so-savage red men, Grover Mudd sauntered into the ailing newsroom. Fuzzy Byron met him at the door. At eleven A.M. the temperature was 92°. The heat wave was another week old. Fans blowing loose paper around the room looked like permanent fixtures. So did the flies buzzing through the open windows.

"What's news, Fuzzy?"

"Mr. Howard wants to see you."

"That's not news."

Fuzzy put the yellow papers to his nose. Between his failing eyesight and his perpetual hangover he delivered most of the day's news from what he heard. "The city is facing a deficit of one million six hundred thousand dollars, so one thousand four hundred city workers are going without pay and threatening to strike. In order to save money, street lamps will be extinguished at midnight every night."

"Put us back in the black, so to speak."

Fuzzy laughed and shuffled his papers as the two of them shuffled through the newsroom. "Wets and drys are still debating repeal, calling each other names. The big vote is Tuesday. Couple more things, they're kind of fuzzy here. Judge Parks ruled that merchandise slot machines are gambling machines and illegal from now on, but Mayor Mahoney and the new chief of police say they're not. Yesterday police stopped some men in a truck with a load of slot machines, but Public Safety Commissioner McDonald arrived on the scene and let them go. He denied they were related to him. Then you got this envelope here, and would you like to hear about the monkey from Omaha?" Fuzzy handed Grover a large envelope.

"What's this?"

"St. Sauver sent it over."

"Really? It's too thin to be a bomb." Grover opened it up and removed the papers inside. "It's the coroner's report on the Kendrigan twins. Maybe St. Sauver is serious about that commissioner's job." Grover read it.

Fuzzy waited. "What's it say?"

"Sand. Both had their necks broken, but sand permeated their bodies. An unusually fine, white sand, that's what it says. They had sand in their navels, and sand in their socks. The same sand was found in their nostrils, and even in the corners of their eyes. Since they were apparently playing in sand before they died, and Pig's Eye is surrounded by swampland, St. Sauver concludes they were murdered somewhere else and dumped in the lake."

"Battle Creek Park. Aren't the caves and cliffs over there filled with sand?" asked Fuzzy.

"Yeah, but that doesn't make sense. Kill them in the park, then drag them across Point Douglas Road, through the brush, and throw them in the lake. Hell of a lot of work."

"Doesn't the creek wash into the lake? They could have been thrown in the creek."

"By the end of the summer that creek isn't deep enough to wash the dirt off your toes. No, more likely they were murdered upstream and thrown into the river, then washed into the lake."

"And the sand?"

"Cliff climbing, Mound Park, Cherokee Park, mushroom caves, Yoerg's beer caves, and a hundred sandbars along the way. Anything else?"

"Just the monkey from Omaha," Fuzzy told him.

"What about it?"

They arrived at Grover's office, where Harv Bennett was blocking the doorway. He was a good reporter but Grover always thought him something of a bellyacher, and though he never came out and said it Grover suspected he had wanted the columnist job when it was open. Having listened impatiently to Fuzzy Byron's rendition of the news, Bennett stepped forward and spoke up. "What's the word, Grover, were we sold out? What do you know?"

"I don't know any more than you do, Harv."

"Don't you want to hear about the monkey from Omaha?" Fuzzy asked again.

"Listen, Grover," said Bennett, nudging Fuzzy out of the conversation, "you've got to get off this cops-and-robbers kick and give us some ink on this so-called merger, this sellout."

"C'mon," Grover shot back, "we've been running full-page ads explaining the whole lousy deal."

"They look like ads, like an act of desperation. You know how to make people mad. It's what you do best. So why not make a few thousand people mad at the ungrateful bastards who own this paper."

"I think the deal has already been cut. A few columns from me isn't going to change things."

"Are you on their side?" Harv Bennett asked the question with some hostility. "Are they feeding you under the table?"

"Their side? I've called the *North Star Press* everything but a newspaper. I'll be the first guy they ax."

"Don't you want to hear about the monkey?" asked Fuzzy, nudging his way back in.

"Now look, Grover," Harv Bennett went on, "I got a wife and four kids." He began counting on his fingers. "I used to make four hundred and eighty dollars a month. They tried this merger flimflam three years ago. We took a pay cut and they dropped it. That summer we took part of our vacations without pay. We doubled up on jobs. Some of us were doing three and four jobs around here, while you columnists rode the gravy train. We agreed to another pay cut last year, and we took another pay cut this year. Ten and fifteen percent at a crack. I'm down to a hundred and thirty dollars a month, Grover."

"I really have to tell you about the monkey, Grover."

Harv Bennett went ape. "Will you shut up, you goddamn wino!"

But for the whirling of the fans the newsroom fell
silent.

Fuzzy Byron removed his thick glasses and rubbed
his pitiful eyes. He focused them as well as he could on
Harv Bennett. "To call me a wino is to understate the
facts, but I am also an artist. My work will live a thousand years. However, Mr. Bennett, you are a reporter.
You write words. People read them. Then they wrap
garbage in them and throw them away."

"An artist," scoffed Bennett. "We saw the house you
painted on Grand Avenue."

Fuzzy Byron put his glasses back on and faded away.

"I don't think that was necessary, Harv."

"Well, dammit," he told Grover, "my friends have
been laid off and that ugly drunk is still working here."

"He gets paid out of petty cash. What's he talking
about, anyway?"

"The zoo in Omaha," Bennett explained disgustedly.
"They had this male gorilla named Casey that was hung
like an elephant. He'd been hard for six weeks.
Wouldn't come down. Medical wonder. Omaha Zoo
got a lot of complaints. He did things in front of girls.
So they got the bright idea of shipping Casey up here
to Como Zoo, to see if he'll mate with our female ape,
Tanya."

"That's true?" Grover burst. The story was a crack-
up. "I thought St. Sauver was joking. Why don't they
just put a dollar in his hand and drop him off on St.
Peter Street?"

"Forget the monkey, Mudd, none of us can afford to
lose our jobs here."

"And why the hell are you crying to me about this?"

Grover's short temper was about to explode when
Harv Bennett turned misty-eyed diplomat. "What I'm
trying to say is this deal stinks and we'd appreciate it

if you'd show more concern. The *North Star Press* has been trying for years to make this a one-newspaper town, and there's not a city in this country the size of St. Paul that has only one newspaper. Walt Howard respects you. Talk to him for us, will you? And give us a little ink." Bennett wiped the sweat from his red face and went back to work.

The editor's door was open. Grover knocked.

Walt Howard stood at his desk with his few remaining troops in front of him. He glanced over their heads at Grover, then ignored him and went back to passing out assignments. A big copper fan was humming in the window. The papers on Mr. Howard's desk were weighted down in an orderly fashion. When he was done with them his people scurried from the office, squeezing past Grover as if he had a contagious disease. "Come in, Mudd."

If there was one thing Grover hated it was being called Mudd, just plain Mudd.

A degree from the University of Minnesota hung on the dirty white wall behind the editor's desk. On a side wall the sun streaming through the window fell across pictures of Walt Howard and Minnesota's greats. Walt Howard and former secretary of state Frank B. Kellogg. Walt Howard with United States Supreme Court Justice Pierce Butler, and United States Solicitor General William Mitchell. A young Walt Howard pictured with railroad baron James J. Hill and Archbishop John Ireland. The handsomely framed photos took up half the wall. A picture of his wife was on his desk. "Sit down, Mudd."

Grover sank into a soft leather chair and wondered if his old swivel had ever been in such condition.

Walt Howard remained standing. He was tall and slim; his silver hair was neatly combed back. Behind the wire-rimmed glasses were wise gray eyes with experience written all over them. Written in newsprint. "Anything new on those two boys?"

"I have a copy of the coroner's report. I'll write it up."

The editor of the *St. Paul Frontier News* seemed cold and uninterested. He picked up a bulletin. "This is just off the wire, a big prison break at the Indiana State Penitentiary in Michigan City. Ten long-termers walked right out the front door. They're considered armed and dangerous. I'm going to run it across the top."

"If they're smart they'll catch the first train to St. Paul."

Mr. Howard put down the bulletin and handed Grover another sheet. "Yesterday the Minneapolis City Council passed an ordinance banning men's swim trunks without tops. Anybody caught swimming at city lakes with a bare chest will be fined. Why don't you see if 'Grover's Corner' can have some fun with our friends across the river."

Grover read the anachronism. "I'm sure I'll have no trouble getting a column out of this." He laid the paper on the edge of the desk. "But I really don't think you called me into your office to discuss the Mill City's retreat to the nineteenth century."

"No, I didn't." Walt Howard sat at his desk. "Once again, as you have undoubtedly heard, negotiations are under way to sell the *Frontier News* to the North Star Press Company. It may take a few months but I believe this time the sale will go through."

"So the *North Star Press* is going to get everything they want," Grover said without hesitation.

"There's a depression out there, Mudd. Newspapers aren't above its effects. Over two hundred dailies across the country have gone under this year. The *Frontier News* hasn't made money in years."

Grover went on. "The *North Star Press* gets complete domination over the city, complete domination over the advertising. Set their own rates. No choice. You want a St. Paul newspaper, pay the *North Star Press*."

"The deal our owners are trying to strike is this," Walt Howard patiently explained. "The *North Star* would own the paper but the *Frontier News* would continue to act and publish independently. Hundreds of people would keep their jobs."

"Of course they would," stated Grover. "To throw them out of work now would run smack into the NRA, wouldn't it? A program the two papers have patriotically supported. How long would a charade like that last? One year? Two? Until after the election of '36? The fact is, while our people were marching in that gigantic parade they were being sold down the river."

The editor continued as if Grover Mudd were not interrupting him. "And if the *Frontier News* were to cease publication, the *North Star Press* would absorb as many of our employees as possible."

"And how does that work?" Grover asked rhetorically. "Is the *North Star Press* going to put two reporters at every typewriter? Will two men sit at each linotype, occupy each press station?"

Walt Howard pulled a handkerchief from his breast pocket and removed his glasses to clean them. The paper was through. Grover could see it in his eyes.

"And what becomes of you?" Grover asked.

"I've been offered an executive editorial position with the *North Star*. They're good people. I began my career with them."

"And 'Grover's Corner'?"

The St. Paul editor folded his handkerchief and pressed it back in his pocket. He adjusted the glasses to his face. "You are in a precarious position, Mudd. The other paper likes to accentuate the positive. That's not exactly your forte, is it?"

"I was born and raised in St. Paul. I think, over the years, I've written some of the most positive things published about the future prospects of this city, and this state. Or have you forgotten those pieces?"

"No, I haven't forgotten, Mudd. You've done some fine work. I also can't forget that every year on December twenty-sixth, right in the middle of the holiday season, you feel compelled to remind everybody, through your column, that this is the anniversary of that infamous day back in 1863 when thirty-eight Indians were hanged by the neck in Mankato, Minnesota, making it the largest mass execution in American history. Are we going to see a similar piece this year?"

"What I thought I would do this year, in order to accentuate the positive, is point out that the good people of Minnesota had every intention of hanging three hundred Indians, until President Lincoln put a stop to it."

"How many times, Mudd, have you reminded our readers that in 1920 Minnesota led the nation in lynchings?"

"It was those three negroes they strung up in Duluth that pushed us over the top. Hardly my fault people in this state have a penchant for swinging men from the neck, not to mention a few women we've dangled from a rope. A bit strange considering capital punishment was abolished in Minnesota over twenty years ago. If it hadn't been for some fancy footwork by the feds we could have added Roger Touhy's name to our list. I think it only positive someone point out this peculiar proclivity of ours."

"History is a funny thing, Mudd. Much of it comes to us secondhand—point of view, assumption, conjecture, theory. We Americans like to wash our history, rinse it out and hang it up to dry, hope it comes out nice and white. Excuse the pun, but you keep throwing mud on the laundry."

"Perhaps I could just ring up the Chamber of Commerce every morning and beg them for the big scoop."

Walt Howard responded quickly. "How come when

Secretary of State Kellogg, former St. Paul lawyer, won the Nobel Peace Prize, no word of it could be found in 'Grover's Corner'? And what of that literary gang from the Kilmarnock Bookshop you ran around with? Sinclair Lewis, the first American to win the Nobel Prize for literature and we didn't read one congratulatory word from his friend Grover Mudd. Scott Fitzgerald, another pal of yours, why have we never seen a column on him? Remember when this heat wave began? I called you in here and asked for something on a lake, any one of our ten thousand lakes. Do you remember what you wrote?"

"Yes, I do," Grover answered. "My mail was never heavier."

"You handed in one of the most nauseating articles I've ever read."

"There was an avalanche of complaints from the people living around Lake Phalen about the drinking parties going on out there. The police did their usual nothing so I thought it was time somebody said something."

"I plugged my nose and ran that piece, Mudd. Every repugnant euphemism. I print everything you write. That will be your undoing."

Grover felt the conversation was trite. He was direct. "Is the murder of those two boys going to be St. Paul's undoing? Or are you really going to let it pass?"

Mr. Howard took a pensive pause. "My editorial on the killings will be in tomorrow's paper."

"On the editorial page?" asked Grover.

"Where else?"

"On the front page," Grover told him. "Where it belongs."

"You said yourself they weren't gangland killings."

"So what, they don't count?" Grover was mad. For the *Frontier News*, time was running out. The back of his shirt was sticking to the leather. He leaned forward, caught his breath, muffled a cough, and calmed himself.

"Put 'Grover's Corner' on the front page. I'll take the heat."

"Yeah, my foot. I take enough crap about your column on the back pages. Those Moral Rearmament people on my butt. There's some battle-ax of a schoolteacher on the East Side ready to lead a crusade against us. She writes me threatening letters every week, never forgetting your name."

"Your editorials on the front page couldn't be ignored," said Grover, pleading his case. "The *North Star* will never give you this chance."

"I know you never finished college, Mudd, so let me finish it for you. The front page is for the news, and the sports page is for the sports. The funnies page is where we put the comic strips, and the editorial page is where we place the editorials, our opinions. When we place our opinions on the front page we cross the line. We are no longer reporting the news, we are trying to make the news. We don't cross the line, Mudd." Walt Howard smoothed away the beading perspiration above his lips. "You're not the only one who cares. I have met with the owners of both papers and we discussed in length our crime and corruption problem and a newspaper's role in covering it."

"The owners of the *Frontier News* live in Chicago, and the owners of the *North Star Press* live in New York," Grover reminded him. "To them this is just a horse-drawn hick town. Soon to become a one-paper hick town."

"You have two types of readers, Mudd. Those who love your butt, and those who hate your guts." Suddenly there was some feeling in the editor's voice, frustration with a touch of anger. "In the upcoming months don't let your popularity slide too much the wrong way." The man in charge of the dying newspaper gathered business in front of him. He picked up a fountain pen.

The meeting was over. Grover knew it. He stood and

walked to the door. Then he stopped and turned. "Which way is the wrong way?"

"I haven't decided yet. Get out of here."

No joy, no misery passes unnoticed. They live among the hard facts of life, reality, as it is called. It is the reality of a swamp and they are the frogs who have nothing better to do than to croak. The more they croak the more real life becomes. Newspapermen—the quacks who have their fingers on the pulse of the world. A constant atmosphere of calamity. It's marvelous. It's as if the barometer never changed, as if the flag were always at half-mast.

Grover Mudd closed the book, *Tropic of Cancer*. His workday was done. He had a window seat on the Rondo–Stryker. The words on his lap were written by a young expatriate in Paris named Henry Miller. Just released in Europe, the writing had already been branded obscene in America and banned. Grover bought the novel wrapped in brown paper in the backroom of the Kilmarnock Bookshop. The sex in it was great. He would proudly add it to his collection of banned books. With pangs of regret Grover gazed out at his hometown and remembered dreams deferred: the trains at Gare St. Lazare; blue novels; red wine and sidewalk cafés; beautiful women on beautiful boulevards with beautiful names he couldn't pronounce. But the trolley didn't pass by the Cathedral of Notre Dame, it rolled by the Cathedral of Saint Paul, then struck west on Rondo Avenue.

It was a quiet ride. The main thoroughfare was up on University Avenue while Rondo Avenue cut through a neighborhood called Cornmeal Valley. The misnomer conjured up scenes of New York's Harlem, or State Street in Chicago, but St. Paul's negro district was not those places. The area was only half colored at most, and there was a seedy charm to the joints along the way. Signs hanging from modest wood structures with peeling paint and grimy windows offered Barb BQ and Chili, Chicken and Ribs, Beer and Dance. Vacant lots collected junk. Tired Victorian houses climbed the curbless side streets where weeds grew on the boulevards and unpruned trees crowded the rooftops. At the police substation on Western Avenue the fire hydrant was open, and uniformed officers squirted frolicking children.

Grover hopped off at St. Albans Street and dropped into the neighborhood co-op store, where he bought a bag of groceries. Then he trekked a few blocks south where, crossing a dirt patch called Holcombe Park, he seemed dwarfed by church steeples. Every denomination had a block staked out. Through the tree branches he could see the green domes of the cathedral. Cornmeal Valley was tucked neatly behind the great church and ran parallel to opulent Summit Avenue only a few blocks away.

It was a three-story brownstone row house on St. Albans Street he turned into. Heavy black balconies hung from the second floor and gave the place a French flavor. Dormer windows accented the third floor. At ground level concrete steps led to round porches that sat in the shade of boulevard trees. The grass needed cutting. A path of dirt tore through the lawn to the rear. Grover mounted the steps of the corner house. A breeze whispered by, the tease of a cool front coming through. The heat was dissipating with the setting sun. The humidity was dropping. He stepped into the hallway and knocked on a flimsy screen door at the foot of a narrow staircase.

The day's events had unsettled Grover. The Pig's Eye murders were already inching off the front page. The owners of the paper were selling out. His friend Fuzzy had been humiliated. A boyhood friend, Tommy Carroll, had been identified as a gangland member. Grover needed a drink. He coughed into a closed fist, wiped the water from his eyes, and knocked again.

The boy gave the screen a hard shove. Grover jumped aside. The door swung in a half-circle and slapped the bricks. The little boy stepped back. His clean white T-shirt was tucked snugly into his trousers. His baggy pants were neatly cuffed at the bottom. He was barefoot. "Hi, Grober. She ina kishen. Washa brung?"

"Food." He pulled the screen door shut behind him.

"Can'y?"

Grover reached into the bag and found a Baby Ruth bar. The boy's face lit up. "Go outside and eat it or your mother will kill me."

Brody took the candy in both hands and darted past him. The screen door slapped the bricks again. Grover pulled it shut.

A dime-store throw rug lay on the hardwood floor. Tan shades hung over the curtainless windows. The couch was tattered in spots; a blanket covered it. Healthy potted plants sat on end tables that were nicked along the edges. One table, missing a leg, was supported with an orange crate. The lamps looked as if they belonged in a hotel. What made the shabby furniture stand out was the cleanliness of the place. The floors were clean and waxed, the tables dust-free and polished. The chairs were brushed. Only a toy or two broke the order of the room. He found Stormy in the kitchen. Grover set the groceries on the table. "Hi ya, Brown Eyes."

"Hi, Grover. I heard you give Brody that candy. I asked you not to do that. What's in the bag?"

"Some things to nibble on and enough chocolate to keep you choking for a week."

"I got you some more apples from the hotel. They're in the icebox. They're some more of the good ones from Washington."

"You're going to get caught smuggling things out of there one of these days and find yourself without a job."

"Everybody steals from the hotel. Just little stuff. Have you eaten yet?"

"No, but you don't have to bother. I just thought I'd stop and say hello on my way home."

Two years earlier he had been attending a press luncheon at the Hotel Saint Paul, up the street from the *Frontier News*. After boring and hypocritical speeches on civic responsibility he was invited to a private party in a ninth-floor suite, where the real refreshments were being served. Grover left the party after an hour. He was not drunk, but two shots of his favorite moonshine allowed his very own personal depression to set in. His eyes were cast down on the plush red carpeting as he shuffled along the hallway to the elevator. A colored girl was stuffing sheets into a laundry bag. They were alone. He paid no attention to her. He pushed the bronze button, slipped his hands into his pockets, and waited. His recent divorce had his head in a whirl. He did not miss the lousy bitch, but he could already feel distance growing between himself and his son. His daughter was too young to understand.

"Grover's Corner" was gaining notoriety, but he had doubts about keeping up the pace, turning out five columns a week with the sharpness and frankness he prided himself in. Urbane he wasn't. He couldn't quote the rules of grammar, his spelling was atrocious, his vocabulary was limited, he didn't always know where the comma went, but he believed if he wrote with his heart and his guts people would read him.

The elevator was taking forever. He glanced up at the arrow. It was still five floors away. Then, in the softness and sweet innocence of a child's voice, he was asked, "Are you Grover Mudd, the newspaperman?"

Her chestnut eyes caught his, then shied away, embarrassed at having asked the question. She was tall and slender, curvedly slender, not skinny, and not taller than him, but tall for a girl. Her striped maid uniform was clean and pressed and it fit her perfectly, showing off her figure. He put her age in the early twenties. It was her hair that impressed him right off. It was negro hair, yet it was somehow different: longer and glimmering black. She wore it down over her shoulders and it had a controlled wildness to it, meticulously cared for. Grover never thought of colored girls as pretty—he rarely gave colored people much thought at all—but this girl was pretty. "Yes, I am. How did you know that?" His picture had not been in the paper in years. He did not have his face at the top of his column as others did, those banalities sketched in America's newspapers sucking on a pipe with the tops of their heads chopped off, brainless, like the insipid claptrap that ran in their space.

"It says so on your name tag," she told him.

He had forgotten about the formal piece of paper pinned to his coat. Grover sheepishly removed it and dropped it in his pocket, feeling for the moment like sucking on a pipe.

"I read the *Frontier News* all the time," she went on. Her shyness was charming. She glanced down or away whenever she spoke, then caught his eyes at the end of each sentence. "You're funny. 'Grover's Corner' makes me laugh. I read it to my little boy. He doesn't understand, but he laughs too."

"What's your name?"

"Stormy Day."

Grover smiled. "I've seen a lot of those, but I've never met one before."

"My father named me after his favorite racehorse." She laughed. It was an infectious laugh, and Grover laughed along with her.

The next time he had business at the hotel he made it a point to see if she was working and say hello. The time after that he was not sure if he was at the Saint Paul on business or just to see her pretty face and hear her laugh. It was not long before he found out where she lived, and that she lived alone with her little boy.

He made up his mind to stop by and see her one day.
He did not know why. It would be a short visit. Of that
he was sure. He had been visiting for two years now.

Stormy roamed the house barefoot in her maid uniform. He rarely saw her in anything else. Her own
wardrobe consisted of several antiquated dresses and a
purple Sunday dress, but even the Sunday dress was
provincial and worn. Grover often thought about buying her new clothes; then he would set the thought
aside. New clothes were for going out.

The summer evening wore on quickly for Grover
Mudd. She and the boy made him feel good in a way
the whiskey never could. Stormy made them a big sup-
per. He made them laugh. When dark came Grover
dragged Brody to the bedroom and tossed him in bed.
He slept in his underwear. His bed sheets and pillowcase
were sanitary white and wrinkle-free, just like in a hotel.
Grover covered him with the sheets. The boy kicked
them off.

"Too hot," he said. "Can't sleep."

Grover sat on the edge of the bed. Stormy stood in
the doorway. The child's paintings were taped to the
wall.

"I know how you feel, kid," Grover told him. "When
I was a boy, on hot summer nights my daddy would
pack up the bed gear and we'd go sleep down on the
riverbank. Catch the cool air coming off the water."

"Dinna ya get mugged?"

"Oh, no. A lot of people slept down there then. It
was one big powwow."

"We'd get mugged."

"Yes, today we'd get mugged." Grover said good
night, got up, and turned out the light. She took his
hand and they walked to the living room. "I'd better
be going, Stormy. It's getting late."

"Can't you stay and talk?"

"Maybe for a bit."

The words had been spoken a hundred times before,

part of a game they played. They sat on the couch. A soft lamp was left burning across the room. The shades on the open bay windows were pulled three-quarters down. A breeze with some long-lost coolness to it drifted in off St. Albans Street. They talked in hushed tones, intimate voices, almost in whispers.

Grover talked of his ex-wife, how he married only half in love and ended up half hating the woman. He shared with Stormy the uncomfortable feeling he had around his children, that awful silence that came with not knowing what to say. He dreaded his visiting rights. Take them to the park, take them to the zoo, take them anywhere they could entertain themselves. He wondered aloud how it was he got along better with her child than he did his own. He wished he loved his children as much as he despised his ex-wife. Grover went on for an hour.

Stormy asked about the sale of the paper. She said it was silly. She said it was st*uuu*pid. He loved the way she talked, often drawling the "u" for emphasis. Short "u" or long "u," Stormy let it drawl. Love became l*uuu*v. Beautiful became bea*uuu*tiful. Grover told her about his meeting with Walt Howard.

"Doesn't he like you, Grover?"

"He puts up with me."

"But yo*uuu* said he got you your job."

"That was a long time ago. After the war. He was a big-shot reporter with the *Frontier News* and he came to interview me. Then he went out of his way to get me a job with the paper. My only qualifications were three years towards an English degree. I thought Walt Howard was the greatest guy in the world, with the exception of that tiny flaw in his speech."

"What flaw?"

"His lips are unable to form the word Grover. He's called me Mudd from the first day we met. 'Send that Mudd kid in here.' 'Sloppy work, Mudd.' 'Where in hell did you learn how to write, Mudd?' 'How would

you like a shot at your own column, Mudd?' I was pretty
touchy about it when I first started, kept seeing my
father's name screaming from the papers. I was never
sure if Walt Howard ever made the connection between
Mudd the soldier and Mudd the old engineer in the
train wreck. Fifteen years and he's never once called
me Grover."

Stormy smiled and held his arm. She was a good
listener. Grover knew how much he meant to her, and
he was growing concerned. She meant a great deal more
to him than he had ever planned.

Stormy talked of growing up in St. Louis, and of the
boy who got her pregnant at seventeen. "There's two
types of colored people," she told Grover. "Light-
skinned and dark-skinned. Light-skinned ones get
treated better, and they get better jobs. Because I'm
dark-skinned, and they found out the boy that got me
pregnant was dark-skinned, I got sent away." Her cou-
sin had a friend who worked at a hotel in St. Paul and
had a room to rent. So Stormy Day left the Gateway
to the West in disgrace and disgust and moved far up
the river to Minnesota. She liked St. Paul and could
not always understand why Grover spoke badly of it.
The people did not speak with that Missouri twang that
smacked of prejudice. The avenues that tunneled
through the tall trees made every neighborhood seem
welcoming, even though most of them were restricted.
She was not Catholic but she never missed Sunday mass
at the cathedral. The church was the most beautiful
thing she had ever seen. She knew God could be found
there. After walking the mile in her purple dress she
would take her place in a back pew, stare up into the
great dome and shed tears with the figures in the
stained-glass windows. She asked God to forgive her,
punish her if he must, but give her little boy a better
life.

For Grover Mudd it was as awkward as the first time
he ever touched her. The closeness to Stormy's body

set butterflies free in his stomach. His knees went weak. He was fifteen again. He touched her face. She murmured and leaned into him. She unbuttoned his shirt.

"It's okay, Grover."

He knew it was okay, but even after two years he could not go on without her permission. Her hair still fascinated him, its deceptive look, its velvety softness. She called it nappy and said it took an hour to fix every morning. He ran his fingers through the thick curls, nudged her close, and kissed her. She slid her arms around him. There was a freshness about her. Her perfume was special, a touch of that fancy fragrance the rich ladies at the hotel wore. He kissed her again and Stormy drew his tongue into her mouth. They stretched gently out on the couch. Grover laid his body across hers. He loved the kissing. They could go on for hours, never parting lips. Outside the uproarious city was still, or their heavy breathing made it seem that way. The night air was cooling. For the first time in months his clothes were not sticking to his skin. Grover inched the uniform up over her knees, slowly up her thighs, up to her waist. He slid his hands behind her and down her panties. Her legs spread. He cupped her hips into his. Stormy drew his tongue in deeper. She held it there for the longest time, then tore away and hugged his head. They lay motionless.

"You missed the last trolley, Grover."

"The last trolley" were the last words in the game they played. Grover came to his knees and massaged her legs. He could not take his eyes off them, the youth, the length, the midnight sleekness. Then, like a child who begins opening a present before he is supposed to, Grover tugged the wrapping back into place and smoothed away the wrinkles. He helped her to her feet. They embraced. Kissed. Danced slowly to music that was not playing. Stormy turned out the lamp.

A huge oak tree stood in the backyard. Its branches swayed in the wind like a gospel choir, throwing shad-

ows against the bedroom wall that looked like giant
arms, black arms reaching for something they could
never have, rooted to the same spot for generations to
come.

Stormy turned down the sheets. They embraced again
at the foot of the bed. She was frail, so fragile he could
have snapped her with a hug. It made him want to
protect her more. Grover undid the buttons on the back
of her uniform. The dress slipped to the floor and she
stepped out of it. Standing only in her panties she put
her arms around his neck and toyed with his hair. He
toyed with her breast. They were fully rounded and
delicate with large dark nipples.

Stormy undressed him teasingly. She rubbed him
through his underwear before stripping him completely.
Then she handled him softly, lovingly. Grover per-
suaded her into bed with little effort. She was strikingly
beautiful, lying on her back, one leg bent slightly over
the other, one hand stroking his face. He wished he
could love her every night, but St. Paul would not let
him—or was it Saint Mudd standing in his way? His
fingers ringed her panties, drew them to her knees, her
ankles; he tossed them to the floor. Grover Mudd
climbed on top of her and whispered kisses over her
innocent face, her lovely neck, her shapely shoulders.
He inched his lips lower and lower. He took a nipple
into his mouth and took his time. He inched lower. Her
tummy was flat and firm. He kissed it, tongued it, and
went on. He rubbed his hands over her hips and when
he got between her legs he paused. He teased her. He
kissed her thighs. Another second of anticipation. He
passed a finger over her. She drew a sharp breath. Then
he covered her with his mouth and tasted her. She
moaned and repeated his name. She told him no man
had ever done that to her before, that he was the only
one who ever cared about her pleasure.

Stormy returned the pleasure when Grover rolled
over. She moved down on him slow, put the head to

her mouth and drew moist circles with her tongue. She worked her way to her knees and took him deep into her mouth, rocked her whole body to and fro. It was too much. Grover made her stop. He rolled her over. He laid his head on her stomach. She stroked his hair. They were silent. When he began to work his way down for more she urged him back to her face and told him with her shy brown eyes that she could wait no longer, the teasing was at its peak. She was moist and warm and he could never get over how easy she drew him in, how right it was with this woman. She reached behind and forced him deeper. Her hips moved with a graceful rhythm. Their mouths were inseparable.

For minutes after it was over they lay kissing, refusing to part. It was Grover who exhausted first. He flopped to his back and ached for a cigarette. He could not keep from comparing Stormy's lovemaking to that of his ex-wife. A more materialistic woman never lived than the one he had spent ten years with. Ten years of sporadic sex and she never let one drop get away from her. She did not want the sheets messed. The woman had tissues stuffed between her legs before Grover could get the damn thing out. They used to count to three together and he would withdraw while she would stuff. Then off to the bathroom she would waddle like a penguin, tissues between her legs and a silly grin on her face. *"Now don't look, Grover."* Ten years!

Stormy let the come run down her legs. She said she liked the way it felt. Sometimes she asked him to rub it in. He asked about the sheets once and she made him feel foolish by laughing out, "Wh*ooo* cares?"

Grover leaned on his elbow and propped his head up. His other hand played with her breast. He knew there would be a second time. Sometimes a third and fourth time. Sometimes after they climaxed he would stay hard and stay in her until they climaxed again.

She reached up and ran a finger across his upper lip. "Did you know there's a Clark Gable movie at the State

Theater. Fifteen cents. Any seat, anytime, anybody."

"I'm pretty busy of late, Stormy, with all the layoffs and cutbacks we've had. The movie will be there for a while."

"I understand, Grover."

"Do you?"

"Would you lose your job 'cause of me?"

He smiled, kissed her, wrapped her in his arms. "If I lose my job it won't have anything to do with you."

"We could go over to Minneapolis, Grover. Nobody knows you there."

"What would we do in Minneapolis?"

"We would go to a fancy restaurant with lots of candles. There's places like that in Minneapolis that would let us in, Grover. I've heard so. Then after that we could go to a movie. Then we would row a boat out on Lake Calhoun and look at the stars. And when we got home we would be so tired we'd just flop in bed and fall asleep in each other's arms."

"Do you have these dreams often?"

"They're just little dreams, Grover."

She looked hurt and Grover knew he had said the wrong thing. He was the kind of guy who always said the wrong thing. "I'm only joking you, Brown Eyes. You hang onto your dreams and we'll see."

"I understand, Grover."

In Minnesota the passing of summertime weather to autumn is not measured in days, it is measured in hours. The night wind blew cool. Leaves on the big oak snapped at each other. Thunder rumbled in the distance. A September chill set in. Summer was over. Grover pulled the sheets over them and eased on top of her. "We'll see," he said again. He took her face in his hands and brushed her forehead with a kiss, and was soon inside her again.

Grover woke before dawn with retching spasms. He hung his head over the floor and gagged. He had a violent dream but could not remember what it was about. It was not like the old dreams. Then she was on his mind, the gorgeous blonde from the kidnapping trial. Was she in the dream? He could not remember. Stormy's hand was on his shoulder. She understood. With her on top they made love again in a half-sleep.

She fixed him breakfast in the wee hours. Then Grover left the house and started for the corner. Lightning bolts split the dark. If he caught the first trolley of the morning he could grab a few more hours of sleep before work. The thunder was on top of him now. He broke into a run that hurt his chest. The clouds opened up. Down it came.

Grover Mudd ran through Cornmeal Valley with rain pouring over him. He'd bet his last dollar the Big Holy Spook had something to do with it.

Nina the Ballerina

Beyond the turn of the century, through the Roaring Twenties, and into the Great Depression, the city clung to its Victorian past. But the mansions, the shaded parkways, the streets of wedged brick, the beautiful lakes, the very name itself, were all a sprawling façade. St. Paul was born a lusty town.

Soldiers at a new fort, fur traders rich with pelts, whiskey-loving Indians. And the first whores came up the river. Then came an invasion of lumbermen, who raped the pine-laden state of two-thirds of its trees and floated them downstream to build St. Paul and St. Louis and a hundred towns in between. The logs flowed south and the whores flowed north. Next came the railroads and the robber barons. Iron ore and iron men. Swedish farmers, German brewers, and Irish politicians. And the whores came up the river.

The long shiny Cadillac swung off River Drive onto West Seventh Street and angled through town, rushing by the lush green hills of Highland Park and the medieval Jacob Schmidt Brewery. It sailed past gothic Ancker Hospital, which handled city and county emergencies, and circled the bluff behind the Northern States Power High Bridge Plant. Then it dropped into downtown at Seven Corners, the most chaotic intersection in the city.

Seven streets came together and carved the buildings into arrowheads. Small businesses lined the sidewalks.

Traffic was snarled. No less than eight streetcars man-aged to trolley through the intersection at the same time without crossing wires. The bright sun shining over the web of cables gave the corner a checkerboard look. Pedestrians, like ants, darted through the traffic. There was one traffic cop. Occasionally he blew his whistle. Once in a while he raised a paw and growled.

The black Caddy nudged a sharp right turn. It skirted the public baths, then dropped again, this time into the historic Irvine Park neighborhood. Roxanne Schultz rolled down the rear window of the limousine. It was a brisk autumn day, one of those wonderful Indian-summer days when kids played hooky and footballs played catch with the clouds. The trees were splashed with dazzling colors. The air had a fresh bite to it. Roxanne admired the historic homes with their tall iron gates and rolling green lawns. They slowed in front of the well-preserved home of Alexander Ramsey, Min-nesota's first governor. Gardeners were busy raking away the October leaves and burning them before the untidiness could be recorded. The red and orange of the maples, shades of yellow from the elms, and dif-ferent browns of the oaks were gathered in piles and set ablaze. Thick ashes rose to the sky behind roofs of golden shingles and sailed away in the pre-arctic breeze.

The chauffeur turned left and the Cadillac rolled to a stop. It parked on the wrong side of the street in front of the house at 147 Washington Street, where the fancy neighborhood came to an abrupt end, where stately homes met unsaintly homes in the Under the Hill Dis-trict at the foot of the cliffs below City Hall. The black-capped chauffeur jumped from the car and opened the door for the boss's girl. Roxanne stepped out.

A crusty building stood like death directly across the street, a shivering cold place of dirty gray bricks and expired vines. The ghostly windows had tainted yellow shades hanging behind them. The chimney was at the front of the roof and Roxanne could imagine the kind of smoke that went through the stack. Goose bumps ran up her arms. It was the Ramsey County Morgue.

Looming next door was a rambling structure four stories high that climbed the cliffs along Steep Street, which dropped off Kellogg Boulevard like a trapdoor and met Washington Street at the bottom. Bars decorated most of the windows, and out front was a line of rusty black cars, turned sharply to the curb. The infamous St. Paul Police Station.

Roxanne put on her white gloves and checked the hem of her turquoise dress. "Do I look all right?" she asked the chauffeur.

"Far too good for this place, Miss Roxanne."

"I mean, do I . . ." She stopped. She was being silly. He'd answered her question. She reached into the back seat, drew a large handbag, then turned to the house of Nina Clifford.

Four stairs led to the two-story brownstone. An arched porch sheltered a polished door of Minnesota's finest dark oak. Off to the right another set of stairs followed a railing down to an impregnable door of cast iron. Round, slender columns provided the perpendicular trim. Three of them stroked the front of the house and stuck out over the flat roof like penis heads. A red stone in the shape of a star shone on the roof over the upper bay windows, suggesting that patrons would be watched over; and in a way they were, considering the buildings across the street.

Roxanne made use of the brass knocker. She tapped lightly. A fat colored woman opened the door. They did not speak. Roxanne was ushered into the parlor to wait for the lady of the house.

The room was orderly and spotless but reeked of aging. The musty smell of days gone by lingered on, cigar smoke and rum, spice cologne water and French perfume, good scotch and pine poker chips. The European furniture on the threadbare rug was not antique, it was dead. Heavy curtains were drawn tight over the picture window, blocking out the gorgeous day. Roxanne waited.

On the wall was a large imperious oil painting of a strangely alluring woman, as if the room had been built for the portrait. The fascinating figure had dark, straightforward eyes and rainbow brows. The nose dominated the face, almost to the point of being unattractive, and there was the obligatory enigmatic smile. Dark hair dropped over a low-cut scarlet dress with fine lace trim. The painting was as captivating as the folklore that surrounded the woman who had posed for it. Roxanne recalled the legends as she waited.

She heard no footsteps, just the eerie creak of the doorknob.

Nina Clifford entered the room with a hint of arrogance and a wealth of secrets. She closed the door with a gentle press of the hand and listened for the click of the latch before turning to her guest. She was old. Her thick makeup could not mask the blue-veiny nose or the rumpled face hiding under the ugliest crimson wig Roxanne had ever seen. A beauty mark on her chin looked like an early sign of leprosy. The heavy green dress and the black lace scarf she modeled were French, but pre-war French. Was it possible this old bat was once the most powerful woman in the state? Could she ever have been the enchantress in the painting?

"Hello, Angel."

"You should know my name by now, Miss Clifford. It's Roxanne. Roxanne Schultz. It's German."

"Of course it is, my girl. When I was a young lady I, too, had a German name."

"I'm not one of your girls." She paused. Nina waited. Then Roxanne added a touch of respect: "Miss Clifford."

"I know you're not, my dear. I should be so lucky to have in my care one as pretty as you."

There was something transparent and wicked about Nina Clifford's politeness that set Roxanne's nerves on fire. To Roxanne, Nina was a witch. Yet, there was also something about the ancient whore Roxanne couldn't resist, a motherly quality she not only surrendered to but sometimes sought out. "Thank you, Miss Clifford." Roxanne reached into the handbag. "I have your package." She held out a baseball-size bundle wrapped in green paper.

"Well, this is unusual. I've never known Mr. Rankin to assign deliveries to his women."

"This is a special delivery. A message comes with it. Dag says deliveries may get more difficult, next to impossible."

Nina relieved her of the goodies. "I can handle the local authorities. I always have. Payment will be as usual."

"This may not be local." Roxanne searched her bag for a cigarette. She found one at the bottom. "Machine Gun Kelly is on trial in Oklahoma for the Urschel kidnapping."

"Yes, I've read about it."

"His wife testified that the snatch was planned here, and that they came here after collecting the ransom."

"*Did* they?"

Roxanne watched the cigarette shake between her fingers. "Dag washed the money. Now he has word of a new federal operation with its focus on St. Paul."

"I see. Please tell Mr. Rankin that his efforts and his information are sincerely appreciated. Payment will be as usual."

"I'm afraid you don't understand, Miss Clifford. The price rises with the risk. Also, Dag feels the madams should be pushing more dope. He needs the cash."

"My lord, how much is he bringing in?"

"As much as he can buy."

"Is it safe? I have a warehouse."

"I don't know where he keeps it, but you're to instruct the houses to push dope. Tell Mr. Gleckman."

"*Am* I, now? Yesterday a police lieutenant came here

and told me that to be safe from raids we must begin serving Old Style Lager Beer. That's not even a local brand. A man up at City Hall tells us what cigarettes to sell. And now Mr. Rankin wants the sparrows pushing dope. Or what?"

"Push the junk, Miss Clifford, not Dag."

The old lady remained a picture of composure, like the painting on the wall. "Do you know how many Dag Rankins have come and gone in my lifetime?"

It was no surprise that Rankin had sent his woman to deal with Nina Clifford. The dickless jerk. The only time he wanted to see Nina was when she could help him dream of manhood again. Roxanne extinguished her smoke in a dime-store ashtray. She was feeling sick. "He'll cut you off, Miss Clifford. That's no idle threat."

"You may want to remind Mr. Rankin that I'm his connection to the local police, and they, too, are beginning to push. Prohibition has been good to them, but those days are coming to an end. We can all profit from this new venture." Nina came to her, stroked her golden hair and wrapped her arm gently in hers. "He must let me help with storage and distribution." She smiled and added, "Payment will be as usual."

"Yes, Miss Clifford."

Nina Clifford walked Roxanne to the front door. "Will you be joining us again, Angel?"

"I don't think I will."

"Oh, but you must come. It's not business, and it's hard to imagine Mr. Rankin without you at his side. You both enjoy it so."

She did enjoy it. But she hated surrendering to this twentieth-century witch and her magic potions. "If Dag insists I come along, I will, but I won't partake."

Nina grinned good-bye as the fat colored woman approached the door.

Roxanne Schultz left the house with a feeling of defeat and shame, of being manipulated, of being treated like a slut from Swede Hollow. She was angry. The

chauffeur opened the door for her, but that was not
respect, that was his goddamn job, and she knew it.
The finer things in life still eluded her. And she knew
it.

Nestled among a plethora of elms, maples, and oaks in
a residential neighborhood below Indian Mound Park
on St. Paul's burgeoning East Side was Mound Park
Elementary School, where the Kendrigan twins once
marched to class. The new building of red clay and white
trim was the picture of tranquillity, situated on a small
bluff where slanting Cypress Street crossed Pacific Avenue. On this fine October day, while Roxanne Schultz
was consigning a cache of opium to one of the great
madams in American history, the president of the local
chapter of Moral Rearmament was conducting a civics
lesson for her sixth-grade class in a corner classroom
on the second floor.

"Miss Pearl," she was asked, "is it true our police
department is on the pad?"

She was a tall, fiftyish spinster with dyed red hair.
She had thirty pupils. They were restless. Outside was
the fleeting beauty of a Minnesota autumn. The sun
sprinkled gold dust on the treetops. The sky was at its
richest blue. Fire-colored leaves broke away from
branches and zigzagged to the ground. A row of screen-
less windows was open, allowing a fresh fall breeze to
drift in off Cypress Street and sharpen the students'
spunk. It was a day for children to savor. The drudgery
of winter would soon be upon them.

"Mr. Irving," responded Miss Pearl with a lofty chin,
"I am not sure what you mean by 'on the pad.' I can
assure you, however, that our police department is a
fine one. They do an excellent job of protecting us."

"Is that why they call it protection money?"

"Mr. Irving, where do you pick up these illicit
terms?"

WALDENBOOKS

ALE   1909   104 6527 01-07-04
             REL 7.6/1.05 29 17:18:21

1 0451176820   7.99
2 0446610313   7.99
REF NO. 923307425 EXP 12/04
3 0091228481203028   5.99
REF DISC   15.98 10% OFF   1.60-
             SUBTOTAL   20.37
INNESOTA 6.5% TAX   1.32
             TOTAL   21.69
             CASH   22.00
             CHANGE   .31
             PV# 0046527

 PREFERRED READERS SAVE EVERY DAY

==========CUSTOMER RECEIPT==========

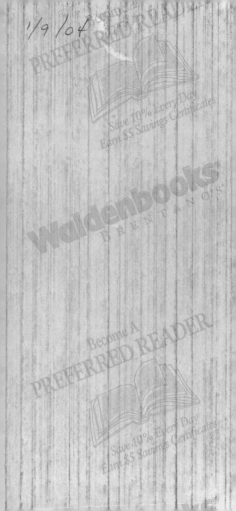

1/9/04

"Jory Ricci tells me them."

"Jory Ricci." Miss Pearl sighed. "Should not I have guessed? Jory, have you been playing cops and robbers again?"

Wild-haired, chubby Jory Ricci leaned across his desk with a snarl. "Oh, sure, blame it on me, Bobby Irving." His stringy suspenders were tangled over his plaid shirt. He looked Teacher defiantly in the eye. "All I was doing was my civics history like ya told me to."

"And what, pray tell," asked Miss Pearl with a roll of her eyes, "are you using for reference?"

"My dad says . . ."

From behind him Kevin Green snapped Jory's suspenders. "Your dad ain't even got a job."

"Knock it off, Green." Jory took a swipe behind him. "Your old man works swing shift at the brewery. What's he know?"

The classroom burst into giggles.

"People, people," cried Miss Pearl, clapping her hands. "Mr. Green, if you wish to speak, raise your hand. Now, Mr. Ricci, I was asking for your source of information pertaining to today's lesson."

"My dad says if ya really wanna know St. Paul history all ya gotta do is read 'Grover's Corner.' "

Miss Pearl just about shit. "Oh, my God!" Her face turned red. Her eyes bulged. The bun in her hair contracted. The glass in her spectacles fogged around the edges. "Grover Mudd is the poorest excuse for a historian who ever picked up a pen. He is an irresponsible, reckless, feckless, alarmist. He is a degenerate."

Kevin Green whispered over Jory Ricci's shoulder. "What's a degenerate?"

"I think it's a reporter or a lawyer," Jory answered.

"Mr. Mudd is a cynic," Miss Pearl went on, coming out of her rage. "He looks on the dark side of everything. His writings should never be published, much less read by schoolchildren."

Jory Ricci argued back. "My dad says everyone in

St. Paul knows what's going on, but Grover Mudd is the only one with enough backbone to write about it."

Across the room Bobby Irving cupped his mouth and mumbled to the boy behind him, "Jory told me, in St. Paul gangsters can fuck in the street."

Miss Pearl ignored the shrieks from girls sitting near Bobby Irving and put an end to the argument. " 'Grover's Corner' will not be discussed in our class. You may tell your parents I do not approve of the *Frontier News*. There is a much better newspaper in town. If we are fortunate, the *Frontier News* will not be with us much longer. Now, people, if we may return to today's lesson." Miss Pearl sat at her desk and paged through the agenda. On the wall behind her were paintings of George Washington and Abraham Lincoln, and hanging between them was a picture of her hero, Anthony Comstock. "You should have your papers completed today. Shall we hear some of them?" She looked over her students. "Miss Larsen, why don't we begin with you. What aspect of our city's history have you chosen?"

"Fort Snelling, Miss Pearl."

"Will you read it, please."

Linda Larsen stood with perfect poise at the side of her desk. She held her paper in front of her at half an arm's length. Her straight-A grades were reflected in her clear speech and articulate manner. " 'Fort Snelling,' by Linda Larsen. Fort Snelling was built on the crest of a bluff where the Minnesota River meets the Mississippi River. It took four years to build, from 1820 to 1824. The job of building the fort was given to Colonel Josiah Snelling. It was built to protect fur traders and settlers from Indians and a possible return of the British. The fort was so strong that, in its long history, it was never attacked. Around the Falls of St. Anthony and the many lakes northwest of Fort Snelling grew the city of Minneapolis. On the seven hills to the northeast grew the city of St. Paul. Divided mostly by the mighty

Mississippi River, they became known as the Twin Cities." She brushed her skirt forward and eased into her desk with discipline and grace.

"That was a very bold reading, Linda."

"Thank you, Miss Pearl."

"People, we should remember when we drive by Fort Snelling that this is where Minnesota, as we know it today, has its roots. Miss Mufflman, what subject have you chosen?"

"The Basilica of Saint Paul, Miss Pearl."

"Will you read it, please."

Cindy Mufflman was shy, religious, studious. Her light brown dress was clean and pressed, but it was worn. She lived with her mother and grandparents. Her father was only a shadowy memory. He had deserted them. It was with some hesitation and a touch of insecurity that Cindy stood at her desk. She had made it through September, the most difficult month. That was the month when her friends figured out for themselves that Cindy Mufflman had no new clothes for the new school year. If only she had grown an inch.

Miss Pearl waited patiently. Cindy spoke in a soft voice. " 'The Basilica of Saint Paul,' by Cindy Mufflman. In 1840 there were settlers living on land that belonged to Fort Snelling. These settlers were called squatters. They were mostly French-Canadian and Swiss. The fort commander ordered them to move. So they moved down the river to an area known only as Pig's Eye Landing. Pig's Eye was the nickname of Pierre Parrant who sold whiskey there."

Cindy was suddenly interrupted by cheers and applause from the boys in the class, who felt obligated to honor Minnesota's forefather of bootlegging.

Miss Pearl rose in her chair and clapped her hands together hard. "Boys, please. I assume, gentlemen, you are applauding Miss Mufflman's research. Please continue, Cindy."

The outburst had startled the girl. She was upset with

herself. Whiskey should have been left out. Boys were so crude. In an even softer voice she read again. "In 1841 Father Lucian Galtier came to the new community and built a little log church that was so poor it reminded people of the stable of Bethlehem. He blessed the new basilica and named it after the Apostle Paul. Pig's Eye Landing then became known as St. Paul. Today, we have a magnificent new cathedral, and Kellogg Boulevard is where the little church used to be." She took her seat and waited for everybody to stop staring at her.

"That was very inspirational, Cindy."

"Thank you, Miss Pearl."

"People, even if you don't like Catholics, you should take a trip to the Cathedral of Saint Paul. It works miracles on the soul." Teacher looked over the class again and settled on a smile. "Mr. Hirte, may we hear from you."

Wendell Hirte was up like a shot. He was the tallest boy in the class. He was the best dressed. Wendell exchanged a prideful grin with Linda Larsen, then began: " 'Lake Phalen,' by Wendell Hirte. Lake Phalen is a large, clear-blue lake located in the northeast corner of St. Paul. It is part of a four-lake system left by receding glaciers. The other three lakes are Round Lake, Lake Gervais, and Keller Lake. Since Lake Phalen is our largest lake it provides much beauty and recreation for the people of St. Paul."

Jory Ricci huddled with Kevin Green. "Is he talking about Piss Lake?"

"Jory Ricci"—Miss Pearl pounded the words out on her desk—"if you will. I shall make it a point to call on you. Hold your tongue until then." She paused. "Go ahead, Wendell."

"Lake Phalen was named after Edward Phalen, an Irish-American soldier stationed at Fort Snelling. After being discharged from the army, Phalen laid claim to property here on the East Side. The creek flowing near his property became known as Phalen Creek. Since the creek flowed from the large lake, the lake was also called Phalen. Today the Hamm's Brewery sits on Mr. Phalen's claim."

"That was very refreshing, Wendell."

"Thank you, Miss Pearl."

"We all enjoy swimming and wading in Lake Phalen. Now we know how it came by its name. People, these are exceptional papers today. Mr. Bradhoff, I believe you were going to tell us about Indians."

"Indian mounds, Miss Pearl." Jeffrey Bradhoff rose. He loved Westerns, as was evident from the cowboy shirt he wore. Tom Mix and his horse, Tony, were going to be live at the Orpheum Theater downtown and his father was taking him. He had been beaming for weeks. Jeffrey did not read or write well but he always received an A for his effort. " 'The Indian Mounds,' by Jeffrey Bradhoff," he read. "In the old days when Injuns died they got buried in big mounds of dirt, and grass grew over them. Gifts and stuff like pipes, and jewelry, and tools, and stuff was buried with them. Some of these big mounds where Injuns got buried was shaped like buffaloes, and snakes, and bears. There used to be over ten thousand Indian mounds in Minnesota. Most of these mounds got plowed up by farmers or were dug up by stupid people. Many of the mounds and stupid people were in St. Paul because it was a great big grave-yard. Now the only mounds in St. Paul are the ones at Indian Mound Park, a few blocks from our school. That is why our school is called Mound Park." He stopped reading and looked up. "Miss Pearl, I got some stuff on Carver's Cave, too. Should I read that?"

"Please do, Jeffrey. You're doing fine."

Jeffrey Bradhoff stuck his head back in the paper. "In the cliffs below the Indian mounds is Carver's Cave. Injuns called it Dwelling of the Great Spirit. In 1766, a explorer named Jonathan Carver came up the Mississippi and he could see the cave from the river because it was so big. You had to travel through the cave in a boat because there was a great big lake in it and Injuns wrote on the walls. When the railroad was built along the river in 1869 they used dynamite and the cave caved in. Today only the mouth of the cave is there and kids ain't post to go in there because hoboes live there." He sat down quickly and folded his hands.

"That was very deep, Jeffrey."

"Thank you, Miss Pearl."

"People, another fascinating thing about the park, from which we get a splendid view of our city, is that you can see every mode of transportation from the bluffs. As you look down at the river you can see the steamboats and barges. Across the river are the hangers and runways of Holman Field. And you can see automobiles rolling along River Drive. You can also see that our city is the greatest railroad center west of Chicago, with nine railroad systems operating twenty-three lines. Four of these railroad systems have their headquarters right here in St. Paul." Miss Pearl removed her spectacles and left them dangling from her neck by a gold chain. She rubbed her temples and sighed. "Mr. Ricci, have you completed the assignment?"

"Yeah. My dad helped me. It's about Lake Phalen, too."

"I see. Well, perhaps you can add something to Mr. Hirte's fine work. Why don't you share with us some of your father's illustrious words."

"Ya want me to read my paper?"

"Please."

Jory Ricci crawled out from behind the desk and brushed the hair from his eyes. He was almost two years older than the other kids, having been held back twice. Half his shirt was untucked. There was too much slack in his suspenders; they kept drooping down his arms, and he kept thumbing them back up. His brown corduroy knickers were government-issued, a sure sign of a family on welfare. His knee-high stockings were held up with rubber bands. One shoe had a hole in the toe. The shoestrings did not match. Jory held the crumpled paper close to the pudgy nose on his baby face. Reading had always been difficult. His handwriting was sloppy. He pronounced every word slowly and deliberately. " 'Lake Phalen,' by Jordan Ricci. My dad says that Grover Mudd says that Lake Phalen was named after a murderer. Ed Phalen's partner was found floating in the muddy Miss' with his head bashed in."

Miss Pearl put her spectacles back on and interrupted him. "Now, Mr. Ricci, Mr. Phalen was never convicted of that crime, and in America a man is innocent until—"

Jory continued. "My dad says that Grover Mudd says that Phalen fled the state and later got his head blown off in California. My dad says that Grover Mudd says that it's right Lake Phalen is named after a murderer because the lake has been murdered by drunken fools pissin' in it."

"Jory, bring me your paper and go stand in the cloak hall."

The classroom was in disarray. Hysterics. With few exceptions the boys were spitting up laughter. Kevin Green could feel a sideache coming on as he clung to his desk and tried to control himself. Most of the girls put on precocious acts of disgust.

Jory Ricci traipsed triumphantly up to the desk and handed Teacher his paper. "Thank you, Miss Pearl."

Kevin Green went to the floor. "Grover's Corner" had read "urinating into the water by the light of the silvery moon," but Jory Ricci said "pissin' in it." Right in class. He not only said it, he wrote it down and handed it in. "Thank you, Miss Pearl." The Green boy was on his back with his knees up to his chest and his arms wrapped around his sides trying to keep the laughter from cracking his ribs. "Thank you, Miss Pearl."

Jory Ricci was banished to the cloak hall, the Siberia of elementary school classrooms. With some heavy

pounding on her desk and a look in her eyes that must
have matched the look in Edward Phalen's eyes as he
bashed his partner's head in, Miss Pearl restored order.

Kevin Green climbed back into his seat and looked
around for someplace to wipe away the snag he had
dangling from his nose.

Teacher regained her composure. She glanced out
the window at the city she loved and gave a few moments' thought to the next letter she was going to send
Walt Howard. Returning to the civics lesson she called
on the most sanctimonious child she could find. "Cathy
McGovern, will you read your paper, please."

"Yes, Miss Pearl." Pigtailed, freckle-faced, and
dressed in baby blue, Cathy McGovern stood in an
attempt to put St. Paul history back on the high road.
" 'Andrew J. Volstead,' by Cathy McGovern. Andrew
J. Volstead was a Republican lawyer from Granite
Falls, Minnesota. He was elected to the United States
Congress in 1903 and served for almost twenty years.
Mr. Volstead wrote the Eighteenth Amendment to the
U.S. Constitution that said alcohol is bad and should
be prohibited. It passed in 1919 and all the saloons in
America had to close. Then he wrote the Volstead Act
so people who made and sold alcohol could be prose-
cuted. Because of his courageous fight against drinking,
Mr. Volstead was defeated for reelection in 1922. So
he came here to St. Paul to be an advisor for the Northwest Dry Enforcement District at the Federal Courts
Building downtown. In a statewide election last month
Minnesota became one of a bunch of states with no
shame that voted to repeal Prohibition. But they need
thirty-six states to do it and they are still seven states
short. So Mr. Volstead, and the Anti-Saloon League,
and the Moral Rearmament people in our city continue
to fight a twenty-first amendment to our constitution
that would bring drinking and crime back to St. Paul."

Miss Pearl, faith restored, spirits soaring, clapped her
hands together below her chin. With an ear-to-ear smile

she proclaimed, "And it's people like Mr. Volstead and his friends that make St. Paul, Minnesota, such a wonderful place to live."

On that note a huge fart noise could be heard ripping through the cloak hall.

Nina Clifford did not dance around the law. She danced in front of it. Literally. There was a timid knock at her door. She flicked on the porch light and answered. It was a boy. "My, you're out late tonight."

"I have some newspapers I couldn't sell today. Would you like to buy them, Miss Clifford?"

"How many?"

"Four *Frontier*s and a *North Star*."

She reached into the deep pocket of her Oriental robe. "Here is a dime for the papers, and a penny for you."

"Thank you, Miss Clifford." The boy leaped down the stairs and was lost in the dark.

Once upon a time her establishment was the talk of the underworld. From New York to California, if you were a visitor with class and you visited such places, when you visited St. Paul you visited Nina Clifford's. But that was once upon a time.

Nina waltzed upstairs to the old Presidential Suite and removed her robe. She lit a row of candles and rolled back the red velvet curtains that hung over the spacious bay windows. Broken rays of a street lamp slanted across the darkness and fell over a thin rose carpet with a black floral design. The long, hot summer was gone. Autumn was upon Nina's house. A crisp northwesterly blew fallen leaves down Washington Street and into the gutter. Clouds a child might draw scudded the midnight sky and played peekaboo with the harvest moon. Too soon the snow would come, that angelic-looking white stuff. The thought of it made for a melancholy whore. She had seen so many snows.

Across the street excited little heads began to appear in the windows. Thieves clenched the bars and jostled for a better view. Officers on the upper floors scurried to their balcony seats. Drunk-tank denizens sobered up for the show. A few saints looked across the way in disgusted wonderment. Next door the morgue came to life. When the house was sold out and the balletomanes were seated, Nina placed Tchaikovsky's *Swan Lake* on the phonograph and delicately set the needle.

As the ice went out in the spring of 1884, a princely steamer pushed up the river to St. Paul, and off the plank stepped a frustrated ballerina and part-time businesswoman named Hannah Steinbrecker. She was a dark-haired beauty with firm shoulders and a disarming smile. The future queen of the city was determined to bring a piece of culture to the ruggedness of Minnesota. As expected, Miss Steinbrecker found St. Paul's appetite for the fine arts small, but the thirst for female flesh was unquenchable. The winters were cold, but the political climate was warm. By the 1890s, Hannah Steinbrecker was Nina Clifford, and the house of erotic saints she built on Washington Street was doing an ungodly amount of business.

Nina cued the orchestra. Music played. The volume was kept at a whisper. The rich burnished tones of the Vienna Philharmonic filled the room. Like a true prima ballerina she began her nocturnal dance in the fifth position. Her arthritic feet were close together, with the front heel attempting to touch the toe of the back foot. Her knobby knees were weakly turned out, her plump poundage unevenly dispersed. She was wearing her faded white tutu over silver slippers and black fishnet tights. A thick blond wig hung down over her sagging shoulders. The ballet began.

Nina did a demi-plié, then a battement tendu with her right foot; a demi-plié, then a battement tendu with her left foot. She executed a sequence of turns on knuckled toes, not bad pirouettes for her age. Holding her arms out in second position she went into her chaînés, spinning by torn scarlet wallpaper, spinning under a crystal chandelier. She kept her balance.

Throughout St. Paul's history a whore could be had for a bag of peanuts, but in her prime years Nina asked, and received, a hundred dollars for the privilege of entering her house. In her luxurious sitting room guests would relax with a glass of Mumm's champagne and a Cuban cigar while they contemplated the eroticism to come. In her parlor, powerful Democrats gathered to plot local and national strategy. They discussed the whos and hows to tighten their grip on City Hall. They mapped plans for presidential campaigns. The groundwork for the election of 1892, which sent Grover Cleveland back to the White House, was laid down in her swank bawdyhouse, and it was during his second term the grateful president appointed St. Paul alderman Richard T. O'Connor to the powerful position of United States marshal. And Marshal O'Connor took care of Nina. Yes, it was a hundred dollars for the privilege of visiting the house of Nina Clifford, and slurping her champagne, and smoking her cigars, and licking her girls, and picking a president. But that was in her prime.

Bathed in orange candlelight and drenched in a melody, the ancient ballerina spun to a halt at center stage and wobbled in her memories. The legs had seventy-five-plus years on them. She dropped a shoulder, and the strap of her tutu looped over it. Her swollen fingers passed over her wrinkled face and down her turkey neck and embraced the blue bows where the straps met the dress. With all the grace she could afford, Nina stripped to the waist. Her breasts tumbled out, her potbelly too. Her flabby arms assumed the third position, raised high, fingertips almost touching, the palms of her hands facing each other, her head slightly forward. She did a frappé left and a frappé right, she twirled and twirled. Her tits

bounced about like soggy white coconuts; her love han-
dles waved to the audience.

Oh, no, it had not always been like this. Nina Clifford
once prided herself on having the firmest tits and flattest
tummy in town. She believed that in her youth she was
prettier than any girl who ever worked for her, perhaps
even as pretty as the angel-faced blonde who delivered
the package. But that was in her youth. The violins
played on.

In the glow of the street lamp, the dancing septu-
agenarian kicked a silver slipper into the bay window.
It bounced off the glass and fell to the floor. The other
slipper followed. Playing the part of the naughty little
girl, she put a finger in her mouth, winked at the man
in the moon, and watched her tutu slip to the floor.
Then the crusty ballerina was in the air with a change-
ment de pied, leaving her skirt below. The audience
roared. Anna Pavlova rolled over in her grave.

Hard times had befallen the queen of the city. Soiled
doves still spread their wings for Nina Clifford, but they
were not the charming, cultured beauties she had once
employed. It was the opium den in the basement that
supported her in her old age, and she had no control
over the supply.

The orchestra played on, but the dying swan was
dizzy. No more turns. She put her thumbs in her tights,
like a Texas cowboy, and slowly peeled them from her
legs. They flew to the ceiling, floated down over the
chandelier, hung there.

She had given almost fifty years of her life to this
Irish-run town and, in the end, she was taking orders
from the German moll of a two-bit Chicago bootlegger
with no balls. The city had changed. It was wide open.
Too wide open. St. Paul was a powder keg on a downward spiral, like a ballerina who never made it. Sooner
or later a match would ignite the fuse.

The Vienna Philharmonic reached the crescendo.
Nina turned her back to the audience. Her pink panties

illuminated the night. She stepped out of them, ignored the pleas of the crowd to turn around. The madam did not believe in showing that part of herself. Some things had to be left to a man's imagination—or his pocketbook. Her hands cupped her breasts. She closed her eyes and absorbed the coda. The swan song came to an end, only a scratching sound. There was faint applause. Was it from across the street, or from another time and place? It was midnight. The street lamp went out. The curtain fell.

Good night, ballerina.

Dag the Wag

It was Halloween, and for six dark hours St. Paul was at the mercy of goblins. No home was safe. Doors and windows were smashed, fences uprooted. By midnight the police switchboard had received fifteen hundred vandalism calls. Extra operators manned the lines. In addition to the normal twelve radio squads, twelve additional squads were put on patrol in the residential neighborhoods. But their cars were not radio-equipped and they had to phone in after each call. Hundreds of ornamental street lamps were destroyed by rifle fire. Bonfires were built at busy intersections. Flying rocks broke through streetcar windows. Planks with nails driven through them were tossed onto roadways. Fire hydrants were turned on, flooding the streets and lowering the water pressure.

On Grand Avenue, firemen were pulling a blazing automobile off the trolley tracks when the tow cable snapped and injured three people.

Where Summit Avenue ended at the park on River Drive a bonfire was built with parked cars. As the flames rose over the river between Saint Thomas College and Saint Paul Seminary, motorists were ordered from their vehicles and then had to watch helplessly as their cars were destroyed. A roadster deliberately jumped the curb and chased pedestrians down the sidewalk.

When the fires were finally extinguished, and the lunatic moon bowed to the rising sun, there were no arrests. A thousand Halloween vandals vanished in the night. Like ghosts.

Grover Mudd walked up Robert Street to Kellogg Boulevard. It was cloudy and chilly. The night before, while the city was riotously celebrating Halloween, he had been celebrating his thirty-ninth birthday. Alone.

The new boulevard was expansive but not quite complete. The lanes were unmarked and the only thing controlling traffic was a moveable stop sign. With two bad-weather months left in the year, St. Paul had already set a record for traffic deaths: sixty. Only New York and Chicago had more. Grover was careful not to add his name to the list. He waited for the speeding trucks to clear, then dashed across the street to the grassy median. He caught his breath next to a newly planted pine tree, then beat the cars to the sidewalk.

A new city park that would overlook the Mississippi River was supposed to run along the boulevard, but the city had run out of money. So it was a muddy parking lot. Where Father Galtier's poor little church used to stand, Fords and Chevys now stood. Grover squeezed between the cars. He leaned on the railing that ran along the cliff tops and coughed until his breathing came under control.

"It's that shit you drink, Mudd. Stuff'll kill you."

Grover looked below the Robert Street Bridge to the Lower Landing, where the city was born. Tugboats were in a line facing south. The November wind off the river blew cold. Winter would be early. "It's freezing out here," he said.

"It's a nice day. Won't be another one like it until March."

Grover fished a hankie from his coat pocket and wiped his mouth. "No arrests last night?"

Gil St. Sauver glanced over at him. "We couldn't make any arrests because we didn't dare leave districts unpatrolled while we brought prisoners downtown."

"I could see the flames from my room. It was kind of pretty, but I couldn't get my toilet to flush."

They stood without talking and watched the river traffic. On the far bank steel cranes swung over the water at American Hoist & Derrick. Sparks flew in the windows of Valley Iron Works. A locomotive chugged by the Rock Island freight house and started across the lift bridge.

"What's news, Mudd?"

Grover thought November an ugly month. Bare trees lined Harriet Island. The bath house was closed. Caged animals shivered in the dog pound. "Machine Gun Kelly and his wife got life. Virginia voted for repeal. Only four more states needed. Prohibition will be dead by the end of the year. Mayor Mahoney voted no on a resolution asking the War Department for a battleship to be named for our city. He said he didn't believe it appropriate to put the name of a saint on a warship. He'd rather see our name on something else."

"Paper sold?"

"No, just talk. What's news with you?"

"Commissioner McDonald says he's going to lay off fifty-five cops due to lack of funds, and we've got three cops in the hospital as a result of last night's fun and games. By the way, we got a photo of an Indiana con. He's got a mug like yours."

"Better dressed?"

"Seriously. The guy looks like you."

"And the Pig's Eye murders?"

"Still an open case."

Grover felt a wisecrack coming on but held it in. Whatever it was St. Sauver wanted to talk about would have to be dragged out of him. "Any new leads?"

"Nope. Same old puzzle. Sand."

"Sand is sand."

"I hate to cold-water you, Mudd, but sand isn't sand. Not this sand."

"What do you mean?"

"It's an extremely fine, white sand. We've compared it to every grain of sand along the cliffs. No match. We've checked the caves, we've checked city and county beaches. We dredged up sand from the bottom of the river. No luck." A tug sounded its whistle. Heavy barges crossed under the Wabasha Street Bridge and raced past Raspberry Island. Grain spilled over the tops. St. Sauver changed the subject. "The Gophers had a hell of a season, didn't they?"

"You a big football fan?"

"I can remember watching you play at old Northrop Field."

"Christ, that was almost twenty years ago."

"Yeah, I was just a beat cop then." Downtown, a sharp bend in the Mississippi cut St. Paul off from a part of its west side. The High Bridge, the Wabasha Street Bridge, and the Robert Street Bridge sewed them back together. The veteran cop stared at the fine homes along Cherokee Heights on the wayward side of the river. "I've been reading your column. There's been some good things in it lately."

"You didn't call me up here to pat me on the back."

"There's no reason we can't work together in certain areas."

"Cats don't run with dogs."

"They do when they're chasing rats."

"Or an election in the spring?" The sun broke through the clouds. Grover closed his eyes, raised his head, and showered in the warmth. "I hear G-men are in town."

St. Sauver turned back to him. "They've set up shop in the basement of the Federal Courts Building. That's all I know. Whether they believe it or not—and I'm sure they don't—some of us would like to help. I just got back from a meeting in Chicago where I let them know that."

"What's news in Chicago?"

"The feds put Touhy away for kidnapping Jake Factor."

"That's old news. Why should it concern us?"

"Chicago has a new problem, similar to one we've encountered. With Prohibition coming to an end, the bootleggers are turning to dope. Chicago cops collared some of Touhy's gang with a ton of the junk. They sang a sweet song about a friend in St. Paul."

"And who would that be?"

"Dag Rankin. Know him?"

"I've heard about him. Don't know that I've ever seen him."

"He's smuggling dope. City's being flooded with it."

"How much stuff are we talking about?"

"Mounds of it. The head whores are pushing it hard, so you can bet your ass Nina Clifford has a hand in it."

"C'mon. That old bat hasn't had any say in this town since the war ended."

"She's up to her fat nose in junk. I know what goes on in that basement of hers."

"Then why don't you raid the place? It's not like you have to go very far."

"With her connections? By the time we got across the street that house would be cleaner than the White House. She owns a warehouse down on Sibley. I checked it out. Place is clean. There's nothing I'd like more than to bust that old witch. She's ruined more cops than Al Capone."

"Forgetting what she did to your father, I think you're wasting your time. She's just a piece of folklore that forgot to die."

"It's Rankin I want. Nina's personal." St. Sauver paused, then lowered his voice almost to a whisper. "That coroner's report on the Kendrigan twins I sent you—there's something I cut out. Off the record?"

Grover agreed. "Sure. Off the record."

"The mongoloid had raw opium under his fingernails."

Grover thought about that long and hard. Children with dope. Bootleggers in their heyday had never stooped so low. "That's some sandbox those kids were into. I suppose I could do a column on dope and mention those under investigation."

"Don't waste your time. Article like that they'd frame and hang on the wall."

An awkward silence fell over them, the silence of antagonists too proud to admit they need each other. A train passed below. A *Frontier News* truck followed the Mississippi up River Drive.

"I don't know what else I can do." The sun disappeared behind the clouds again and the afternoon wind off the river chilled Grover to the bone. "I've got to get back, we're short on help these days." He turned to walk off.

"Say, Mudd?"

Grover stopped. "Yeah?"

"I heard a great story when I was in Chicago."

"About who?"

About Dag Rankin. The gangster had a handicap no man should have. He kept telling himself Roxanne and Nina were the only ones who knew about it, but he did not believe that. Others had to know. What were they saying behind his back? Who would dare talk about it openly? He would kill anybody who did. He would do to them what he should have done to that Chicago cop. On a cold November evening Dag Rankin limped into Nina Clifford's opium den with these thoughts in mind. It was these thoughts he came to forget.

Roxanne was at his side. She was not happy, yet it was she who had brought him here the first time so his spirits could rise again, if nothing else would.

When he was stretched out and comfortable Nina came to him wearing a Japanese kimono and the ugliest black wig he had ever seen. He wanted to laugh, but he feared her, this treacherous and aged woman, this guardian of godless secrets. He'd love to be rid of the witch, but she had a spell cast over the police department. Without her he couldn't trust them. Nina Clifford held the pipe in her hands and the fragrance of unimaginable pleasure brought tears to his eyes. He smoked and the pain vanished. He breathed deep and found euphoria. He held the magic in his lungs and his problems melted away. The sensual pleasures returned. Gone were the sleepless nights and the hateful days. Forgotten was the dark alley behind 33rd Street.

With Capone busted and the gangs in disarray, the morale of the Chicago Police Department was high. They hit Dag Rankin's 33rd Street place on a Saturday night. The doors were kicked in; whistles blew, and nightsticks swung through the air. In a lifetime of crime Dag Rankin had never been nabbed, but there he stood on the balcony watching his patrons clubbed and his club ransacked. Rankin dashed into his second-floor office and bolted the door. He could hear the law trooping up the stairs. They threw their combined weight against the door and it cracked down the middle. Dag Rankin tore open the office window and searched the alleyway. It was dark and smelled of week-old garbage and dead felines. As far as he could tell it was deserted.

"Open up, Dag, or we'll huff and we'll puff and we'll blow the fucking door down!" The door splintered again. A black-uniformed shoulder with sergeant's stripes on it wiggled in. Rankin leaped to the ledge. He gave the alley another look. Then he jumped.

He might have skipped out of town if it hadn't been for the cat shit. He hit the blacktop with both feet and went into a shoulder roll like his older brothers taught him to do when he was a boy, like he had done during so many escapes while growing up in the slums of DeKalb Street Bottom. It was when he was coming out of the roll and scrambling to his feet that he stepped in

the shit and his leg slipped out from under him. He
grabbed his ankle and tried to wring out the pain. There
was no time. His office was flooded with cops. They
were at the window. Dag Rankin hop-sprinted down
the alley like a fox who had just jerked his foot from
the jaws of the trap.

He might have made a clean break of it had it not
been for the experience of Officer Hawkeye Flannigan.
When the raid began, the tall Chicago cop with the
sharp beak and narrow eyes rushed to the corner of the
building at the far end of the alley to stop any turds
that tried to escape the flush. Sure enough, Dag Rankin
had skipped to within a foot of the street when Flannigan arrived on the scene and dropped the plunger.
Rankin had no gun and there was no going through this
cop. He pivoted on his good foot and doubled back up
the alley. A pile of garbage cans was stacked below the
fire escape of the adjacent building. He leaped into the
trash and pawed his way to the top. His arms prayed
for the ladder and he was able to claw the bottom rung
and hoist himself up. Then Dag Rankin began his last
climb in the Windy City.

And he might have gone over the top if Officer Flannigan had not been such a lazy son of a bitch. The
sharpshooting police officer had no intention of chasing
a shoestring gangster over West Side rooftops. His rea-
soning was barbaric and simple: Why go up when he
can come down? The Chicago cop drew his .38 Special,
extended his long arm upward, took aim, and smiled.
The bang echoed back and forth between the brick walls
like cannon fire. Cats scurried from old hiding places
to new hiding places. The echo faded. A thud hit the
pavement. Silence. A second later, a cop leaning out
the office window was heard to say, "Old Hawkeye got
him."

Old Hawkeye had indeed gotten him. The shot more
than lived up to Officer Flannigan's reputation and far
exceeded his own expectations. A single bullet entered

Dag Rankin's lower left buttocks, journeyed through the flesh and exited through his testicles, blowing away the right one and doing damage to the left. Although he had to wait for the hospital to confirm his accuracy, standing in the alleyway over his fallen prey Hawkeye Flannigan knew he had outdone himself. It showed on his face.

What showed on Dag Rankin's face was a contortion of pain, shock, and immense fear as he lay on his side in the prison ward of Cook County Hospital. After weeks of putting it off, doctors finally informed him that his limp wag was perpetual. He broke down and cried. He threw violent tantrums in the spirit of a crazed child and had to be strapped to the bed. For days on end he swore to God—he swore to anybody who would listen—he was going to kill Hawkeye Flannigan. He knew in his heart Chicago cops had orders to shoot gangsters in the balls. He had daily fantasies about how he would take Officer Flannigan on a one-way ride, torture him, castrate him, murder the cop that murdered his dick.

The wound was not talked about in open court, but everybody involved knew about the little mobster with the little problem. When it came time to sentence Dag Rankin the judge showed mercy and gave him two to three years at the state pen in Joliet. He was paroled sixteen months later. But before he could be released he was robbed of another pleasure, the pleasure of killing Officer Flannigan. Old Hawkeye fell to submachine-gun fire from a trio of bank robbers. It was said that if he could have drawn his gun in time his legend would have grown by three. As it was, he was laid to rest with full honors, just like thirteen other Chicago policemen killed in the line of duty that year.

With everybody in the Chicago underworld aware of his handicap, and his hopes of torturing Officer Flannigan shot down, there was no point to remaining in Chicago. Dag Rankin could never be a big man in the big city. So he limped four hundred miles northwest, to the sainted city of gangsters, where he could at least pretend there was something left of his manhood. His nightclub experience and Touhy gang money enabled him to take over the Hollyhocks Club down by the river, and he quickly transformed the sprawling farm into the most exclusive dining and gambling spot in St. Paul. Valet parkers met Cadillac limousines at the door. Tuxedos and evening dresses were mandatory. Rankin set up an office and apartment on the third floor of his spacious speakeasy and the wheel of fortune spun.

He dappered Danny Hogan's Chrysler with dynamite, then took control of his bootlegging operation. He cut sweetheart deals with the others. Dutch Otto at the Royal Cigar Store could keep his gambling interest, and Jap Gleckman of Pickwick Café fame could run all the bordellos his heart desired. Nina Clifford came cheap. Whiskey and dope. St. Paul was a jewel on the Mississippi. Rankin found power he had never dreamed of in Chicago.

During the waning euphoria in the lair of Nina Clifford, Dag Rankin had different dreams. Vivid sex dreams. He was in a castle on Lake Michigan, surrounded by naked women. Behind his gem-studded throne were giant phallic symbols carved of ivory. Monuments to his prowess. He was growing bored and restless when a thousand trumpets sounded and the massive doors at the end of the great hall swung open. The maidens formed an aisle, dropped to the floor, and bowed in awe and respect. It was Empress Roxanne of Germany, who had been banished by the Nazi leader because of her overpowering beauty. Her golden hair was the glimmering sunlight, her blue eyes were the heavens, her fair skin was worthy only of a goddess. She came to him, fell to her knees, and wept. She had a problem only King Dag's delicate touch could solve.

Then the blissful sleep was over. Dag Rankin

emerged from his dream to find his hand between his
legs, wishfully rubbing his ball.

The story of Hawkeye Flannigan's legendary shot and
the gangster with the limp wag was a popular one among
Chicago cops. When the assistant chief from St. Paul
arrived in Chicago a few years later to meet with federal
officials, the legendary story skipped into his ears. Then,
on a chilly day in November, it found its way into the
ever-open, ever-sardonic ears of Grover Mudd. And
from Grover's ears it was not far to "Grover's Corner."

During the autumn months there was a marked
change in his daily column. Grover wrote about the
ridiculous inadequacies of the Ramsey County Prosecutor's Office, and about a state law that said the defendant's attorney had the right to address the jury last
and the prosecutors had no right of rebuttal. He wrote
of another Minnesota law that said any crime that carried a sentence of ten years or more, such as armed
robbery, forgery, and grand larceny, had to reach the
courts through a grand-jury indictment, causing a back-
log of felony charges to be reduced, or dropped alto-
gether. "Grover's Corner" detailed a Wisconsin law
designed to attack the nation's crime problem by agree-
ing to return fleeing offenders to states that recipro-
cated. Wisconsin's neighbor, Minnesota, refused to
cooperate. Grover produced satirical pieces about Minnesota's state highway patrol, which had no authority
to arrest except in traffic cases. They could arrest a
drunken driver, but not a bank robber or a murderer.
He churned out articles about the embarrassingly small
and outdated firearms the St. Paul police were equipped
with; about the few and dilapidated squad cars they
drove; about the fact that they could not overpower the
most diminutive gang even if they could muster up the
nerve to try. For six weeks Grover Mudd was on a roll;
a roll even his worst enemies were impressed with. But

the story of the impotent gangster was too good to let pass. He sat down to his typewriter with a euphemistic meanness he had not felt since the Piss Lake column.

With serious reservations, *Frontier News* Editor Walt Howard plugged his nose and ran the piece in "Grover's Corner."

MONKEY BUSINESS
by Grover Mudd

Our city has seen the arrival of two new monkeys, both with unique problems, though their problems point in different directions.

Our latest addition is a gorilla named Casey, who moved to our Como Zoo from the city of Omaha. This rare and treasured beast arrived with excellent references, but with a problem that was an out-and-up embarrassment in Nebraska. Officials there thought we might be able to solve Casey's dilemma with our female gorilla, Tanya. So far this has not happened.

The other monkey is an ape named Dag, who came to St. Paul from the city of Chicago. Dag's references do not stack up to Casey's, but then neither does his problem. It seems Dag the Ape is a minion of the Terrible Touhy gang who tried to strike out on his own before tragedy struck a part of him down.

We'll come back to this calamity later.

Casey's problem began during the long, hot summer. The big boy was locked in a cage all by his lonesome and forced to watch those pretty Nebraska girls, dressed in their Sunday best, parade by his bars. Casey got so worked up his natural instincts took over. Now, the Omaha Zoo is a family zoo and the natural instincts of a lonely adult male gorilla were not considered proper. The 6-foot, 300-pound gorilla was removed from his public cage and put into isolation, but still there was no letdown. Then Omaha heard about our Tanya, and about St. Paul's jungle moral standards. Casey's bags were packed and he was put on the first train north.

Now, back to Dag the Ape. His problems began when he opened a speakeasy on Chicago's West Side. Unlike St. Paul cops, the Chicago police frown on such places, and they paid a surprise visit to Dag's nest one night. The ape fled out an upper window and was swinging from fire escape to fire escape when a police officer known for his marksmanship brought him to the ground with one incredible shot. Dag has not been a whole ape since. The bullet passed through his lower hip and blew a small but very important part of him away. With the exception of a noticeable limp Dag appears to have recovered from his wound, but in truth, what pretty girls did for Casey they will never be able to do for Dag.

Casey was met at Union Depot by Mayor Mahoney. When reporters pointed out a striking resemblance, the mayor denied that he was a relative and mumbled something profane about Darwin's theories. With a police escort, Casey was taken to Como Zoo to meet Tanya, but—like many blind dates— things have not worked out. After two months Casey still cowers in one corner of the cage while Tanya hurls insults at him from another.

Things have worked out much better for Dag. He owns his own club off River Drive and is making quite a name for himself in the rackets business.

Omaha would like Casey back after he gets Tanya in a family way. But it looks like Dag will be doing it to us for some time to come. Just another case where St. Paul has the wrong ape behind bars.

Foxy Roxy

The breakout at the Indiana State Penitentiary in September of 1933 was gaining in notoriety with every passing week. The escape was planned and funded on the outside by a recently released inmate who got the money for the job by robbing a bank in Indianapolis. After supplying the means to the men inside, he was arrested in Ohio and thrown into a county jail to await extradition to Indiana. Meanwhile, his gang broke out of the state pen without a hitch, only to find their leader locked up in a small town called Lima. To raise funds for his breakout the gang robbed a bank in St. Marys, Ohio. A week later they burst into the Lima jail, killed the sheriff, and freed the man who had helped free them. This was only the beginning of their audacious ways. In the month of October they raided two police stations for weapons, robbed a bank in Greencastle, Indiana, of seventy-five thousand dollars, and hit another bank in Racine, Wisconsin, for untold thousands. By November the nation's list of the Ten Most Wanted had eight of their names on it. At the top of the list was the gang's leader, the man who started it all.

With a Lucky Strike dangling from his lips, Grover Mudd banged away on his reliable Remington. The Indiana gang was a newspaper's dream. Good copy. The public may not have loved these outlaws, but they loved reading about them.

Fuzzy Byron poked his head into the corner office. "I have the photo you asked for, Grover. Just came in. It's a bit fuzzy to me, but everyone in the newsroom says it looks like you." He handed over the photograph.

"This is John Dillinger?"

"That's him, Grover."

Grover studied the handsome face. Dillinger was a clean-shaven man with a wisecrack smile and a big dimple in his chin. His hair was thicker than Grover's, but lighter in color. The gangster had an athletic look about him, and it was said he was once a gifted shortstop, who could have played pro ball. Dillinger was into his thirties, not that much younger than Grover Mudd; but, as Grover stared at the picture in his hands and noted the resemblance, he knew he had not looked that good in over a decade. "I think he looks more like you, Fuzzy."

"Couldn't say. I haven't been able to focus on a mirror in years. I guess I'm lucky in that respect."

"Have you got somewhere to eat on Turkey Day?"

"The Salvation Army. Best meal in town. Care to join me?"

"Sorry, Fuzzy. I've got two dinners to wolf down now." Grover propped the photo of Public Enemy #1 next to his typewriter and went back to work. He could not have ordered better material. It made him forget about the no-class crooks who owned St. Paul. But the lapse was short-lived.

"Sorry to bother you, Grover," said Fuzzy Byron, sticking his head back in the office. "Mr. Howard wants you."

Grover blew smoke in Dillinger's face. "Is he mad?"

"No, but he has visitors."

As always, the editor's door was open. Walt Howard stood behind his desk with his hands on his hips. He did not look mad, but he did look serious. A Buggs Palooka type was seated in the leather chair next to the desk. Grover had seen the face before, but could not place it—a homely man, dressed to kill. A long black coat covered his double-breasted pinstripe suit. He had an ivory tie around his neck, with a silver silk scarf draped over his shoulders. His manicured fingers were tapping a ritzy homburg on his lap. His spats wore the shine of newness.

"Close the door, Mudd."

Grover acknowledged his editor's request and reached for the door.

She had been blocked from his view when he first walked in, but as the door swung closed she was revealed, sitting with quiet grace in a corner chair. It was the Scandinavian goddess from the kidnapping trial, even more dangerously beautiful than he remembered. She was wearing a pink dress with red and white flounce. The fringe was just below her knees and one gorgeous leg was crossed over the other; from it dangled a thinly strapped high heel of winter white. Her arms were folded around her red coat as if someone might try to take it from her. She glanced up at Grover and he locked on her eyes, fox eyes in noon blue. Her lovely face blushed and she looked away. He was staring at her, but did not realize it.

"Mudd?"

Grover was in shock. His heart was beating fast, stoking the fire in his chest. He turned to Mr. Howard. "Yes?"

"Mudd, this is Dag Rankin."

Double shock. Grover's first inclination was to laugh. What could this palooka possibly have to say for himself?

Walt Howard continued with a touch of skepticism in his voice. Grover knew it well. "Mr. Rankin says he's a nightclub owner, a prominent St. Paul businessman. He believes he was the subject matter of one of your columns. Mr. Rankin says you defamed him. Libelous writing he calls it. Malice aforethought."

Grover sneered down at Rankin and his two-bit urbanity, sized him up, got a good whiff of the cologne he was wearing. He wondered how a guy who smelled so bad could smell so good. "Dag Rankin is a no-good, lousy bum. Who cares?"

Rankin smiled up at Grover, a mean smile that showed off his sharp teeth. "So you're the jerk who writes 'Grover's Corner.' The infamous Grover Mudd. What an appropriate name."

"Why don't you tell me again what it is you're asking for?" Walt Howard interceded.

"What I am demanding, as a prominent citizen," said Rankin, "is a full retraction, a public apology, an explanation to your readers that the story was pure fiction and was not meant to hurt anybody. Of course, Mudd's dismissal is a foregone conclusion."

"And in return?" the editor asked.

"I've already explained the legal implications. My lawyers eat guys like you for lunch. In return for the public apology, I would agree not to bring the matter before the courts. Also, I understand your newspaper is experiencing some financial difficulties. I might be in a position to help."

Walt Howard shook his head in amazement. "Well, Mr. Rankin, I won't deny that's an attractive offer. Not only is my paper saved from ruin, but I get rid of Grover Mudd, too. Quite a deal. What do you think, Mudd?"

"I think we should get to the bottom of this," snorted Grover. "Buggs, will you stand up and drop your pants?"

Rankin was out of his chair with amazing quickness for a man who could not walk straight. With the face of a madman he grabbed Grover by the throat. Grover gave him a hard shove and sent him tumbling over the chair to the floor. Walt Howard stepped between them as Rankin awkwardly struggled to his feet.

Grover backed off, caught his breath, and held his words. The old ache crept up his back.

Don't run, Grover

He refused to be bullied, but at the same time he did not want to make a scene in front of the girl. She was on her feet, too, and closer to him. Grover could hardly keep his eyes from her. The monkey column might have brought him trouble, but it had also brought him face to face with the most beautiful woman he'd ever seen. He could smell her perfume, a fragrance he would never forget.

Dag Rankin popped his hat back into shape and brushed away the dust. He tried in vain to control his own heavy breathing. "I'm disappointed, Mr. Howard. I'd heard many fine things about you. I can't imagine why a man of your integrity would employ a piece of slime like Grover Mudd."

"I stand by my people. I think it's about time you left, Mr. Rankin."

"I'll leave. But I won't wait long for that retraction." Rankin buttoned his coat. "And make sure you spell my name right."

Grover looked into the eyes of his found-again love. "And how do I spell your name?"

She seemed taken aback by the question, surprised someone had acknowledged her presence. With a trace of hesitation she answered, "Roxanne."

"What's your last name, Roxanne?"

"Schultz."

"Schultz," exclaimed a surprised Grover. "That's German." He was not sure what it was he said, but the eyes of a fox became the eyes of a tiger. Where Rankin's threats failed, she succeeded. Her hate cut through Grover's thick skin and stung his heart.

Dag Rankin took her arm and they were at the door. Grover stepped aside.

"It's bad enough you slander a highly respected businessman all over your newspaper, then push a cripple over a chair," Rankin told him. "Now you insult my girl."

The sob story had no effect on Grover, but the phrase
"my girl" made him want to vomit.

Rankin leaned into him and lowered his voice. "Write
the apology, Mudd, or you may have written your
obituary."

The words sent a chill up Grover's spine. But not
because they were muttered by this impotent palooka.
Grover Mudd had had his obituary written long before
he ever heard the name Dag Rankin.

Special Agent Steff Koslowski spent Thanksgiving evening in the basement of the Federal Courts Building
with a turkey sandwich and a glass of fishy-tasting water.
The agents had makeshift jail cells constructed from a
pair of storage rooms, where the federal fugitives they
apprehended spent the night before being taken to
Union Depot first thing in the morning. St. Paul police
were told nothing, even though Steff's conversation
with Gil St. Sauver had been a positive one. He was
impressed with the sincerity of the assistant chief's offer
to help. No crooked cop could be that smooth. He felt
bad having to snub the man.

The basement office was cold and damp. Only one
window decorated the place, a window with wrought-
iron bars on the outside, and a corner broken out of
the glass, allowing the freezing winds of November to
shoot through. Steff sat shivering at a gray metal desk,
feeling like a common jailer. Two penny-ante holdup
men from Detroit were snoring in the holding tanks.
There was no trace of Homer Van Meter and his pals.
When reports put them in Chicago, Steff was overjoyed.
But his orders were to stay put.

The lonely G-man looked around for a rag to stuff
through the hole in the window, but the cellar was bare.
He opened the desk drawer and found a newspaper in
it, the one he was saving. He flipped to the back page
and ripped out "Grover's Corner." Steff wanted to send

the monkey column home to his father. It was his kind of humor. As he crumpled the paper into a big wad and pulled his chair over to the window, he thought about the feast they would be having back in the old neighborhood.

Standing on the chair and peering through the bars, Steff could see the first snow flurries of winter circling the bare trees in Rice Park. Street lamps punctuated the absence of people. The water fountain was shut off. Paths that crisscrossed the lawn were deserted. Across the way the library's cold stone and sprawling Renaissance style choked his view of the river bluffs and imprisoned him in desolation. It was a frigid city. No, not a city at all. More like one of those icy enclaves where the fairy princess is held in captivity after being kidnapped. He stuffed the broken glass with the *Frontier News*.

Most of Steff's three months in this crook's haven had been spent trying to keep track of the cash, much of the money linked directly to the Chicago syndicate. St. Paul was the fencing capital of America. Millions of dollars of hot money was exchanged for cool money. Stolen goods were traded for fresh currency. The bureau traced bills from the Oklahoma kidnapping to St. Paul, and just by tabbing the city's cash flow they knew the Hamm ransom had yet to be passed. Steff had seen more cold, hard cash in the last ninety days than most people saw in a lifetime. The scope of the city's venality was finally being realized back in Washington. Behind a storm of Victorian architecture was a storm of Machiavellian corruption. Two more inspectors were arriving on the morning train. More agents were being transferred from the Chicago office.

Special Agent Koslowski sat at the desk again and pulled the phone in front of him. He wanted to call home, but there were rules. After staring at Ma Bell for a minute he lifted the handset, and instead of dialing the operator he unscrewed the mouthpiece. The parts and wires fell into his palms. He smiled at them the way a sculptor smiles at clay. Boy, what he could do to a telephone if only they'd let him.

———————

It was snowing hard now. A wonderful wet snow. Huge flakes tumbled out of the night sky and whitened a gray world. Roxanne Schultz lost her thoughts in this pristine beauty as they drove up to the Tudor mansion across the parkway from Lake Phalen. Fancy cars lined the street. The yard looked like a parking lot. The sweet sound of jazz spilled out of the house and danced with the snowflakes. She paused at the front door to admire the splendor of it all. Then Dag Rankin took his exquisite golden girl by the arm and rang the bell.

Alvin Karpis, dressed like a Pilgrim, greeted them. "Ya like the threads, Mr. Rankin? Minnehaha Costumes. Great, aren't they?"

They were among the last to arrive. The party was in full swing. It was a G-man's dream, or nightmare, a smoke-filled house decorated with wall-to-wall gangsters. If a bomb were to go off under the place the Midwest crime rate would drop in half.

For many it was a Thanksgiving costume party. Homer Van Meter was draped in buckskins, with a single feather sticking out the back of his headband, and war paint smeared on his face. Tommy Carroll was decked out like an Indian chief with a full war bonnet over his scalp and a Thompson submachine gun under his arm. In another corner gathered the Pilgrims, the Barker-Karpis gang and Baby Face Nelson in buckled shoes and bloused knickers under black coats with wide white collars. On their heads were floppy black hats, and on their arms were their women, dressed in seventeenth-century garb. A live band left over from the Jazz Age controlled the tempo of things from the foot of an ornate staircase.

St. Paul's nightlife was well represented. Jap Gleckman had brought his girls. A pair of them were dressed like turkeys. At a pillory in the parlor the whores took turns locking up their arms and heads. And the music swung.

Over where the hallway melted into the library, Chief Carroll threw his arm around Indian brave Van Meter. "There's a fucking orgy upstairs."

"What other kind of orgy is there?"

"I'm going up. Keep an eye on my wife, Homer. I don't want no one touching her."

Homer Van Meter had to pass on the orgy. His feather was bent. The festering sores were eating away his dick. He chewed the corn off the cob and looked across the steamy hall at Dag Rankin. So he had problems in his pants, too. Maybe they could work together. Minnesota had the finest medical facilities in the world. With Rankin's money and connections they should be able to find a good penis doctor. Maybe they could drive down to the Mayo Clinic one weekend and have a look. The music went limp. The band took a break.

As the party wore on Dag Rankin took Alvin Karpis aside and left Roxanne alone to fend off horny Puritans. "Tell me, Alvin, where do you get the loot for all this?"

"Where do you think?"

"I really don't know. Word out of Chicago is you and your trigger-happy boys hit a pair of messengers from the Federal Reserve Bank, and all you got for your troubles was a bag of postcards."

"Yeah, well, don't believe everything you hear."

"I have a job in mind. Something you're better at."

"Like what?"

"Another snatch."

"You must be joking. We still haven't converted the Hamm money."

"Wash money too fast and you'll end up like the Kellys."

"I don't like it," Karpis protested. "We need cash now."

"So do I. So get rid of Van Meter and Nelson. I've already got the pigeon marked, and I don't want any screwups. This time we're going to double the ransom."

"It's too risky."

"Then try cashing your postcards."

By the time Dag Rankin had convinced Alvin Karpis to dump Nelson and Van Meter and do another job for him, Tommy Carroll was all orgied out. He saw the Barker brothers at the top of the stairs, undressing a wild turkey, but he couldn't find his wife. He felt his way back to the library, where he curled up in front of the fireplace with his submachine gun and had a fireside chat with Homer Van Meter. Snowflakes twinkled in the bay windows.

"Karpis is a fuckup," Van Meter told him. "And those Barkers can't spit without crying to their fat mamma for permission. I'm telling you, Tommy, stick with me and sooner or later we'll tie up with Dillinger."

"Do you really know him?"

"We did seven years together at Michigan City. He was the best friend I ever had. I put the word out in Chicago. I know he'll come here. And this guy knows how to hit banks. That's what we should be doing, hitting banks. I got a top-notch jug marker and he tells me there's one in Minneapolis ripe for picking."

"No, that's too close to home," Carroll reminded him.

"Ah, hell, it might as well be New Jersey. Those people in Minneapolis get lost every time they come stumbling across the river."

"There's been too many jobs over there lately."

"And why is that? Because the coppers are a bunch of sob sisters who don't do nothing more than stand at the bridges and cry in the river."

"What about Nelson?" The band struck a sour note.

Later that evening, after Alvin Karpis and Homer Van Meter secretly agreed to go their separate ways,

Dag Rankin cornered gambling kingpin Dutch Otto. "Do you read the *Frontier News*, Dutch?"

"Yeah, sometimes."

"What do you know about Grover Mudd?"

"I know he likes to have fun with us. But he's harmless."

"I mean, what do you know about him personally?"

"Not much. He was a big war hero. Won some kind of French medal."

"I'd consider it a personal favor if you could find out everything there is to know about him."

"Such as?"

"Where does he live? Married? Children? A girl? When does he go to work? How does he get there? Little things like that."

"Sure, Dag, I'll put somebody on it. As soon as you tell me and the boys in Chicago what you plan on doing with all that dope you're stashing."

Meanwhile, back in the library, Homer Van Meter stood behind an overstuffed sofa and tried to explain his theories of reincarnation to fellow intellects gathered around the fire—Baby Face Nelson and his whiskey-soaked brain, sleepy Tommy Carroll and his tommy gun, Alvin Karpis and the Barker brothers, as sloshed as Plymouth Rock, plus assorted molls, wives, and whores. "When I die," Van Meter explained, "I don't want to be buried, ya see. I want to be thrown to the wolves. Really. There's wolf packs up by the boundary waters and they'll eat your body. So instead of dying, you go on living as part of the wolf."

"Wolf shit," cried Nelson. "You end up wolf shit!"

"You got no respect for the dead, do you, Baby Face?"

"I told you for the last time never to call me that."

Van Meter grinned, then broke into an Eddie Cantor imitation. "Baby Face, you've got the cutest little baby face. I'm up in heaven when I'm in your fond embrace . . ."

"I'll put you up in heaven, fucker." Nelson ripped the tommy gun out of the hands of Carroll and leveled it at the malicious songster. Van Meter dropped behind the sofa. Nelson opened fire. The whole party hit the floor as the drunken Pilgrim raked the couch and then the bookshelves behind it. The women screamed, the bullets flew. A horde of drunken braves jumped him from behind and wrestled the submachine gun from his arms. An angry pall fell over the room as everyone but Van Meter slowly rose to their feet and stared in awe at the smoking sofa with its guts hanging out. Even a suddenly silent Nelson realized what it was he had done.

Then Homer the Gnomer, the Indian, sprang from behind the sofa like a jack-in-the-box, singing, "Baby Face, you've got the cutest little baby face . . ."

"I'll kill him!" screamed Nelson, struggling to get free. "I'll kill him!"

"Throw him in the lake," Karpis ordered.

"Throw him to the wolves," yelled Van Meter.

They hoisted the baby-faced paleface above their heads and marched him out the front door. The band quit and left.

The shooting was too much for Roxanne. She put on her coat and boots and slipped away. The snow was coming straight down. Powdery layers of it coated the earth. She tramped down the parkway and made her way across Shore Drive and into Phalen Park. The riotous Indians and a few Pilgrim friends were returning from the dousing of Nelson.

Roxanne stood at the water's edge with her hands pressed in the pockets of her coat and breathed wintry air so pure her eyes frosted. The lake was not yet frozen, making it a great black hole in a sea of illumination. Reeds, tall above the water, caught the heavy flakes and bowed in her direction. The snowflakes crowned her queenly hair and melted over her gleaming cheeks. When she was a little girl, still living on the farm, she would go out to the fields on winter days and lie on her

back in the unbroken snow and stare into the endless
sky. Everything on earth was silent white. The sky was
breathless blue. The solitude was heavenly. Then she
would sweep her arms and legs back and forth, and
when she got up the imprint of an angel was planted in
the snow. It had been a long time since Roxanne had
lain with angels. These days the opium was as close as
she could get.

But this night was heavenlike on this sugar-coated
lake. She recalled the article in "Grover's Corner" and
wondered how a man could be so cynical that even the
simple beauty of a park was twisted into something ugly.
She tried to explain that to Dag Rankin on the day he
read the monkey column. The rage he went into was
the worst she had ever seen. His fury seemed impossible
to control. But she did it. She reasoned with him. Ca-
joled him. It was her idea to go to the paper and demand
an apology. Perhaps, as Rankin told her afterward, that
was a mistake. She knew the likes of Grover Mudd. He
was Dag Rankin with balls. There would be no apology.
At best they would both forget it. You can fight City
Hall, but you can't fight a newspaper. Not even a dying
one.

Headlights passed over her and Roxanne turned to
the house. A black squad car cut through the white
night. The police drove by the mansion and shined a
spotlight on it. The revelers in the windows waved. The
cops kept going.

As the snow continued to fall on that uniquely American holiday, Roxanne heard the tinkle of rain, then
saw a shadowy figure. It was Baby Face Nelson. In the
midnight whiteness on the snowcapped shore the drippy
little Pilgrim stood pissing into the icy water.

And the spirits of gangsters danced across the lake.

Saint Nicholas

In December of 1933 Utah became the thirty-sixth state to vote for repeal, and Prohibition was laid to rest. "Sweet Adeline" became the national anthem.

On Christmas Eve, Grover Mudd dragged Fuzzy Byron up to Bo Kelly's Tavern on Seven Corners, where good old moonshine was still being served. The death of Prohibition meant little in St. Paul since, even at the height of it, anyone with a compass from a Cracker Jacks box could find a drink being served. What Grover Mudd really wanted to celebrate was a decision he had reached. They sat at the bar and ordered a couple of 13s.

Behind the bar was a giant painting of blood-red Lucifer with his nasty horns, cloven hoofs, a forked tail, and a long pitchfork he used to keep rebellious sinners in line. The big white smile across his fanged face made Grover believe the Big Holy Spook had posed for the blasphemous thing.

The drinks were poured. Grover laid two bits on the bar and hoisted his glass. "Fuzzy, my boy, the American do-gooders, good God-loving Christians one and all, told us Prohibition would put an end to crime, but instead, we created organized crime and spilled more blood than whiskey." He looked the devil in the eye. "Here's to you, Lucifer. You're a hell of a guy." They downed their drinks and ordered another round.

"Are there other cities like St. Paul, Grover? Where crooks can hide?"

"Joplin, Missouri, is known as a safe town for gangs. Hot Springs, Arkansas, is where they spend their vacations. I hear Toledo is a bad place, too, but they don't offer the security and fringe benefits we do."

"How does a system like that get started?"

"Politics. It was those wily Irish who did it. Your Scandinavians went into farming, the Germans grabbed the labor jobs, and when nobody was looking the Irish stole all the civil-service jobs. Dick O'Connor had an alliance with the Bourbon Democrats—James J. Hill, William Hamm, and Otto Bremer and his brother, who own the Schmidt Brewery. They had this lovable old fellow named Bob Smith, and for twenty years they propped him up and ran him for Mayor until he was literally too old to stand. Whenever he was in office Dick O'Connor was the real mayor. His brother, John, the police chief, controlled all the gambling and bawdy-houses."

"Why did the people keep voting for them?"

"They didn't. Every few years the reformers would throw them out of office and put some well-meaning souls in there. Chief O'Connor would resign and take all his detectives with him. Then mysterious crime waves would break out, especially along Summit Avenue, where the rich contributors lived. Once they even robbed the new chief's office. Another time they got Nina Clifford to show a new police chief how he could earn a thousand dollars a crack by granting bawdy-houses privileges. Do you know Gil St. Sauver, the cop? It was his father. With Nina's help the O'Connors framed him and the poor son of a bitch ended up in Stillwater. Then people would scream bloody murder. *'This never happened when Bob Smith was mayor.'* Next election the Cardinal would prop up Bob Smith and send the old war-horse into battle. With a little help from floaters it worked every time."

"What's a floater?"

"A bunch of derelicts they'd bring over from Minneapolis on Election Day to vote. They not only floated from polling place to polling place, these guys floated from booth to booth. Twenty-five guys could cast over a thousand votes. Then the Big Fellow would be back as police chief and he'd crack down on vice until the joints understood that the price of staying open just went up. And he'd put out the word to the gangs: St. Paul is safe again as long as you check in, spend money, and commit all your crimes outside the city limits."

"Would John Dillinger come here?"

"Hell, he's probably in the booth behind us."

Fuzzy Byron spun his stool around, and Grover spit up his drink. It felt good to laugh, took his mind off things. As the weeks passed Grover gave little thought to the threat made by Dag Rankin, but he was haunted by the angel-faced girl, the Scandinavian goddess who was really German. He could not understand why she got so upset. Grover had nothing against Germans. Still, for all her haunting beauty, she did not figure in the decision he had made.

After visiting his children Grover Mudd spent the nicest Thanksgiving of his life with Stormy and the boy, and he stayed the night, the slender kitten in his arms. That was the night he began putting his feelings in proper perspective. Roxanne Schultz was only an infatuation, one of those unobtainable women men fantasize about. It was Stormy Day he loved. It was Stormy who loved him. He knew in his heart she was the only person who made him happy. He also knew he had to make up for two years of callous neglect. To hell with St. Paul. Grover Mudd was going to marry a colored girl.

He ordered another drink.

———————

'Twas the night before Christmas . . .

Roxanne Schultz got off the Payne Avenue streetcar at Minnehaha Avenue, where Hamm's Brewery was ablaze in light. Not even the holidays could slow the production of beer. The icy wind cut through her silk stockings. A few lonely snowflakes swirled about her face. She pulled a thick wool hat down over her ears. Winter's seasonal siege had begun. Snow crunched under her boots as she followed Payne Avenue past East Side tenements to a vacant lot and a foot-beaten path that led to the edge of the ravine.

> *The moon on the breast of the new-fallen snow*
> *Gave the luster of midday to objects below . . .*

Roxanne looked down upon the shantytown outlined in white. The slum she had climbed out of. With garbage and debris buried under a foot of snow, the place reminded her of the friendly village in her first-grade reader. The early hunters and trappers found the ravine comfortable in the winter and cool in the summer, but gazing down at it now Roxanne knew there were few comforts to be found in the ramshackle surroundings.

She got on the old Indian trail that zigzagged to the bottom, the zigzaggedy trail, the children called it, and clung to the trees as she half walked, half slid down to the railroad tracks. The tracks were kept clear and, as she carefully made her way across them in the dark, she remembered the balancing act she used to do with her girlfriends, pretending they were the high-wire stars in the circus. Roxanne climbed down a long stairway made of railroad ties that was sometimes lost in the deep snowdrifts that plagued the hollow. Another flight of stairs brought her down to the creek and to a trail she could walk with her eyes closed.

Water that discharged from a big pipe in the side of the brewery kept the stream flowing, so that even in the worst winters Phalen Creek only froze along the edges. Spoiled ice-water raced over broken bottles, tin

cans, and wads of newspaper and disappeared in the
reeking redolence of a manmade tunnel. A goat was
chewing on a salt carton. There was a dead cat on the
bank, the top half of it frozen stiff, the other half wag-
ging its tail in the water. Roxanne crossed over a derelict
bridge and made her way along a snow-packed road
that ran by the shoddy houses. Silver birches hung over
her. Broken picket fences tried in vain to define front
yards. One of the two-family shacks had frozen laundry
hanging on the porch. Candles were burning in some
of the windows, and a few of the larger places displayed
scrawny evergreens decorated with strings of popcorn.
In the distance she could hear an accordion struggling
with "Silent Night." Christmas had come to Swede
Hollow.

A naked birch tree stood in her front yard. The stairs
that climbed up to the door had not yet been cleared
of snow. The house was set on posts, and had been
whitewashed that summer, putting a pretty face on poverty. Roxanne paused before entering and stared at the
Hamm mansion on the high bluff over the back porch.
It was dark this year. She wondered if that had something to do with the kidnapping. The society page said
the family was looking to move. Perhaps they were tired
of the view. She pushed open the door and called for
her mother.

Not a creature was stirring, not even a mouse;
The stockings were hung by the chimney with care,
In hopes that Saint Nicholas soon would be there. . . .

Saint Nicholas, patron saint of brewers, children, and
poor souls, could not have found a more appropriate
haunt: a two-room shanty of broken slats and crumbling
plaster. The only light came from a wood-burning stove
in the front room, where the old lady had the couch
close to the fire. Pillows supported her back, and blankets covered her legs.

"I knew my little girl would not forget her mamma on tonight of all nights. Did you bring the dream stuff?"

"You know I did." Roxanne found her mother's appearance unbelievable: a woman near sixty looking eighty years old, bathed in sweat, with a scarf over her head and glassy gray eyes swimming in melancholy so black the sun would be shamed. That is what the dream stuff did.

The old lady pulled a cigar box from under the covers and flipped open the lid. "You see. I knew you would come tonight. Will you do it, Roxy? Your mamma's shaking too bad."

The wind sang a chilly song under the planks as Roxanne removed her mittens and stood before the fire. The heat felt good, but the bright blaze was intoxicating. Days gone by loomed in the flames. She saw herself nine years old again. The sun was coming up. She had to go to the outhouse. She stepped onto the back porch. Her eyes were not awake yet. A bare foot hit her in the head and knocked her down. It was her father. Swinging back and forth. Hanging in the dawn.

"Please, Roxy. It's Christmas."

Her mother's weepy voice pulled her from the fire. She hadn't meant to make her beg. Roxanne, like a peddler, drew the pack from her coat. She mixed the solution and filled the syringe. She cleaned her mother's trembling arm with alcohol from the kit and then held it tight, because it was like the precarious branches on the birch trees outside the house, just trying to hang on till spring. Roxanne popped the needle through the skin and pumped a little warmth into a cold life, shot a little heroin into her mother's shivering veins.

And mamma in her 'kerchief, and I in my cap,
Had just settled our brains for a long winter's nap . . .

The whistling wind caused a clatter on the roof. The logs in the fire toppled into ash. A train rumbled through the ravine. The needle came out.

"You are a saint, Roxy."

"This can't go on, Mamma. The price is sky-high. An ounce can cost a hundred dollars or more."

"Somebody is getting rich, yah, baby?" The old lady chuckled. "It's the winters, Roxy. They're so damn miserable. I have stomach pangs, and there is shooting pain in my legs."

"I want to put you in the Mound Park Sanatorium. I have the money. If you need it they'll put you on morphine."

"Like your brother was on the morphine. No, little girl. Wretch that I am, I will die in this godawful hole."

"I can come more often."

"No, not in the winter. It is so difficult to get down here. If you could just send the dream stuff while the weather is bad."

"Is that nice Polack family still living next door?"

"Oh, no. Mexicans. The hollow is being overrun by them. And they're so dirty, Roxanne."

"How many of our friends are left?"

"Only Mrs. Hokanson. She brings coffee every day and we talk. Most of politics. These Swedes, they are so proud of the governor. He is doing a good job, yah?"

"You know I don't like politics."

"Oh, but you should. In the old country they did not like politics, so now look what that little Hitler is doing to them."

"Daddy liked politics. What did it get him?"

"It got us Floyd Olson and Franklin Roosevelt, and it'll get a new mayor and new commissioners, and some day the peoples will not have to live in the hollows. The Farmer-Labor party was born of the blood of men like your father." The old woman put her quivering fingers to her daughter's face. "You turned out so pretty. Your papa and brother would be proud. Be proud, Roxy."

She rested her head on the pillow and closed her troubled eyes.

And away they all flew like the down of a thistle. . . .

Roxanne Schultz stood at the broken gate in the front yard. It was late. The candles in the windows were out. The swing shift from the brewery was going home amongst joyous shouts of season's greetings. Up on Sixth Street, where the hills of the East Side came to a peak, the bells of Sacred Heart Church were celebrating a birth. She gazed through watery eyes at a rat in the middle of the creek, gnawing through a leaky bundle of garbage. It was wrapped in newspaper and Roxanne could make out the big words *FRONTIER NEWS*. The biting cold slapped her face. She started through the snow as the first tear rolled down her cheek. She would cry to the top of the hill. Then she would stop.

"Happy Christmas to all, and to all a good night."

When they left Bo Kelly's Tavern, Grover Mudd was only slightly less plastered than his friend Fuzzy. Two drunkards lurching homeward. They staggered over to St. Peter Street, blowing their fire-laden breath into the freezing air. The sidewalk was dusted with fresh snow. Christmas decorations lit up the night. Street lamps were wrapped in tinsel. The street was festooned with holly from hotel to hotel, or bawdyhouse to bawdyhouse, with illuminated red bells hung in the middle. Then the real bells sang and the city went black. It was midnight. The last trolley of the evening clanged by in front of them. Sparks flew off the cables. In the frosty darkness Grover turned Fuzzy around and, motherly, buttoned his coat. "How'd a nice guy like you end up in St. Paul?"

"Looking back it's a bit fuzzy, but I think I was riding the rails and I literally fell off the train. I thought I was in Chicago. Never found an easier place to get a drink. So I stayed."

"And you were a painter?"

"An artist, Grover. When I had my eyes I could paint the wind, landscapes so gorgeous city slickers would cry at the sight of them."

"I saw the house you painted on Grand Avenue. Everyone in town went to see it."

"A work of art."

"It sure was. Only she wanted the house white and the shutters black. Not the other way around. It looked like a giant negative."

"The colors got fuzzy. Besides, I tried to tell the old bitch black and white don't mix."

"Don't say that."

Grover and Fuzzy stumbled by the Union Bus Depot, where late holiday arrivals stood at the dark curb with their suitcases and watched the two drunken fools trip across Seventh Street.

"How'd you end up in St. Paul, Grover?"

"I was born here. Goddammit. I was going to get out. Write the great American novel like every other reporter in the world. Now I write about palookas for the local yokels. I may be the only reporter in history who went to war and couldn't get a decent column out of it, much less a book."

"What was the name of that medal you won over there?"

"The Croix de Guerre."

"The Cross of Courage."

"Where'd you learn French?"

"When I was young I studied in Paris."

"You're a real wonder, Fuzzy."

"Now I'm a bum. When are you going to do a column on me?"

"When you're sober you don't talk, and when you're drunk you talk drunk talk."

"Drunk talk? Grover, my boy, not one beguiling word has ever passed these lips."

"C'mon, some of your stories defy the law of gravity."

"In stating my past to you, Grover Mudd, who I have chosen to be my Boswell, I have never exaggerated my existence, nor have I deluded my accomplishments. Take that day in Boston."

"This ain't the Boston museum story again, is it?"

"It was cold, much like tonight, and I was passing by this famous art museum, though its name escapes me now. I had to pee, much like tonight, so I walked inside to use the john. There it was. Hanging on the wall."

"The john?"

"No, Grover boy, my painting. *Ontario Hills*. And right down in the corner, it was fuzzy but I could see it, it said, 'Chester D. Byron.' I reached out to touch it. Two guards grabbed me. They called me a bum. Said the painting was worth thousands and threw me out. Thousands. Want to know a secret, Grover, between me and you?"

"Sure, Fuzzy, our secret."

"They didn't get them all. I got the best ones hid."

"I have a confession, Fuzzy. I lied. I did write a book."

"No lie?"

"*The Great American Great War Novel*, by Grover Mudd. Sold millions."

"Well, I'll be."

"The original handwritten manuscript is displayed in a glass case at the famous Huntington Library in Pasadena, California. Armed guards watch it around the clock."

"That's really something, Grover. And now you're a bum like me."

Grover laughed. It was a retching laugh that induced severe coughing. He tripped into a brick wall. Fuzzy held him up and patted his back. Grover wiped the blood-speckled froth from his lips with the back of his hand. He regained his intoxicated composure and they moved on, up St. Peter Street.

They floundered across Ninth Street, past Mother Merrill's Café, where the lonely shared Christmas dinner, past Assumption Church, where candlelight was flickering in the stained-glass windows and a sad German hymn floated over the steeples. Grover searched the snowdrifts for the Big Holy Spook. He made a snowball. "I know you're in there, Spook. Come out, come out." There was no answer, only a poignant tune from a faraway land. They moved along.

Up on the hill, under the snowcapped domes of Saint Paul's Cathedral, midnight mass was under way, and more glorious carols hailing the birth of Christ spilled out of the church and blessed the two inebriated agnostics passing below.

Grover hauled Fuzzy up to the door of Granny Walker's boardinghouse and pushed him inside. The lobby was pitch black and they both tumbled over a chair and fell to the floor. A light switch flicked at the end of the hall. Then came the unmistakable sound of a shotgun being cocked.

"Don't shoot, Granny, it's only me and Fuzzy."

"Who's me?" came a not-so-sweet voice.

"Grover Mudd of the *Frontier News*." There were footsteps in the hall, and the sudden glare of the overhead light nearly blinded him, but he could make out the double barrels under his nose. "C'mon, Granny, put that away, I'm just bringing Fuzzy home."

"I thought you were after my girls."

"For Christ's sake, we just passed every whorehouse in town, why would we want your girls?"

She lowered the gun. "This ain't his damn home, and you know I don't let in no one after midnight." She was a sixtyish woman, round and sturdy with bits of rags tied to her head in a sorry attempt to put curls into her stringy gray hair. Granny Walker had the reputation of a benevolent witch. Besides the boardinghouse, she also owned a dry-cleaning shop where the freezing poor could usually find a pair of socks, if not a warm coat. And Granny Walker had another reputation. She had been legally married eight different times. One marriage lasted only a day. Where doctors and lawyers hung their diplomas on the wall, Granny hung her Minnesota marriage certificates. Grover did a piece on her once and she was so flattered by it she wanted a piece of him. "Are you too drunk to even stand up?"

Grover got to his feet and hoisted Fuzzy. "Where's his room?"

Granny stared through Fuzzy and talked to Grover. "Did this little mutt tell you he has a room here?"

"This is where he stays."

"When he pays he stays."

"I pay my rent each and every month," Fuzzy babbled. "Most important thing in my life."

Granny plugged the shotgun into Fuzzy's belly. "That's a cock-and-bull story. He hasn't paid me in a month of Sundays. I've been letting him sleep in the hall."

Fuzzy was getting heavy and Grover was getting sick. "How much for tonight, Granny?"

"A flop is fifty cents, a room is a dollar."

Grover fished five bucks from his pocket and handed it to her. "Give him a room for a week. Which way?"

"Last door on the right," she told him.

Grover carried Fuzzy down the hallway, stepping over sleeping bodies. He'd just reached the door when Granny, in her sweetest voice, called to him.

"And where will you sleep tonight, Grover Mudd?"

Grover stopped and turned, holding Fuzzy halfway

off the floor. Granny was leaning on the countertop, doing her old-fashioned best to look sexy. She palmed the rags in her hair and squeezed the shotgun barrel like a whore squeezing a high-buck penis, and in her day she was probably sexy as sin. But her days had been blown away. Grover was too sick to laugh and too drunk to cry. "Well, Granny, where do you suggest?"

"There's a room right next to your friend."

Grover looked across the hall. Granny's door was cracked open and a speck of light peeked out. He turned back. "I would, Granny, but sure as it snows in the wintertime I'd end up a certificate on your wall." He kicked open the door. The room smelled of Borax.

"And if in the morning God should call, tell him I'm painting St. Paul," Fuzzy cried out.

Grover dropped him on a pallid mattress.

Chester D. Byron muttered something about gorgeous landscapes and melting colors, then dozed off.

"Merry Christmas, Fuzzy." And Grover Mudd left the old wino snoring in his spit.

Baby Face

On the frigid Friday afternoon of December 29, Homer Van Meter led his leaderless gang across the Franklin Avenue Bridge and descended on downtown Minneapolis over ice-slicked streets. Baby Face Nelson was riding shotgun. Trailing them in a twelve-cylinder Auburn was Tommy Carroll, and a new recruit named Red Hurlocker. The temperature was below zero. Up the river the Falls of Saint Anthony, which Father Louis Hennepin had named in honor of his patron saint, had turned to glass. The first blizzard of the winter season blew through the day after Christmas, leaving behind plunging temperatures and snowdrifts five feet high. As hard as he tried, Van Meter could not beg warm air from the heater of the black Chevy coupé he had bought from a used-car dealer.

"How much did you pay for this piece a shit?"

"Fifty-five bucks."

"Sucker. Homer Van Sucker."

"It's only gotta last one day."

"Mind telling me why we didn't get the Auby wheels and let those two clowns ride this hay wagon? We're the brains of this outfit."

"Tommy's a better wheelman."

"Hor'shit."

"He's the only one that didn't queer the Sioux Falls job, or the post-office job, or the Chicago job. So I told him he could drive it."

"Those jobs were smooth as a duck's ass."

"What? You crazy or something? We've left a trail of blood across three states. The feds got flyers of us in every police station in the country. The only thing keeping us off the front page is Dillinger."

"Yeah, the greedy bastard."

"If you ever talk to him like that he'll cut off your balls."

"Who cut off yours?"

"What?"

"Word is you and Rankin got no balls. Hahahaha-haha."

"Who told you that?"

"Did you see that broad of his? What a tomato. Wonder how they do it."

"Who said I got no balls?"

"It was in 'Grover's Corner.' Big headline—'Homer Van Meter Got No Peter.' Hahahahahahahahaha."

"You lying piece a shit."

"What's a matter, Homer, the old flag don't rise anymore? Hahahahahaha!"

Frederick Ricci was a railroad worker, unemployed for almost two years. The bank took his home. Deep in debt, he was forced, with much humiliation, to move his family—wife and son, Jory—from Minneapolis to his mother-in-law's house in the Mound Park neighborhood of St. Paul. He was a big man. He'd fought in the Great War. And he was loud, a character much like his chubby, precocious son. He blamed himself for a lot of Jory's troubles in school. Although teachers like Miss Pearl could be a little more understanding, it would help if he had a job. Franklin Roosevelt and the New Deal gave him hope.

With money humbly borrowed he bought his son a pair of ice skates for Christmas, but the blustery weather prevented the boy from trying them out. Finally, on the afternoon of December 29, Frederick Ricci borrowed

his brother's black Chevy coupé so he could take Jory
ice-skating across town at Como Park.

"We don't have to go all the way to Como," Jory
told his father as they climbed into the car.

"The whole lake has been plowed for the winter carnival. They're billing it as the largest skating rink in the
world. We've gotta go today. I don't know when I can
get the car again."

The streets were treacherous, the intersections dangerous. Seeing over the snowdrifts was sometimes impossible. "Three days," Frederick Ricci grumbled as
he drove along, "and the city still hasn't got the streets
plowed."

"They ran out of money," Jory reminded him.

"They stuffed the money in their pockets, that's what
they did. I'll bet the streets are plowed in Minneapolis."

"Did you hear the two cities are going to merge, Dad?
They're going to call it Minnehaha. 'Minne' for Minneapolis and 'haha' for St. Paul."

His father cracked up. "Ha ha for St. Paul."

The Chevy coupé snuck behind the State Capitol, cut
through Frogtown, then headed out Como Avenue toward the park. In a borrowed car, with a Christmas
present bought on borrowed money, Frederick Ricci
clung to a small measure of fatherly pride. His favorite
song was playing on the radio: "Brother, Can You
Spare a Dime?"

––––––––––

It was not long before Assistant Chief St. Sauver grew
sick of babysitting Patrolman Emil Gunderson. To put
him out of sight and out of mind, and keep his name
out of the news, Gunderson was assigned to the Ramsey
County Jail behind City Hall, where he underwent a
conversion of sorts. Instead of beating the snot out of
the prisoners, he took their money and supplied them
with dope for weekend parties. But these narcotics or-
gies grew so wild and popular they eventually earned

space on the front page of the *Frontier News* and the *North Star Press*. Since Gunderson's sponsorship could not be proved, and it was virtually impossible to fire a police officer, Gil St. Sauver transferred the big cop to the dispatcher's office at the Rondo Substation on the corner of Rondo Street and Western Avenue. Not far from Como Park.

———————

Tire tracks ran through the alley, but it had not been plowed. Snowdrifts climbed the walls. Homer Van Meter parked there behind the bank and followed Baby Face Nelson out of the car. A gust of freezing wind blew flurries between the buildings and numbed their cheeks. They hid tommy guns under their long coats and dropped extra clips into their pockets. They hid their faces behind thick fur collars, then ducked around the corner to Hennepin Avenue.

Traffic was snarled. The sidewalks were crowded. Road crews were lifting snow piles off the curbs. Nelson stopped and grabbed Van Meter by the arm. "I thought you said you cased this place."

"I did."

"Christ almighty, it looks like a big fishbowl."

"What's a matter, Baby Face, no balls?" Homer Van Meter sounded tougher than he felt. When he'd cased it a week before, things were quiet, and he could not remember the glass front being so large. But this was the Friday before the holiday weekend. The bank had to be steaming with cash.

The big Auburn pulled into a NO PARKING zone at the front door. Tommy Carroll and Red Hurlocker stepped out.

Even if he'd wanted to, Van Meter knew it was too late to call things off. He dropped his hand under his coat and fingered the trigger. Tommy Carroll took up his position on the sidewalk, and Homer Van Meter & Company went through the front door.

The lobby was busy. Lines formed at every teller's window. The floor was slushy from tracked-in snow. Decorative balconies with gold railings ran below the lofty ceiling. Homer Van Meter gaped up at them with his mouth hanging open. Now he knew. They were in the wrong bank.

Nelson unleashed his Thompson, pointed it in the air, and fired off a round. "Everybody hit the floor."

During the screaming and scrambling, plaster fell from the wounded ceiling and hit Van Meter over the head. "Damn you!" he shouted. "I told you not to do that."

Nelson fired off another round. "Hit the floor!" People dived in the muck. The alarm went off.

Red Hurlocker got busy cleaning out the drawers as Van Meter leaped the counter and darted into a walk-in vault. There were no piles of money stacked on shelves, only a line of small safes with combination locks. He was ready to drag a banker in with him when he heard shots coming from the street. With bells ringing in his ears Homer Van Meter rushed out of the vault and vaulted the counter.

Red Hurlocker was out the front door and into the Auburn.

Tommy Carroll was covering the car's rear, blasting away at a squad car down at the corner.

Baby Face Nelson was on the sidewalk shooting up Hennepin Avenue.

Van Meter got through the front door just in time to see a bloody cop fall in the icy gutter. Another squad car approached from the opposite direction. Van Meter sprayed the corner with bullets and the car swerved across the ice into a curb. Two cops leaped out and returned the fire until a rolling streetcar got sandwiched in the shootout. The motorman jumped from the trolley and the passengers leaped for cover.

Tommy Carroll sprang up behind the steering wheel of the Auburn and used the runaway trolley for cover as he roared past the cops and steered for the river.

When Homer Van Meter saw that half of his gang had gotten away he yelled, "Back door!" and he and Baby Face Nelson dashed through the bank, hurdled the customers on the floor, and busted out a rear exit. It was all snow and ice, and they lost their balance and pitched into the white stuff. The tommy guns flew out of their hands. One of the guns went off and creased a back tire on the getaway car. They scrambled to their feet, collected their hardware, and stumbled to the car.

"I'll drive," declared Baby Face Nelson.

"I'll drive. It's my car." Van Meter shoved Nelson across the seat.

The Chevy skidded through the snow to the end of the alley, but the exit was sealed with a wall of hard, chunky snow the plows had just left behind. The bank alarm was still ringing. The scream of police sirens was deafening.

"Back up," yelled Nelson. "I told you to let me drive."

Van Meter threw the car in reverse and skidded back down the alley, but a squad car blocked that exit and a pair of Minneapolis cops jumped out with .38s in hand.

Nelson leaped from the car and let them have it. In the hailstorm of bullets that followed one officer doubled over into the snow, and the other crawled back into the squad car clutching his leg. Baby Face Nelson jumped back into the car. "Run it!"

Van Meter put the pedal to the metal and the car fishtailed down the slippery alley and burst through the wall of snow at the end. They slid sideways across the street. Then Homer Van Meter drove like a crazy man for the nearest bridge.

The Mill City ground to a halt. Father Louis Hennepin's avenue displayed the red badge of courage across its proud white way. Five cops soaked in blood were strewn about the snowy street.

The bullet-speckled Chevy thumped its way into St. Paul and through the State Fair Grounds. By the time they reached Como Park the crippled tire was working its way off the rim. They were forced to stop. Homer Van Meter and Baby Face Nelson got out of the car and stomped up and down to keep warm.

"Where's the spare?" Nelson wanted to know.

"Ain't no spare."

"You bought a car for a bank job with no spare?"

"We wouldn't need a spare if you hadn't set off the alarms."

"Shit-for-brains. Homer Van Shit-for-brains."

"Talk about it, Baby Face. Last job I do with you. I'm heading back to Chicago and tie up with Dillinger."

"You wouldn't know John Dillinger from Herbert Hoover."

"We'll see. At least he knows how to hit a bank."

"It's sure as shit *you* don't. All you did was get us stuck out here in iceland like a pair of sitting ducks."

"Sitting penguins," said Van Meter, correcting him.

At the same time as Homer Van Meter and Baby Face Nelson were stepping out of their black Chevy coupé, Frederick Ricci and his son, Jory, were stepping into theirs. The outing was disappointing. Only a corner of the lake was cleared of snow. The ice was choppy. There were no other people skating. It was too cold for fun.

Frederick Ricci slid behind the wheel. The seat was hard as stone. His frustration was reaching the boiling point. "This goddamn city can't do a freezing thing right," he swore. "Twin Cities, hah. If these cities are twins, St. Paul should have been strangled at birth."

"I had fun, Dad. It's just a little cold."

Frederick Ricci took his gloves off and put his hand to his forehead, almost in tears. "I try, son. I really try." He hit the starter and coaxed the engine into turning over. He blew his breath into his hands, pulled his cap down over his ears, put the gloves back on, and pulled out.

He had only driven a block when he approached a parked car off to his left. The rear tire on the street side was flat and two men were arguing over it. He stopped in the middle of the road and rolled down his window. "Do you fellas need a hand?" he asked.

The two men froze, amazed, as if someone had sneaked up on them. "I'll give you a hand across the chops, buster," the short, pudgy man finally said.

"Beat it," grumbled the skinny man.

Frederick Ricci was taken aback by the sharp rebuke and watchfully inched away. Then the tall, skinny man was yelling at him. "Scram, asshole, if ya know what's good for ya."

Jory leaned over his father's lap. "Look at the back fender, Dad. Looks like bullet holes."

He nudged his son away. "I'll get their plate numbers and we'll get out of here." He crept forward, stuck his head out the window and took a good look at the rear license plate.

The short man was furious. "Son of a bitch," he yelled, and he reached into the car.

Frederick Ricci was rightly suspicious, but he was also naïve enough to believe the pudgy man was, at worst, going after a tire iron. He had gotten three letters of the license plate when he heard the roaring staccato of automatic gunfire and saw glass exploding around him. There was a slug to his face, followed by a crack across his shoulders. He slumped across the seat and heard Jory scream in terror. Another punch slammed through his guts, and an unbearable cramp gripped his leg. His cap fell to the floor. His gray coat turned soggy black. His ear was against the cold leather, but something warm was running under it. He heard car doors slam, then a rubbery thumping noise that faded away like an echo. He tried to call his son's name.

Jory Ricci was in shock. Blood streaked his face. His

mittens were dripping with it. His father's bloody face
was resting next to his leg with a guttural mumble bub-
bling out his lips. The boy tried to calm himself. He
pulled the stocking hat off his head and pressed it to
his shrieking mouth. He had not been shot. His wounds
came from the flying glass. Glass was in his hair, and
cuts marred his forehead. The gangsters were gone.
Most of the blood he saw was his father's. Jory stuffed
his hat under his father's bleeding head. He clawed his
way over the bullet-riddled body and took control of
the steering wheel. The car was rolling, the engine still
running. All that was left of the windshield were a few
sharp edges jutting out of the frame. His thinking was
muddled. Ancker Hospital was near by, but he didn't
know how to get there. Then he remembered the police
had a substation at Rondo and Western. That would
be the best place to go.

Jory had never driven a car before, and it was much
harder to steer than he had imagined. The city blocks
seemed like miles, and everybody was in his way. The
tears dripping from his eyes mixed with the blood dropping from his forehead, and the freezing wind smeared
both of them across his baby face. He raced down Como
Avenue to Western and cut through the seedy Frogtown
neighborhood, and finally slammed to a halt at Rondo
between lampposts labeled POLICE.

The boy bolted up the stairs and through the door.
The front desk was unmanned. He could hear the
squelching static of a two-way radio coming from below
a short flight of stairs. He leaped down them and burst
into the dispatcher's room, and into the coat buttons
of the largest cop he had ever seen. His Sam Browne
belt was stretched tight over the wide shoulders and
thick waist of his green winter overcoat. He reeked of
wet wool. His big gun handle stared Jory in the face.
His britches were neatly tucked into a pair of black
leather boots with knee-high shafts and wide brass
buckles. Above one of the coat pockets was a police

badge and a whistle; above the other hung a sharp-shooter pin. Below it the name tag read GUNDERSON. The giant patrolman glared down at him in disbelief, as did the other cops in the room.

For the first time since the shooting young Jory Ricci took a good look at himself. His mittens and coat were soaked with blood. His trousers were streaked. His overshoes were dripping red snow onto an already muddy floor. His face felt wet and sticky. Still in shock, he gazed up into the unfriendly eyes of Emil Gunderson. "Shot. Gang . . . gangsters . . . shot my dad. In the car . . ."

Patrolman Emil Gunderson put his hand on the boy's shoulder and squeezed hard. "Check it out," he ordered. Two cops ran from the room.

Jory added confusion to his fright. The big cop's thumb dug into his chest. Nobody moved to help him. Nobody asked about the gangsters. They just stared at him with contemptuous faces. The only sounds came from the squawking chatter of a tin speaker. Then Jory heard running footsteps in the hallway, and an out-of-breath cop was standing next to him with hate in his voice.

"It's the Chevy coupé, shot all to hell. His partner got it good. Didn't see the loot."

Emil Gunderson grabbed Jory by the throat. "You've got a lot of balls, you son of a bitchin' cop killer."

"No. Some gangsters shot my dad," Jory choked out.

"Your dad," screamed Gunderson. "Two of the cops you shot in Minneapolis just died, Baby Face." With that he heaved the boy across the room and into a brick wall.

Jory Ricci slid to the floor and began to weep. "Two men shot my dad."

Patrolman Gunderson put the steel shank of his boot across the boy's mouth and bounced his head off the bricks. He swift-kicked him in the pit of the stomach, and the other cops joined in.

While St. Paul's finest were putting the boot to his son on the muddy floor of the dispatcher's office, Frederick Ricci slowly bled to death on the frozen seat of a borrowed Chevy; gazing through a shattered windshield at an overcast sky, he died believing that in Roosevelt's New Deal he'd been dealt the joker. But he did not die in vain. If Nina Clifford was right, and St. Paul was a powder keg on a downward spiral, then the unemployed railroad worker from Minneapolis—when he closed his teary eyes for the last time—was the match that ignited the fuse.

Saint Walt

Editor Walt Howard sat alone in his office. The new year was only minutes away. The newsroom was dark. The paper had been put to bed. A kerosene lamp was glowing in front of him. He picked up the announcement and read it again. Had he failed?

THE "FRONTIER NEWS"
CARRIES ON

Ownership of the "Frontier News" was transferred Friday to the North Star Press Co.

The "Frontier News" will continue publication, not in any sense as an appendage of the "North Star Press," but as an independent, progressive newspaper designed to give service to the citizens of St. Paul and the state of Minnesota.

The announcement would run on the front page, above the fold. He set it aside. Spread under the flickering light was the story of the Riccis, father and son, as told by four different newspapers. There was a police report, and the coroner's report. Two Minneapolis policemen were dead. Three others were in Hennepin County Hospital. Jory Ricci was recovering at Ancker Hospital. Walt Howard lived near Como Park. If it had been summertime, with the windows open, he'd have heard the shots. Or he might have been the one to stop and offer help. What has a city become when a helping hand is greeted by machine-gun fire? This story was going to be more than newsprint and a black-and-white montage on the front page.

The Front Page

The struggling editor removed his glasses and cleaned them. The paper was finished. He had less than a year.

Walt Howard had been with the *Frontier News* since the end of the war, a St. Paul newsman even longer. He had known them all—John and Richard O'Connor, James J. Hill, Archbishop John Ireland. To a young reporter they were venerable giants. To an aging editor looking back they were a puzzle. The O'Connors were easy enough to piece together, but what about Hill, and Hamm, and Bremer? How could businessmen with so much foresight condone a system that would one day put a stranglehold on the city? And what of the archbishop who counted the donations? Did he turn his back to get his cathedral built? Why did he systematically destroy all of his papers?

Mr. Howard wandered through the deserted newsroom and into Grover's Corner. He stepped over newspapers stacked on the floor and leaned against the window. Rags were stuffed in the bottom. Frost trimmed the pane. What was it Saint Mudd saw out there?

Steam rose from the manholes. Icicles hung from the *North Star Press*. Snowflakes danced around the street lamps the way gangsters danced around the law. An old man bundled in winter garb was pulling a horse and cart over the icy bricks, a lonely vestige of a St. Paul the proud editor once knew. Up at City Hall, lights were burning on the top floor, and a shadowy figure floated past the windows. A janitor pushing a broom. He stopped and put his face to the glass. Was he looking down at the *Frontier News*?

Standing resolute in Grover's Corner the embattled editor mapped out a course that would steer through apathy and fly against the fierce winter wind. This bold

new course was for a schoolboy laid up in the hospital
with no daddy coming to see him. It was for a couple
of Irish boys tied together like animals and floating
upside down in a city lake. It was for the children of
police officers standing in cemeteries praying last good-
byes to their fallen fathers. He'd had a son once. If he
had lived . . . No, that was not fair to Grover Mudd.

It was midnight. The street lamps went out. The horse
clip-clopped through the dark. A hundred whistles
sounded in the train yards. Diffident fireworks exploded
over Harriet Island. The church bells of St. Paul rang
in the new year.

Walt Howard had heard enough. A lump swelled in
his throat, and a hatred found its way to his heart. "Now
we cross the line."

BOOK TWO

Winter Spring 1934

We are put here to become saints.

—Dorothy Day

Saint Anne

Grover Mudd ate lunch at Mother Merrill's Café. He skipped dessert and left a dime tip on the counter next to his plate. Out in the snow-mantled city the sidewalks were bustling with bundled people. The icy winds of winter were back. His gloves were wearing thin and he needed a new coat. He buttoned up and went window-shopping for winter clothes. He hoped the January thaw would arrive on schedule.

Grover spotted her coming out of the Golden Rule Department Store. She had a box under her arm. He ducked into a doorway out of the wind and watched her cross the street. She followed the crowd up the sidewalk and passed him by. Grover fell in line and followed her with no idea what he was going to say. The sidewalks were slippery with ice. She hurried to make the light, crossed Wabasha Street, and moved past the Saint Francis Hotel toward the Orpheum Theater. Grover had to wait for traffic. Then he carefully trotted across the street and slowed to a walk before calling her name, "Roxanne."

She stopped and turned to an ornate sidewalk clock with big Roman numerals, the fat black hands frozen for the winter. Standing under the theater marquee, she watched him approach.

Grover put a hand to his throat to suppress a cough. "I thought it was you," he said, stilling his breath. She was even prettier than he had tried to forget, her blond hair tossed slightly by the breeze, her cheeks apple red with the cold. "Grover Mudd, the *Frontier News*. Remember?"

"Yes, I remember," she said in a bitter voice. The movie house was showing *Son of Kong*. The big ape growled down at them from a poster.

Grover stumbled for words. "Listen, Roxanne, Miss Schultz, I want to . . . well, you know . . . kind of apologize for that remark I made last time we met. I didn't mean anything by it. In fact, the whole scene was rather ugly, and I'm sorry you had to be a part of it."

"You're wasting your breath, Mr. Mudd. I'm not the one you slandered all over your newspaper."

"Call me Grover. My friends do."

"You don't have any friends."

"How would you know that?"

"I know you." People were brushing by them. She stepped closer. He could see her crystal breath in the freezing air, smell her cool perfume. He felt the cold, cutting edge of her words as she spoke. "You sanctimonious bastard. You ought to be shot."

Her steely tongue surprised him. "That's mighty righteous talk for a palooka's moll."

"I'm sure you like them deaf and dumb."

"That's right, blondie. Busty and stupid, that's the way Grover Mudd likes his women. Not a brain in their heads. Let me tell you something else about your type . . ." He jerked a glove to his mouth and threw an arm around the clock post as the cough cut up his chest and burned his throat. He hung there a moment, embarrassed and weakened.

She was wearing white mittens, and she pressed the warm wool to the side of his face. "Are you all right?" she asked. It was a soft, tender voice full of caring. And for a second—and it was only a second—Grover saw in her eyes compassion and understanding, a sympathetic union of sorts. For a brief moment their differences melted away, because somehow she knew. His destiny was written across her angel face. She must have seen it, too. She pulled her hand away.

A trolley rolled by and the bells rang in his ears. "It's just a cold. Damn winters are killing me."

"You should get out of this climate. My brother . . ." She stopped and dropped her head.

Grover yanked the big red handkerchief from his pocket and wiped his mouth. He leaned his back against the clock post and stared at her. "I can't figure it out, dame like you. Brainy, brassy, beautiful. Why him?"

He made her uncomfortable. She looked up at him confused, as if she wanted to run, wanted to stand and fight. "You're a newspaperman," she said with only a trace of bitterness. "Everything you touch turns to black and white. You divide the world into gangsters and saints. It must be heaven, believing life is that simple." She seemed lost for words. "He's a very dangerous man, Grover Mudd. Don't play games with him." She turned and hurried away.

He called after her. "It's no game, Roxy. Tell him his answer will be on the front page tomorrow, and the day after, and the day after that." She was gone. Grover looked up at King Kong's son. "You and your big dick." He grabbed the frozen clock and coughed into the old engineer's handkerchief.

When the type was set and the switch was thrown the newspapers shot off the press at machine-gun pace. The printers wore earplugs. The clatter was deafening.

Outside, ice crystals twinkled in the dark. It was three o'clock in the morning. The rusty *Frontier News* trucks turned over their sleepy engines. Thick exhaust poured into the freezing air. They crept into a line around Fourth Street.

Inside, the newspapers were folded, stacked, and bundled. The big garage doors were thrown open and the news was tossed into the back of a waiting truck.

Then the truck crunched out over the snow-packed street.

Up on the third floor of the *Frontier News* it was black, except for a dim light in a corner office. The silhouettes of a proud editor and a loyal columnist slipped into their coats. It was done. The launching of a crusade. The first truck rolled down the street, and they watched it disappear in a swirl of smoke as it ventured into the icy dark.

———————

On the day after her second encounter with Grover Mudd, Roxanne Schultz visited the Art Deco bar at the Commodore Hotel and waited for her lunch date to arrive. It was a small bar, teeming with elegance reflected in mirrored walls and a black lacquered ceiling with gold-leaf domes. The ocean-liner design of the place included a stately white bar with a brass rail and a black marble top. Candles glowed in the corners. Classical piano music waltzed out of the lounge. Roxanne sat on a white leather couch in the back, where, through the side door, she could watch people passing through the gold lobby. The lunch crowd had departed. One couple was enjoying a quiet drink near the foyer. Roxanne ordered a Chablis and unfolded the newspaper on the mirror top of the coffee table.

THE ST. PAUL FRONTIER NEWS

* Page One * Monday, January 8, 1934
* Two Cents *

WHO SHOT FREDERICK RICCI?

Ten days ago an innocent citizen of St. Paul was riddled with machine-gun slugs as he sat in his automobile. Frederick Ricci, 39, an unemployed railroad worker, died outside the Rondo Substation while waiting in vain for police to rush him to the hospital.

BUT THE MOST DIS-HEARTENING ASPECT OF THIS OUTRAGE IS THE MATTER-OF-FACT WAY IT HAS BEEN ACCEPTED BY THE PO-LICE—AND TO SOME EXTENT BY THE PUB-LIC.

This apathy is, no doubt, the aftermath of a long series of gang outrages that began with the organization of crim-inals to profit from Prohibi-tion. The people of St. Paul have become hardened to even the most outrageous crimes. Like the ambush murder of two policemen at Laurel and St. Albans; the bombing of underworld leader Danny Hogan; the kidnapping of William Hamm, Jr.; the Swift's pay-roll robbery and murder; the Kendrigan murders at Pig's Eye Lake; the widespread rioting last Halloween; and now the murder of Frede-rick Ricci—to mention just a few of the more notorious crimes.

Today, St. Paul enjoys an unenviable reputation throughout the nation as a hangout for gangs and a ran-cid town.

The arrival of legal liquor means the gangs that got rich and fat off bootlegging will be driven to other crimes to earn the easy money they require. We have already seen them go into bank robbery and kidnapping.

WE WILL SEE A LOT MORE UNLESS THE PO-LICE, WITH PUBLIC SUPPORT, TURN LEGAL FOR A CHANGE AND DRIVE THE GANGS OUT.

—EDITOR,
    THE FRONTIER NEWS

Roxanne put the paper aside, the words of Grover Mudd ringing in her ears. The *Frontier News* was going after Dag Rankin and everybody like him. Add to that a federal investigation, and to *that*, volatile city elections in the spring, and St. Paul was adding up to an unsafe place to live.

Nina Clifford swept through the lobby as if she owned the place and somebody was trying to steal it from her. Balanced on her head was an ugly brown wig with a tint of copper. The waiter, dressed in tails, helped her out of her heavy fur coat. "The white wine will be fine, Roscoe."

"Yes, Miss Clifford. And may I say what a pleasure it is having you here again."

"Thank you, dear. You are sweet." She nestled into the couch, beside Roxanne. Two salesmen eyed them from the lobby. Nina waved. "They say Sinclair Lewis used to hang out here, and that pretty Fitzgerald boy who used to write those wonderful stories about St. Paul. Personally, I don't like the place. Too many mirrors. How's your sex problem, Angel?"

Roxanne was embarrassed by the question. "You caught me at an unguarded moment. I really don't care to discuss it."

"Don't be embarrassed. You are so young. It'll happen again, and when it does your body, mind, and soul will come alive as never before. No narcotic can do that." Nina's drink was served and she thanked the waiter.

"Did you read today's paper?" Roxanne asked.

"The *North Star* or the *Frontier*?"

"The *Frontier*."

"Yes, I did. Interesting, wasn't it? I mean, being on the front page."

"Do you think anything will come of it?"

"There was a so-called cleanup campaign by the newspapers back in 1913, I believe it was, the year Chief St. Sauver went off to prison. You see, in the old days we had Ordinance Number Ten. The first week of each month we house madams would march down to the courthouse and dutifully pay our fines, which were based on the amount of business we did."

"Whores on parade?"

"If you like. The system worked. We made money and the city made money. After the police-chief scandal the papers raised a fuss and the houses were closed for ten days. A few flatfoot cops got fired. The mayor made a wonderful speech. Then we all went back to work.

Things are much different this time. In my day a girl could walk from one end of this city to the other end and the worst thing that might happen to her is some man might forget to tip his hat, and even that was rare. Today, it's kidnappings, gang fights, and murder. People should be upset. It never happened under the old guard."

"Do you know these people at the *Frontier News*?"

"Mr. Howard has been around a long time. We don't travel in the same social circles, but I'm sure he knows the whole story and is not afraid to print it."

"And Grover Mudd?"

Nina smiled and clapped her hands together. " 'Grover's Corner.' I never miss it. Delightful writing."

Roxanne sensed a wicked glee in the old lady. "Do you know him?"

"Oh, I feel as if I do. Every time he mentioned me in his column, business went through the roof." A sad look came over her face. "He doesn't write about me anymore. A long time ago I sent him a thank-you note along with an invitation, but he didn't bite."

The two women ordered sandwiches and more wine, and as the afternoon wore on Roxanne felt sympathy for this living relic. Old age is cruel. Much more cruel for women. Much more cruel still for women of the street. For every Mary Magdalene there are a thousand Nina Cliffords.

"And the church," Roxanne asked later, "did they ever try to clean things up?"

"Some pretty sermons. For years it was understood in this town that if there was ever a referendum on getting rid of the prostitutes, or getting rid of the Catholics—the church was gone. I always believed the people were on our side, and that Saint Anne, the patron saint of women, was watching over us."

"Not to mention a police chief?"

"The Big Fellow?" Nina put her hand to her heart

and laughed. "My girls called him Pee-Wee." She chortled again at the private joke. "When he died, over four thousand people attended his funeral at the cathedral. Of course, half of them probably had outstanding warrants, but it was touching nonetheless. No, it was his brother, Richard, the Cardinal, who wielded the real power."

"Why did they call him the Cardinal?"

"It had to do with Archbishop Ireland. They hated each other. It went way back to when Richard was a boy and got booted out of Father Ireland's cathedral school. He spent his whole life outfoxing the old priest. Anyway, after Rome made John Ireland a bishop, O'Connor's cronies started calling Richard the Cardinal. It really stuck in the archbishop's craw."

Roxanne could see Nina Clifford was getting drunk. Her speech was slurred and her eyes were watery. She was talking to the wine.

"But the Cardinal is dead now," the madam groaned. "The Big Fellow is dead. The railroad barons are gone. It was sometime around the Great War that my cards collapsed. I don't remember how or why. I just looked in the mirror one day and I was old and my house smelled stale. I know you don't think much of this old lady, angel face, but I've given away so much money over the years it makes me cry. It may not get me into heaven, but when I arrive at the Pearly Gates Saint Peter will have to take note of the cash I poured into the construction of that cathedral over my house. Attention will have to be paid to the hundreds of orphans I found homes for. I was going to build the city a whole damned orphanage, but they wouldn't let me put my name on it." She wiped a tear from her eye. "And when James J. Hill had a cash-flow problem, Nina had the cash. Do you think I'll be remembered with the same reverence as he? I gave over fifty years of my life to this town and all I ever got was a street named after me." She drew a handkerchief from her bag and blew her nose. "Puny little side street behind the church. First name only."

"Nina Clifford," Roxanne begged, "look into your crystal ball and tell me what you see."

"Why, Roxanne Schultz, I do believe you're worried about that pretty behind of yours. Is that what this lunch is about?" She took hold of Roxanne's hand. "You have good reason to worry. I hope I don't live to see it, but I see a sober-faced, upright, banal little city where the houses are a thing of the past, and working girls are confined to Frogtown, or Lowertown, or whatever part of town is out of favor with society at the time. I see once powerful men going to jail. And a few women, too. Have you ever been in jail, Angel?"

"I spent a year and a day at Shakopee. When I got out Danny Hogan got me a job waiting tables at the Green Lantern. After he was killed, Dag offered some of us jobs at the Hollyhocks Club."

"Poor Dapper Danny. He was a saint, he was. To this day I sometimes sit and wonder what kind of person would be low enough to kill that way. I guess we'll never know." The venerable whore polished off another glass of wine. "The *Frontier News* is dying. You can't blame them for wanting to go out in a blaze of glory. It's harmless now, but one more outrageous crime would validate everything that newspaper says, and then we are all through."

On the morning after Nina Clifford looked into her crystal ball, Alvin Karpis and Freddie Barker started up their car on Dunlap Street off Summit Avenue. Karpis checked his watch. It was eight-thirty A.M. The low white sky had warmed up to 10°. The heater was on "hot." A pair of machine guns rested on the seat between them. Freddie Barker was staring over his shoulder at the rear window. Alvin Karpis kept his eyes on the rearview mirror.

"He just turned off Summit," said Barker. "Here he comes."

"Right on time. Did you see Doc?"

"He was right behind him, kept going straight."

A big blue Lincoln cruised by them. It turned left on Goodrich Avenue and pulled to the curb in front of a schoolhouse. A little girl kissed the man driving good-bye and climbed out of the car to join her classmates marching up the walk.

"Cute kid," said Barker.

Karpis pulled out and followed the Lincoln down Goodrich. "She's probably spoiled rotten." They rolled along the quiet street past fine homes and a boulevard of naked trees sprinkled with snow.

At Lexington Parkway the Lincoln stopped for a stop sign. A tan Plymouth broke in front of it and blocked its path. Three doors swung open and three gun-wielding men swung out.

Alvin Karpis closed in from behind. "Now we've got the filthy rich son of a bitch."

Saint Agnes

Walt Howard poked his head into Grover's Corner. "Tell me everything you know about Edward Bremer."

Grover Mudd leaned back in his chair and rattled off what came to mind. "He's president of Commercial State Bank. I've never met him. Seen him a couple times. Big guy. Mid-thirties. Handsome, but snooty-looking. Scion of a wealthy family. His father, Adolph Bremer, is head of the Jacob Schmidt Brewing Company. His uncle, Otto Bremer, is chairman of the board of American National Bank. They're big-shot Democrats, personal friends of President Roosevelt and Governor Olson. I heard the family forked out three hundred grand to help get Roosevelt elected."

"You're on the story."

"What story?"

"Edward Bremer was kidnapped yesterday."

"You're joking."

"Nope. Snatched him just like Hamm."

Grover jumped from his chair and clapped his hands. "Oh, that's beautiful."

"Beautiful? You have a sick mind, Mudd." They hurried through the newsroom to the editor's office.

"Can't you see the beautiful irony of it?" Grover asked. "Otto and Adolph Bremer and William Hamm, Sr., were three of the biggest backers of the O'Connor System. Now their families have become its biggest victims."

"Do you suppose you could contain your glee long enough to get out to the Bremer mansion?"

"Which one?"

"That monstrosity of stone, across the street from the brewery."

"Is that where they grabbed him?"

"He dropped his daughter off at the Summit School on Goodrich about eight-thirty yesterday morning. He never made it to work. They figure he was nabbed a few blocks from the school. We haven't heard of any witnesses yet. His car was found two miles north of the city. There was blood in it. He's either dead, or he didn't go without a fight."

"Ransom?"

"Two hundred thousand dollars. Twice what they wanted for Hamm."

"What are the police saying?"

"Get this. Our new chief admitted hearing rumors of the reported kidnapping, and is making every effort to run them down. I figure the family is trying to keep the cops out of it. What's your guess?"

"If the feds are on it—and with the White House connection, you can bet they are—they're not going to let St. Paul cops near the Bremers."

"Get a camera and get going. Feed everything to Harv Bennett. He'll write it up."

Grover Mudd skipped through the newsroom with newfound energy. "What a way to kick off an editorial campaign on crime."

Walt Howard shouted after him. "And if you talk to the Bremer family, try to look crestfallen, will you?"

Once again the sober-faced city was spawning national headlines. And front-page editorials.

ST. PAUL MUST END ITS REIGN OF TERROR

Never has St. Paul stood more aghast, more indignant, more stunned. Edward G. Bremer has been kidnapped.

Now six St. Paulites have been kidnapped in less than three years. Not even Chicago has been disgraced by six abductions in three years.

Why is St. Paul singled out for gangster raids? An average citizen could easily find a reason for this by a simple visit to police headquarters. In a department that numbers only 172 patrolmen and 23 detectives, there are 48 men of higher rank, including 9 ex-police chiefs; approximately one "officer" to every four "privates." There are commissioners, assistant commissioners, chiefs, assistant chiefs, inspectors, assistant inspectors, captains, lieutenants, and sergeants to give orders—and very few men to carry them out.

THE POLITICAL SETUP IS THERE. THE DEPARTMENT IS PERMEATED WITH IT. We'll never be able to fight on equal terms with criminals until political influence and interference are removed from the police department. The system by which an able police chief passes out of the picture as soon as a new mayor is elected is all wrong.

This latest kidnapping outrage can not become a nine days' wonder to be forgotten for the next sensational event. St. Paul has got to clean house and make itself no longer hospitable to gangsters.

Above all we have to catch a few of these kidnappers and discourage this highly prosperous racket. Even Chicago has been able to lay hands on a few of the big shots. The record here to date is a big fat ZERO.

—EDITOR,
THE FRONTIER NEWS

Ten days after they grabbed Edward Bremer, Alvin Karpis and Freddie Barker met at the Hollyhocks Club with Dag Rankin. Downstairs was fun and games, and people danced among spinning roulette wheels. Upstairs was all business.

The kingpin of St. Paul's underworld poured Canadian whiskey and talked. "Things are not going well, gentlemen. This job should have been wrapped up by now. I'm disappointed. I've given you boys a free hand in my town. I didn't even say anything about that song-

and-dance number you did in South St. Paul last summer."

"That was outside the city limits," Karpis reminded him. "Those are the rules."

"The rules are what I say they are. Secondly, Como Park is not outside the city limits."

"Those nitwits aren't with us anymore. We had nothing to do with that job."

"That surprises me," Rankin told them, "because, after I read how they found Mr. Bremer's car, I would have sworn those trigger-happy lunatics were operating with you again."

"The whole job's been queered," complained Barker. "This Bremer guy is a pain in the ass. All he does is bellyache day and night. At least Hamm was jake."

"This Bremer fellow was a big mistake, Rankin."

"It's *Mr.* Rankin, Mr. Karpis."

"Yeah, I forgot," apologized Karpis. "Anyway, there ain't no way Old Man Bremer is going to cough up two hundred grand for his kid, and if you had to baby-sit this jerk-off you'd know why. I say we take half and unload the bastard."

"The reason it has been so difficult to arrange payment of the ransom is because the family believes he is dead. There was enough blood in his car to choke a vampire."

"He tried to get away when we grabbed him," argued Barker, "so we crowned him one, and he bleeds like a stuck pig. He's jake now."

Dag Rankin dropped a newspaper in front of them. "The *Frontier News* found an eyewitness, a nurse at a bus stop who saw the actual snatch. Grover Mudd tracked down a milkman who saw the whole setup and even remembered a license-plate number, printed on yesterday's front page. Now today I read in 'Grover's Corner' that Mr. Bremer is being held in the Hill District. Not that I want to know the details, but please tell me you're not holding him in St. Paul."

Alvin Karpis looked at Barker a moment, then answered. "He's guessing. We got him in Bensenville, outside Chicago. Same as Hamm. We're not dumb enough to hold him here."

"No, but you are dumb enough to haul him across three state lines and ensure a federal investigation." Rankin tore the paper off the table and looked at the article again.

BREMER MAY BE HELD IN HILL DISTRICT
Right Under Nose of St. Paul Police
by Grover Mudd

The byline set his blood boiling. For once the columnist was wrong, but Dag Rankin found little satisfaction in that. He would not be satisfied until Grover Mudd was dead wrong.

"The feds are a joke," sneered Barker.

"A joke?" snapped Rankin. "The feds put Capone away. The feds collared Machine Gun Kelly. Roger Touhy is in prison. Last week John Dillinger and his whole mob were arrested in Arizona without a shot fired. Nobody's laughing anymore. You so-called pros have seen to it that the Bremer family can't go anywhere without a pack of G-men on their tails. I have no choice but to personally make arrangements for payment of the ransom." He threw down the newspaper. "There won't be any more mistakes."

Freddie Barker shook his head. "No dice. Any plans gotta be talked over with Ma in Chicago."

Dag Rankin grinned. A mean, dirty grin. "I find it peculiar that a bunch of grown men can't make a decision without running to Mommy."

Freddie Barker jumped out of his chair, but Karpis caught his arm. "Sit down, Freddie." Karpis pulled Barker back into the chair and tried hard to control his own temper. "Listen, Rankin, the snatch game was your idea. We took care of Hamm for you and thought that was the end of it. You muscled us into this Bremer job and we didn't like it from the start. Frankly, I don't know why you did either job. Well, we're in it for the loot, and only the loot. We got Bremer and we're gonna arrange the payoff, not you. Don't worry, we'll drop off your cut."

"I have a much better idea, Karpis. You keep my cut, if you manage to get anything at all. Then you get your motley gang out of Minnesota and don't ever come back. Because if Dag Rankin ever hears you're in his city again you'll end up floating facedown in a bog, and by the time the leeches get done with your carcasses Mommy won't ever know what became of her boys."

Karpis and Barker stormed out of the Hollyhocks Club. It was dark and cold. They drove silently along the frozen Mississippi until Alvin Karpis turned his beady eyes on Freddie Barker and smiled. "Pretty tough talk for a guy with no balls."

The pair of kidnappers roared with laughter all the way to the St. Croix River, where they crossed the bridge to Wisconsin and headed for Chicago.

The January thaw lasted a scant two days. Under cloudy skies the temperature climbed to 40° one day and 42° the next. Then the clouds disappeared, the warmth escaped, and the mercury dropped below freezing again. Edward Bremer remained missing.

Snow was swirling outside the bedroom window. Newspaper was stuffed around the frame. The huge oak tree in the backyard was ghostly white in the night. "Are those spider toes of yours warm enough?"

"I ain't got spider toes." Stormy Day squirmed closer to him and tucked the covers under her chin. The night-time temperature was below zero and the fat-piped radiator was hot and noisy. "I'm gonna have to steal another blanket from the hotel, Grover. It never got cold like this in St. Louis." She had a ratty sweater on over her nightgown and was wearing a pair of socks. He pressed his body to hers and threw an arm over her shoulders.

Grover Mudd had begun with lousy credit and graduated to no credit. It was a safe bet they were not going to have a large church wedding, so he decided to make it up to Stormy with a ring, a five-hundred-dollar diamond that would knock her eyes out. Grover did not have the money, but he figured if he saved every penny, cut out the booze and cut back on cigarettes, skipped a few lunches and lost a few pounds, he could surprise her in the spring. Marriage was the last thing she expected. In the meantime he had to get more life insurance, which meant another phony doctor's report. It was frustrating, but he was not going to change his mind.

"Do you miss St. Louis?" Grover asked her.

"No. I only remember the shantytowns."

"Don't you miss Brody's father?"

"That wasn't love, Grover. You're the first man I've ever loved. A long time ago in St. Louis I thought I was in love with a white boy. He was rich and my mamma would clean his folks' house, and lots of times I would go with her and help. He told me I was the prettiest negro girl he had ever seen. He was always telling me how pretty I was. He asked me to come over one day and we were alone. We were kissing and stuff on his bed and he took off all my clothes. Then he got undressed and got on top of me. He was scared and I told him it was okay. He really wanted to, I could tell, but he wouldn't do it. Then he got mad and told me to get dressed, and I was supposed to wait till I got married. That's what he kept telling me, but I know why he wouldn't do it."

"When did you first realize that you were treated different? I mean, not different, but, you know . . ."

"I understand, Grover. When I was a little girl I thought niggers were negro people that were bad. I was told if I wasn't a good little girl the niggers were gonna come and get me. Then one day I went to the farmer's market with Mamma and this white man tried to sell us some rotten food. Mamma started yelling at him and he called Mamma a nigger bitch. She told me all white folks call us that. They did in St. Louis, but I don't think they do in St. Paul. Do they, Grover?"

"No, that's the difference between North and South. Down there they say it. Up here we only think it." The heater kicked on again. Newspaper crackled in the window. Grover smiled at the thought of her face on the day he proposed, the day her eyes would fall on a diamond of her very own. Easter Sunday, that would be a good day, he decided.

"What do you think Mr. Bremer is doing tonight?" Stormy asked.

"If he's still alive—and I'm beginning to doubt it— I imagine he's in pretty rough shape. It's hard to feel sorry for a banker, but I guess I do."

"I'd be scared to go into a bank. I wouldn't know what to do."

"They're like whores. Just hold out your money. They'll take it from there."

"It's good what Mr. Howard's been writing on the front page about bank robbers and kidnappers. Lots of people at the hotel are talking about it, and the *Frontier* is selling out in the lobby. Do you help him write it, Grover?"

"He doesn't need any help. He's more worked up about this than I could have hoped for. For a change everybody is urging him to be cautious, play it safe."

"Safe it ain'ts in the city of gangsters and saints." Stormy laughed at her impromptu poem. "Do you know what tonight is, Grover?"

"A cold night in January."

"It's Saint Agnes' Eve," she told him.

"That one escapes me."

"Saint Agnes was a Roman Catholic girl who lived in the time after Jesus died. She got beheaded because she absolutely ref*uuu*sed to marry. According to legend, this is the night a young woman will dream of her future husband."

They talked and joked and made love until they forgot about the cold, until they fell asleep wrapped in each other's arms.

Stormy Day did not have any dreams that night.

Creepy Karpis

In the basement of the Federal Courts Building, Special Agent Steff Koslowski sat at a long table pushed against a cold, gray wall and sorted through pictures of known criminals. He kept the photos of Homer Van Meter and Baby Face Nelson in front of him and that's where he placed his bets, but some of his colleagues were now giving odds on a frumpy old lady named Ma Barker and her sons, and their partner in crime, Alvin Karpis.

The FBI had to admit they had made a mistake. The Bremer kidnapping was so similar to the Hamm kidnapping it was obvious the same men were behind it, and that could hardly be Roger Touhy since he was now behind bars. John Dillinger and his gang were locked up in Arizona while Indiana, Wisconsin, and Ohio fought over extradition rights. Machine Gun Kelly and his gang had been put away, and two key agents who had worked on that Oklahoma kidnapping flew to St. Paul to take charge of the Bremer case.

Staking out the Bremer homes and tailing friends and family proved as fruitless as Steff knew it would be. So, with nothing to lose, he brought to the agents in charge his ideas for an eavesdropping operation the likes of which had never been tried before.

Up until then the only way to record a telephone conversation had been to put a Dictograph microphone up to the earpiece. This was so cumbersome it was impractical, and the recording it made was usually worthless. The electrical wizard explained in detail how he could tap right into the phone wires and record the actual telephone conversation on aluminum records using what he called a pamograph machine. He also told them he was converting a fire-alarm teletype machine that he hoped would be able to record all numbers dialed from a tapped phone and print them out, day and night, on a white ticker tape similar to that in a broker's office. With these instruments in place the agents could keep their distance from the Bremer family but, at the same time, record their calls. Steff's superiors listened carefully and were so impressed with his inventiveness they gave him the go-ahead. But the wiretapping debut had to be postponed. In Washington, United States Attorney General Homer Cummings stated publicly that St. Paul was not a pleasant place to live, but he promised to stay out of the Bremer case until the banker was released. The G-men in St. Paul were ordered to back off, leaving them to do what everyone else was doing. Waiting.

Steff Koslowski rubbed his tired eyes. The monster boiler kicked in with a bang. Everybody jumped. The tension in the basement was palpable. Steff settled back into his chair. He sipped lukewarm coffee and picked up the *Frontier News*. Daily for two weeks the paper had continued its front-page assault, calling police and city officials everything but human. But on this day, at the request of the Bremer family, the editorials stopped. In a statement printed on the front page, editor Walt Howard explained that the paper's cleanup campaign was planned—and, in fact, had begun running—before the kidnapping. But out of concern for Edward Bremer's safety he would respect the family's request. He vowed that the front-page editorials would return. In place of the editorial was an open letter from white-haired Adolph Bremer.

TO THE PARTIES HOLDING MY SON
AND TO EDWARD G. BREMER

All city, state, and federal authorities have consented to allow me, in my own way for a limited time, to seek the return of my son.

To convince you that there is no catch in this effort of mine I can see but one way to work out our negotiations. Edward will have to select someone, regardless of where he may be located in the United States. Have Edward write this party a letter in his own handwriting referring to this notice in the press so that I will know he has read it. Enclose with Edward's letter your instructions to be carried out.

If I have not heard from Edward within three days and three nights, I shall understand that you do not wish to deal with me and I will feel I am released from any obligations contained in this note.

———

After consulting with Ma Barker in Chicago, Alvin Karpis and Freddie Barker returned to St. Paul and answered Adolph Bremer's letter with specific run-around-the-state instructions on how the bagman was to make the payoff, the full two hundred thousand dollars in five- and ten-dollar bills. Then, in a kidnapping plagued with mistakes, Karpis made one of his biggest mistakes in a small way. On the morning of February 6, at a hardware store at Seven Corners, he bought four flashlights and made a pass at the girl behind the counter.

That night they fitted the flashlights with red lenses and lined them up along a gravel road in rural southern Minnesota. It was the signal for the bagman. And, before the sun came up, Alvin Karpis and Freddie Barker were back in Bensonville, Illinois, with the ransom paid in full.

At noon they shoved a blindfolded Edward Bremer into the backseat of another new sedan and, one last time, set out on the eight-hour trip to Minnesota. It was a long silent ride through the never-ending farm fields of Wisconsin, which in the dead of winter seemed only a white wasteland. Alvin Karpis drove. Doc Barker rode shotgun. Freddie Barker was in the back with Edward Bremer, who was cramped on the freezing floor behind the driver's seat.

Halfway through the trip Doc Barker checked the gas gauge. "We're near empty," he said. "Pull into that field over there."

Doc Barker got out, popped the trunk, and drained four cans of gasoline into the tank. Then he made an even bigger mistake than Alvin Karpis had made in the hardware store. With his greasy fingers he tossed the empty red gas cans into the frozen white farm field. They drove away.

At eight o'clock that night, with the mid-winter stars twinkling over hills of drifting snow, the gang got ready to say their good-byes. And what could be more touching than kidnappers saying good-bye to the victim? Karpis pulled off the road. City lights sparkled in the distance.

"Now listen, Ed," Freddie Barker said, "if you ever get into trouble like this again and we're in the neighborhood, you just give us a call and we'll come help ya. And I mean this serious. We'll never rob a Bremer bank, and from now on all we drink is Schmidt Beer."

Alvin Karpis stuck his head over the back seat. "Ditto up here, Ed. Truth is, you Bremers are square shooters. From now on we vote straight Democrat. Tell Honest Adolph I said that."

"Now here's what we want you to do, Ed," explained Freddie Barker, as if he were talking to a child. "You're about a half-mile from Rochester. Just follow the lights. When we pull away you count real loud to fifteen, then take off your blindfold. Here's a few bucks." He stuffed some bills into Bremer's coat pocket. "There's a nine-forty bus to St. Paul. You'll be home in front of the fireplace in two hours." He helped the still-hurting banker out of the car.

"It's been swellelegant," Doc Barker called.

Freddie Barker stood Bremer alongside the road, then got back in the car.

Karpis rolled down his window. "Say, Ed. While you're in town there you might want to stop in at the Mayo Clinic and have that bump on your head looked at."

Edward Bremer began counting.

"Not yet, Ed, we ain't left. Now start again."

The sedan pulled away, leaving the St. Paul bank president counting to fifteen in the dark, freezing cold.

It was their last snatch job and, having successfully completed it, the Barker-Karpis gang left Minnesota. The Barkers, who had a date with death at the hands of the FBI, would never come back. Creepy Alvin Karpis, who had a date with J. Edgar Hoover, would return two years later—in handcuffs.

After Edward Bremer's release Governor Olson declared war on crime. On February 8 he called for the establishment of a state bureau of criminal apprehension and the immediate construction of a state police broadcasting system. He drafted the National Guard Aviation Service as a major unit in the anticrime war, and asked that the state highway patrol be given more power. He proposed new laws that required municipalities to adopt ordinances compelling hotelkeepers and landlords to report to police all new tenants and the license numbers of their automobiles.

The four flashlights used in the payoff were found beside the road, and the FBI traced them to the hardware store on Seven Corners. Steff Koslowski showed the girl behind the counter his collection of mug shots. She passed on Van Meter and Nelson, but positively identified Alvin Karpis.

A farmer in Wisconsin found the gas cans in his field and called the county sheriff, who in turn notified the FBI. At their labs in Washington they lifted the fingerprints of Doc Barker.

Only one day after Bremer's release, pictures of Ma Barker and her boys lined the front pages of America. A nationwide hunt was under way, with the focus on Steff Koslowski's beloved Chicago. His orders: Stay put.

The elevator at the *Frontier News* got stuck again. Fuzzy Byron coaxed it to the third floor and, when the doors creaked open, the biggest, meanest cop anybody there could ever remember seeing marched through the newsroom the way the Nazis marched through Berlin. Patrolman Emil Gunderson's dark green uniform was immaculate and bursting at the seams with perverse pride. Bullets sparkled on his belt. His spit-polished boots hit the floor like a storm trooper's all the way to Walt Howard's office, where he walked in unannounced and slammed an envelope to the desk.

THE ST. PAUL FRONTIER NEWS
* Page One * Friday, February 10, 1934
* Two Cents *

NO MUZZLE FOR US

MANY attempts have been made in past years to intimidate the "Frontier News"—boycott, libel, closing up of news sources, and even physical violence and death threats. None has ever worked.

THE *FRONTIER NEWS* REFUSES TO BE INTIMIDATED.

Nor will it be hushed by the following legal document served yesterday.

Dear Sir:

Under the powers given the Commissioner of Public Safety I hereby summon you to appear at a hearing to be held in the office of the Mayor of the City of St. Paul in the courthouse in this city on February 13, 1934, at 10 A.M., and to be prepared to answer questions relative to your charges printed in the "Frontier News" concerning the conduct of the police department. You are to bring with you any documentary evidence in your possession.

Yours very truly,

John H. McDonald

Commissioner of Public Safety

Neither the heavy legal bologna nor the fact that the document was served by a big bad policeman frightens this newspaper. But it demands that instead of a star-chamber session behind the closed doors of the office of Mayor Mahoney, who dictated the appointment of the present police chief, the inquiry be an open one in the council chamber, or any other public place that Commissioner McDonald desires.

Under the administration of the present commissioner of public safety there have been three major kidnappings. Innocent victims have been machine-gunned down in the parks. Gambling and prostitution are flourishing.

IT IS HIGH TIME FOR A SHOWDOWN.

—EDITOR

THE FRONTIER NEWS

Saint Valentine

Minnesota means "land of sky-tinted waters," and the price for living among these prodigal waters is winter. The state was born from a glacier. By Minnesota standards it was a mild winter, with average snowfall and normal temperatures. But that came to an end on February 14. It was Saint Valentine's Day, and Minnesota was about to be massacred.

For Grover Mudd it began as just another gray winter morning. The mercury was hovering near 40° as he walked the last block to work. Hopes of an early spring could be sniffed in the air. But snow flurries started circling his office window when he sat down to his desk at ten-thirty A.M. He thought nothing of it. He tucked a sheet of paper in his trusty Remington and checked his notes.

The showdown at the mayor's office was a bust. Walt Howard was left standing in the reception room for an hour before being told the hearing was postponed. Instead, Mayor Mahoney issued a report that claimed his police were busier than ever. Grover decided to begin his column by quoting His Honor.

There are no criminals here. That's all politics. For fifteen years the "Frontier News" has been hatching criminals, and now they throw them in our lap. There are no criminals here. They got Machine Gun Kelly in Memphis. They got Dillinger in Arizona. The Barker gang is from Chicago; everybody knows that. These fellows come here to visit our lakes. We have ten thousand lakes and a resort for every crook.

With a mayor like Mahoney a columnist needed little imagination. The filing deadline for the city's spring election had come and gone, and a new record was set. Two hundred fifty-five people had filed for the offices of mayor, commissioners, and comptroller. A lawyer named Mark H. Gehan was beginning to pick up valuable support for a run at mayor, but in St. Paul it was the commissioner of public safety who wielded the real power. The O'Connors had set it up that way. Near the bottom of the long list of candidates for that office was the name of Gil St. Sauver. Grover hammered out his column and paid no attention to the weather outside his window.

By eleven o'clock the snowfall was heavy and swirling. At eleven-thirty a severe blizzard warning was issued. By noon it was snowing sideways, whipped by winds of up to 75 miles per hour. An arctic cold slammed into town and the mercury plunged from a respectable 40° to −13° in less than two hours.

Grover Mudd did not finish his writing. He stood at the window, mesmerized by the fury of the storm. Below him, Fourth Street was paralyzed. Across the way horizontal waves of snow crashed into the North Star Press. Then he thought about his girl. He called up the hotel and was told the help was not allowed to receive calls and that most of them had been sent home early.

Most of them?

Grover hung up. Was Stormy one of those sent home? If she wasn't, would they put her up for the night? He knew the boy would be safe with neighbors, but would that stop Stormy from trying to get to him? Would she be foolish enough to try and walk all the way to St. Albans Street? He had to find out.

Grover pulled on his overshoes. The buckles were broken so he slipped his trousers over them. He wrestled into his coat, buttoned it up to his neck, and pulled the flap of his cap down over his ears. As he tugged his threadbare gloves over his fingers and stomped through

the newsroom he heard a wise guy crack, "Good rid-
dance, fool."

The Hotel Saint Paul was only two blocks away.
Grover found the going fun. Traffic was frozen. The
banana-yellow trolleys were plastered white and stood
abandoned in the middle of the street. Cars slid to the
bottom of the hill and were left tangled in the drifting
snow. Grover Mudd felt like a child again. He put his
head down and pretended he was carrying a football.
He sliced through the wind, rammed over the flakes,
and crashed through the drifts. He did some fancy
broken-field running and dived across St. Peter Street.
His lungs collapsed, his stomach cramped, his knees
buckled at the lobby door. Grover fell into the hotel
feeling old and sick. He had been foolish. People were
staring at him. He cleared his throat and recaptured his
breath.

Grover took the cargo elevator to the basement and
followed the concrete floor to housekeeping, where he
found Stormy's boss, a stout colored woman named
Hildy, removing clean linen from the shelves and stack-
ing it in neat piles on a countertop. She saw Grover
coming and busied herself even more.

"Hildy, did Stormy go home yet?"

"Stormy Day didn't come in today."

Grover was not only surprised by her answer, he did
not like the tone of her voice. "That girl hasn't missed
a day of work in two years," he told her.

"She gonna miss lots of days now."

"What does that mean?"

"She went and got herself fired."

"Fired. For what?"

"Ain't my place to say. But I warned 'em. I warns
all my girls."

"Warn them about what?"

"No matter now."

"Don't play games with me, Hildy."

"I got a good job here, Grover Mudd, and I live

pretty good. Got me a son that's gonna go to a real college next year. Proud of that boy. So if the boss folks say don't tell about it, I don't tell about it. I'd be suggesting you go talk to Stormy Day."

"I'd be doing just that, Hildy dear, but in case you haven't looked out a window of late, I can't exactly go roller-skating over there."

"I knows that. And there's gonna be a thousand and a thousand more people trying to get into this hotel tonight, so let me do my job and you go talk to Stormy Day when you can."

Grover turned away in frustration and was ready to leave.

"Maybe ain't my place to say, Grover Mudd." She did not look at him, kept counting the bed sheets with her eyes. "She's a peach. But I don't think she's yours to be pickin'."

Grover floundered through the rising snow to the buried intersection of Fourth and St. Peter. The furious wind tore at his back. *Fired.* Did it have something to do with him? The normally jolly Hildy seemed to think so.

The once-bustling sidewalks were ghostly. Grover shielded his face with his gloves and looked down Fourth Street toward the two newspapers. Visibility was nearing zero. Still, he could see himself riding out the monster snowstorm with his feet kicked up in his slovenly, cozy office, swapping drinks and stories with Fuzzy Byron. At night, with the storm wreaking havoc over the town, he would curl up next to the radiator with *Ann Vickers*, the latest work of Sinclair Lewis. Read himself to sleep. No need to fight his way back to work in the morning. A fierce wind blew him toward the *Frontier News*, but he turned in to it and set out for Stormy's house. *Ann Vickers* would have to find someone else to sleep with.

Grover figured it to be one and a half, perhaps two miles at the most, and the shortest distance would be a straight line down Dayton Avenue from behind the cathedral to St. Albans Street. He trudged through the blizzard to the tunnel under Cathedral Hill, where he thought he could take respite, but gale-force winds shot through the underground passage like thunder out of hell. A trolley car in the tunnel was left for dead. He would have to climb the stairs and go around the church. He groped his way to a green railing, slanting down a hill of unbroken white. Grover grabbed on for his life and pounded and pulled his way up, focusing on the cross atop the dome.

At the top of the hill, at the foot of the great church, Grover doubled over to bag his precious breath. Snow pelted his face. He had traveled only half a mile from the hotel but the fun had long gone out of the adventure. Then he heard it, or thought he did. An eerie voice in the storm. It was so faint that Grover at first believed he was imagining it, but through the howling wind he heard it again.

"The time has come! The time has come! The time has come!"

There was no mistaking the call. It was the Big Holy Spook, shouting damnations four blocks away.

Grover shook his head. "Amazing." He looked up. Before him, bold and impregnable in the middle of hell's fury, was the Cathedral of Saint Paul. Through swirling oceans of snow it shined warm and inviting, like a heavenly message saying that in this ungodly weather even a Grover Mudd would be welcome. He tramped around the cathedral, and with his back to the church and his face to the wind, trod on through the whitecapped waves of Dayton Avenue.

The snow was lightest at the center of the street, but even some of that was up to his knees. When his cheeks and nose could take no more blistering he turned and stumbled backward; then he would turn again, afraid of becoming disoriented. Frozen trees were dismembered by the wind. Ice and snow ripped down power lines, and if it had not been for the dancing sparks he would never have seen the hot wires across his path. He plodded up the bank of a yard and around the mishmash of twisted electricity, but on his way back to the missing street he faltered and pitched face first into the white stuff. Cough spasms came and went. His joints were freezing. His face was stinging with pain. Grover lay there. He guessed he was halfway to St. Albans Street, and at the halfway point it was difficult for him to say what was worse, the frightening ferocity of the storm or the intensity of the fire burning in his lungs. The combination was killing him. Something in the back of his mind, or in the ache of his back, told him he had taken this walk once before. He thought about those Jack London stories he read as a kid, of leather-hearted men freezing to death in the white silence of the Yukon. He could see the headline in the *Frontier News*.

KILLER BLIZZARD TAKES GROVER MUDD
Columnist Found Dead with
Head Buried in Snow in Cornmeal Valley
What Was He Doing There?

The onslaught continued. The morning glimpse of an early spring was a whiteout. The brunt of the storm beat him while he was down. But Grover Mudd got up. Coughing and shivering, he climbed to his feet. His legs were iron-heavy and bone-weary, but he braved the worst Minnesota had to offer and slogged his way to St. Albans Street, and two hours after he had left the hotel he pushed through Stormy's door and dropped to the floor at the boy's feet.

"Whatcha' doin', Grober? Look like a snowman."

Grover looked at Brody's thick wool socks and thought how warm they must be. He kicked the door closed like a mule and stayed on the floor until he stopped heaving. Ice bridged his eyebrows. He wiped his stone-red face and stood. "Where's your mother?"

"She ina bedrum cryin'."

Feeling like a stick man and breathing like a monster, Grover peeled off his hat and gloves. "Why, what did you do now?"

"Din do nothin'. She got no job."

Grover's fingers were numb and he could not get a grip on his overshoes. The boy pulled them off with a rolling laugh across the floor. "I wanna go out an' play, Grober."

"You open that door and I'll string you up by your toes." In his stiff stocking feet, with the fringes of his hair frozen white and the blizzard still dripping from his coat, Grover shuffled into the bedroom.

She sat up on the bed, dried her teary eyes, and looked at him. "Grover, what are you doing here?"

"I was in the neighborhood, thought I'd drop by."

She was wearing her old purple dress; her hair was mussed, her eyes were red, and for all the hell he had just been through, he knew from her anguished face that she was suffering twice the misery and humiliation.

"I lost my job, Grover."

"I know. What happened?"

"They'll tell the other hotels and no one will give me a job."

"Stop crying and tell me what happened."

"We can't work nowhere else, you know."

"Tell me how you got fired, dammit."

Stormy wiped her eyes again and fought back the sobs. "We were checking out and they stopped us and searched us. They found a spoon from the kitchen in my purse and they fired me. Said don't ever come back or they would have me arrested."

"Jesus Christ, a spoon?"

"Brody uses them to dig in the yard and he bends them and loses them."

"A spoon?"

"They told me there's lots of white people need jobs."

"What's the manager's name?"

"Hildy's my boss."

"No, the hotel manager? The big shot?"

"His name is Mr. Healy, but he don't deal with us."

"He'll deal with me."

"No, Grover, yo*uuu*'ll get in trouble."

He took her face in his hands and gently brushed away the falling tears.

"Who's the prettiest girl in the world?"

"Stormy is."

"And who loves you, Stormy?"

"Grover Mudd *luuuv*s me." She threw her arms around his waist and sobbed into the snowflakes on his coat.

He stroked her hair and kissed her forehead. "I'll go talk sweet to Mr. Healy and see what I can do."

Grover knew it would be two days before anybody went anywhere, and he looked forward to the warmth and relaxation of being snowbound with his girl. Then he heard the little boy yell from the other room. "Grober, there snow comin' ina win'ows."

On the glacier-ravaged night when Grover Mudd found tender loving refuge in the house of Stormy Day, Roxanne Schultz took dreamy redoubt in the winter-dark lair of Nina Clifford. Outside the blizzard raged on. One minute the basement window on Washington Street was buried in a sea of white, while the next minute the arctic wind picked up the horde of giant flakes and pitched them at the door. The old bawdy-house moaned and groaned. A blow job that shook the foundation.

Roxanne smoked the magic, and the basement window became a crystal ball enveloping a white night of swirling opium, and floating into it she was swept up in the storm and carried away.

The crazy wind pushed her up Steep Street and blew

her by City Hall, where she laughed at lost faces staring out the windows in terrified wonder. She swept through Lowertown and danced over Smith Park, where bums lay drunk and dying in the severe drifting.

Up Payne Avenue to the busy brewery she flew, where the smoke from the stack was inhaled by the storm, and the train that ran through the building was frozen to the track; down through Swede Hollow, where the roaring wind got trapped in the gulch and tore at the shanties like a caged lion, and Mamma sat frightened and alone in front of a timid fire and dreamed of her fallen men and prayed for help.

The swirling opium carried Roxanne out over the icy Mississippi and whirled her by the caves where the helpless homeless sat curled against the rock while Indian legends whistled in the wind. She followed the river up past the Hollyhocks Club and saw Dag Rankin laughing in the window, as if the blizzard were some great ruse that had snared his patrons and would not let them leave until the last jack came up black. She shot over the Ford plant, where acres of cars were buried in hard slabs of snow. She cut through a park where the pines were shelved in white. Down Summit Avenue she whirled, past the pretentious homes and the manicured lawns that were buried for the season.

Roxanne Schultz blew into the blinding whiteness of the colored district where, over St. Albans Street, she sensed the sweet aroma of forbidden love. A cold pang of jealousy marched up her spine. Then he was in her dream, the newspaperman with the wrenching cough, smelling of whiskey and waving a gun. He was crying, and she felt wonderful about it.

She went twirling over Oakland Cemetery. The trees were naked and bent, and small winter birds were blown off the branches and slammed against the tombs.

Hovering above the State Capitol, she saw the golden horses at the base of the dome saddled in ice, and in the snowy chariot the figure of Prosperity had adversity flung in her face.

Roxanne followed the storm of opium down St. Peter Street, where a woman's warmth was bought and paid for. The neon lights were busted and dark, and the heavy advertisement signs that hung over the doors were torn from the hinges and tossed about like autumn leaves in a breeze. A fallen angel was sitting in a doorway, tears frozen on her face, and even if the freezing whore could find the strength to knock she would not be heard.

Roxanne smuggled by the battered castle that was the federal government and saw maps and guns and frustrated men far away from home. She skipped across Rice Park and blew through the library, through a thousand books she would never read and a mountain of knowledge she would never climb.

Over the snowy cliffs she went, rushing by the police station, where an assistant saint sat plotting campaign strategy, and down to the morgue, where those who perished in the storm would come to thaw out.

Then Roxanne Schultz floated through the crystal ball back into the soft warm den of Nina Clifford, where dreams were made and prayers were answered. If only for an hour.

On his lunch hour Grover Mudd hurried up to the hotel and found his way to J. V. Healy's outer office, where an unattractive nose-up-in-the-air secretary instructed him to sit and wait. He picked up the paper. Grover had guessed right. It took two days for the city to dig itself out. And he wasn't too far off about the headline in the *Frontier News*.

STORM DEATH TOLL RISES TO 34
Blizzard Being Called Worst of the Century
Sub-Zero Temps to Continue

Another memorable performance in Minnesota's theater of seasons. He tossed the paper aside. "Grover's Corner" was not in it. The first deadline he had failed to meet. He'd tried to phone the column in, but the lines were down. Walt Howard camped out in his office and made sure the presses kept rolling. He continued his front-page attack on city government by detailing the five-month-long process for closing a disorderly house. He compared in print the inefficiency of the St. Paul Police Department to the high efficiency of the Milwaukee Police Department, and listed the reasons.

That morning Mr. Howard made a speech to the entire staff, praising them for their dedication and hard work during the blizzard. "If this is a dying newspaper," he told them, "I never would have guessed it these past two days."

Those were the spoken words, but Grover could hear the unspoken part loud and clear. "I'm proud of all of you, except that lazy, good-for-nothing bastard Grover Mudd, who spent the last two days in bed with a girl he's not even married to, and missed a deadline everybody else busted their ass to make."

A loud buzzer sounded on the desk and Grover jumped. "Mr. Mudd," Nose-up-in-the-Air said, "Mr. Healy will see you now."

J. V. Healy was a smallish man with a red face, one of those pontifical manager types. He was fingering a gold fountain pen. Grover stood in front of his desk, thinking how easy it would be to lift his pompous ass out of the chair and beat the pulp out of him, wipe his bloody nose on the shaggy white rug under his feet. It was a pretty fancy office he was in, but then it was a pretty fancy hotel.

"So you're Grover Mudd. My own taste runs to the *North Star Press*, but the *Frontier* is on sale in the lobby. What can I do for you?"

"I'm not here on business. This is kind of personal. There was a girl got fired . . . I mean, one of your

employees was relieved of her duties here a few days
back."

"Dismissed. For what reason?"

"They said she took a spoon from the kitchen."

"Did she?"

"Maybe she did, maybe she didn't. What's a spoon
to a place like this?"

"You said it was personal. Sweetheart of yours?"

"Friend of a friend."

"A colored maid, if my memory serves me correctly."

"That's right. I'd like you to consider hiring her
back."

"Whatever for?"

"Because she's on her own and she has a little boy
to feed, that's whatever for."

"My God, Mr. Mudd, you sound like Eleanor
Roosevelt."

"There's only two businesses in this town that will
hire them. The hotels and the railroad. Now, she can
hardly go to work for the railroad."

"Mr. Mudd, it may have been only a spoon to you,
but to me it is a one-thousand-dollar-a-month problem.
That is how much property we are losing to theft. Our
rich guests steal from us. Our cheap guests steal from
us. Our employees, whom we pay well, steal from us.
Bums sneak in the back door and steal from us. There
are many people out there looking for work, and if you
work for J. V. Healy and you get caught stealing, you
are through. Case closed."

"Horse meat."

"What?"

"The restaurant here serves horse meat," Grover told
him.

"You're insane. This hotel houses the finest restaurant in the Twin Cities."

"I have information that you've been passing horse
meat off as steak."

"You're making that up."

"I'm going to write it."

"You wouldn't dare."

"Big headline right next to 'Sister Ruth's Kitchen': 'Hotel Saint Paul Serves Prime Stallion, Chopped Mare, Palfrey Cuisine.' "

"We'll sue the *Frontier* for their last penny."

"Too late. The *North Star* already got it."

"My God, what kind of newspaperman are you?"

"The worst kind there is. On the other hand, you could pick up the *Frontier News* one day and find a sparkling piece in *Grover's Corner* about the first-rate Hotel Saint Paul and the charismatic manager who runs it with an iron fist."

"You would write that?"

"It would be horseshit, but I'd write it."

"And all I have to do is hire back this colored. That's interesting."

"What's it going to be?"

"I want to see the article first."

"You're going to get filly fillet first. Don't push me."

"I want a photograph along with the article."

"I want a pay raise for the girl."

"Don't push me, Mr. Mudd. You can leave her name with my secretary, but that article better be glowing, or I'll run her thieving behind right back out of here." Grover stomped out of the office, leaving the hotel manager shouting after him: "I'll send a photograph over, if somebody didn't steal it."

He stepped into the frost-encrusted city with mixed feelings inside, but only one feeling outside. Under a steely blue sky it was −19°. The severe, clear cold cut right to his bones. His breath did somersaults in front of him. Grover Mudd hurried along St. Peter Street, where the snow piles were six feet high. He had gotten Stormy's job back, but he still had to write an article about a horse's ass. Now all he had to do was figure out how to make it glow.

The Cuke and the Spook

When the blizzard finished plastering St. Paul, Washington began. United States Attorney General Homer Cummings called Minnesota's capital the "poison spot of the nation . . . a haven for criminals . . . a citadel of crime." He listed St. Paul as "needing a cleanup more than any other city with which I am acquainted," and added: "In St. Paul segments of the police department have our confidence, and other segments do not."

On Capitol Hill the city came under attack by Senator Royal S. Copeland of New York, head of a special Senate crime-investigation committee, who announced he would seek an additional $25,000 and come to St. Paul himself with his special committee to investigate crime conditions. The senator declared the sift would "tear the lid off the Midwest underworld."

"Politics," screamed Mayor Mahoney, demanding apologies. "That's all politics."

It was a brutal midnight. The winter sky was glass-clear. Downtown, shards of ice on Gothic towers glittered with northern stars. Church bells were frozen. The blizzard of the century was followed by the cold wave of the century. The temperature was −31°.

Homer Van Meter hated being cooped up inside. It reminded him of the pen. In the cold that followed the blizzard he went to bed early to help pass the time. But on this, the coldest night of all, sleep proved elusive.

His mind drifted to news about his old cell mate at Michigan City. After John Dillinger's arrest in Arizona three states fought fiercely for the rights to him. Indiana and Ohio wanted to seat him in the electric chair, while Wisconsin only wanted to throw him in the slammer for twenty years. When the dust finally settled in the West, Dillinger was transferred to an escape-proof jail at Crown Point, Indiana.

From his room on St. Peter Street Homer Van Meter could hear the deadly cold outside his window. The sound of icy silence. The Fords and Chevys would not start. The streetcars would not run. Nobody was foolish enough to walk the sidewalks below. Baby Face Nelson was in Chicago. The only sound this night came from the room next door, where his friend Tommy Carroll and Tommy's shapely wife were going at it hot and heavy. Every time she moaned the thin walls moaned with her, and Van Meter's plague-stricken dick grew an inch thicker, and with the stiffness came the pain of stretching sores. He tried jerking off but it hurt when he squeezed it. Then she screamed. He screamed. The walls broke into orgasm. Homer Van Meter leaped out of bed.

He jumped into his pants and tucked his lumpy flag-pole of an aching penis into place, careful not to catch it on the zipper. He counted the money in his pocket. There would have to be another job soon. Van Meter grabbed a snub-nosed .38 off the chest of drawers, stroked the tiny shaft, slid it under his belt, and was out the door.

In his horny hurry he forgot about the freezing weather. No cap covered his pixy ears. No gloves protected his sticky fingers. His overcoat was long and warm, but his light shoes and thin socks could not fend off the blowing snow. A newspaper stand stood frozen to the curb. Homer Van Meter bobbed in front of it and read the headline across the *Frontier News*.

U.S. MAPS CLEANUP HERE

In a twin story below, Mayor Mahoney received an answer from Attorney General Cummings.

"I MEANT WHAT I SAID!"

The cold was excruciating. The wind was deadly. The minutes were outstretched and painful. Van Meter watched his breath swirl in front of him. His spit was instant ice. He was still hard. Or was it frozen? He pounded his zipper. Yelled for help. It was not frozen. Still, he needed something warm to put it in. In the record-breaking cold Homer Van Meter limped down St. Peter Street in search of love. He checked his cash again. Just enough to treat himself at the fabled house under the shadow of City Hall, and so what if it was not what it used to be, it was still the best ass in town.

Homer Van Meter ran down to Kellogg Boulevard like an Egyptian mummy, stiff arms, stiff legs, stiff dick. He monstered across the street, frosty white and deserted, and plowed down Steep Street past the police station. Then he wobbled up the stairs and palmed the frozen door.

The robust colored woman answered. She jumped back and grabbed her heart at the sight of what appeared to be an escapee from the morgue across the street. Something right off the slab. He pushed his way in. She ran for help.

Homer Van Meter put his back to the door and walked it closed. The heat was heaven, but the thawing out was hell. His ears, his fingers, his toes tingled with a thousand needles that, if touched, would shatter. But he had made it to the house of Nina Clifford. Icicles over his eyebrows dripped down his face like tears.

In his corner office on the third floor of the *Frontier News*, Grover Mudd, in coat and gloves, sat atop a stack of newspapers next to the radiator, pecking at his typewriter between drinks. The newsroom was dark and vacant. He pounded on the pipes and cracked jokes about the *North Star Press* not paying the heating bill.

Fuzzy Byron passed him the bottle. "Somebody read me your column on that hotel manager. There was enough syrup over it to kill a pancake. I hope you at least got free room and board for life."

"It'll never happen again."

"What are you writing about tonight?"

"A boyhood friend, Tommy Carroll," Grover explained to Fuzzy, who was sitting on the floor trying to stay warm.

"There's a Tommy in every neighborhood, isn't there?"

"Tommy's daddy and mine worked for the railroad. In our Grand Avenue youth we'd mix with the Summit Avenue crowd. A wonderful combination of the haves and have-nots. We ran with kids whose grandfathers founded Minnesota—Griggs, Ordway, Weyerhaeuser, Shepard—most of these kids had streets named after them. Early in our high school years Tommy and I drifted apart. It was obvious even then that someone had thrown the switch in the track and we were headed in different directions. His father was a jerk. Treated the kid like dirt. I can't remember the last time I saw Tommy. All I know of him today is what I read in the newspapers."

"What about your mother, Grover? You never talk about her."

Grover punched a couple of typewriter keys, then sucked more warmth out of the bottle. "According to my notes here," he said, wiping his mouth, "Tommy Carroll was arrested in St. Paul last September after a car accident by no less than five uniformed policemen. In his possession was one forty-five-caliber automatic pistol with extra clips, one Thompson submachine gun, and one sawed-off shotgun. Two days later Tommy is released, his guns are returned to him, and he goes merrily on his way. Our police chief explained to me that state law covers only the offense of carrying 'concealed' weapons. Two days after that federal agents identify Tommy Carroll as the man wanted for thirty-three post-office robberies in Minnesota and Wisconsin, as the gunman who kept a thousand people at bay in the Sioux Falls bank robbery, and as one of the machine-gun–crazed robbers in South St. Paul. Then, in December, after trying to rob a Minneapolis bank, Tommy Carroll blasts his way down Hennepin Avenue. Two more cops dead." Grover read as he typed. " 'Your hometown has treated you and your friends well, hasn't it, Tommy? Today you blaze across the front page. But today's front page is what the winos vomit in tomorrow. News doesn't last, Tommy.' "

"Paintings, Grover. Paintings last." Fuzzy wiped an 80-proof tear from the corner of his eye. "I was born in Albany, New York," he muttered, "of good New England stock. Met Whistler in England when I was young. A poet of a man he was. And Winslow Homer and John La Farge. I painted at their studios in New York City. Such great artists. They admired my work. I was young, but they admired my work even then." He stared into the small pool of water forming under the radiator. "I could paint the wind, then."

"How come you never got rich and got married?"

"It was the establishment that didn't like me. I didn't fit into their stinking art world. Besides, there's no money in painting, unless you're dead. That reminds me, the first is coming up. I have to pay my rent."

"And marriage?" Grover asked again.

"Can you really look at this ugly mug and ask that?"

"Better off, Fuzzy. The first time out is a shocker. You marry a twenty-one-year-old beauty, and ten years later you find yourself married to a fat slob." Grover had another swig of their favorite moonshine and passed the bottle. He blew his whiskey breath into his gloves and clapped them together. He stretched his fingers and searched the keys for another sentence. "When we got married she had a Scottish terrier named Coolidge that slept on the bed at night. Did you ever try to make love to a woman who carried on a running conversation with a dog? 'Oh, look what he's doing now, Coolidge.' I took to smothering her mouth with mine so she would shut up and I could get off. Know what finally led to the divorce?"

Fuzzy Byron spit laughter. "What?"

"Coolidge used to stand in the driveway and bark at the car when I'd come home from work. My ex-wife thought that was so cute. One day after I parked he lifted his leg and did a number on the wheels. My Studebaker Dictator. I loved that car. Next day I come home and there's Coolidge in the driveway. I gunned the Dictator and tried to run the mutt over. Missed."

"I can't see much, Grover Mudd, but I can see you can be a mean son of a bitch."

Grover rested his arms on top of the typewriter. He was tired. His red eyes were growing heavy. "I remember the first time it happened, just out of the service. Some wiseguy smarted off to me. I stared right through him. I wanted to kill that disrespectful bastard, and he could read that in my eyes. It worked. He backed down. He apologized. I tried it again and again. It worked. War taught me how to kill with my eyes." Grover wiped his runny nose with the back of his glove. "But over the years it wore off, or I let it wear off. Or maybe over the years people just got tired of hearing about our war."

Fuzzy Byron shook his head in resignation. "I saw Gettysburg once. So beautiful I couldn't imagine what happened there. So sad I couldn't paint it. There is no God." He handed Grover the Stearns County 13.

"I'm inclined to agree with you." Grover took a small

swig, saving the last swallow for his friend. "They're going to stop making this stuff, Fuzzy."

"I'll bet I drink the last bottle." Fuzzy Byron got to his knees and ran his long fingers over the frosty window. "Nobody can paint like Jack Frost," he said. "So simple. A window for canvas. Ice for paint." Again he seemed choked with emotion. "When I was young I painted oceans melting into the land, rolling meadows, and a lonely little brook. At times like that I believed in God. He must live in New York."

"Minnesota is God's country."

"God's country," Fuzzy coughed out. "Get me a bottle of white and I could paint the whole freezing state in an hour."

"Speaking of an hour, I've got to finish this." Grover read out the last lines of his column as he pecked at the keys. " 'I suspect I will see you one more time, Tommy Carroll. The day they drop your bullet-ridden body into an unmarked grave. I will be there. Not to goggle at a dead gangster, or pay my respects to a boy I used to run with. Just covering a story.' "

Nina Clifford breezed in, sporting the ugliest white wig Homer Van Meter had ever seen. She sized up this frozen twig come calling. In her day she would have had him snapped in two and deposited in the alley for knocking on her door. In the winter of her life she took whatever blew in.

"I want the best ya got," Van Meter stuttered out. "I got a pocket full of jack and a pantsful of love." He fumbled open his coat so she could see the bulge between his pockets. The man was a walking, talking erection.

"The best is one hundred dollars," Nina announced matter-of-factly.

"Stop dreaming, Grandma. Those days are long

gone. The best ya got. Twenty bucks. Four hours. Anything goes.''

"The best is one hundred dollars."

"Then give me second-best."

"The second best is one hundred dollars."

"Then, goddammit, tell me what I can have for
twenty bucks."

"There's a pair of chickens living in the old carriage
house."

Van Meter's blood was boiling. He thawed in seconds. He wanted to grab her wrinkled neck and wring
it like a chicken's, but lurking around a corner was
bound to be an ape of some sort. Besides, his throbbing
dick was tickling his belly button and his pants were
damp. He grinned through the agony. "Miss Clifford,"
he whimpered, "I'm a long way from home. Fort
Wayne, Indiana. I'm cold and I was rude. I humbly
apologize. I walked a good way to be here tonight because I know you only got the best, and in these troubled times I just got to make sure I get my dollar's
worth."

"I am an old woman," the elderly whore said with
just the right touch of sincerity. "Forgive me, and welcome to St. Paul. Since you have come so far I insist
you have my very best at less than half my usual rate
—twenty dollars, one hour or one shot, whichever
comes first. Take it or leave it." Nina smiled. Homer
Van Meter handed over his wad. "Up the stairs," she
told him, "third door on the left. Knock before entering. Leave your shoes in the hall."

The room smelled of perfume and pumice. The dirty
blue wallpaper featured four-in-hand carriages and
teams of stallions like those found in Currier and Ives
prints. A four-poster bed from the Victorian era was
covered with a thick red spread.

She said her name was Valerie, and he was the most
handsome man to call on her in weeks. They shook
hands. Van Meter stood in his crusty stocking feet and

sized her up. Big tits and a big ass. He liked that. A little old, late thirties, but a clear face and bunchy black hair. She had on a ratty gray robe that looked like something a grandmother would be found dead in, and thick white socks with tiny flowers. But what the hell, it was cold.

Van Meter slipped his overcoat off his shoulders and let it drop to the floor. He put his hands on his hips. "Do you take it in the ass?"

She rolled her eyes and smacked her lips. "You don't beat around the bush, do you, Slim?"

"I do that too, but I prefer the back door. You game?"

"Doggy style? Yes. Up the old alley? Not on your life."

"Turn out the lights," Van Meter ordered.

Valerie retouched her makeup in the mirror over the dresser. She dipped a washcloth in a basin of water and wrung it out. "First you have to wash yourself. Then I have to check you."

"Check me for what?"

"Crabs. Lice. The Loch Ness monster. Whatever."

"You ain't checking me for shit. Shut off the lights and bend over."

"House rules, Slim."

"There's only one rule, and I coughed up twenty big ones for it."

"You're a real charmer, Slim, but rules are rules." She tossed him the wet cloth. He threw it back at her. It hit her shoulder and hung there. She licked her lips, folded the washcloth in her hands, eased up to him, and wiped the last speck of ice from his eyebrow. "Don't be bashful, Slim," she seductively whispered. "I was sucking wienies on St. Peter Street while other kids were still sucking their thumbs. Now let ol' Val have a look-see." She planted a sloppy kiss over his mouth and honked his crotch.

Van Meter shrieked. He threw her on the bed and

dived for the light switch. It was pitch black. He jumped
on the bed. She wasn't there. The lights came on.

Ol' Val was at the switch. "Last chance, Slim. Show
or blow."

"I paid twenty bucks for your ass," he cried until his
lungs hurt. There was fire in his eyes and saliva drooling
down his chin. He stripped off his shirt and socks.

Valerie swung the door open and stepped into the
hall. "Miss Clifford," she called. Nina was at her side.
"He won't show. Wants to play bronco buster."

"I paid twenty bucks for her ass, Grandma."

"He reminds me of one of those cuckoo birds that
pops out of the clock on the hour," Nina remarked to
Valerie. She stuck two fingers in her mouth and gave
a whistle. The house quaked. The ape was coming.

Homer Van Meter drew his pistol and crouched into
a defensive position. From the sound of the footsteps
he expected Paul Bunyan. What he got was the Big
Holy Spook. He filled the doorway with his massive
shoulders. His fat black face blotted out the ceiling. He
chomped on his big red tongue and clenched his giant
fist.

A lump swelled in Van Meter's throat. Out of fear
he sprang for the door like a cat, then fell like a swatted
fly. The Spook grabbed hold of his twiggy arms and
squeezed until the gun dropped to the floor. He lifted
Van Meter by his ears and set him on his knees, then
stepped around behind and knelt on the backs of his
legs. Van Meter was squealing.

Nina snapped her fingers.

Valerie stooped down, unzipped his pants, and
tugged on his underwear. "Oh, Christ!" she cried out,
falling back on her ass. "It looks like a stick of cherry-
vanilla ice cream."

"Yes, and it's melting," exclaimed Nina. "Scoop it
back in his pants and get it out of here."

The Spook let go and Homer Van Meter dropped
facedown in pain and humiliation. Nina's heavy black

shoes were under his nose. He could smell the leather, could count the stripes on the laces. Her words fell on his ears like mushy snowballs. "You get your diseased ass out of my house or I'll set fire to it." She skirted away.

The Spook was still breathing down on him. Van Meter stretched out his long arm and latched onto the .38. He rolled to his back and pointed it right between the tree-trunk legs of the Big Holy Spook and fired once, thus welcoming the street preacher to Dag Rankin's exclusive club for unique cripples. The cry of the banshee reverberated through the rafters. Scared the pants off Homer Van Meter. He leaped from his trousers and dove into the hall. He somersaulted down the stairs, flew out the door, and sailed up Steep Street.

Over the past forty years the St. Paul police had heard some strange noises come out of Nina Clifford's place, but nothing could match the frightening wail now piercing the frigid sky. They rushed to the windows to see snow tumbling from Nina's roof while some beanpole of a man in his underwear went skipping by the station like a jackrabbit out of hell.

Winter's icy breath grabbed Homer Van Meter's face and twisted it. The frozen sidewalk burned his feet. The wind cut through his bare shoulders and gutted his ribs. Shelter in seconds was a must. The police station was unthinkable. The morgue was unbearable. His knees buckled at Kellogg Boulevard. A lamp was glowing in the lobby of City Hall. Fire from heaven. Headlights from a lonely car lit up his frosty red frame as he stumbled across the street and zigzagged into the Art Deco building. He was still perpendicular.

Mahoney Bologna

When the cold spell broke so did Mayor Mahoney. With a tough election less than two months away, and the United States Attorney General calling his city every name in the book, and Senator Copeland threatening to bring his special investigative committee to St. Paul; with the *Frontier News* pounding away at him every day on the front page, and state bureaucrats screaming in his ear about the bad publicity hurting tourism; with the arrival of March and unsolved murders and unsolved kidnappings remaining unsolved, His Honor the Mayor ordered a grand-jury investigation of his police department. The investigation was to begin immediately and wrap up its business in four to five weeks. Short and sweet. Sweet enough to be well under way during the primary, and short enough to be over with and forgotten before the general election.

"You're Grover Mudd, aren't you?"

"Yes, I am," Grover told the elevator operator.

"What floor?"

"Lobby."

"You can sink a lot lower than that," the man sneered.

Grover stepped into the lobby. If an elevator door could slam, that one did. He was at the City Hall and county courthouse.

Because of the stock-market crash the cost of labor and materials for the jazzy twenty-story building was

much less than expected. As a result the Art Deco work
was finished with expensive woods and marble, and fine
artistic details. On the six bronze elevator doors before
which Grover stood, themes of history and industrial
growth were portrayed in a flat relief style—an Indian
and a tepee, a worker carrying a power tool, a farmer,
a factory, a gavel and a Bible. It was the man with the
gavel and Bible Grover Mudd had come to see.

While doing a follow-up on his Tommy Carroll column he'd learned that police weren't the only ones
letting gangsters go on their merry way. Some municipal
judges had it down to an art. During a brawl on Seven
Corners a criminal lawyer named Charles Keefer was
arrested with a loaded revolver in his pocket instead of
draped proudly and legally over his shoulder like any
smart citizen in Minnesota would do. He was charged
with carrying a concealed weapon. Judge Maxwell Clayton sentenced him to thirty days at the Como Park
Workhouse. After serving only four days Keefer was
secretly released by the same Judge Clayton. The release was legal. As Grover learned, the law permitted
municipal judges to publicly sentence an offender one
minute and secretly release him the next. Judge Maxwell Clayton had done it repeatedly. So Grover Mudd
came to the courthouse to interview the judge with the
peculiar sentencing guidelines. But, alas, there was no
judge to be found. On the morning the grand-jury investigation was announced, the overworked magistrate
decided to take a four-week vacation in Florida.

From the lobby Grover shuffled into Memorial Hall,
which was dedicated to the Ramsey County soldiers
who lost their lives in the Great War. The blue marble
hall extended upward three stories to a gold-leaf ceiling.
Sixteen hollow bronze shafts lighted from within provided a spectacular soaring effect and served to highlight
the names of the soldiers inscribed on the wall. Grover
Mudd, reading the names of the dead, forgot himself.
A statue was on order from a famous Swedish sculptor,

an American Indian god of peace weighing fifty-five tons and standing thirty-six feet high, but where the god of peace was supposed to stand there now stood only a greasy concession stand.

Grover needed cigarettes. "Pack of Luckies."

On the food-stained counter was a stack of punch-boards and a dice box. Between the sundry items against the wall was a crusty hot plate. The stocky man who ran the stand was even more crusty. He had a filthy apron tied over his beer belly and an unshaven face that sized up each customer. "Ain't you Grover Mudd?"

"Let me try a cup of that coffee, too."

"You got no friends around here." The surly man slapped the cigarettes on the counter. "Twelve cents."

Grover dropped the exact change on the counter a coin at a time. "You were at the old City Hall, weren't you?"

"What of it?"

"Yeah, the more things change," Grover muttered. "Just out of curiosity, what kind of rent do you pay for this stand?"

"Two hundred bucks a year. Check the records."

"What was the last year you paid it?"

"Blow it out your ass, Mudd."

"I see you're selling bottled beer."

"Been legal a year now. It was in all the papers."

"Do you have an on-sale beer license?"

"Blow it out your ass, Mudd."

"I don't see a cigarette license posted, or a restaurant license for that food you're serving."

"Blow it out your ass, Mudd."

"That looks like marijuana next to those sweet rolls. Did you know the city banned the sale of marijuana two weeks ago?"

"Don't go into effect for ninety days."

"Any running water besides what you piss on the floor?"

The slob dipped a cup in a pail of water, shook it dry, filled it with coffee, and slammed it on the counter. "Ten cents."

Grover made no attempt to hide his disgust. "What am I supposed to do with that, drink it or scrub my typewriter keys?"

"Drink it, Mudd. Then blow it out your ass."

Grover Mudd left City Hall and wandered toward a jewelry store on Seventh Street. It was a dreary afternoon, cloudy and still. The temperature was just above freezing. The snowdrifts were dirty black. The streets were slush-brown. Stone-infested potholes were everywhere. At the Orpheum Theater he paused to read the illustrated movie poster. Clark Gable and Claudette Colbert were starring in *It Happened One Night*. He thought how much Stormy Day would love to see it.

The jewelry store disappointed him. Grover did not like the selection of wedding rings, or the price tags attached to them. He remembered a pawnshop on Jackson Street in Lowertown that displayed some real beauties in the window. Outside again, he checked his watch. Grover felt a pang in his chest and swallowed hard. He lit another cigarette, then cut back to Fourth Street.

The campaign for the primary election was well under way. The newspapers were fat with political ads; debates preempted local radio shows; there were so many candidates it was almost a joke. Along the streets that Grover walked, picture posters and slogans were pasted to every street lamp. Flyers were tucked under windshield wipers, while others blew up the sanded sidewalks and settled in the slush. Mayor Mahoney was picking up sympathy support. He continued to hammer home the idea that the city's problems were caused by the local newspapers. He lashed out at the politicians in Washington, reminding them that after two full years the kidnapping of the Lindbergh baby was unsolved, too. Even with that, independent lawyer Mark H. Gehan was coming on strong. In the closely watched race for public safety commissioner, Gil St. Sauver was running a smart campaign, keeping Commissioner McDonald on the ropes.

The Moral Rearmament people were picketing the *Frontier News*, demanding Christian ethics from the newspaper. Some of the signs they were parading had Grover's name on them, his last name spelled with one "D."

Grover loped down the other side of the street and was passing the front door of the other paper when he saw it on the newsstand. The front page of the *North Star Press*. Grover ripped the paper off the stand and held it up to his disbelieving eyes. There in big, bold black and white above the fold was a photograph of Como Zoo's two gorillas, Casey and Tanya. They had only been photographed from the waist up, but Casey was clearly humped over Tanya's back, and both had their tongues hanging out. The caption below the picture read: "At Long Last, Sweethearts Embrace!" Journalism in Minnesota would never be the same. Grover Mudd looked up at the windows of the *North Star Press*. "Fucking monkeys."

He tossed the paper back on the stand. He thought he heard his name called through the traffic. Thinking the protesters had spotted him, he paid no attention. He continued on his way when he heard it again, this time loud and clear. Grover looked up. It was Fuzzy Byron, shouting from a third-floor window of the *Frontier News*. "He escaped, Grover."

Grover couldn't make it out. He tossed his cigarette. A streetcar clanged by in front of him. Car tires spun in the winter muck. He climbed a bank of snow and shouted back. "What?"

"He escaped!" Fuzzy yelled again. "John Dillinger broke out of that jail in Indiana. He's on the loose."

A crowd gathered. "When did this happen?"

"This morning," answered Fuzzy.

"They claimed Houdini couldn't get out of that jail," a man on the street complained.

"Ask him how," a lady in the crowd ordered.

"How'd he do it?" Grover shouted.

"Hang on," cried Fuzzy. He turned in to the office. The traffic on the sidewalk below Grover came to a halt as the news spread. Passing cars slowed and looked up. Reporter Harv Bennett appeared in the window with Fuzzy Byron, reading him the news off the wire. Fuzzy relayed it to Grover Mudd standing below on a mountain of dirty snow. "It says he used a wooden gun. Locked up all the jailers. Went through six barred doors. Got by fifty guards, and one squad of National Guardsmen." Fuzzy turned for more information. "It says he stole the sheriff's car, a Ford V-8. Got a plate number here."

"Which way was he heading?" Grover wanted to know.

"Chicago," Fuzzy reported. "But Chicago police are saying he might come here." Harv Bennett collected another bulletin and read it to him. Fuzzy leaned far out the window. "Says here, Grover, Mayor Mahoney has sent police to watch the bridges."

The news swept down Fourth Street like the Saint Valentine's Day blizzard. Dillinger is coming.

The big black Caddy rolled into the "No Parking" zone. A fugitive-felon-turned-chauffeur opened the back door, and Dag Rankin hobbled out with an overnight bag. Roxanne followed him out of the car with only her purse in hand.

"Wait for her," Rankin told his man. "And while I'm gone get that information on Mudd. I'm tired of waiting for it."

With the first rays of spring sun reflecting off the sparkling stone walls, the snow was disappearing faster than gang leaders called before a grand jury. Icy water ran down the sidewalks, and the crisp clean air smelled of new beginnings. Dag Rankin took his girl by the arm and they marched up the stairs past the colonnaded façade and through the heavy bronze doors of St. Paul's Union Depot.

During the first week of the grand-jury investigation gambling kingpin Dutch Otto was asked to take the stand. Unfortunately, the appearance conflicted with his Florida vacation and he was unable to make it. In the second week of questioning bawdyhouse boss Jap Gleckman received a written invitation, but he had a business convention in Miami and sent his regrets. Nina Clifford showed up and testified. After a fascinating rendition of the city's nocturnal history that held jurors spellbound, she reminded one of the investigators about the night he came to her house with handcuffs and marmalade and asked for Gretchen with the big lips. Nina was dismissed with no further questions. It was in the third week of the investigation that Dag Rankin was summoned to City Hall.

Iron chandeliers dangled from a lofty ceiling punctuated with dusty skylights, allowing the sunshine to follow them inside. Roxanne could not remember a time, day or night, when the train station had not been crowded. Long lines formed at the ticket windows, and each time the loudspeakers echoed departures and destinations a thousand anxious eyes would focus on the rotund clocks dangling at each end of the marble hall. Dag Rankin already had his ticket. Roxanne was mad, frustrated, scared. They brushed by the lines and started down the long corridor to the gates.

"What if the grand jury calls me?"

"They're not going to call you," Rankin told her. "I got a man inside and he showed me the list of witnesses. It all adds up to zero."

"Then why are you going to Florida?"

"Business, I keep telling you. I'll be in Miami a week, Havana a week, then I'll be on my way home. This cockeyed investigation will be over with and the news-papers will be officially discredited." They stopped at a newsstand, where Rankin flipped the man a nickel. "Keep it," he said, grabbing a *Frontier News* off the rack.

RECORD NUMBERS TO VOTE IN PRIMARY
75,000 Expected to Go to Polls Today

Above the headline was another editorial, this one already predicting a whitewash by the grand jury and demanding a complete investigation. In capital letters was a list of witnesses who'd skipped town, and a para-graph about honest men not disappearing when called by a grand jury. The editorial closed with another lam-basting of the police department, and a suggestion that suspicious characters be reported *not* to the local police, but to the FBI. Their telephone number in the basement of the Federal Courts Building was printed in large bold type.

"Slimy bastards," muttered Rankin. "When the city's done with them, I'll fix their ass good."

"It's easy for you to talk tough on your way to Flor-ida," Roxanne told him, her voice quivering with emo-tion. "I've seen a witch-hunt in this town before, during the war. They'll do it again. I know they will."

"Do what again?"

"They called themselves the Minnesota Commission of Public Safety," Roxanne told him, talking fast. "It was the governor, the attorney general, and five ap-pointed cronies. The legislature gave them dictator rights. I'm scared and I don't want to stay here."

"This is no witch-hunt and there is no war. There's an election coming up and this is just some of Maho-ney's bologna."

They continued through the depot, dodging scattered luggage. The smell of fried food permeated the air. Along one wall stood a group of soldiers with duffel bags at their feet, and eyeing them along the wooden benches was a spattering of depot whores.

"They created their own police force called the Home Guard, just like that Gestapo Hitler's got," Roxanne went on, the childhood memories coming faster than the words. "They hated everything German. They raided German churches. They quit teaching German in the schools. Mamma's got a heavy German accent, but the people in the hollow left us alone as long as we said our last name was Smith. But then the Home Guard starting going block to block, and when they got to the hollow they went door to door. Mamma and I hid in the woods and the old Swedes wouldn't tell them where we were. Then we bought war bonds with money we needed for food and showed them to everybody, and we pasted those idiotic, patriotic posters in our windows, praying they'd leave us alone."

"Roxanne, my love," Rankin said dispassionately, "you're upsetting yourself over nothing."

"You know the Guardian Building on Minnesota Street? It used to be the Germania Life Insurance Company. They made them change the name and take down that big statue of Germania that used to sit on top. They called sauerkraut 'liberty cabbage' and hamburger 'Salisbury steak.' Everything Germans have done for this city, for this state, and they ended up beaten, spit on, lynched."

They reached their gate, the bold gate numbers posted as at a racetrack. The train was not boarding yet. Rankin checked his watch. Roxanne sat on a wood bench and wiped her forehead.

"I've never seen you like this, doll. You were always the cool one. If you're all that worried about this thing, go stay with Nina. She went down and testified and made fools out of them. While you're at it, bring her that package I left you and tell her if she don't start coming up with the dough I'm going to cut her off. I'm going to cut them all off."

A locomotive roared into the station, and the squealing brakes sent a shiver up Roxanne's spine. She could smell the scorching metal on metal and the wisps of engine smoke that drifted inside. Her head was aching. She looked around, avoiding his eyes. In the corner stood a family of European immigrants with fear and hope carved on their faces, their meager belongings stacked at their feet—too provincial for German, perhaps Polish—searching the crowd for a face they knew long ago in the old country.

The skylights went dark. The sun was under a cloud. Boarding for the southbound train was announced.

"I have to go, doll. How about a big kiss?" Rankin asked.

She did not move from the bench, but looked him square in the eye and he had his answer. He got in line, limped through the gate, and disappeared in the hissing steam.

All the people going places, dreams arriving and dreams departing. The daughter of the German immigrants got up to leave. In front of her was a big poster hailing California as the Sunshine State. She looked at the giant trains out on the tracks. She turned and looked through the depot tunnel to the speck of a city outside the doors. Roxanne Schultz took a small step then stopped in frustration. Chewing gum stuck like glue to the bottom of her shoe.

———

Frontier News editor Walt Howard slipped into his sweater. He rolled the pilfered document into a paper telescope and aimed it out his office window. The snow was falling heavy and wet now, wiping out the first attempt at spring. The daylight slipped slowly away. The street lamps popped on. It was Friday evening. The grand jury, hastily called and operating behind closed doors, had abruptly completed its work. A source at City Hall had filched a copy of the report and now it was in Walt Howard's hands. Just as he had guessed, had gone as far to predict on his front page: a whitewash, pure and simple.

He thought wistfully back to the week before, when he went to cast his vote in the city primary and had to stand in line for nearly two hours. Pride, involvement, and civic responsibility were returning to St. Paul. Seventy-five thousand people were expected to go to the polls that day, but more than eighty-two thousand showed up. At some locations the city ran out of official ballots, and voters were asked to write their choices on blank pieces of paper. When the ballots were counted it was Mayor Mahoney vs. lawyer Mark H. Gehan, as expected. Unexpected, and much to the delight of many, Assistant Police Chief Gil St. Sauver led all votegetters in his bid to be the next commissioner of public safety while current commissioner McDonald was ousted for good. The primary election was a beacon of hope in a stormy town, and Walt Howard knew in his heart that day he and his paper had played a major role in setting that beacon aglow.

But now the crusading editor was sick. He slapped the sugar-coated report across his knee. In a dramatic move, the grand-jury foreman was going on radio Saturday afternoon to read the findings. Unless something happened, the *Frontier News* front-page editorial campaign would be officially discredited and lawlessness in St. Paul would be given a new lease on life.

The next day something happened.

Gun Number One

At twelve-fifteen P.M. on Saturday, March 31, grand-jury foreman William Burrows sat down to a microphone at the KSTP radio studio housed in the Hotel Saint Paul. An hour earlier he had presented the grand jury's final report to Judge Kenneth Brill at the Ramsey County Courthouse. In an unprecedented broadcast he was now going to read the anxiously awaited findings to the people of the Twin Cities.

The message in the front-page editorials was beginning to register with the good citizens of St. Paul—at least, it did with Adelaide Meidlinger, known to her tenants as Addy. As manager of the Lincoln Court Apartments in the fashionable Hill District she rented Suite 303 to a Mr. and Mrs. Carl Hellman. But they were a suspicious couple from the start. Neither of them worked. Their shades were drawn day and night. They only used the back stairwell. Raunchy-looking men and women came calling at all hours, and they, too, would use only the back stairs. She learned from neighbors that Mr. Hellman rented a garage down the alley in which he parked a large Hudson sedan, never taking it out. Instead of reporting her suspicions to the police, on Saturday morning Mrs. Meidlinger called the Federal Courts Building.

Around ten-thirty A.M. Steff Koslowski and fellow agent Rufus Coulter arrived in their out-of-tune Ford to question her. Since the *Frontier News* began its editorial campaign, the number of calls coming into the G-men's office had quadrupled. Many of them were routine police calls, but several led to the arrest of federal fugitives. What Steff found interesting about this report was the location of the Lincoln Court Apartments: Lincoln Avenue and Lexington Parkway, a half-block north of Goodrich Avenue, where Edward Bremer was grabbed. Steff came armed with pictures of the Barker-Karpis gang, but the lady manager swore it was none of them. The description she gave of Mr. Hellman was so general—tall, dark hair, suspicious-looking—it could have fit every other man at the Justice Department.

At eleven-fifteen Agent Rosser Knowles showed up to assist in a stakeout. Steff Koslowski, along with Agent Coulter, parked their car on busy Lexington Parkway so that they were in position to watch the front of the building and, at the same time, keep an eye on the alley with the rented garage. Agent Knowles parked on Lincoln Avenue, where he could watch the door to the back stairwell and the driveway off the alley. The G-men, used to the routine, sat in their cars and waited.

It was the day before Easter and the new blanket of snow was already melting on the streets. Sitting in the warm spring sun, Steff Koslowski thought of how his family back in Chicago would be getting ready for church the next morning, and then, after a flowery mass, would return home to a scrumptious dinner. Another holiday missed. Another day in St. Paul. A soft wind breezed through the bare trees. He tuned the car radio to KSTP and they listened to orchestra music until twelve-fifteen, when the *World Report* came on.

Mrs. Meidlinger was right about the shades in 303. They were drawn tight. Nobody peeked out.

At twelve-thirty the sound man cued the grand-jury foreman, and Mr. Burrows calmly explained into the microphone how they had conducted a complete and thorough investigation, and any inability to find evidence was due to a lack of funds and no facilities for carrying on a widespread investigation. Then he had a sip of water, cleared his throat and read the findings.

"We believe there is no justification for any charges that an excess of crime exists here. We believe further that a comparison with other large cities will prove that St. Paul cannot be shown in an unfavorable light.

"Charges of official incompetence and neglect—these charges have not been sustained by evidence. Charges of collusion between police and underworld—no evidence of centralized graft has been found.

"Gambling—evidence has been produced to prove that there has been gambling in St. Paul. In all likelihood there still is gambling going on. If any citizen has knowledge of gambling, it is just as much his duty to furnish such evidence as it is the duty of the police to stop it. No evidence has been produced to show that gambling was permitted to continue in any place after the police officials became aware of its operation.

"Newspaper campaign—the jury took cognizance of the grave charges made daily on the front page of the *St. Paul Frontier News*. The statements relied upon and recited in these editorials are not proved and in most instances are shown to be inaccurate.

"In the judgement of this jury, this, the editorial campaign, is not the way to secure either the wholehearted effort of the police to suppress crime or to secure a change in police administration. Publication of articles such as these, particularly if not warranted by the facts, serves as notice to crooks that this is a city in which they can safely operate. Information brought to the grand jury shows that the state of Minnesota, widely advertised and famous as a summer resort playground, is damaged by such unwarranted publicity.

"We commend the practice of alert newspapers to uncover official wrongdoing. But in justice to the reputation of the city—unwarranted undermining of public confidence should be condemned."

Back on Lexington Parkway Steff Koslowski and Rufus Coulter were laughing so hard tears were streaming down their faces. They watched Rosser Knowles giggle his way around the corner and over to the car. He leaned in the window and it was all he could do to spit out, "Are you guys listening to what I'm listening to?" Steff reached for the radio knob and turned it up.

Mr. Burrows was still going strong. "Your present police department is essentially honest."

The three federal agents went into hysterics.

The grand-jury foreman, unaware he was being drowned out by laughter in the Hill District, droned on. "The fact is well established that our police force is undermanned, underpaid, and inefficiently equipped compared with cities of similar population and area. This fact in itself would not excuse corrupt practices or neglect of duty, but in our judgement trouble does not exist with the present personnel."

Agent Knowles pounded on the roof. "Turn it off before somebody calls the cops on us."

Steff turned the radio off and wiped his eyes. "Christ, I haven't had a laugh like that since I hit this crazy town."

Agent Coulter was still chuckling. "What should we do about the James Gang up in 303?"

Steff looked up at the blank windows. "Well, we know it's not Karpis or the Barkers, so let's handle this the old-fashioned way. Knock on the door and tell them to get out of town by sundown."

They stood on the parkway and waited for a break in traffic. Slush spattered the cuffs of their pants. The three G-men, all laughed out, crossed the street, hurried up the shoveled walkway and entered the Lincoln Court Apartments.

Rosser Knowles positioned himself on the top stair of the front stairwell, unbuttoned his coat and watched his two colleagues walk down the third-floor hallway. Rufus Coulter stopped in front of 303 and unbuttoned his coat. Steff Koslowski continued down the hall, to where he could cover the back stairs.

Agent Coulter knocked on the door. There was no answer. He knocked again.

A woman's voice came from inside. "Who is it?"

"We're federal investigators," Coulter said with a great deal of authority. "We'd like to speak with Carl Hellman."

There was no response.

Steff heard footsteps coming up the back stairs. He signaled the others then moved down the hall.

It was a tall, slouchy man whose overcoat hung on his skinny frame like a wet blanket on a clothesline. His head was down and his hands were stuffed deep in his pockets. He climbed slowly up the stairs as if he didn't have a care in the world. Steff stood at the top and silently waited for him. When the man got within two steps he finally looked up. Steff knew the face in an instant. He had been living with it for seven months—the pointed ears, the missing teeth, the funny haircut. And if Steff Koslowski was quick to recognize him, Homer Van Meter was even quicker to spot a G-man. His hand flew out of his coat with a .45 so fast Steff had no time to go for his gun. He lunged forward and shoved Van Meter hard. They tumbled and wrestled down three flights of stairs. Steff bolted out the back door as a bullet shot by his ear. He went into a shoulder roll and came up with his gun drawn. Van Meter came out shooting. Steff knelt on one knee, held his gun with both hands, and for the first time in his life fired at a live target.

Van Meter ducked, jumped, then ducked again.

Afraid he was being outgunned, the ghostly gangster spun around and fled through the building.

Now there was machine-gun fire coming from upstairs.

Steff pursued Van Meter down the first-floor hallway and out the front door. The skinny fugitive jumped into a Ford coupé and made off. Steff wanted to shoot at the car but there was too much traffic, and he wanted to go after him but there was a gun battle raging on the third floor. He ducked inside and sprinted up the stairs, where he found Agent Knowles crouched at the top and Agent Coulter pinned in a niche in the wall. "He went down the back," cried Knowles. "Go around."

Steff raced back down the stairs and out the front door and hurdled through the snow to the corner of the building. A woman was backing a Hudson sedan out of the garage they had been watching, and standing in the alley covering their escape was the suspicious Mr. Hellman. His face had been on every front page in the country. His name dominated the headlines. His long black coat was wide open and he had a machine gun tucked under his arm. With a series of short bursts he kept Agents Coulter and Knowles pinned in the back stairwell.

Steff Koslowski shouted no warning, showed no hesitation. He raised his gun and fired one shot.

Dillinger flinched.

Steff squeezed the trigger again, but this time his pistol was empty. John Dillinger's machine gun was not. Steff dived behind the building and into the sticky snow as a long, loud volley of slugs tore the bricks to chips and rained down on his back. Then he heard the car tearing through the slush. He ran to the alley only to see the big Hudson, carrying Public Enemy #1, disappear at the end of the block. A trail of blood speckled the snow where John Dillinger had stood.

Agents Coulter and Knowles rushed out. "Get to a

phone," Coulter shouted. "We're going after them."
They ran for the car.

Steff pounded on the manager's door.

"Go away," she yelled from inside.

"This is Agent Koslowski. The shooting is over. I
need to use the phone."

Mrs. Meidlinger unbolted the door, peeked out, then
pulled Steff in, slamming the door behind him. "This
has never happened at the Lincoln Court before," she
protested, in the understatement of her life.

Steff tracked snow across her polished floor and
picked up the phone, and, as he dialed and listened to
the ringing at the other end, his mind was only beginning to grasp the truth. In the last five minutes he had
wrestled with, and shot it out with, Homer Van Meter.
He had come within spitting range of John Dillinger,
had him cold, but he'd missed. Or had he?

Mrs. Meidlinger had her radio on. It was tuned to
KSTP, where grand-jury foreman William Burrows was
finishing the report. "The United States Attorney General has spoken uncharacteristically of the city of St.
Paul but has steadfastly refused to amplify or clarify his
statements. Until the attorney general sees fit to be
more specific, there is no evidence of failure on the part
of the St. Paul police authorities to do their duty."

At four o'clock Saturday afternoon the *St. Paul Frontier
News* hit the street with a special edition, which
promptly sold out. Editor Walt Howard put out extras
and they sold out. In Minnesota the front page was
destined to become a collector's item.

THE ST. PAUL FRONTIER NEWS

* Page One * Saturday, March 31, 1934 * Two Cents *

MACHINE GUNS BLAZE AS JURY WHITEWASHES POLICE

Report Finds Little Crime, Raps *Frontier News;* Police Essentially Honest

Two Men, Woman in Gang Blast Way to Freedom as G-Men Stumble on Lair

———

As predicted in the *Frontier News* on March 18, the grand jury today brought in a "whitewash" report on the St. Paul Police Department . . .

Acting allegedly on a tip that "suspicious" men and women were occupying a fashionable Hill District apartment, federal agents today walked unsuspectingly into a mob of machine-gun "heavies," staged a five-minute gun battle, and lost their quarry . . .

Saint Albans

In Suite 303 of the Lincoln Court Apartments the FBI found snapshots of John Dillinger, letters written by John Dillinger, and fingerprints left behind by John Dillinger. They also found a St. Peter Street address.

It was a dingy second-story flat at the top of a long, dark stairwell. There was one window. It overlooked the street. Steff Koslowski searched the place with Agent Rufus Coulter and a new arrival from Chicago, Agent Sol Wellmen. Agent Rosser Knowles watched the door from outside. It was Sunday morning.

Several notebooks were crammed with pencil-drawn maps that detailed the back roads in and out of the Twin Cities. The agents found two revolvers under the bed, and various machine-gun parts in a cardboard box. Filthy as the place was, it did not look lived-in, more like a dumping ground. Steff and Coulter settled in and waited. Agent Wellmen joined Rosser Knowles outside in the car and did the same.

Steff Koslowski had not slept well, had really had no sleep at all. His mind kept racing over the events leading up to the shootout. A half-block from where Edward Bremer was snatched. He should have brought an army. And if they had been patient, had stayed in their cars another five minutes, they would have seen Van Meter arrive. Then walking down the hall and approaching a suspect with his gun buried under two layers of clothes. He had messed up. Mistakes his father never would have made. Mistakes his grandfather would find inexcusable.

Steff stood to the side of the window and exchanged hand signals with the agents in the car. He looked over the street, a street that could match Chicago decadence for decadence. This morning it was fairly quiet for such a street, though he thought he heard a preacher shouting damnations far away. Up on the hill a line of cars was circling the cathedral and the Polish boy from the Windy City thought of the Catholic upbringing he'd left behind.

Just before noon the agents in the car spotted a colored girl coming up the walk. She pushed through the front door and started up the stairs. They sounded the horn twice.

There would be no fiasco like the day before. Steff and Coulter took cover, drew their guns and listened to the key slide into the lock. The door pushed open. The girl stepped in.

Steff Koslowski leveled his gun at her chest. "Hold it right there, sister."

She was startled. She backed up against the wall as if she was going to cry.

"Put the purse down."

She dropped the purse to the floor and cupped her hands under her chin. At the foot of the stairs two more agents were pointing guns up at her.

Coulter picked up her bag and searched it. "It's clean," he said, and he threw it back at her.

Steff lowered his gun. "Who are you?"

"Stormy Day," she whispered.

"What are you doing here?"

"Maid service. I clean houses."

"You clean houses on Easter Sunday?"

"I went to church this morning," she told Steff defensively. "I clean houses every weekend."

"And you're suppose to clean this place up?" Coulter asked skeptically.

"The man said I don't have to clean. He just wants me to pick up some things. The man gave me ten dollars."

"What things does he want?" Steff asked.

"Some clothes and some shaving stuff. He says he's going out of town."

"Didn't you find that suspicious?"

"Ain't my place to ask."

It was obvious to Steff she was nothing more than a frightened cleaning woman, but for some reason he felt it necessary to speak harshly. "How are you supposed to get these things to this man?"

"He said he'd get them at my house later."

"Where's that?"

"St. Albans Street."

Steff shot an inquisitive glance at his partner.

"It's off Rondo," Coulter informed him. "Negro district."

"We've got a car outside," Steff told her. "We'll all go over to St. Albans Street and wait for the man to come and get his things."

———————

Grover Mudd stood outside the house he was paying for. Dinner was over. As usual he had been made to feel an unwelcome guest, but this was a holiday and coming to dinner was one of those American things that had to be done. He did not eat much, preferring to save room for Stormy's meal.

An elm tree shaded the front of the house. Upstairs, overlooking the street, were the windows to the master bedroom, where the walls were papered with excuses and sex was something that had to be wrestled for. On the front porch was a swing where he used to take refuge from the fighting. A black iron mailbox that collected alimony checks was screwed to a porch beam. If the porch were removed the house would resemble a children's drawing: A-framed, painted yellow, trimmed in

failing colors, with something crooked about it. After
the war the bank mortgaged the storybook house to a
Grover Mudd bedecked in medals, but now he was only
a divorced reporter behind in his payments and they
treated him with less respect than the gangsters who
held them up.

The melting snow was sloppy brown. Grass was
springing to life on the banks and around the trees.
Grover moved up the walk to the driveway and saw his
beloved Studebaker Dictator sitting outside the garage.
It looked moribund, streaked with mud, and now in the
uncaring hands of ex-in-laws, ex-neighbors, and ex-
friends. Cars are not made of metal, Grover thought,
cars are built out of memories, and all the dirt in the
world couldn't cover the joy he once got from that
Studebaker. He shoved his hand in his coat pocket and
grabbed on to the only thing that really mattered now.
The case with the wedding ring. What would they say?
What would they say when Grover Mudd took a negro
girl for his wife?

The sun popped through the clouds and Grover got
caught up in the optimism of spring. He glanced at his
watch. Time was getting on. He muffled a cough. He
leaped a muddy puddle and set off for the trolley stop.

In the spring the snowman melts last. On St. Albans
Street the snowman outside Stormy Day's window was
surrendering to the sun. The smiling pebbles had fallen
from his face. His twiggy arms were drooping. His chest
was slowly dripping away.

Special Agent Steff Koslowski watched this melting
man from the bay window. Agents Coulter, Knowles,
and Wellmen took up positions on the side of the house
and in a car out front. The girl sent her little boy to a
neighbor's house. She was still scared and was unable
to identify any of the faces in the mug shots they showed
her. "He's a cute boy," the G-man said, trying to make

conversation. "Where's his father?" She looked down and away and Steff knew the answer. "Did you have something planned for today?"

"I'm supposed to be making dinner."

"Are you expecting anyone besides this man?"

"Maybe later."

"Your sweetheart?"

"Just a friend."

The girl kept a warm and welcome house. Steff had never before been in the home of a colored person. He could not help but compare the St. Paul negro district to the slums off State Street in Chicago. Here there were few signs of real decay, and the area was only half colored at best; whites lived and worked amongst them. In Chicago no white man in his right mind would walk down Smoketown. And there was something else about this girl. The innocent face. The soft eyes. She was pretty. The most attractive colored girl he'd ever seen. If only she'd comb her wild hair. Steff Koslowski shook the thought from his head. The city was starting to get to him. "St. Albans Street," he asked her, "weren't there a couple of cops massacred here a few years ago?"

"Down on Laurel," Stormy told him. "I didn't live here then."

For an hour Steff tried to make small talk with no success. Then a Terraplane sedan pulled to the curb in front of the row house. A slender man was behind the wheel, and a woman sat beside him. Steff backed away from the window, far enough not to be spotted. They sat in the car and talked for nearly ten minutes and Steff began to think they would have to change the plan and move against them. Then the man stepped out of the car. It was not Dillinger or Van Meter, not Baby Face Nelson or Creepy Alvin Karpis. It was not one of the Barker brothers. Steff felt a tinge of disappointment. But as the man approached the house he could see they had a big fish after all. It was Tommy Carroll.

Steff Koslowski drew his gun and stepped behind the door.

"Remember what I told you," he instructed Stormy. "Don't let him in. Give him his things and get out of the way."

There was a rap at the door. Stormy squeezed the bundle of clothes. She gave the G-man a desperate look, then she opened it. "Here's your things," she almost screamed. Stormy Day shoved the bundle in Tommy Carroll's arms and slammed the door in his face.

Steff knocked her aside and tore the door open again, but before he could yell "Stop!" there was gunfire and he saw Tommy Carroll jerk down the stairs like a hooked worm and drop to the sidewalk beside the melting snowman. His wife came screaming from the car and cradled his bleeding head in her lap.

Steff Koslowski stood on the stoop with his unfired gun at his side. Agents Wellmen, Knowles, and Coulter were posed nearby with smoking pistols and callous faces. The gangster's dirty wash had landed in a puddle. The pretty young maid was crying in the doorway while across the street her little boy gazed out the window.

It was Easter Sunday. Once again death had come to St. Albans Street.

Grover Mudd was furious. There was no joyful greeting. No Easter dinner. What he found on his arrival was the chalk outline of a man's body on the blood-stained sidewalk. The girl he wanted to marry was in hysterics, and Brody was stammering on about the shooting.

Grover stood in the bay window and focused his angry eyes on the crippled snowman. "Why didn't you get to a phone and call me?"

"They wouldn't let me talk to no one," Stormy cried. "They were real ruuude, and they were scary. They dress real nice and they talk real educated-like, but they got faces that don't smile and they use guns just like gangsters."

"You're not going to spend any more weekends cleaning houses."

"I need the money, Grover, and you can't stop me."

"I'll give you the goddamn money."

"I don't want your money, Grover."

"No, you'd rather spend your weekends picking up after any Buggs Palooka with a hot ten-spot to unload."

"I got nothing else to do on weekends."

Grover ignored the remark. He grabbed her by the shoulders and squeezed hard. "You're not cleaning houses anymore. That's final. Now get some dinner on the table."

"I ain't your slave!"

Grover slapped her across the face and she fell to the couch. It was the first time he'd ever lifted a finger against her. Brody sat in a chair with fear on his face and a lone tear trickling down his cheek. Stormy did not lash back, or even sigh. Instead, she composed herself and looked him in the eyes. She said nothing, but the shyness was gone.

Grover felt sick. The sickness in his stomach this time instead of his chest. Her big brown eyes tore his heart out. The little boy reduced him to nothing. He remembered the terrible fights he'd had with his ex-wife, and he wanted to drop to his knees and confess his love to Stormy, explain to her there was no comparison, tell her a better woman never lived, no city could tear them apart. But he didn't. He sat in his guilt and shame, folded his hands between his knees, and dropped his head.

There was a passionate desperation to their lovemaking that night. In the hour before dawn Grover Mudd sat on the edge of the bed and smoked a cigarette. He dug through his coat pocket and found the small case with the wedding ring. He opened it and watched the diamond sparkle in the dark. *What would they say?*

She was asleep, her thick nappy hair floating on the pillow like a black cloud, her face turned serenely away. Grover kissed her neck. He brushed his fingers across her naked shoulders and let them linger down her side until they came to a tender rest in the small of her back.

Farewell, Carroll

On the evening of April 2, Herbert Franz, a sixty-year-old grocer from Luxembourg, was on his way to church for confession when he was struck by a car on University Avenue and knocked into a freezing puddle of water. He lay in the water for fifteen minutes before a squad car with two St. Paul police officers arrived. In his broken English Mr. Franz tried to explain his injuries. The officers promptly concluded that he was intoxicated and left him lying in the water for another fifteen minutes until a police ambulance arrived. Mr. Franz begged to be taken to nearby Bethesda Hospital, but since the police officers had declared him drunk they insisted he be taken to Ancker Hospital. There it was found he was perfectly sober and he was treated for deep cuts, a broken left leg, and exposure. When the police discovered their mistake they told Mr. Franz and hospital officials not to talk to reporters. The *Frontier News* already had the story.

On the evening of April 3, Herman Peterson, a sixty-eight-year-old St. Paul man, failed to return home. He had recently suffered a stroke and his health was not good. At eleven-fifteen P.M. his family called the hospitals and police headquarters, but they reported that nobody answering Mr. Peterson's description had been picked up. At one-thirty A.M. Mr. Peterson's son went down to police headquarters and requested a search. One squad car and two officers spent the rest of the night searching for Herman Peterson with no luck. At eleven-forty-five the following morning, Ancker Hospital reported that Mr. Peterson had just arrived in a police ambulance, having been in a cell at police headquarters since ten-thirty-five the night before. He had suffered a second stroke, with paralysis, which police officials diagnosed as intoxication. He died a few days later of pneumonia. Walt Howard ran the story on the front page in place of his daily editorial.

On April 4, a barber in Hastings, Minnesota, reported he had shaved the notorious John Dillinger. Late that night St. Paul police received a hot tip that Dillinger was staying at Hastings' leading hotel. Sixteen of St. Paul's finest crammed into a line of squad cars and raced twenty-five miles down Trunk Highway 61 to the sleepy river town. Arriving at two-thirty in the morning, they surrounded the hotel and routed everybody into the street. After the rooms had been ransacked, Dillinger turned out to be Mr. A. J. Hall, a traveling marshmallow salesman. Among those forced to join the pajama parade were St. Paul municipal judge Maxwell Clayton and a shapely female companion, both sporting Florida suntans. Marshmallows were had by all.

Grover Mudd turned his collar to the freezing rain and hurried into Oakland Cemetery through the Sycamore Street gate. The saturated grass over the graves was yellow with thatch. The last patches of snow were black and hard.

It was a medieval cemetery littered with baroque monuments, Celtic crosses, and Athenian temples. The grounds were hilly and the road serpentine. The spooky elms of spring looked as dead as the bodies at their roots. The pines were limp from the weight of the sleet.

Watching Grover hurry by was the Angel of Death, a haunting statue of a naked woman with giant wings, the palm of one hand facing heaven, the palm of the other hand facing hell. On her pedestal were the words THAT ANNUNCIATION MEN CALL DEATH.

They were gathered on the backside of a hill with a
view of the blighted neighborhood that ran behind the
State Capitol. A preacher was reading from the Bible.
The sobbing widow stood handcuffed to a detective. On
a nearby path was a Concord buggy with a matched
pair of horses. A teamster held the reins. Two gravediggers were leaning on shovels. The coffin was in front
of them. A wreath, losing its color in the cold rain,
decorated the top of the pine box. Around the open
grave the fresh dirt was slop.

Grover Mudd took a place next to Tommy Carroll's
father. He remembered him as a mean man, but now
he looked only feeble and miserable, dressed in the
standard railroad outfit, black boots and a dirty overcoat thrown over gray striped overalls. Grover put his
hands to his mouth and coughed. The old man looked
at him, then turned away in a breath of contempt. The
meanness was still there. It showed in the deep lines
around his eyes. He was retired now, which meant he
sat around and drank his pension, or walked down to
the depot and talked of the good old days, now that he
no longer had to bust his ass on an eighteen-hour shift.
The only semblance of respect for his dead son was the
greasy cap he held in his hand.

"Just covering a story?"

"I'm afraid so, Mr. Carroll."

"Is this the part where I'm supposed to say he was a
good boy?"

"If you like."

"He was a shit," the old man said loud and clear.

The preacher stopped.

"Hurry on with your babble," Carroll ordered him,
"we're all getting wet." He bowed his head a bit, more
to keep the sleet out of his face than out of respect for
the service.

The preacher went back to the Bible. The weather
beat down on the pine box as Grover listened to the

Scriptures. To him the reading meant little. He was sure that to Tommy Carroll it meant even less.

Mr. Carroll paid no attention. "G-men got him," he said to Grover. "Put a hole in his head the size of a silver dollar. You should have seen it. They think his dolly over there knows where Dillinger is. I'll bet she knows where a lot of money is."

The thought of it made Grover mad. "Maybe it was all that love and understanding you showed him when he was growing up."

"Don't start with me, wise guy. Your daddy pampered you like the Prince of Wales and you turned out to be a shit, too. Did you know your mommy was a depot whore? She worked the Great Northern line between here and Butte."

"Yes, I know that."

"Huh, spit on my boy. You ain't nothing but the son of a whore. Weren't for shits like Tommy, shits like you would be out of work. You're all a bunch of crooks."

Again the preacher stopped, more baffled than shocked.

"All right," Mr. Carroll told him, "that's enough preaching. Throw him in the ground and let's get the hell out of here." He waved at the young girl. "Kiss the box good-bye, dolly." The old man reached in his pocket. "Here, Preacher, take two dollars for your troubles."

Mrs. Tommy Carroll knelt in the muck. In a poignant tableau she kissed her fingertips and touched the casket. She's pretty, Grover thought. Nothing is quite as beautiful as brides and widows.

"I hope they bury that shit newspaper of yours deeper than they buried my shit boy," the old man told him walking away.

The gravediggers attached a rope to the casket. The cop led the grieving widow down the hill. The preacher was gone.

Grover marched through the blustery rain to a humble hillside called Soldier's Rest, where simple headstones resembled milestones of the ancient world. The grass seemed greener, the trees taller and bold. Here were buried old soldiers who battled the Chippewa near Sunrise River, who fought their American brothers at Shiloh and Gettysburg. In fresher graves rested veterans of the Spanish-American War. For a wedding gift, Grover's ex-father-in-law gave him a plot here. The lousy bastard.

"Wrap me in old newspapers," Grover Mudd wished on Soldier's Rest, "and bury me in a field of dandelions on a sunny day."

The Great Debate

Homer Van Meter followed the river by the Ford plant and stuck his arm out the coupé window in mock salute. "Best getaway car in America," the grateful gangster shouted. He swung down the muddy road to the Hollyhocks Club. Baby Face Nelson was with him. The afternoon sky was stormy. It would be raining soon.

"Getaway," Nelson scoffed. "You got my best friend killed."

"Tommy hated your guts."

"If I'd been there, there'd been feds splattered all over the street."

"If you'd been there we'd all be dead." Homer Van Meter parked in front of the club and shut off the engine. A limousine was the only car out front. His crotch hurt. He squeezed his zipper.

"So what do you want with Rankin?" Nelson asked.

"Maybe he can help us."

"Yeah, he'll help us split our loot. That dickless bastard takes a fifty-percent cut right off the top. Besides, I heard he ran to Florida."

"He's back."

"That's where we should be. Florida. Sunshine. Women."

"We're going to Wisconsin," Van Meter reminded him.

"Wisconsin," grumbled Nelson. "What are we suppose to dick there?"

"Frogs. It'll be a step up for you. Wait here." Van Meter got out of the car and hobbled into the club.

On the third floor of the Hollyhocks Club Dag Rankin sat at his desk and tried to wipe a headache from his brow. The Big Holy Spook went bellowing out the office door and down the stairs. Damnations shook the house. Rankin looked over at a skeleton hanging in the corner and wondered if Jesse James ever had trouble finding good help.

The information Rankin had been impatiently waiting for, the girl's name he had been wanting for months, was in front of him. The newspapers were pasted with the shooting of Tommy Carroll, like the pieces of a puzzle magically gluing themselves together. He now understood why such information was so hard to come by. He at least had Grover Mudd, if not the *Frontier News*, by the neck. Now all he needed was a knife. In his own righteous way the Big Holy Spook turned down the job, but their kind always stuck together. Then the puzzle continued to work its magic. Homer Van Meter knifed through the door.

"Christ, he almost saw me. That crazy nigger tried to kill me one night down at Nina Clifford's. Do you know him?"

"He works for me," said Rankin, unpleasantly surprised by his visitor. "He keeps tabs on Nina, among other chores. With my generous offerings he hopes to build his own little chapel one day."

"That preacher's a lunatic," Van Meter said, closing the door. He approached Rankin's desk with the trepidation of a job applicant. He brushed his coat clean and polished his shoes on the backs of his pant legs. "My name is Homer Van Meter. We kinda met at a party last year. The big Thanksgiving bash on Lake Phalen." He stuck out his hand.

"I know who you are." Rankin ignored the twitching hand over his desk. He scribbled doodles across the

Frontier News. "You and your boys sure are making a mess of things. There used to be rules in this town."

"Yes, sir, Mr. Rankin, and we stuck by them rules, but St. Paul ain't safe no more. It's crawling with G-men, and now there's that election coming up."

"Where's Dillinger?"

"Minneapolis. Some doc fixed up his leg. Nothing serious."

"He won't be safe over there."

"Right. One of the boys knows of a resort up in the north woods. We're going there soon as J.D. is feeling better."

"So what do you want from me?"

Van Meter didn't know what to do with his hands. He buried them in his pockets. He folded them in front of him. He scratched his crotch. He avoided looking Dag Rankin in the eyes, focusing instead on the skeleton in the corner. "Looks like a doctor's office," he said snickering. "Whose bones?"

"Charlie Pitts."

"What's a Charlie Pitts?"

"Charlie was one of the James Gang. He bought it in the Northfield raid," Rankin explained. "Posse put a hole right through his chest. See where the bones are broken there? They packed his body on ice and put him on display at the State Capitol. People lined up for blocks to see him. Then he got sold to a doctor who wanted the skeleton." Rankin laughed at the thought of it. "Anyway, I picked him up at an auction and brought him home. Might be there's a lesson in that story for you and your friend Dillinger."

Homer Van Meter stared hard at the skeleton. "No, I don't think that's gonna happen to us."

"Well, I'm not going to debate it with you. What do you want from me?"

"My dick needs fixing."

"What?"

"It's syphilis," Van Meter blurted out. "They say it

drives you crazy. They say Capone's got it. I read in a newspaper that you got kind of the same problem. So I was thinking maybe you know some doctors. Like they say, that Mayo Clinic can do miracles but it costs lots of money. We've got some big jobs lined up, so I was thinking maybe we could help each other."

Rankin's head boiled. His face caught fire. He stood and limped slowly around the desk. Van Meter held his ground. Dag Rankin reached up and delivered a sharp backhand to Van Meter's jaw that sent him sprawling across the floor to the corner, where Charlie Pitts kicked him in the face. Rankin stepped up and kicked him in the ass. The floored gangster reached into his pocket and drew his gun. He pointed it up at Rankin. Homer Van Meter's eyes wept with humiliation.

Dag Rankin knew the feeling. He thought fast and disarmed him with a smile. "What are you going to do, Homer, blow my balls off?"

Outside, the sky looked ominous. Baby Face Nelson was leaning on the horn. The seconds ticked by. Van Meter eased up. He lowered the gun and grinned. Dag Rankin reached out a hand and helped the hapless gangster to his feet. Rankin was still smiling. Homer Van Meter smiled. Charlie Pitts was smiling.

"I think I can solve your problem, Mr. Van Meter. Modern medicine is wonderful," Rankin said limping back to his desk. "They cured me, but it was expensive."

"You got all cured? At that Mayo Clinic, right? I can get you the money."

"You really aren't my style, but perhaps we can work something out."

"I'd do anything if you could help me."

"Anything?"

"Anything, Mr. Rankin."

Dag Rankin picked up a copy of the *Frontier News* and once again checked the St. Albans Street address.

"I think the first thing we should do is take care of that nigger bitch that set up our friend Tommy Carroll."

———————

Jory Ricci rode his big red bicycle down Payne Avenue to the edge of Swede Hollow. The streets were bumpy and full of sand. Repair crews were patching the potholes. In the rusty wire basket over the handle bars was a clean shirt in which the boy had wrapped a can of chicken noodle soup and a bottle of Coca-Cola. He was running away from home. The clouds in the sky were daunting and the air was cool, but the snow was gone. Thick white smoke billowed out of Hamm's towering stack. Jory watched a train rumble through the brewery. He watched trucks loaded with beer join the late-afternoon traffic. The mansion on the hill across the way looked haunted.

The boy was sick of being in trouble. Being in a class with younger kids was humiliating. His days in school were spent standing in the cloak hall. The rules at his grandmother's house were choking him. His mother had taken an evening job at a department store downtown. Some times Jory would wake up late at night and see his father standing at the door. Other times machine-gun fire shot through his dreams.

Phalen Creek was high and fast. The banks were squalid. The trees were still bare. The brush was dead and yellow. Wet winter garbage stretched down the hillside. The shanties were crumbling. Jory thought he might hide in the hollow, but there were rats down there and stories about bums living in the woods. He could go live in the caves along the tracks, but there were the Kendrigan twins. They had gone to play on the tracks. Running away was much easier to plan than it was to do.

She came from behind him like a blond breeze, sweet-smelling and fresh, and smiled at him in the kindest way. The prettiest woman he'd ever seen. If she had wings she would be what an angel must look like. She swept by him to the edge of the ravine. Jory watched her zigzag down to the tracks, then down the stairs carved into the hill to the creek. She wore nice clothes. When she crossed a rickety bridge over the water and slipped in the muck Jory felt sorry and wanted to race down and help. Her slacks were filthy now and looked awful on such a beautiful lady. Jory got off his bike. The pretty lady wiped her hands like it didn't really matter and kept on going. She was easy to track through the hollow because her golden hair glowed like a beacon. Jory watched her navigate the oozy path along the creek until she came to a dirty white shack. She entered without knocking. He couldn't believe a heavenly beauty like that lived down there.

Jory climbed back on his bike and debated whether to go on. He heard a car backfire. He remembered skating with his father. The stormy sky looked deathly. A raindrop slapped his face. Jory Ricci pedaled home.

Grover Mudd hopped off the University Avenue trolley at Snelling. It was the night of the great debate. Searchlights swept the evening sky. Traffic was bumper to bumper. An illuminated banner over Liberty Hall read MAHONEY VS. GEHAN. Cops guarded the door. The big clock hanging from Midway State Bank read eight-ten. Grover was late.

If Seven Corners downtown was the most chaotic intersection west of Chicago, then the intersection of Snelling and University avenues, in the heart of St. Paul's Midway District, was the busiest. At this intersection twenty lanes of automobile and trolley traffic came together at an eyesore of used-car lots, drugstores, branch banks, and Montgomery Ward. It was joked that more Minnesotans were killed at Snelling and University than were killed in Europe during the Great War.

A large crowd smothered the entrance to Liberty
Hall. They were blocking the sidewalk and spilling into
the street. Signs touting the virtues of the two candidates were waved enthusiastically over heads. Much of
the sidewalk was torn up for repairs. A hard afternoon
rain left small lakes in the gutters where the sewers had
backed up. Raindrops were still dripping from store-
window awnings.

Grover waded into the sea of people only to hear the
cops yell there was no more room inside. They ordered
the revelers away from the door. Shouts of disappointment and anger cut the festivities. Grover reached for
his press pass and tried to squeeze his way forward but
caught a sharp elbow in the chest and fell backward
into the bunch. He was shoved again as things turned
ugly.

A rope was thrown over a street lamp, and a dummy
of Mayor Mahoney was hoisted into the air to hang in
effigy. Minutes later another dummy was strung up on
an adjacent lamp. But it wasn't Mark H. Gehan. It was
Walt Howard. Somebody put a match to the newspaper
feet and the editor's pants went up in flames amidst a
cacophony of cheers and outrage.

Grover Mudd put away his press pass. Again he tried
pushing his way to the door. This time a hand reached
out and grabbed his coat collar and jerked him backward, choking him. Grover snapped. He turned and
shoved the stranger violently into the crowd. A sharp
blow felled his shoulders. Someone was beating him
with a MAHONEY FOR MAYOR sign. Grover was on the
ground, his breath already gone. He covered his head
from the jungle of legs tripping over him. He heard a
woman crying.

Grover rammed through the bedlam on his knees.
He repeatedly tried to stand but the belligerent crush
kept him down. He reached the edge of the mob only
to be tripped into a flooded gutter. What little wind he
could hold in his lungs was again knocked out of him.

One leg got soaked. Getting to his feet, he lost a shoe in the water but did not bother looking for it. In the bright light he saw chunks of concrete flung at Liberty Hall. A brilliant flash whitened the night, a searchlight exploding with the noise of a bomb. Grover cupped his ears. Glass rained down on him like hail. The world was a shade darker.

Grover was dizzy. He stumbled to the end of the block and clung to a police callbox. He felt like vomiting. The taste of blood ringed his mouth. His throat was fire hot. From the corner of Snelling he gazed down University Avenue at a horde of screwballs gone wild. Mahoney supporters stomping on Gehan voters. Backers of Gehan flailing away at Mahoney campaign workers. Cops, swinging billy clubs, skirted the rabble. Sirens were screaming in the distance. On a billboard, overlooking the riotous intersection, a smiling baker was holding up a loaf of Taystee Bread, double wrapped, sliced or plain. Grover Mudd needed a drink.

Travel on the avenues was impossible now. The popping colors of the traffic lights meant nothing. Car doors were flung open where drivers had entered the fight. Others cowered behind their steering wheels. Grover limped to a pedestrian island in the middle of the street. He bent over and rested. When he looked up again he saw a searchlight sweep past the Winnipeg Tavern. He'd heard of it. Everybody'd heard of it.

It was a basement club. Grover crept down the narrow stairs and sat near the bottom. He felt near death. His shoulders ached. His clothes were wet. Tiny nuggets of glass clung to his hair. The ankle above his bare foot was swelling. Breathing was difficult. Suddenly, a pair of bare tits was in his face, as in a bad sex dream.

"I have an extra drink here," the waitress said. "It's gin. You look like you could use it."

"I hate gin," Grover wheezed.

"Take it. No charge." She handed him the drink and bounced away.

The gin tasted terrible, but felt good going down. Grover wiped the water from his eyes. He lit a cigarette, leaned back on the stairs, and waited for his breath to catch up with him. The dingy tavern had a cement floor that looked sticky black. The lighting was yellow and dim. Through the smoke Grover could see a creaky stage of two-by-fours and planks. Tables and chairs crowded out from there. A bar ran along the wall. Crates of Hamm's and Schmidt were stacked behind it. The window blocks just below the ceiling were boarded up. The stale air had nowhere to go. The place could handle a hundred people, and tonight it was teeming.

Some of the patrons looked on their last dime. Others were dressed to kill—the Buggs Palooka ilk and their outwardly sophisticated ladies. The climate was loud. The name of the game was drink, shout, and pound on the table.

Where the corner of the bar met the corner of the stage two cops were standing in full uniform, their caps cocked forward. One was scrawny and unshaven. The other was huge. Grover recognized him as Emil Gunderson, the big cop who'd slapped the subpoena on Walt Howard's desk, who put the boot to Jory Ricci. A muscular German shepherd was at his feet. No leash.

A stubby comedian in a shamrock-green suit was winding up his act on stage. "What does the perfect woman look like?" he asked in a high staccato voice. He answered himself. "About three feet tall, no teeth, and a flat head to set your beer on." The tavern shook with laughter. The stubby joker took his bows, dodged some peanuts, and leaped off stage. The next act leaped on. The crowd roared its approval.

The girls wore gray striped overalls, buckled over their bare shoulders, the kind of clothes Grover's father spent his life in. Stripper number one was a tall redhead with a sharp nose—not pretty, but not unpleasant to look at.

It was stripper number two who caught Grover. She

had honeysuckle hair with creamy white skin and a smile that glowed through the haze. Her brilliant green eyes had the innocent gleam of a young girl good enough to live next door to anybody.

Grover stood.

The girls danced to make-believe music and the unorganized drumroll of the drinkers. The buckles unsnapped, the bibs fell, four tits toppled out and flopped about. The redhead had the big tits. Honeysuckle's were high and pointed. It did not surprise Grover that Redhead Tits was going to shed every inch of clothing she had on in front of a Minnesota wolfpack, but the idea of Honeysuckle Tits doing it unsettled him. Not only was she going to strip, she seemed to be loving every second of it. A twinkle of joy showed in her eyes, her smile was real, and when her overalls hit the floor she swung her whole heart and soul into her wild hips and black panties.

Grover backed up a stair for a better view.

Now the beer bottles were clanging in unison. So were the girls. The panties slid down their legs in the slowest manner possible and were flung to the wolves. The athletic duo bent into an arched handstand and thrust their bushy cunts at the pack. When the howling subsided they landed on their feet. Redhead Tits stuck two fingers in her lips and whistled for help. Patrolman Gunderson grabbed his dog by the scruff of the neck and hoisted him on stage. The stripper rolled the German Shepherd on his back. The crowd cheered as she pointed out his sex. Honeysuckle Tits dropped to her knees between the dog's hind legs and grabbed his feet like a farmer grabbing a plow. The dog squirmed like a worm. The girl wet her lips with her long hooked tongue and turned her bright eyes on her fans as if debating the issue. Should she or shouldn't she? The answer came in pennies and nickels, hats, and a banana. The pack got to their feet and stomped the floor, their fists in the air. It was raining beer.

"Do it! Do it! Do it!"

Grover couldn't see. Didn't want to see. Didn't want to miss it. He backed up another stair and stood on his toes. His ankle ached. The brave police dog looked like a helpless puppy. The shepherd turned to his master for help, but none was forthcoming. Then Redhead Tits peeled the banana and a minute later the Winnipeg Tavern exploded in an orgasm of cheers. The exhibition beggared description. Sodom and Gomorrah at the height of their depravity boasted of nothing so vile. The dives of San Francisco's Barbary Coast and New York's old Bowery in their palmiest days had nothing so low. On the night of the great debate, in the watery eyes of Grover Mudd, the city of St. Paul reached the pinnacle of disgust.

———————

On the night of the great debate Stormy Day made her way from the back of the trolley, tears still in her eyes. She stepped off the Rondo–Stryker at St. Albans Street. It was late. The co-op store was closed. There were no groceries in the house. Brody was with neighbors. She worried about not being a good mother. How would she be able to raise two children? Again, shame overcame her and tears rolled down her face. She hurried south, toward home.

It was a cool and spooky night. In the distance the illuminated domes of Saint Paul's Cathedral shone through big black trees, their naked branches clawing at a howling breeze that still had a winter bite to it. The sidewalks were wet, creating eerie shadows. Stormy had to hurry before the street lamps went out. She walked with the fear women walk with after dark. But it wasn't gangsters she was afraid of. It was God.

In her heart Stormy Day really believed she was a good person, but she did bad things, or maybe bad things just happened to her.

The woman at work said it would be safe and easy,

and that it was the right thing to do. She'd be run out
of St. Paul as fast as she'd been run out of St. Louis.
So earlier that evening Stormy scraped the money together and went over to the address she was given.

It was a big, ugly house off Trunk Highway 12 on the
East Side. A pretty school building was lit up across
the street and Stormy could imagine children playfully
marching to class. All she knew of the neighborhood
was that Indians were buried somewhere nearby. She
knocked at the back door and gave the name she was
told to give. The man said he was a doctor and asked
her to wait in his office. But it wasn't a doctor's office.
It was a backroom off a back alley, and he wasn't a real
doctor, he was just a pin artist. When he left the room
Stormy Day got down from the table and ran.

She would go to the cathedral in the morning. She
would look into the great dome and pray. She couldn't
go through with it, and if God was fair he would have
to take that into consideration with her plea for for-
giveness. She crossed the deserted street to Holcombe
Park, upset and scared.

Facing her at the edge of the park was a car parked
on the wrong side of the street. She thought she saw a
skinny shadow behind the wheel. Stormy hurried by.
She was only two blocks from home. She heard the car
door open and close, then the shuffle of footsteps behind
her. She didn't turn around. Now she was scared to
death. She walked even faster.

In St. Louis they had been wrong. They said the child
she was bearing was a thing of shame. Dark shame.
But Brody was the most important thing in her life.
Her life had little meaning until he was born, in St.
Paul. She wanted to get home, get to the neighbors,
give him a kiss and hug him, wrap him in her arms. But
now God was hinting that wasn't going to happen, and
she was more frightened than she'd ever been in her
life. The footsteps were right behind her. The wind and
the trees were making a terrible noise. She questioned

how God could be so cruel. She said a prayer for her little boy. Then the lights went out on St. Albans Street. The cross atop the cathedral's dome looked like a star in the sky that was shining down on her. Stormy Day wiped the tears from her eyes. She stopped and turned. "Grover?"

Saint Stormy

It always rains when someone you love dies. Grover Mudd limped out of the elevator and into the newsroom. "What's news, Fuzzy?" He removed his trench coat and shook off the raindrops as he headed for his corner.

Fuzzy Byron followed him with crumpled bulletins. "Feds arrested a Minneapolis doctor for treating John Dillinger. They think he's still around town. Ten anticrime bills were approved by the House of Representatives and now head for the Senate where swift approval is expected. It'll be a federal crime to assault or kill a federal officer, to rob a federal bank, and to flee from one state to another to avoid prosecution. FBI will have new powers, including the right to carry arms at any time. Also, J. Edgar Hoover is sending Assistant Director Hugh Clegg to St. Paul to take charge of the office here."

"What else?"

"Locally, somebody stood up at the City Council meeting and made a motion that the city's name be changed back to Pig's Eye. Mahoney and Gehan blame each other for last night's riot."

"Is that it?"

"One more item, kind of fuzzy here. A couple of kids spearing for carp found the body of a negro girl floating in the river off Harriet Island. She may have jumped off the High Bridge."

"Who was she?"

"No I.D. yet, but she had on a maid uniform like they wear at the hotels."

A spear ripped through Grover's heart. His face paled. "Where's the body now?"

"Down at the morgue. Where else?"

Grover muttered something inaudible and left Fuzzy Byron holding the news. He walked gravely into his office, tossed his coat at a hook on the wall, and slouched into his chair. What were the odds? She was at work. He would call her. They were not allowed to receive calls. He could walk up there. She would think he was being silly. Grover watched the raindrops splatter against the window. Then he darted out of the office and tore through the newsroom. The elevator was too slow. He took the stairs.

When he hit the street the wind and rain intensified. The first thunder of spring rumbled over the bluffs. He'd forgotten his coat. It was cold. Grover hurried over to Kellogg Boulevard and dodged traffic to Steep Street, where he limped down the hill, past a line of rusty police cars. At Washington Street he slowed to a brisk walk to save his breath. Nina Clifford's house was dark but he thought he saw a curtain move. Grover put a hand to his chest and hustled up the stairs and through the front door of the Ramsey County Morgue. He was coughing as he approached the front desk.

A sloppy-looking fat boy was leaning back in his chair with a Montgomery Ward catalogue on his lap; the catalogue was open to women's undergarments. He looked up at Grover and waited for him to stop coughing. "Still raining?"

"Is the coroner in? Bjorkland's his name, isn't it?"

"Doc's busy. What do you want?"

"My name is Grover Mudd. I'm with the *Frontier News*."

"No shit? You're Grover Mudd?"

"Can you tell the doctor I'd like to talk to him?"

"Oh, yeah, he'd like to talk to you."

The fat boy got up and walked to the hallway. Grover followed. It was a long, narrow hall with bare light bulbs that hung from the ceiling by electric cords. Grover stood at the end of the checkerboard floor and waited as the fat boy shouted his way along.

"Hey, Doc, Grover Mudd is here from the newspaper. You remember? He wrote that story about the crook with no wiener. And about people peeing in Phalen. And about that monkey at Como Zoo that was hard for a month. Remember? You said it was impossible."

A gruff voice barked in the office. "He's here?"

"Yeah. Grover Mudd," the fat boy answered.

The county coroner stepped into the hall. He was a short, portly fellow, and it was obvious to Grover the overblown boy and he were related. The stubby coroner waddled down the hall with an outstretched arm. "So, you're Mudd. Doc Bjorkland here."

"Call me Grover."

"Oh, sure, Grover." They shook hands. "Me and the little lady get the *North Star* at home, but we read the *Frontier* here at the shop. Say, you boys aren't going to fold up on us, are you?"

"It's pretty much day-to-day now."

"A shame to hear that." Doc Bjorkland reached up, put his arm around Grover's shoulder, and spoke in hushed tones. "Let me give you some advice here, Mudd. I'd tell Mr. Howard to stop with the front-page stuff. I know it sells newspapers, but it's not going to change things. Believe me. I've been cutting up stiffs in this town for thirty years. You're just going to make a lot of the wrong people mad." He slapped Grover on the back and became his jovial self again. "But then you've cut up a few people yourself, haven't you?" The coroner let out a good laugh as they moved down the hall. "Now, what can I do for you, Mudd?"

"It's Grover. I was told there was a girl brought in today that jumped off the High Bridge."

"That colored girl? She's no jumper. Somebody strangled her. Threw her in the river. Like those Kendrigan twins last summer, only I figure this was kind of like a copycat murder. Not nearly as clean. Didn't break the neck. No sand. From the markings on the body I'd say her killer was awful weak or she put up one hell of a fight. You can quote me on that, Grover. My name's been in the paper lots of times but folks don't always know how to pronounce it. It's like New York. Beeyork. Bjorkland. My people came over from Sweden. Maybe you can take a paragraph to explain that."

"I'll see your name is spelled right."

"Yeah, too bad it's a colored girl. White girl, you'd have a big story on your hands."

"Can I quote you on that?"

"What? That a joke?"

"Can I see the body?"

"Oh, sure, Grover. I got her downstairs on a corner slab. I try to keep the darkies separate. Don't want the white meat complaining." He belted out another laugh as they started down a flight of stairs at the end of the hall.

In the basement Doc Bjorkland ushered Grover into a side room. "Now this here is our waiting room, Grover. We've fixed it up real nice for the bereaved. I'll wheel the corpus delicti down to this window in the hallway and that's where you view it, from behind the glass there. That's the procedure. Don't you want to take notes on this, Grover?"

"No, I think I'll remember."

"I'll give you a holler when I'm ready." The coroner disappeared.

The room was depressing. The walls were grimy green and badly stained. Electric cords poked through the plaster and ran along the floor. A Red Cross poster of Clara Barton was taped next to the door. A Bible lay on a small table, along with an ashtray and a pitcher of water with a dead cockroach floating in it. Grover lit a cigarette. Years on the paper and he'd never been to the morgue. He picked up the Bible and wondered if there was anything in it worth reading. His shirt was wet. He had the chills. He was starting to sweat. The doc called his name. Grover Mudd put the Scriptures back on the table and stepped into the hall.

"No smoking out here, Grover."

Grover turned back to the room and shot his cigarette at the roach in the water then walked down the hall to the viewing window.

On the other side of the glass Doc Bjorkland stood over the white sheet that covered the body on the porcelain table. Behind him was a basement window. The rain was coming down hard. Three bare light bulbs hung low over the display table and caused Grover to squint. The stench of formaldehyde nauseated him. Then he saw it. A foot sticking out of the sheet.

Spider toes

Grover came unnerved. The aching pain marched up his back. He told himself they all had toes like that.

"This is her, Grover." The coroner pulled back the sheet.

Her nappy hair was matted and filled with sludge. Her face was bloated, the neck twisted. Her once-beautiful black skin was ash gray; the eyes were swollen closed. Dead people were supposed to look at peace. Stormy Day did not look peaceful. Stormy looked murdered. Grover pressed his hands and face to the window and closed his eyes.

Don't run, Grover

"Your first stiff?" The coroner's voice was muffled by the glass. "You probably don't want to see the rest of her, then. It happens. Actually, she had a pretty face for a colored girl."

Don't run, Grover

He opened his eyes and took another look.

Doc Bjorkland kept talking. "There's something else.

Don't know if you want to print this. It's really a double homicide. This bitch was pregnant."

Grover ran. He stumbled up the basement stairs and down the hall to the front door, where he burst into the rain, slipped on the stairs, and tumbled to the sidewalk. Grover picked himself up. His hands were badly scraped. At Nina Clifford's an old whore was watching him from the bay window. He tripped his way to the corner and up Steep Street past the police station. At Kellogg Boulevard he did not stop for cars. A taxi braked for him and skidded sideways toward City Hall. Grover shoved off the hood and jumped to the curb as the horn sounded. He ran down the parking lot where Father Galtier's poor little church had once stood. The next four blocks were a downhill blur. Grover fought to keep his balance across Jackson Street, past the post-office building, across Sibley Street and under the Union Depot walkway, across Wacouta and Broadway, oblivious to the traffic and weather. By the time he reached the foot of the Third Street Bridge his clothes were soaked, his chest was caving in, his throat was swallowing nails, breath was almost impossible to come by. But Grover ran, ran up the walk and onto the bridge that spanned the railroad yard where his father once drove the locomotives. It was a quarter-mile long and straight uphill to the bluffs of the East Side. Blinding cracks of lightning illuminated the black clouds. The last rays of daylight disappeared from the noon sky. He ran from street lamp to street lamp until thunder rocked the span and sent him crashing to the railing. Cars bounced over potholes and drenched his feet with muck. In his mind he could hear the Big Holy Spook shouting, "The time has come! The time has come!"

Grover Mudd kept running, up the bridge to Mound Boulevard. He glanced down at the shrinking city, then ran on, higher and higher, along the boulevard to Bluff Playground. The football field was ankle-deep in slop. He splashed across it and wanted to keep on going but

his body would not let him. Grover wrapped his arms
around the goalpost and collapsed. His chest and throat
opened up. He gagged and choked. He threw up blood.
A barrage of thunder shook the earth. Rockets of lightning lit up the sky. The rain washed his face clean.
Grover hugged the goalpost and pulled himself up. He
caught his second wind and ran.

He staggered across Plum Street and Cherry Street
and into Indian Mound Park. He lurched over the bluff
that housed the cave where the Great Spirit dwelled.
His legs and chest begged him to stop. Again he turned.
The city was shrinking below him. Higher he climbed,
through the park to the first Indian mound. It was the
smallest of the graves and he faltered around it and fell
off the retaining wall to the road. Grover got up. He
tripped over the gravel to the wall on the other side.
Before him stood the largest mound in the park. Tears
streamed down his face with the rain. Blood spewed
from his mouth. His hands were cracked and red. His
legs had nothing left. The ghostly mound loomed before
him like a mountain. Children used it as a place to play.
A swath of mud rolled over the top. Grover stepped
on the grave and dropped. Faces swirled in the
puddles—black-faced Stormy, red-faced twins, baby-
faced soldiers dying in a trench.

Grover wormed his way to the top of the mound and
rested there on all fours like a wounded animal. He
was as high as a man could climb in St. Paul. He looked
to the city below, the cathedral, the capitol, City Hall,
the *Frontier News*, the *North Star Press*, silhouettes in
the storm. When lightning split the dark the bridges
were skeletons across the water. Tugboats pushed
empty barges up the river. Trains chugged along the
tracks, undaunted by the weather. Grover struggled to
his feet and wavered in the wind. What strength he
could muster he put in his voice. "Goddamn you," he
wheezed. "God damns every one of you," he roared.
He fell backward and tumbled down the mound, and

facedown at the bottom he beat his fist into the mud. "God damns every one of you," he wept out.

Then heavenly voices whispered in his ear. "It's Saint Mudd you really hate."

"Shut up," Grover cried.

"All she wanted was to be taken to a Clark Gable movie."

I understand, Grover

"Shut up," he ordered the voices.

"All she wanted was to eat at a fancy restaurant with lots of candles."

I understand, Grover

He covered his ears. "Shut up!"

Safe it ain'ts in the city of gangsters and saints

"SHUT UP! SHUT UP! SHUT UP!"

A torrent of rain swept over the park. And Grover Mudd cried himself sick at the foot of the ancient Indian graves.

Saint Elmo

In the Sunday edition of the *Frontier News*, Special Agent Steff Koslowski read about the murder of the pretty hotel maid. He remembered how frightened she had been, how cooperative she was, how rudely they had treated her. He noted the cause of death and ripped the article from the paper.

Steff had been looking forward to his first weekend off in months, but it was such a rotten day—cold, windy, and wet—he wasn't upset when the phone rang that morning and he was summoned to headquarters. Every agent assigned to St. Paul was crowded into the basement of the Federal Courts Building. There was not enough space for them in the boiler room, which doubled as a conference room, so they filed into the hallway and gathered at the foot of the stairs.

Assistant Director Hugh Clegg, now in charge of the St. Paul office, was a stocky, muscular man who might have been more comfortable barking orders on the sideline of a football field. He stepped up the stairs to speak and the G-men fell silent. Mr. Clegg waved a crumpled map in his hands. "Melvin Purvis phoned me from our Chicago office. He has reliable information that John Dillinger and his gang are holed up at a lakefront lodge called Little Bohemia in northern Wisconsin, about two hundred miles from here. Gang members at the lodge have been tentatively identified as John Dillinger, Homer Van Meter, George 'Baby Face' Nelson, and two to four unknowns, plus girlfriends. Mr.

Purvis has chartered two planes. His teams will be leaving within the hour. Two more teams are driving up from Chicago. With such short notice I've only been able to get my hands on one plane. It can take seven of us. We're leaving only a skeleton crew here. The rest of you will be driving there. The closest town is called Rhinelander, fifty miles south of the lodge. We rendezvous at the airfield there. Coulter, Knowles, Wellmen, and Koslowski, I want you on the plane with me. You've got shootout experience."

Fly? As the other agents rounded up weapons and ammunition, Steff Koslowski made his way to the assistant director. "Mr. Clegg, sir, I've never flown before." He stumbled for the right words. "What I mean is, sir, I've done extensive driving for the bureau and my talents may be more attuned to the wheel of an automobile."

Mr. Clegg squeezed his shoulder in a fatherly manner. "You're coming with me, Steff. You'll love it."

Special Agent Koslowski put his hand to his belly and once again swallowed his breakfast.

St. Paul's Holman Field was on the wayward side of the river. The G-men sped across the Robert Street Bridge and slid to a halt at the hangar. The dispiriting drizzle continued to fall. If the sun had been shining and he'd had time for sightseeing Steff might have noticed how wide the river was at this point, or how tall the bluffs of the East Side really were. But his attention was drawn to the aircraft on the runway, a lumbering high-wing monoplane with the name ELMO painted on the fuselage. The pilot, a fortyish heavy-set fellow with a wet, grizzly beard, was wiping grease from his hands. He was wearing a flight jacket and a skipper's hat. To Steff he looked like a broken-down version of the assistant director, who ran up and introduced himself. A few words were exchanged, then Hugh Clegg waved his team over.

"This is our pilot, Ivar Dorn," Mr. Clegg announced.

"Mr. Dorn says there's only room in the cabin for six. Steff, since this is your maiden voyage, you can ride up in the co-pilot's seat. Let's go, men."

Everything was happening so fast Steff had no time to argue. They removed the weapons from the cars and threw them in the plane. Steff crawled through the cabin to the cramped cockpit.

The pilot extended his stubby hand. "Name's Ivar."

"Steff Koslowski, how do you do." He shook his hand.

"You a Polack?"

The agent sighed. "Of Polish descent. Chicago."

"Well, set your ass in here, Chicago, and don't touch anything."

"It doesn't look like very good flying weather," Steff complained, squeezing into the seat. "Don't you think we should wait?"

"Naa. Old *Elmo*'ll fly through anything."

"Can you fly above the rain? I've heard of that."

"What do you think this is, a spaceship? Besides, *Elmo* don't like high altitudes."

"Just out of curiosity, who was old *Elmo* here named after?"

"Saint Elmo, patron saint of pilots. He'll be smiling over us."

Steff watched with a nervous stomach as Dorn's fat fingers worked the instruments. The engine sputtered, then rumbled into gear. The pilot reached into his coat for a bottle of whiskey and downed a swig. He offered the bottle to Steff.

"No thanks," Steff told him. "Isn't that moonshine?"

"Sure is," said Ivar Dorn, capping the bottle. "New legal stuff taste like pony piss."

"Where do you get it? Not that we care anymore."

Pilot Dorn pointed across the river. "Do you see that big cathedral up there on the hill? That's the only place in St. Paul you *can't* get moonshine whiskey." They wheeled down the runway. "Strap yourself in, Chicago, we're taking off."

"Already?" Steff pulled on the safety belt until he couldn't breathe and grabbed the bouncing seat. They rolled down the strip faster than he could ever remember moving, lifted into the air, and sailed over the river higher than he'd ever been before. He stared down at the dark Mississippi and for the moment was captivated by the chunks of ice racing downstream.

Then Pilot Dorn brought him out of it. "Uh-oh, we must be heavier than I thought."

The airplane tilted left and the frightened G-man was suddenly flying sideways. "Climb, *Elmo*, climb," he heard the pilot order. Steff saw the jagged cliffs of the East Side coming at him. He covered his eyes with both hands, lifted his feet and screamed, "Climb, *Elmo*, climb!"

Elmo leveled off, cleared the bluffs, darted between the trees of Indian Mound Park, skimmed a few roof-tops, then banked east through the rain.

The Chicago landlubber had always imagined flying to be like gliding on a cloud, a magic carpet ride, but this was worse than the potholes of St. Paul. If he didn't vomit out the window over the Gopher State he'd surely end up doing it over the Badger State.

"I figure we'll follow Twelve across the St. Croix," Pilot Dorn told him, "then veer north towards Rhinelander. Check the map and see what runs up that way."

Steff studied the smudgy map the pilot tossed in his lap. "This is a road map."

"Of course it is. How the hell you think we're gonna get there?"

"Don't you have charts and compasses and stuff like that?"

"Hey, you wanna fly it, mac? If not, stick your nose in that map and find Trunk Highway Twelve."

"Christ's sake, Lindbergh found Paris without a front window."

"Anybody can find Paris. Try and find Rhinelander, Wisconsin, in a rainstorm."

The cockpit was breezy and cold and chills set in as Steff tried to follow the lines on the map.

"A lot of guns back there," Dorn noted. "Who you boys after?"

"Can't say."

"Dillinger?"

"Can't say."

"I hope he gets away. Nothing personal."

"Doesn't this thing have a heater?"

"Waste of power."

They flew low, shot across the scenic St. Croix River, which divided Minnesota and Wisconsin, and soared over its tributaries. Steff could see massive scars along the banks, stubs of a thousand tree trunks and canyons of erosion, the sorry signature of the packed-up-and-left lumber industry.

"Most of the trees you see down there are second growth," Dorn said, educating his passenger. "Thirty years ago that land was naked as a jaybird. Lumberjacks stripped it like a whore, ran the logs down the tributaries to the St. Croix, then pushed them into the Mississippi at Point Douglas."

As they scurried north, large patches of snow appeared in the fields below. Then, further north, the snow disappeared beneath a lush forest. Fog shrouded the lakes and sifted through the evergreens. A slender ribbon of tar snaked through the woods. Steff Koslowski had never seen anything like it and could not help but wonder what barren South Dakota might have looked like from the air, or the streets of his own Windy City. Sometimes the blacktop would suddenly end and he would try to follow a naked path with the dirty map. After two hours his head was throbbing. Pilot Dorn punched his arm.

"That must be Rhinelander down there. Do you see anything that looks like an airfield?"

Steff squinted. "I don't see anything that looks like a town."

"There's the airfield."

"Where?"

"That strip of mud between the snow."

"You're going to land on that?"

"Grab your socks, Chicago, I'm putting down."

"You're joking?"

Old *Elmo* dropped out of the cold, rainy sky and bounced off the soggy earth three times before taking hold. The airplane ran the length of the field, spun twice and lost a wheel. The doors were kicked out and seven of J. Edgar Hoover's finest men scrambled into the woods for relief.

The train was supposed to whistle on its way through Moorhead but the locomotive roared by the station without a single shout. The bell above the boiler plate remained silent. The blazing headlight and the red marker lamp cut a rainbow through the midnight shower and Engine 3137 with its rolling stock rolled into the dark where the Red River raged.

Grover Mudd was at the bridge. It had been a bad winter of heavy snow, and spring came surprisingly early. When the downpour pushed the swollen river over the brink the center span got washed away. Grover built a blockade from crossties. While he tried hopelessly to ignite a torch the rails below his feet began to hum. The train was coming. He hustled down the tracks to the nearest crossing.

Dag Rankin and Roxanne Schultz were at the crossing, seated placidly in a waxy Studs Bearcat convertible. The top was down but it was not raining on them. Roxanne was sipping champagne, and there was a heavenly glow about her golden hair. Rankin leaned over the door. "Stand in front of the headlights, Mudd. He'll be able to see you better."

Grover edged into the light between the rails.

"I've got a package on that train, so you better stop him, or you're a dead man, Mudd."

Roxanne stood behind the windshield. "Saint Mudd, my brother had a cough like yours and he's dead now."

But it was the clamor of 3137 that weakened his knees. Grover waved frantically at the blinding light bearing down on him, but it did not slow. He jumped from its path, and the earsplitting locomotive bellowed by. Grover was up and running, running alongside the cab, faster than he'd ever run in his life. He was stung by the intense heat of the boiler and he felt the power of the driving wheels as they raced for the bridge. His father was asleep at the throttle, his puffy round face drooling over his belly, a dog-eared copy of *Jack London Stories* on his lap. Grover could smell his shaving spice and see the years of engine grease ground into his hands. His pin-striped cap cut into his gray sideburns. His trainman's overalls were frayed and faded.

"Wake up, Daddy. The bridge is out. Goddamn Red River floods every year. You told me so." The old engineer did not stir, and Grover Mudd could see his father slipping away. "Wake up, Daddy. My chest hurts and I can't run like I used to."

Grover fell behind, lost sight of his father. The coal tender passed him by and he found himself staggering beside the hopper cars. "Please wake up, Daddy. The bridge is out and there's nobody to see it."

Grover wheezed, stumbled, tumbled down an embankment and into the thicket. He got to his knees and watched the lighted passenger cars cruise by, and at the last window of the last car was Stormy Day with her delicate hands on the glass and her fair ebony face glistening behind raindrops. Her terrified eyes met his for the last time and a life filled with happiness whirled down the track and drowned in the night.

EXTRA! EXTRA!
GROVER MUDD'S FATHER KILLS 21
Lazy Engineer Falls Asleep at Throttle
55 Injured in Red River Railroad Tragedy

"Newspapers lie! Newspapers lie! Newspapers lie!"
Grover Mudd cried himself awake. He sat up in bed
and wiped the tears from his eyes. It was dark. He was
lost. What was the time? Was he at home? His memory
woke up. Grover Mudd had no home. Grover had a
room. An old nurse had ordered him to sleep. She left
him a small Bible and said she would be back. But
when? How long ago had she been there? Medicine
lined the nightstand, a bottle of green syrup, a jar of
camphor oil, gray chalky tablets, yellow pills, a sticky
spoon, half a glass of water. The sheets were wet from
head to foot. The pillow was soaked. He swung his feet
to the floor and dropped his head between his knees.
Nails tore at his lungs and spewed up his throat, but
there was no blood this time. His hands shook profusely
as he smoked. He could hear rain dancing on the avenue
below. His thoughts returned to the nightmare.

Every state has its legendary tycoon. Minnesota has
James J. Hill. His baronial, thirty-two-room, craggy red
sandstone mansion stands as a monument to success on
Summit Avenue across the street from the Cathedral
of Saint Paul. Legend has it the poor boy from Canada
came to Minnesota as a young man, rose to prominence
in the burgeoning transportation business, and built a
railroad. But he was not one of those robber barons.
Oh, heavens, no. He made his fortune with tremendous
foresight, wise planning, and good old-fashioned hard
work. His overriding concern was to provide better
transportation for the people of the Northwest. He
treated the men who built the Great Northern Railroad
fairly and compassionately, caring deeply for his employees, from the junior executives under his wing to
the colored porters serving the coaches. Like most leg-

ends, it's a crock of shit. As the farmers put it, "First
came the grasshoppers, then came Jim Hill."

Grover tossed the sheets and pillow aside and sunk
into the bare mattress. "Of course he fell asleep. He
was old before he reached middle age. You worked him
eighteen hours a day, you son-of-a-bitchin' robber
baron."

Solace came to the engineer's son when the Empire
Builder died a slow, crude, painful death. James J. Hill,
with all the money in the world, bled to death from
hemorrhoids. Not even the Mayo brothers, summoned
from their clinic in Rochester, could save his bloody
ass.

Grover Mudd folded his arms to squeeze away the
chills. He stared at the watermarked ceiling. Somewhere on the other side was everyone he had ever loved.
Never once had he knocked on that door on St. Albans
Street when she was not there. He closed his eyes and,
for the first time in years, whispered a prayer.

"Take care of her, Daddy. Please take care of her."

When the planes arrived from Chicago the agents were
seventeen strong. Melvin Purvis was there. Steff Koslowski had not seen him since his transfer to Sioux Falls.
He was a diminutive man, but tougher than the walls
of Leavenworth. He yielded command to Hugh Clegg.

Residents of Little Bohemia were still free to come
and go, and, throughout the summer-vacation land,
word that Dillinger's mob was staying at the lodge
spread like wildfire. The original raid was scheduled for
four A.M., but at the Rhinelander airfield, agents got
word the gangsters were leaving that night. The G-men
could not wait for the reinforcements driving up. In a
rush they commandeered three cars in town and set out
north on Route 51.

Steff got scrunched in the back seat of an overworked
Dodge, but before they covered twenty miles it broke

down. They crawled out and, with weapons in hand, hopped on the running boards of the other two cars and sped off. The rain turned to sleet. The old lumber road was a sheet of mud that splashed over Steff's feet and froze his toes. His hands were numb, it was difficult to hang on, and he was afraid that when it came time to pull the trigger of the shotgun he was carrying it would be physically impossible. Ten wild miles later that car broke down. Daylight was gone. The north wind whistled through the pines. Steff Koslowski and his fellow agents walked like statues to the only operable machine left and climbed aboard. Seventeen heavily armed men now rode in and on one V-8 Ford. Limited to ten miles per hour, it was after nine o'clock when they arrived at neighboring Birchwood Lodge and made final plans. Steff tossed his socks in the trash and scraped the icy muck from his shoes.

The G-men were told Little Bohemia sat right on the edge of Little Star Lake, which was anything but little. Since there were no boats out this time of the year, escape by water was impossible. A tavern highlighted e front of the lodge, but—this being a Sunday evening d the off season—business would be minimal. The an was simple: Surround the lodge on three sides and rce them out. When the shooting started the owner vas to usher family and customers to the basement.

The woodland that stretches across the north of Michigan, Wisconsin, and Minnesota is a wonderland of pristine beauty, divided into national forests, state parks, and majestic Indian reservations. Yet, because of its massive scope and density, it is some of the most treacherous land in America. At night it is a spooky land with no tolerance for the naïve.

The federal agents parked the car in a ditch off the road and crept through the woods toward Little Bohemia Lodge. Steff Koslowski led a team of four to the right flank. Then the worst that could happen happened. A pair of dogs in front of the lodge began bark-

ing. Nobody had said anything about dogs. Surprise was
gone. The G-men scurried through the trees to their
positions, but on his side of the lodge Steff tripped over
a barbed-wire fence. It ripped his coat and pant legs
and gashed the backs of his freezing hands. Nobody
had said anything about a fence.

At the same time as the dogs were barking and Steff
was swearing, five men appeared on the front porch.
They looked more curious than dangerous, but in the
dark it was impossible to tell if they were armed. Steff
could barely hear Hugh Clegg when he ordered them
to raise their hands. Perhaps the men on the porch did
not hear him either, or they arrogantly chose to ignore
the warning. Three of them strolled casually to a car
and jumped in. Steff faintly heard Purvis or Clegg order
them to stop, but the engine turned over and the car
began to roll. As the miserable G-man pulled the last
barb from his arm Mr. Clegg yelled, "Fire." That Steff
Koslowski heard loud and clear, and more out of anger
and frustration than duty he shouldered the shotgun
and blasted the car.

Every agent there must have felt the same way. In
seconds the machine was riddled. Two shadowy figures
stumbled out the doors and collapsed. A third man
disappeared below the shattered windshield. The two
men left on the porch ducked inside and an army of
gunfire poured out of Little Bohemia Lodge.

The shooting seemed to come from every window.
Steff pumped shells into the windows nearest him. From
the barrages being laid down from inside it was obvious
the gang had as much firepower as the agents, and Steff
knew from experience the gangsters would utilize every
slug. A constant stream of bullets whistled over his head
and ricocheted through the forest. His adrenaline
flowed, his body thawed, and every tiny misery was
forgotten as he returned fire at will. This is what being
a G-man was all about. At long last he felt like a comic-
book hero.

The heaviest part of the gun battle was over in minutes but potshots continued off and on for hours, though it was often difficult to tell who was doing the shooting. Tear gas was lobbed through the windows. When it became apparent the gangsters were not coming out the G-men settled in for a vigil. Hugh Clegg sent two men back to Birchwood Lodge to call Rhinelander and check on the progress of the agents driving from Chicago and St. Paul.

The rain stopped and the temperature dropped. An eerie pall fell over the north woods. Stars began peeking through the clouds. Throughout the long night Steff could hear the wounded men near the rattled car groan for help. With three of them down out front and Little Bohemia blown to pieces, he reasoned most of the Dillinger gang was dead or dying. Then one of the wounded in the driveway cried out for his mother in a childlike voice and Steff Koslowski had the most disturbing, most frightening thought of his life. He closed his mind to it and fired another useless shot into the lodge.

At dawn the agents driving up from Chicago and St. Paul arrived and blocked the roads. Tear gas pouring out of the lodge had every man in the woods choking. Mr. Clegg ordered a cease-fire. Minutes later a voice was heard inside. "If you'll stop your dad-blame shooting we'll come out." Two frightened men appeared on the porch with their hands held high. Tears were streaming down their bloated red faces.

At the same time a pickup truck slammed to a halt behind the front line. The haggard man who jumped out was as worn as the agents, his face ashen white, his hands trembling. "The raid was supposed to be at four A.M.," he cried. "Look what you've done to my home."

"Who are you?" demanded Purvis.

"Emil Wanatka. This is my lodge, everything I have in the world. And now what are you doing to my bartenders?"

"Those aren't Dillinger's men?" asked Hugh Clegg of the two men on the porch.

"Of course not," answered the distraught owner. "Dillinger escaped hours ago. They shot your men down at Birchwood Lodge and stole the car. I thought you knew. The whole gang is running loose. There's been shooting all night from here to Rhinelander."

"You're crazy," screamed Purvis. "They're in that cabin, goddammit."

"No, they're not," one of the bartenders blurted out. "Their girlfriends are crying in the basement but the men jumped out the back windows last night."

Hugh Clegg pointed at the ambushed car. "Then who in God's name is bleeding all over the drive?"

Emil Wanatka crept over to the car. The agents cautiously followed.

"These boys are from the CCC camp. My God, what have you men done?"

Steff Koslowski was sick. He rubbed the sting from his eyes and looked inside the car. The lodge owner was right. A boy, maybe eighteen, was sprawled across the front seat in a pair of muddy overalls. Blisters showed on his outstretched palms. Steff could picture him at the camp with a shovel in his hands and a wide grin across his face, proud to be a part of the New Deal. But the G-men shattered his dream along with his forehead.

The shaken agent made his way through the silver birches to the back of the lodge, only to find it did not drop into the water as they had been told. Little Bohemia was a good thirty yards from the huge lake, with a steep bank to shield the view. A montage of footprints in the slush led around the lake and into the woods. Steff wiped the sweat from his brow. His clothes were wet and torn. He had the shivers. His hands were still bleeding. He could not feel his feet. He slid down the muddy bank to the edge of the water and, with the shotgun across his lap, sat there in shame as the sun came up over Little Star Lake.

The clouds were gone. The sky was ice blue. It was the dawning of a beautiful day. Steff Koslowski gazed into the rising sun and in his mind's eye saw the finale of the great escape. They were at the Rhinelander airfield, John Dillinger and his band of merry men, introducing themselves and signing autographs for Pilot Dorn. Then the Indiana desperadoes climbed aboard the airplane and, with Ivar Dorn happy at the controls and Homer Van Meter safe at his side, they sailed into the wild blue yonder, where Saint Elmo smiled over them.

Saint Hollyhocks

Out there somewhere was a handful of nameless, faceless people whose only job was to make his life miserable. The trenches had been only the prologue. Grover
Mudd was convinced of that. They went to work on
him right after the war when he wanted to join the
expatriate writers in Paris, but they made him return
home and take a job. They told him to marry and not
worry about love: It would come. Have children: They
make life whole. The thing of it was, they made him
believe it. Every single time a doubt arose they
squashed it, smothered him in guilt. And, when he
strayed, when he went out of his way to find a shred
of truth, an iota of happiness, they were there—there
to haul him back to the abyss of misery and toss him
in. If only he could find them. A name, a face, something to aim at. If he could pump a few slugs into their
heads he would be free. A happy man.

Grover sat on the bed in his underwear, his hands
folded over his knees like an orphan in yet another new
home. The sun was coming up on a dreary day. Another
night of sleep had passed him by. The medicine on the
nightstand was untouched. The bedding was stained and
rancid. He dressed in wrinkled clothes, downed two
beers for breakfast, and chased them with a shot of his
favorite moonshine.

The closet was dark and smelly. Mouse droppings
ringed the floor. The odor of mothballs took him back
to the morgue. Grover pulled out and regrouped. On

the closet floor lay his forfeited youth. He mounted a second charge and rescued the duffel bag from the dark and dumped his war on the floor. Pushing medals aside, the ex-marine pricked his finger on a pin. It drew blood and he swore like a madman. Then he found what he was looking for. It was tucked snugly into the neatly folded uniform where he had stashed it years ago. He loaded it and stuffed it under his belt. Grover hung the Croix de Guerre from his neck and threw on the coat. He straightened the ribbons and decorations and adjusted the unit crest. But he had gained too much weight to button up. With fever in his head, booze in his blood, and vengeance in his heart, Lieutenant Grover Mudd lit out the door to clean up St. Paul.

He caught the first clanger of the morning and told the conductor to wake him at St. Peter Street. An early edition of the *North Star Press* was on the rear seat.

GEHAN WINS BY 255 VOTES
Mayor Race Closest in City's History
St. Sauver Wings into Public Safety Office

Grover used the paper for a pillow and bellied out on the backseat. When it seemed he was sleeping for the first time in weeks he was grabbed by the shoulders, half helped, half shoved off the trolley, and dropped, half blind, on to "Sodom Street" at dawn.

The dingy bars were locked tight. The whorehouse hotels were closed for the day. The sidewalks were deserted. Drizzle was off and on. A hungry dog limped across the street and ducked behind a flophouse. Grover drew his gun and, semi-delirious and semi-drunk, sauntered down St. Peter to a showdown on Eighth Street.

But the intersection was silent. The Big Holy Spook was nowhere in sight. There was no one to shoot. He sat down in the gutter and prayed a cop would show up. Any flatfoot would do. A sheet of newspaper blew

by. Grover made up his mind to wait for the Spook.
Then he got tired and left.

He caught a streetcar going out West Seventh Street
and got himself thrown off at River Drive. The cold,
damp air was clearing his head, and his eyesight was
returning to normal. On the rising bluff across the river
he could see the old fort rotting away in the morning
rain. Grover Mudd turned and hiked up to the Hollyhocks Club.

The sloppy parking lot was empty. The only hint of
life in this desolate corner of the city came from the
morning whistle at the Ford plant up the river. Grover
drew his gun, slopped up to the house and kicked in
the front door. Nobody was there to greet him. The
chairs were turned upside down on the tables. The
shades were down. The bar was covered with a white
sheet. He tracked mud across the polished floors and
kicked at anything in his way.

Roxanne Schultz was upstairs in the master bedroom.
She was clearing her angel face of makeup at the vanity
when she heard the commotion downstairs. A cleaning
boy, she figured, and not a very quiet one. She had just
slipped into her nightgown. It was time for bed. Rankin
was in Chicago. But then the stomping hit the stairs, a
slow awkward stomp, and she knew he was back already, beating up on the furniture because he didn't
dare beat up on her. She was sick of his tantrums, and
the winds beckoning her to California blew stronger
every day.

She leaned forward to clean her eyelids and saw him
in the mirror, an unkempt man in a stale uniform with
a strange pistol in his hand. Her first thought was of
burglary. His face was pale. His hair was dripping wet.
Bags hung from his sad red eyes. Big as he was, he
somehow looked starved. She kept a loaded derringer
in the jewel drawer and was about to go for it when
she recognized him as the man from "Grover's Corner."

She finished off her lashes and calmly addressed him in the mirror. "Up early, Saint Mudd? Or haven't you gone to bed yet?"

"No," he slurred out. "I suppose you're not surprised by men walking into your bedroom. Where's that dickless wonder of yours?"

"Mr. Rankin is still in Florida," she lied. "I'll tell him you asked."

"And he didn't take you? Poor doll. Even old Nina used to take her favorite whores to Florida in the winter."

It was a caustic gift she knew he possessed, his uncanny ability to find and exploit the weakest point of even the strongest person. Grover Mudd knew how to hurt people, and she wanted to hurt back. "Speaking of whores, we were all brokenhearted to read about your little concubine."

She ducked fast. The gun smashed the mirror. Bits of glass sprayed her hair. A smart remark about seven years of bad luck came to mind but she had no time to use it. His hand flew across her face and she flew across the room. Her mouth stung. She could taste blood. She was furious. Men did not hit her.

"Did he kill her?" He was almost crying.

She turned to confront him. "You saints and your storybook ways. Just don't know what to do when reality strikes." He knocked her to the floor. She tried to get up but he was on top of her, slapping at her face. She covered her head and most of the blows hit her hands. Blood trickled down her chin.

"Did he kill her? Did he kill her?" he kept shouting. He grabbed her nightgown with both hands and flung her across the room.

Roxanne landed at the foot of the bed and hit her head against the post. She ran her fingers across her forehead, felt a bump but found no bleeding. She was shocked and exhausted. She hated him. She wanted that derringer. One shot was all she needed. Men did not treat her like this. She got to her feet. He was coming at her, more staggering than attacking. She raised her arm to strike him but he caught her hand above her head and forced her to the sheets. His leg came down hard between hers. He was heavier than he looked, smelled of rainwater and whiskey, and she was no match for the strength in his thick arms. He grabbed her hair as if he were going to yank the roots from her head, and stuck his nose within an inch of her face. His eyes were the fiery red eyes of a drunken maniac. Now she was more scared than angry. Her only defense was to knee him in the groin, but he had her legs pinned with his. She closed her eyes and clenched her teeth. His hands were reaching for her neck. She would be strangled by a dying columnist for a dying newspaper. Murdered in St. Paul, Minnesota. Never to see California. She wanted to cry for the pitiful life she had led.

She was wrong. His hands grabbed her cheeks and twisted her head. He dropped his mouth over hers. His beard scratched her face and smeared the blood across her lips. She could not breathe. He kneed her nightgown up to her thighs and she knew what he wanted was even worse than murder. With every ounce of strength she had she dug her fingers into his hair and pulled his face away from hers. "Never!" she screamed.

He reared back and slapped her hard, slapped her again, and once again. He was crazed. It was impossible to fight back, but she vowed to kill him. Then his hands were at the neckline of her nightgown and he ripped it to her waist. Her breasts were exposed. He violently yanked the nightgown up over her hips, tearing it as she squirmed. She could feel his trousers against her bare legs. She was not going to let it happen. For a second she was free. But he was too quick. He had only let go of her to position himself. His hands went under her and her panties were cut to her knees. She rolled to her side and saw her panties flung to the floor. This had happened once before. She was a girl in Swede

Hollow. Again she felt helpless. Vulnerable. She took so much pride in her strength. She could hear his trousers being undone. She buried her face in the pillow. Then he had her hair again, forced her over, and smothered her mouth with his. She could not beat him anymore. He forced her hands over her head and crawled between her legs. Her only hope was that in his drunken rage he would be limp. But then he poked at her thighs and she swore at herself for being so stupid. He was a fucking newspaperman, and his dick was stiffer than he was. It was going to happen. She squeezed, but he pushed her apart and went in deep and hard, sucking the bloody tongue from her mouth and driving her hips into the mattress. Her arms were pinned above her head. Her mouth was his. The Cross of Courage gashed her nipples. He spread her legs wide and penetrated her deeper and faster than any man ever had.

The feeling began around her heart. Then she felt it between her legs. It lashed at her knees and spread up to her shoulders. It was a feeling that made her weak, the feeling she grasped for when Rankin pulled his fingers out and let her be. But this time it was stronger, almost overwhelming. She hated this drunken fool attacking her, stripping her of her dignity. She longed to kill him, but even more than that she longed for the feeling. She wanted to feel it without the opium, without Nina Clifford. It was her very own feeling coming on and she was going to have it. There would be plenty of time for hate, for killing. She drew his tongue into her mouth and she knew he felt it, too. He let go of her hands. She wrapped her arms around his back and dug her fingernails into his uniform. For a moment she thought it was going to get away, but she fought to hang on and soon it possessed her, made her quiver with satisfaction, watered her eyes with delight, and, if he had not been muffling her mouth with his, she would have screamed with joy.

He collapsed on top of her, the warm come running

down her legs. The pink satin sheets were bunched up around her head where he had jerked them from the mattress. Her bloodstained nightgown was dangling from her foot. The orgasm made her want to smile, but she remembered it was death and sickness that had brought him here; it was shame that glued them together under the sullen roof of the Hollyhocks Club.

Minutes of silence later he grew tense, stiffened again, and Roxanne believed he was ready to start over. Then his chest heaved and his breathing became loud and harsh. He was trying not to cough, trying not to cry. But bloody saliva drooled from his mouth, and tears fell on her shoulder, splitting her heart in two. Roxanne stroked the back of his head and whispered a kiss in his ear. "You poor son of a bitch."

BOOK THREE

Summer Autumn 1934

It was the duty of a saint to be happy.

—Dorothy Day

Saints Meet Saints

Special Agent Steff Koslowski ducked out of the Federal Courts Building. The May sun was bright and warm and as wide as the sky. In Rice Park the trees were outlined in green. The grass was hungry for water. The birds were back. He rolled up his shirtsleeves, threw his coat over his shoulder, and followed St. Peter down to Fourth Street, where a crippled veteran holding the corner announced Wear a Poppy Week. The American Legion was selling little red poppies, replicas of those in Flanders fields. Steff bought one and pinned it to his shirt.

The G-man from Chicago strolled down to the *Frontier News* and took the elevator to the third floor. He expected one of those newsrooms he saw in the movies—chaos, excitement, people scurrying about, stories rolling off the wires. What he found were vacant desks and unanswered telephones. A handful of reporters banged on typewriters. A crusty old man with thick glasses was trying to bring a bulletin into focus. Steff tapped his shoulder and asked for directions. The old man pointed to a corner office.

He was slouched down in a ragged chair, staring out the window. His wrinkled shirt was untucked, the tie askew. His eyes were bloodshot. The face was puffy and weather-beaten, handsome in an unwholesome way. There was also something vaguely familiar about him. Next to an open bottle of whiskey was an empty glass. The cramped office was a mess. Grover's Corner.

The door was missing. Steff knocked on the wall. Plaster tumbled down the slats.

"What the hell you beating on the wall for?" The voice was hoarse and belligerent.

"I'm sorry, I didn't see a door."

"No door to see."

"Are you Grover Mudd?"

"You a cop?"

"My name is Steff Koslowski. I'm with the Justice Department."

"So you're an educated cop. What do you want, G-man?"

"I've been looking into the murder of a negro girl named Stormy Day. She lived on St. Albans Street. They found her in the river last month."

"I know the details."

"Did you know the girl?"

"What makes you ask?"

"I talked with her neighbors. Your name came up."

"We were friends. Know what I mean?"

"Yes."

"Does that picture upset your self-righteous stomach?"

"I'm sorry about your loss. They sent the boy to St. Louis. He has relatives there who are going to care for him."

"Yes, I know that. I arranged it." The newspaperman looked as if he'd been insulted. "Do you know what you look like, G-man? You look like one of those mannequins I see in the display windows down at the Emporium."

"Do you know you look like John Dillinger?"

"Thank you. Any guy that robs banks and kills bankers can't be all bad."

Steff Koslowski stepped into the office and picked his way to the window; the glass was still streaked with winter dirt. Across the street, window washers were polishing off the *North Star Press*. "Do you know of anyone who might have had reason to kill her?"

"I killed her. She threatened to expose me for what I was. A nigger-lover."

"Have the local authorities questioned you?"

"Don't make me laugh. Which brings us to you, G-man. Why are the feds interested in what happened to a colored girl?"

"Do you know who Homer Van Meter is?"

"A lieutenant of Dillinger's. On the Ten Most Wanted List. Uses St. Paul as a hideout. He was involved in that shootout on Lexington."

"Homer and I were both involved in that shootout. I've been on his tail since September. A real sick case. We nabbed a doctor in Minneapolis for treating Dillinger. This doctor told us Dag Rankin once came to him about his problem, the one you wrote about. Van Meter has a similar problem and he went to this doctor asking the same questions. The doc couldn't help him either, but he steered Van Meter to Rankin a week before the murder. We know Rankin threatened you. We'd love to hang a murder rap on him."

"There's no law against killing colored people."

"If we can't get him for murder, we'll get him for something else."

"Such as?"

"Do you know of Nina Clifford?"

"She's a living legend in these parts."

Steff Koslowski toyed with the poppy in his shirt. "She's on the receiving end of a large opium ring. We're not really interested in her; she's a local problem. We are interested in where she gets her stuff. Right now everything points to Rankin. Chicago is going dry. Word on the street is that it's all going to St. Paul."

Grover shrugged. "St. Sauver's known that for months. It's the worst-kept secret in Minnesota."

"It's imperative we find this stuff."

"That's the best-kept secret in Minnesota."

"We've been following your front-page campaign. There are some areas where we could help each other. I'm meeting your editor today."

"I'll keep you in mind."

Steff moved back to the doorway. "For what it's worth, I admire your work. I sent a couple of your columns home to my father in Chicago."

"Yeah? What does your father do?"

"Just a Polish cop."

"He must be very proud of you. My father worked for the railroad."

An awkward silence stood between them. Steff turned to leave. Then stopped. He wanted to add something. "I met her once," he told Grover, "the day of the Carroll shooting. She was something special." There was no reply. And he left Grover Mudd slouched in his corner.

Editor Walt Howard led Steff Koslowski through the *Frontier News* to a conference room with one big table. Commissioner Gil St. Sauver was seated in the middle. There were no windows. Mr. Howard closed the door.

"What did you find?" St. Sauver asked.

The G-man and the editor took seats across from the commissioner.

"We're in luck," Steff told him. "All the telephone wires at police headquarters enter the building through a single terminal box. It's located in a dusty corner of the basement. Each wire has an identifying tag. I can cut into every wire, one after another, and lead the connection to a control room, preferably on the first floor. It's highly sensitive equipment."

"There's a private room with a steel door on the far end of the first floor," St. Sauver informed him. "It used to be a vault. That will be your control room. You're to be an accounting firm conducting an independent audit of the police department."

"Mr. Clegg tells us you're some kind of electrical

wizard," Walt Howard said to Steff. "Has this kind of operation ever been tried before?"

"We've never tapped wires before, and never an eavesdropping operation of this size. Much of the gadgetry I put together myself."

"Will it work?" St. Sauver asked.

"There have got to be backups," Steff warned. "The actual telephone conversations will be recorded on what we call a pamograph machine. It uses a sapphire needle and makes aluminum records. In my experiments the voices have been as clear as those over a radio."

"But?"

"But we need more," Steff went on. "We have to pick up asides, remarks they might make to others in the room while using the phone. For that we'll use a standard Dictograph and hide the microphones in the phone base, ventilating shafts, lamps, that sort of thing. Then I'll coordinate the Dictograph and the pamograph."

"If they find one of those mikes this entire operation is over," St. Sauver reminded him.

"That's part of your job," Steff told him. "You have to put the suspects in the right office and give them the right job."

St. Sauver leaned back. "Don't worry. A few promotions here, a couple of transfers there, and they'll fall like clay pigeons."

"Let me get this straight," said a befuddled Walt Howard. "You're actually going to promote crooked cops?"

"They'll think they never had it so good. I'll hand them the rope. They can hang themselves."

Walt Howard turned to Steff. "What else do you need?"

"Stenographers. At least six of them, working four-hour shifts twenty-four hours a day. They're to take down every suspicious conversation word for word."

The understaffed editor was pleased. "Over the past

year I think I've laid off twenty of them. Good workers, too. I'll get you the best."

"Some of this equipment I need is expensive," Steff reminded them. "Funding for the FBI is in trouble. Since Little Bohemia we've become the most unpopular organization in Washington. Even Will Rogers is taking swipes at us. He said the way to get Dillinger is let him become an innocent bystander."

"Money was the easiest part," Mr. Howard assured him. "After Bremer was grabbed, Summit Avenue opened its wallet nice and wide. I raised sixty thousand dollars in one night. There's more where that came from if we need it."

"Speaking of money." Gil St. Sauver pulled a piece of paper from his coat pocket and tossed it on the table. "First day on the job I found this note on my desk. Ten thousand dollars in cash if I don't recommend a new police chief to the mayor."

Steff read the note and tossed it back. "Take the money and register it. We'll start with his office."

"We have to get the office of police chief removed from politics," Walt Howard explained. "If we catch the chief dirty it could be the impetus for a referendum in the next election."

Steff Koslowski smiled at the thought. "Has St. Paul ever nailed a police chief?"

Commissioner St. Sauver examined the note again then stuffed it back in his pocket. "Just once," he answered. "A long time ago."

———

With his back to the city, Grover Mudd stood in the sun on the gilded bluff and was seduced by spring's warm touch. Far below, the river was dressed for the occasion with flowers pinned to its banks. The water was low. Children played on Harriet Island. Behind him traffic raced back and forth on Kellogg Boulevard. In the parking lot cars hunted for a space.

He sensed her presence before he saw her. She took hold of the railing and breathed deep. "Three months ago it was thirty below zero," she said into the sunshine. "Only in Minnesota. My God, I hope it's not like last summer."

"Working the wrong side of the street, aren't you, Roxy?"

"Your friend Fuzzy told me you walk up here for lunch sometimes."

"Fuzzy talks too much."

"Avoiding me?"

He avoided her eyes. "I keep expecting car doors to swing open and machine guns to cut me in two."

"Like in the movies?" she asked.

"Yeah, just like in the movies."

"You look like hell."

He turned to her. She was smiling. "You look like heaven." And she did. Her dress was as blue as her eyes, and in the sunshine her hair had that angelic golden glow he'd seen one night in a dream.

"I read Jean Harlow got her third divorce," Roxanne said. "Prettiest girl in the world and she can't find happiness."

"And you, Roxy, what have you found?"

"I don't know." She paused to reflect. "Some women think motherhood grants them sainthood. Sure as hell, I'm not one of them." She stopped. Her brassiness seemed a shade more dull. She lowered her voice to the point of uncertainty. "I'm going to leave him. I'd like to see California."

Grover turned away and coughed into his palms. "Seems these days everybody's answer to everything is California." He coughed again. He closed his watery eyes. When he opened them again the river was like a rainbow.

"What do you take for that cough?" Roxanne wanted to know.

"Whiskey."

"I know something better."

The Gust and the Dust

Homer Van Meter wound the black Ford up the spiral bridge in Hastings. Baby Face Nelson was sharing the ride, a machine gun cocked over his shoulder for the world to see. They crossed the Mississippi River and headed north on Trunk Highway 61 toward St. Paul.

Homer the Gnomer was in mental and physical agony. He had a constant headache. The gang's legend grew with every added day they roamed free, but their nerve and their numbers were shrinking. Little Bohemia had been the closest call yet. The FBI was hot on their trail. Reading about themselves in the papers and magazines was once a thrill. Now it was a bull's-eye painted on their foreheads. John Dillinger was talking about Mexico, but Van Meter wanted the cure he was sure the Mayo Clinic had to offer. Besides, Dag Rankin owed him.

"I wanted to go to Florida," Nelson kept griping, "but, no, you guys wanted to go to Wisconsin, sunshine capital of the Yukon."

"Shut up, Baby Face."

The stolen Ford pushed the speed limit across the endless farm fields south of St. Paul. The windows were down. The sun was baking hot. Through townships with names like Cottage Grove and Inver Grove the ground was plowed, the planting was done, but little was growing. The land was parched.

"What was that?" Nelson asked, jerking his head over his shoulder.

"Sounded like a blowout."

"Blowout, hell. It's a sheriff's car. They're shooting at us."

"I thought I told you to switch the plates."

"I did. I switched them with the Packard."

"You dumb shit," Van Meter screamed, "the Packard was hotter than a whore."

Nelson climbed into the back seat and broke the rear window with the butt of his gun. He opened fire.

Van Meter almost ran down a road-repair crew as he wheeled off the highway onto a dirt road and kicked dust past an oil refinery. He could hear bullets whistling by his ear. They broke onto a wood bridge across the Mississippi that seemed ready to collapse. A train was passing over the tracks above them. The river below was wide and ugly. He passed a car in front of him and sideswiped the railing. The beam dropped into the river and for one terrifying second Homer Van Meter thought the car would drop along with it. He saw only water below. Then he was back in the right lane and off the bridge.

Nelson's machine gun was rolling on the floor. He grabbed for it. "I can't swim, goddammit. No more rivers."

They were hurtling by farm fields again. Nelson reloaded and fired round after round into clouds of powdered earth.

"Is he still back there?" Van Meter asked.

"I can't see through the dirt."

"Then quit wasting bullets."

The hunted gangsters swung onto a paved road. The sheriff's car was gone.

They followed the highway to Concord Street in South St. Paul, a path they knew well. Van Meter steered for the stockyards and pulled into a parking lot. Dust floated above the gravel. Cattle trucks were backed up a mile. Smoke billowed from the Swift's stack. Cows marched by the Armour Star. Hogs kicked up more dirt. Van Meter shut off the engine and wiped his face. "We're gonna have to heist one of these cars. This one's got holes in it."

"Did you really work here once?"

Van Meter looked around, for a moment lost. "Kill floor," he mumbled. "I stunned 'em. I stunned them all." His head was throbbing. The sun was blinding. He closed his eyes and rested his brain. Nelson's squawking was a drumbeat in the distance. Pigeons poked about the car.

"This dust is choking me," Nelson complained, rolling up his window.

Van Meter snapped out of it. "Choked what girl?"

"What?"

"You said I choked somebody."

"You're crazy. I said this dust is choking me."

Homer Van Meter relaxed. "Yeah, right. I heard it ain't rained here in weeks."

"This town is starting to heat up again."

"We'll have to find a new room. St. Sauver made a campaign issue out of Wabasha and St. Peter Street."

"What about your buddy Rankin's place?" Nelson suggested.

"If we go walking into the Hollyhocks Club he'll shoot us on sight."

"I'd love a dick shot at that blond tomato of his."

Homer Van Meter plugged one nostril and blew dusty snot out of the other. "I heard she's a doper."

"Who cares how much brains she's got."

"She smokes hop, you jerk-off. Raw opium. She's a real junkie." He cleared his other nostril. "And I heard she uses that angel face of hers to get others hooked on it for Nina Clifford. That Rankin better be careful."

It was only the third week in May but the temperature had climbed into the nineties. The wind was strong and hot. Dirt hung in the air. Dust storms were sweeping across the Dakotas but it was believed they would not reach the cities.

Grover Mudd kept his back to the police station. The sun, a luminous, dull spot in the sky, was sinking behind the house. The Cathedral of Saint Paul loomed ghostly in the dusty twilight overhead.

Roxanne Schultz knocked on the iron door.

Grover felt criminal. His lungs were worse every day. And a lot of the good inside him died with Stormy Day.

Nina Clifford opened the door, and Roxanne led Grover down the basement stairs, where it was cool and damp.

"Miss Clifford—" Roxanne started.

But Nina Clifford stopped her. "We need no introduction, angel. This, I know, is the sometimes famous, sometimes infamous Grover Mudd."

Grover swallowed his embarrassment. "I'm flattered, Miss Clifford." On the top of her head was a sparkling blue wig, the ugliest wig he'd ever seen. He had often seen her in passing, but up close in her own home she was even more pathetic than he had imagined. "Roxanne said you might have something for my cough."

"And I do, Grover." She took him by the arm and ushered him through a curtain to her magical den. "You know, so many of our fighting men came to me after the war, morphine addicts mostly. You should have come, too. I sometimes think what the Huns did to our boys in battle was nothing compared to what we did to them when they got home."

Grover had always believed that, but this was the first time he had ever heard anybody say it. And even now it was coming from a bawdyhouse queen.

The room looked like a whore's idea of the end of the rainbow. "Tawdry" was inadequate. There were enough tallow candles for a Halloween party. The floor was red, the ceiling black satin. One wall was bamboo and leather, another was fishnetting stuffed with gold cotton. East Asian plants wilted in the corners. The biting odor of the juju weed permeated the nest.

The conversation was trite. She invited them to lie down. Roxanne stretched out on a daybed. Nina led Grover to a woolly couch. He removed his shoes and spread out on his back. The old whore told him the soft, fleecy wool was llama, but it smelled like something from a Woolworth's rug sale.

"I know how you feel, Grover," the madam said, comforting him, "but I assure you everything that goes on in my house was once legal and quite respectable. Society made it bad, not Nina Clifford. I can remember Mrs. Winslow's Soothing Syrup, a ten-percent morphine solution given to crying babies. Shut them right up. The people at Bayer used to sell their heroin at the corner drugstore right alongside their aspirin. And I haven't had Coca-Cola since they took the cocaine out."

Grover Mudd was not reassured. He felt like a child at a dentist's office, only now he had the option of leaving. There was still time. But his chest was on fire and his heart was in pieces. Outside, a torrid wind moaned through the streets. He watched Roxanne across the room.

Nina Clifford set a small ball of opium on the end of a wire, then put a candle to it. When it was stewing well, she carefully packed it into the pipe. Roxanne took the pipe from Nina and smoked the dream-fried drug in a glass bowl over a flame. She smiled over at Grover. Then her dreamy blue eyes turned heavenward. Next stop, lotusland.

Nina Clifford came to him with the pipe and knelt beside the couch. She flirted with her eyes. Grover's stomach twisted. The flame was in his face. What would this witch do to him in an opiated state? She ran a hand up his leg. One more inch, he told himself, and he was out the door. The madam backed off, then held out the pipe. Grover took it in his hands. It was long and awkward. He wanted someone to tell him what to do, but

Roxanne was far away and Nina Clifford's wretchedness made him want to vomit.

Grover inhaled. He could hear the juices in the stem gurgling. The smoke tasted bitter. The smell was over-whelming. His eyes filled with tears, until all he could see were flickering shadows of fear. But soon anguish drifted to calm. He turned to Roxanne. She was closer to him now. He put the pipe to his lips again and breathed deep. It was magic. His cough melted away. His lungs filled with spring winds. His troubles got lost in a gust of poppy dust.

Grover took another wonderful puff, and another.

Nina Clifford disappeared.

And Grover Mudd sailed off to the land of divine enchantment.

———————

That night dust storms came sailing through the Twin Cities. The wind was gusting to fifty miles per hour. On-sweeping clouds of dirt crossed the river.

At the railroad tracks below the steep bluffs of Indian Mound Park, Dag Rankin and the Big Holy Spook covered their faces with dark handkerchiefs in the same manner as the dime-novel bad guys of their youth. The desertlike storm nearly blinded them. Boxcars were passing shadows that smashed to a halt. The speck of a lantern came running their way. A signalman held the light up to the boxcar numbers and slapped the side.

"This is the car. Is this where you want it?" he yelled.

Rankin looked at the Spook. The big preacher searched the cliff behind him, then nodded his head.

"Yeah. Open it up," Rankin ordered.

The railroad man threw the latch and pulled the door aside.

Rankin handed him an envelope and screamed in his ear. "Now get lost for an hour."

The man and the lantern vanished in the dust.

Rankin and the Spook climbed into the boxcar and

out of the storm. They closed the door and searched
the crates with flashlights. Stacked near the front were
five double-decked chests made of mango wood and
stamped ST. PAUL FRUIT CO. Dag Rankin tapped the
top crate. The Big Holy Spook tore open the nailed lid
with his hands. The bounty inside was shaped like large
baseballs and wrapped in green paper, packed twenty
on top, twenty on the bottom. Rankin took one of the
globes in his hands and caressed it the way a Gypsy
would caress her crystal ball. He ripped open the paper
and found a hard skin made from the petals of the
poppy; cracking it open he was seduced by the fragrance. Dag Rankin put the black ball of powder to his
nose and groaned with pleasure. The Spook leaned over
his shoulder and shared the experience.

It was not the smell making them high. A kilo of
crude opium sold for twenty-five dollars. Once it was
converted to heroin and sold on the streets of America,
its value jumped to more than two hundred thousand
dollars. Good-bye, bootlegging. Hello, drug smuggling.

Even in the gut of a dust storm, Dag Rankin believed
things were looking bright and sunny. Soon he would
return to Chicago, a king. His shipments of opium were
delivered like babies. He was controlling the flow and
he was shutting off the tap. The election of Gil St.
Sauver as public safety commissioner turned out to be
a boon instead of a bust. His contacts at the police
department were being promoted. When the storm
passed, only two dark clouds would remain behind. The
St. Paul Frontier News, and Roxanne Schultz.

The crusading newspaper refused to die quietly. The
front-page editorials were relentless. Bawdyhouses
along St. Peter Street, masquerading as hotels, were
exposed. Establishments not abiding by the state's strict
new liquor laws were being detailed. Rankin's only solace was rumors of the paper's imminent death and the
unexplained absence of "Grover's Corner."

Roxanne was slipping away. Something had happened to change her. She was openly spiting him. She left him for days at a time. He thought about having her followed.

The Big Holy Spook threw open the door. The noisy wind snapped punishing prairie dust at their faces. The Spook climbed down and Rankin handed him the first crate. The black man with the black poppy dust disappeared into the black dirt clouds. Then he returned for more.

Saint Lucifer

It was the last day in May. The temperature was 106°.
Never in its recorded history had Minnesota been so
hot. Not a breeze could be begged. Dust coated St.
Paul like a filthy shroud. Down on Fourth Street the
Frontier News was blistering under a cloudless sky.

Grover Mudd plopped into the chair in Walt Howard's office. He grabbed the small fan on the desk and
turned it on his face. A larger fan was blowing in the
corner. "Let me guess," he said to his editor, "page
one is going to be the weather?"

"That, and somebody stole a crocodile from Como
Zoo and threw it in Lake Phalen."

"Poor crocodile."

Walt Howard removed his glasses and wiped away
the moisture. "I have to announce more layoffs today."

Grover sank back in the chair. His shirt stuck to the
leather. He pulled away. "Am I through?"

"No. But I have to let Harv Bennett go. And we
won't be needing Fuzzy anymore."

"Christ, Walt, we pay him out of petty cash."

"There is no more cash."

"Take it out of my salary."

"Fuzzy is through. I'm sorry."

"Now I see how the *North Star Press* intends to absorb our people. By the time they get done with the
Frontier News there won't be anybody left to absorb."

"I'm forced to agree with you. I'm disappointed."

"How long do we have left?"

"I doubt they'll let us run to the end of the year. We're going to begin pushing for a second grand jury."

"We need more evidence."

"For that we're going to have to count on St. Sauver and Koslowski."

Grover was doubtful. "Do you really think these so-called wiretaps are going to amount to anything?"

"Cops making crooked deals and the actual conversations across our front page. It's what we've been praying for."

"You've got a lot more faith in electricity than I do."

"I wish we could bring back the electricity 'Grover's Corner' generated."

Grover Mudd walked to the window. The streets were deep in dirt. Cars were bathed in dust. The reflection of the Frontier Building was no longer visible in the grimy glass of the *North Star Press*. "I don't know what to write anymore."

"We've come a long way," his editor reminded him. "The first grand jury, city elections with record turnouts, a new mayor, new commissioners—we can't stop now."

Grover coughed out the window. He wiped his mouth and stared into the broiling sun. "I don't know. Maybe it's time to end this chapter of my life. Have you ever been to California?"

Later that hot afternoon Fuzzy Byron shuffled into Grover's Corner and lifted his coat from the hook on the wall.

Grover watched him button up. "It's a little warm for a coat, isn't it?"

"I won't be back, Grover. You know that."

"You'll always be welcome here."

"Thank you. I liked it here. In my next life, instead of a painter, I think I'd like to be a newspaperman."

Grover wanted to hand his friend a few dollars but he needed the money for later. A feeling of shame overtook him. "We're all getting together at Bo Kelly's after work," he told Fuzzy. "I'll buy you a drink."

"Maybe I'll be there. Right now I've got some serious walking to do. So long, Grover Mudd."

"Don't walk too far in this heat."

Fuzzy shuffled to the door and stopped. "How will I pay my rent?"

"I'll talk to Granny," Grover said to the old man.

"It's not Granny I'm worried about."

Grover Mudd walked up to Seven Corners, ducking under the shade at every chance. The flaming sun refused to sink into the west. The sidewalks were oven hot.

Bo Kelly's air-cooled tavern was crowded, but Fuzzy Byron was nowhere in sight. Harv Bennett was slouched over the bar. Grover parked on the stool next to him. The big red painting of Lucifer, pitchfork in hand, glared down at them.

Harv Bennett looked up at Grover and laughed. It was a drunken laugh. "My coughing colleague Grover Mudd, ace reporter for the *St. Paul Frontier News.*"

"I'm sorry about your job, Harv."

"No, you're not. You're only happy it wasn't you. And so you should be. In fact, you should be celebrating. Let me buy you a drink." He raised his glass. "Bartender, one for my friend here." The unemployed reporter downed his drink. "And another one for me." He slammed his glass to the bar. "I hate you, Grover Mudd. I've always hated you. Nothing personal. My hatred for you is strictly professional."

The drinks were poured and they drank up.

"What is this stuff?" Grover asked with a cough.

"Legal whiskey. Tastes like shit, but it gets the job done."

Grover cleared his throat. "You were saying?"

"I studied to be a reporter," Harv Bennett cried into his glass. "I actually went to college for it."

"Mistake number one," Grover told him. "College is for people who can't educate themselves."

"And, two months after I landed a job at the *Frontier News*, Walt Howard walks in with his arm around war hero Grover Mudd. 'Show the kid the ropes,' he tells me. You couldn't even type." Harv Bennett finished his drink and pounded on the bar for another. "I tried to join the army," he went on. "They wouldn't take me. My asthma. You must find that painfully ironic." He laughed again, this time a sad, cruel laugh. "And, when they gave you a column that should have been mine, I prayed you'd fall on your face. But you didn't. No, you write the way you talk, like an asshole. The world loves assholes because they say the things the rest of us are afraid to say."

Grover finished his drink. "What are you going to do?"

"I might just pack up the family and head for California. They have newspapers there. Why live here anyway? I ask you. We roast in the summer. We freeze in the winter. It rains all spring. Those beautiful autumns are gone in a wink."

"We hate to lose you. You're good, Harv. Let's face it, most reporters couldn't write their way out of a toilet stall."

"If we knew how to write, we'd be writers."

Grover laughed. "What's the old joke? Inside every reporter is a novel, and that's where it should stay." He signaled for another drink. "The paper is on its last legs. I expect to be on the relief rolls before Christmas. Hell, one-fifth of the state is out of work."

"And I'm sorry," Harv Bennett told him. "I was even sorry about your friend Fuzzy. I was beginning to like that ugly old bastard. He's pretty smart when he's sober. Do you think he was ever a real painter?"

"It's hard to say what he was before he went on the bum. Must have been something."

"Looks like the only person the *North Star Press* is

going to save is Walt Howard. God knows he deserves
it. He's a good man. A good editor. A good husband.
I'll bet he was a good father."

"Walt Howard doesn't have any children," Grover
reminded him.

"Not now. But he had a son once."

"I didn't know that. What happened to him?"

"Got killed in a train wreck."

Grover put down his drink. "What train wreck?"

"I don't remember. It was years ago. Before the
war."

Grover grabbed his arm as if he could squeeze the
information out of him. "What train wreck?"

"I don't remember the details. They put the kid on
a train to visit relatives out west and the train never
made it. I think a bridge washed out, or the engineer
fell asleep, or something like that. Look it up."

The sweltering sun was gone now. Moonlight filtered
past the rusty bars of the lone window just below the
ceiling. The temperature outside was still 82°. Inside
the retired vault it was probably 102°. The steel door
was kept closed and locked. The window had been
nailed shut years ago.

Special Agent Steff Koslowski pulled a hanky from
his trousers and, once again, wiped the perspiration
from his face. His only air came through a dusty vent.
He loosened another button on his shirt. Could he really
be in for three months of this heat? In this room?

The overheated G-man split the last tapped wire and
connected it to the two pamograph machines. He fixed
the pamographs to the Dictograph machine and ran
everything to the monitor telephone unit, a clearing
board for all telephone conversations. Now, by throwing a small switch, various calls could be monitored at
the same time—at least that was his theory.

The biggest question mark was his converted fire-alarm teletype machine. Would it really record the telephone numbers of all calls made out of the building, twenty-four hours a day? Spit them out on ticker tape? There was no way to test this setup.

The microphones were hidden in freshly decorated offices. The wires were all tapped. Gil St. Sauver had handed out promotions with the fanfare of a political campaign. All Steff Koslowski could do now was wait, probably till the next day. He sank into his chair and buried his red face in his sweaty hands. The devil's work in the devil's town.

It had been more than a month now, but still there were nightmares. Little Bohemia was a national disgrace. The FBI was on the line. The haunted agent could see the boy from the CCC camp slumped across the car seat. He saw himself running through the north woods with every tree pointing a machine gun at him. Even now in 100° heat he could feel the wet cold. His ears rang with ricocheting bullets. Shivers overtook him. He jumped from the chair. It was hotter than hell.

Steff dragged the chair over to the wall and stood on it. He grabbed hold of the bars and counted the rusty nailheads in the window. The glass was filthy. The wood frame was painted together like cement. He wiped his eyes with his shirtsleeve and stared hopelessly into the night. A snowplow moved down the center of the street and scraped a layer of dust into the gutter.

At the top of Steep Street a man was moving in and out of the shadows. The figure seemed familiar. He kept jerking his hand to his mouth. Steff wiped away some of the grime and took a harder look. The shadowy man was tentative. He started down the street, then backed up. He crossed to the other side before finally committing himself. Steff rubbed more dirt off the glass. The dark figure passed under a street lamp. It was Grover Mudd.

Steff waited for him to cross over to the police station, but he kept on going, down to the morgue and across the street there. He rested against a railing in front of the brick house. He looked behind him, like a man being followed. Then he clutched the railing and followed it to Nina Clifford's basement door. And Steff Koslowski watched incredulously as Grover Mudd stepped across an invisible line.

"Oh, Lucifer, what have you done?"

A bell rang. Steff turned. The monitor unit lit up like a Christmas tree. An aluminum record spun under the pamograph needle. The Dictograph transmitter crackled with static. White ticker tape came spitting out of the teletype machine. Somewhere in the building a crooked cop was making a telephone call.

Saint Wabasha

The entire Midwest was in the grip of a heat wave that squeezed on through June; 90° was topped every day.

In St. Paul a withering Grover Mudd scribbled notes in the press seats of the hearing room at the State Capitol. Governor Olson's crime bills were being hotly debated. Some of the proposed laws had little or no opposition.

The state would enter into reciprocal agreements with other states for the extradition of criminals.

The court would have discretionary power to deny bail before trial.

All hospitals, physicians, and nurses would be required to report immediately cases of injuries caused by dangerous weapons.

But the unions, growing more powerful with every election, were opposing the establishment of a state police force, claiming it would be used against them. They also argued that some amendments being attached to the crime bills were merely attempts by business groups to thwart union activities. All told, there were thirty-six proposed changes in Minnesota's crime laws.

Grover caught the Wabasha Street trolley at the foot of the capitol, his ears ringing with politics, his shirt wringing with sweat. He took his usual seat in the back and hung his head and arms out the window. The streetcar was packed, over fifty people, lawmakers and clericals on their lunch hour, hopping downtown.

As he sat in the sun Grover's troubled mind tried to

piece together the broken parts of his life. He had read
again the yellowing newspaper accounts of his father's
train wreck. It was painful. The writers of the day were
merciless when it came to the old engineer. The fatal-
ities list read just as Harv Bennett suggested it might.
Among the dead was a small boy. Last name, Howard.
Had Grover Mudd been hired out of pity? He let the
thought of it melt in the heat.

Grover was hungry for lunch, but concerned about
the afternoon tryst to follow. As beautiful as she was,
it still didn't feel right.

The trolley had just gotten under way, jerking down
Wabasha Hill, when Grover was jolted by a dull thump.
The car picked up speed. The dead silence that precip-
itates shock swept over the passengers, followed by a
host of screams. The trolley was running wild. Grover
pulled in his head and arms and grabbed onto the seat
for his life. This was it, he believed—those nameless,
faceless people were after him again. They were not
about to let him get on with his life. No, he was to die
on Wabasha Street outside a seedy saloon, his body
twisted like a pretzel inside the mangled remains of a
banana-yellow streetcar.

The intersections flashed by with the feel of a
newsreel—College Avenue, Tenth Street, West Exchange—Wabasha Street as Grover Mudd had never
seen it before, run through a projector at triple speed.
Automobiles swerved, their brakes screeching mad. Pedestrians jumped from the way. The ruins of the old
State Capitol suggested a monument to some lost civ-
ilization. The façades were off the speakeasies, the café
fronts boasted of air-cooling. And sitting on the sidewalk under a cigar-store awning was Fuzzy Byron. In
a senseless act of desperation Grover Mudd screamed
his name out the window. Fuzzy raised his bottle in
salute as his only friend in the world shot by.

The trolley continued its mad path toward the heart
of the Loop District. Sparks shot off the cables. Grover

put his hands to his ears. A man kicked out a window and jumped. Grover saw him roll in the street.

They roared into the theater district, where movie stars waved good-bye, where Chief Wabasha was born again and running wild on the silver screen. At congested Seventh Street Grover closed his eyes and covered his head. Then, as suddenly as it began, the wild flight was over.

When Grover Mudd opened his eyes it was his lungs that hurt the most. He was in the fetal position. Breathing was difficult. He could see blue sky and a sign that read SAINT FRANCIS HOTEL. He was dead, and Saint Peter was waiting for him to check in.

The trolley was on its side. The back door flopped open. Grover crawled into the sun and dropped to the street. Somebody helped him to his feet. He spat blood from his mouth. His fingers patted his body. Only bumps and bruises.

The wayward trolley had a bashed-in cab. The motorman had jumped to the rear. The coal truck they'd smashed into was separated from its trailer, the load of coal scattered up Wabasha Street and down Seventh. Groans of pain rumbled through the wreckage. A crowd was gathering. A siren was screaming. Grover Mudd had a story to cover. He pulled a notebook from his shirt pocket and found a stubby pencil in his pants pocket, but when he went to write, the lead broke.

———————

"Are you nervous?" she asked him.

"I guess I'm still a little shaken from the accident."

"And nobody got killed?"

"About forty people with injuries," Grover told her. "The one guy who jumped got hurt the worst."

They were at the Lowry Hotel at Fourth and Wabasha, behind City Hall. It was a modest room, but clean and comfortable. The air-cooler was working overtime.

"I had a room at the Hotel Saint Paul overlooking the park," Roxanne Schultz said. "I was surprised when you wouldn't meet me there."

"I just thought this might be less expensive," Grover said, sitting on the edge of the huge bed.

"Did she work there?"

"Yes."

"I thought that might be it. Leave it to me to pick the wrong hotel." Roxanne closed the drapes. "I'm afraid this is as dark as it gets," she said with a nervous laugh. "One of the drawbacks of a daytime affair. I hope you're not modest."

She was beautiful, and playful and sassy, not as subdued as Grover would have liked. Her dress was a cool summer pink. She kicked off her shoes and strolled to the bed. Her perfume was intoxicating. He took her hips in his hands and pressed his face against her tummy. She stroked his hair. His heart was racing. He swallowed a cough. She kissed his head.

Something was stopping him. Grover dropped his arms. She took hold of his face. Her pure blue gaze was heartwarming. She understood.

Roxanne moved back to the window. She parted the drapes and Grover could see the windows of City Hall peeking in on them.

"Dag tells people he's cured." She shook her head in disbelief. "That morning you took me," Roxanne said softly, "was the first time I ever felt pleasure with a man inside me."

"Better than opium?" he asked with a curious smile.

"Better than opium," she assured him.

"Come here."

She didn't come as close this time, teased him with distance. Grover stretched a hand between her legs and inched her dress over her knees. He unfastened her stockings and helped them to the floor. He ran his hands up the backs of her thighs and pulled her close. He stripped her of her panties, then let her dress fall back into place.

They stretched out on the bed.

Her kisses were juicy; she was good with her tongue. His hands filled with her flesh. She squirmed and moaned beneath him. She pulled his ear to her lips and licked it out. The sensation was maddening.

"Do it with your fingers," Roxanne whispered. "Do it now. I don't want to lose it."

Grover knelt back and pushed her dress over her well-rounded hips. Her lovely pink thighs matched her outfit. She spread her legs, not the least bit self-conscious. He parted her cunt with the tip of his finger and she groaned with delight. He teased her some, inching his fingers in a little farther with each stroke. She thrust her hips at his hand, forcing his fingers inside her as far as they could go. With his other hand he stroked her hair.

She asked him to go slow, to go fast. She closed her eyes in delight. She was really a fingers girl, and Grover found it exciting. He pushed them deep inside her, then withdrew them slowly so that just the tips were inside her. And she called for more. And he thrust them deep inside her again. It was taking longer than he expected, but Grover could see she was coming. Slowly but surely it was overtaking her. Her breathing was heavy, her moaning grew loud. She squirmed into him and threw her arms around his neck. Her whole body quivered. He held her close, his fingers stroking her as fast as he could.

She flopped on her back, her legs lifeless. Grover was still fingering her. Roxanne smiled. He pulled his hand away slow, then gently stroked the wet hairs a few more times. Grover Mudd lay down beside her and wrapped her in his arms.

Roxanne Schultz was a happy bundle of energy. It was a side of her he had not expected. She kissed him over and over and told him how great he was. She hiked up her dress, threw her legs over his body and settled on top of him. She took his face in her hands and kissed him again, an electrifying kiss. She brushed his hair back, giving him the feeling he had been a good little lover.

"Mommy's got something special for you."

Roxanne slid down and sat on his knees. She undid his belt buckle and pulled the thin strap slowly through the loops. She dragged his pants halfway down his legs. She stuck her hand in his shorts and Grover was swimming in that sea of sensations a woman's first touch brings. It was only in her hand a minute, then it was in her mouth.

And he truly believed she was doing it out of enjoyment, not to reward him. And he was going to ask her to stop, to finish him by hand. He did not want to come in her mouth. He had never done that sort of thing. But she showed no eagerness to stop, and Grover was beyond control.

She gagged a little but licked him clean. Grover Mudd was half dead. She unbuttoned his shirt and pressed her body over his. His chest could barely stand the pressure. Grover was too tired to complain. He worked her dress up so he could rest it between her legs. His lips were on her neck. His hands clung to her naked hips.

There is something perversely satisfying about fucking another man's woman. The ultimate vengeance. Better than murder. It was an hour later before they were completely naked. They lay side by side, listening to the hum of the air-cooler unit. Grover finally released a pent-up cough.

"Is there a chance you knew my brother?" Roxanne asked him.

"I know what he suffered."

"When I was a little girl on the farm my brother was next to God."

"Are your folks still alive?"

"My mother is."

"Where does she live?"

Roxanne hesitated. "She lives on a farm."

"I wonder how many guys like me and your brother had to put our lives in the hands of a Nina Clifford?"

"How many women?" Roxanne wondered. "Why don't you write something about it? If you're still a writer."

"I hate going into that house," Grover confessed, "but for an hour or two I can be free of every problem in the world. Problems I can no longer remember being without." He covered his face and coughed again. "I wish I were in a field of poppies right now."

"I have some with me." Roxanne rolled over and pulled open her purse on the night table. "It's best when smoked, but eating it will still do the job. Go easy. I have a feeling Nina Clifford won't be in business much longer."

Grover had to ask. "Would she ever sell it to children?"

"Don't be ridiculous. Here, just take a tincture and pop it under your tongue. Feel your problems melt away."

He opened his mouth and she popped the laudanum in as if it were candy. He climbed on top of her and ran his hands up and down her creamy smooth body. The drug tasted like ambrosia. For the first time in a long time Grover Mudd was smiling. "Roxy, this is going to be the wildest time we've ever had in our lives."

Her laugh was erotic.

He parted her legs and slipped inside her, warm and easy.

Roxanne grabbed him and forced him deeper.

Grover pressed his lips over hers. They swapped tongues and sucked the dream drug into their brains.

"Yeah, operator, Cedar 1820."

"Thank you."

"Harry?"

"Yeah."

"Inspector Roache here."

"Hey, Hitler, how ya doin'?"

"Just fine. Listen, I wonder if Dutch has got that board up today."

"C'mon, you know it's up, the horses are running in an hour."

"Better take it down."

"What?"

"Take it down. St. Sauver's gone nuts. There's a war going on over here. The chief is sending a couple boys over there to check you out."

"You'll close us down tighter than a clam's ass."

"Well, just put it back up after they leave."

"See that they get here before the first race."

"I'll take care of it."

The stenographer checked the clock and expanded her notes. Special Agent Steff Koslowski removed his headphones. "Whose number is Cedar 1820?"

Commissioner St. Sauver put his headphones down and rubbed the insults from his ears. "Royal Cigar Store on Wabasha. Dutch Otto. Can we wrap this up by the end of the summer? I can't rebuild a police department until I get the bad apples out. Last week I ordered eighteen plainclothesmen back into uniform and into radio cars. These guys may be crooked cops but they're still cops. They're becoming suspicious. I also ordered all slot machines seized."

"We haven't got the chief on wire yet. In fact, all we've really got are a few lowly inspectors. But we're getting there. I can feel it."

Gil St. Sauver wiped the perspiration from his face and downed a Coke. "The only thing I feel is this damn weather."

Steff leaned back and stuck his face in the fan. "I've heard things aren't much better in Chicago. People are dropping dead like flies." He sipped water from his glass. His face soured. "Nothing personal, Commissioner, but doesn't St. Paul's drinking water taste kind of fishy?"

"No, it tastes fine. It smells fishy. Plug your nose when you drink it." Gil St. Sauver walked to the window. The glass was replaced with a screen. The afternoon sun was blazing. He peeked down Steep Street. "Has there been any mention of Nina Clifford?"

"None," Steff told him. "I really think she's small potatoes."

"I'm going to make that old lady bleed."

Steff joined him at the window, praying for a breeze off the river. "What do you know about Grover Mudd?"

"He's an S.O.B. A mediocre writer mad at the world. Still, I can't help but like him sometimes. He was a good football player before the war."

"Is he sick?"

"He got gassed overseas. It'll get him sooner or later. Why do you ask?"

"Just curious."

An officer on a shiny motorcycle pulled out of the station and roared up the street. St. Sauver tapped Steff's shoulder. "See that?" he said. "I just got my hands on six new motorcycles with radios. I'm training a motorcycle squad now, picked the men myself. I've also got new weapons and new squad cars on order."

"Do you really think you can clean up this town?"

"I know I can. As soon as this operation is out in the open we'll begin raiding those hotels along St. Peter Street."

"I'm having second thoughts about turning these transcripts over to the *Frontier News*," said Steff.

"We promised Walt Howard. That front-page coverage will guarantee us a second grand jury."

"It may cost us some convictions. We've never played this wire game before. It's going to raise a lot of legal questions."

St. Sauver turned and surveyed Steff Koslowski's col-

lection of gadgets and maze of wires. "I want these men
out of my police department and out of my town, and
I'm going to use every trick in the book. Or write a
new book."

The bell rang on the monitor unit. "Here we go
again."

They put headphones on and poured themselves
more fishy water.

"Yeah, operator, Riverview 0923."
"Thank you."
"Hollyhocks Club."
"Who's this talking?"
"Eddie."
"Eddie, Roache here."
"Hey, Hitler, how they hanging?"
"Right where the women like 'em."
"Atta boy."
"Say, Eddie, tell Rankin to take those slot machines
down."
"What did you say?"
"Take the slots and lock 'em up. The chief is sending
some boys out there tonight. St. Sauver is on his ass.
He wants Rankin to know."

Saint Roxanne

The July sun was a blistering 102°. Homer Van Meter was sick. He read the *Frontier News* in shock.

DILLINGER KILLED
IN CHICAGO
Shot Down by G-Men Outside Biograph Theater
Lady in Red Dress Led Public Enemy into Fed Snare

Van Meter shredded the paper and hurled it across St. Peter Street. The news floated over downtown traffic. He rushed back to the newsstand and paid the man for a copy of the *North Star Press*.

JOHN DILLINGER DEAD
Only Two of Gang Remain
Van Meter, "Baby Face" Nelson Still Elude U.S. Manhunt

John Dillinger died in an alley, like a dirty dog. A photograph of him spread out in the back of a wagon blotted the front page. Homer Van Meter was furious. Enraged. He ripped the paper to pieces and whipped it around the busy intersection. The noonday crowd stopped to watch. Once again he returned to the newsstand. "Give me those newspapers."

"What the hell are you doing?"

He pulled his gun. "Give them all to me."

"You got 'em, mac. I sell them, I don't want to be in them."

Van Meter tore the stand apart. He put six bullets through the headlines. People dove for cover. A hundred copies of the *North Star Press* got kicked across St. Peter. The *Frontier News* shot down Seventh Street. Homer Van Meter took off running.

On a residential side street in the Frogtown neighborhood Baby Face Nelson loaded the last of his weapons into the trunk of a stolen car. The asphalt was steaming. The metal of the car burned like fire.

Homer Van Meter approached him from behind. "What's doing?"

Nelson was startled. He turned with a shriek and leaned back on the car. It burned his skin. "Don't ever sneak up on a killer!"

"What are you packing for?"

"Didn't you hear the news? It was on the radio. Freddie and Ma Barker bought it in Florida," Nelson told him. "Feds got 'em. Christ, they're everywhere. Get your gear and rear in the car and let's go."

"And where we gonna go?"

"Mexico."

"On what money?"

"The bank's money."

"What bank is that?"

"The one we're going to rob," Nelson announced. "We'll pick one out in the car."

"Oh, that's brilliant," Van Meter said sardonically. "Unpack it, we're staying here."

"No dice, Homer, I'm in charge now. You got some kind of dick disease. I heard all about it." Nelson leaned his pudgy little body into the trunk of the car and arranged the weapons according to kill power.

Van Meter slammed the trunk lid on his head. Baby yelps from Baby Face were muffled. Van Meter grabbed him by the ass, pulled him from the trunk, and tossed him into the sizzling street where Nelson bounced about like a bug in a frying pan.

"Are you crazy?" Nelson screamed in surprise.

Van Meter kicked him bloody. He gave him an extra kick for John Dillinger. Then he pulled Nelson's pants down to his ankles and dragged his bare ass across the red-hot tar. And the last time Homer Van Meter saw Baby Face Nelson he was bouncing down Frogtown with his pants down.

An hour later Homer Van Meter stood like a scarecrow on the Lake Phalen beach. The water was thick with swimmers. The sand was coated with the blankets of sunbathers. Canoes navigated the channels that led to the other lakes.

Dag Rankin dragged himself from the water and picked up the towel at Van Meter's feet. He buried his wet face in it. His two-piece swimsuit was dripping with confidence. "A new man," he said. "That's what a good swim does to me, makes me a new man. I heard three more people right here in St. Paul dropped dead from the heat today. Isn't it amazing what the heat can do to a person? Like your friend Dillinger. Just went to a movie to beat the heat, and the heat beat him."

"We gotta talk, Mr. Rankin. I need that favor now."

Dag Rankin tossed the towel around his neck the way a lifeguard would. He bowed his head in resignation. "Sorry, Homer, you're too hot to handle. I really suggest you leave St. Paul. You're trouble for all of us. This St. Sauver is starting to make waves."

"I want the cure."

"C'mon, Homer, you're practically Public Enemy Number One. Your picture's been in the paper more than Roosevelt. You can't just waltz into the Mayo Clinic."

Van Meter was agitated, almost desperate. "Word on the street is you've cornered the dope market and cut everybody off. Gonna make you one of the biggest men in the country. I want in."

The sun beat down on Rankin's face, tan and taut,

in stark contrast to Van Meter's pale looks. "A lot of people want in. But out-of-work bootleggers are a dime a dozen, and that's all I need."

"Out-of-work bootleggers never done for you what I done."

"Yes," Rankin agreed, "that's true. What about that crackpot Nelson?"

"He blew town. I'm going it alone."

One of Rankin's men approached and interrupted the conversation. "She's with him now, at the paper."

"Bring the car around," Rankin ordered, controlling his anger. He gathered his clothes and gave Van Meter a second look. "So you want in? I may have another job for you, Homer. A real hero this time."

———————

Grover Mudd parked the company car off Payne Avenue as instructed. The Mexican lady, babbling in Spanish, jumped from the backseat. Roxanne Schultz followed her. She understood enough of the language to be upset. Grover understood nothing.

The women cut through a vacant lot strewn with broken bottles. Grover hurried to keep up with them. The brewery was belching white smoke and the trains steaming out of the beer factory spit coal dust into the hot evening air. The dirty haze stung Grover's eyes and irritated his throat. The heat was like soup. He stopped to cool his breathing. To his amazement the women disappeared over the ravine. Grover rushed to the edge. "Roxanne?"

She paid no attention.

"Roxy," he called again, "don't go down there. That's Swede Hollow."

Grover watched Roxanne follow the Mexican woman down a zigzaggedy trail as if on her way home. He started down after them. Gnats swarmed about his face. The sun was setting. Mosquitoes were waking up for the sticky night ahead. At the railroad tracks Grover saw Roxanne hurry across a rickety bridge and head down the path that ran past the shanties. She seemed to know where she was going. Grover grabbed tree branches and faltered down the hill to the bridge, where he stumbled and fell. His hands stuck in wormy garbage. The slimy creek smelled of sewage. The stench turned his stomach. Grover spit into the woods. He wiped his hands in the weeds and chased after Roxanne.

The Mexican woman stood outside the broken gate, mumbling more Spanish, as Grover approached. She clenched a crucifix in her fist. The whitewashed house looked ready to collapse. The posts that held it above the ground were rotting. The door was open. Grover paused on the stairs. He heard a swirling roar and saw green water gush out of a giant pipe at the foot of the brewery. At the Hamm mansion overhead the windows were closed and the shades were drawn. The long grass was turning yellow.

Inside the shack it was dark and hot, the air stifling. The frail body of an old lady was curled up on a filthy couch like a cowering dog. Roxanne, so out of place, stood to the side. A doctor was packing instruments into his black bag. Grover moved along the wall, staying out of the way.

The doctor closed his bag and stood. He turned to Roxanne. "Daughter?"

"Yes."

"I'm sorry," he said. The doctor took a place of mourning next to Grover. "There's nothing I can do," he whispered.

Grover looked out the door and shook his head. "It's hard to believe these people live down here."

"Haven't you heard?" the doctor asked. "Swede Hollow has been condemned. These people have all been evicted. Commissioner St. Sauver has ordered the fire department to douse the hollow with gasoline and set it ablaze."

Roxanne knelt at her mother's side and took hold of

her hand. The old lady couldn't open her eyes but she smiled at the touch. Her voice was barely audible. "Did you bring Mamma's medicine?"

Roxanne's face collected the tears. Her voice choked with apology. "I couldn't, Mamma. I just couldn't no more."

It was not the dying mother who captured Grover's sympathies; it was the life passing out of her daughter's eyes that tore at his heart. How many sons and daughters felt compelled to lie about their parents? In the sunlight streaming through the open door he reexamined the saintly beauty of Roxanne's face, the rose of her cheeks, the melting of her icy blue eyes. She possessed resplendence no man had a right to. Not Dag Rankin. Not Grover Mudd. He slipped outside, leaving the death scene behind.

The mosquitoes were out in force now. Huge flies buzzed the creek. Grover rolled down his sleeves to protect his arms from the bites. The bewildered poor were lining the path. Through the stink came the smell of malt. He lit a cigarette.

So Gil St. Sauver was going to burn the hollow. And where do the poor go, Mr. Commissioner? Grover began to believe that in his drive to clean up the city the new man in the Public Safety Office was as ruthless as any gangster. St. Sauver had used him, had preyed on his hostilities. He'd spoon-fed him the story of Rankin's impotence knowing damn well the "Monkey Business" column would be the result. And so what if somebody got hurt. It wouldn't be the future commissioner.

Two men stood at the top of the ravine staring down at him. Grover was blinded by the sinking sun and couldn't make out the faces. One of the sinister figures was skinny, the other overdressed, considering the heat. It was not until he turned and limped away that Grover Mudd recognized him.

In the cool summer lair of Nina Clifford the Big Holy Spook was stretched out on the woolly couch. The madam was at his ear. Valerie the whore was at his feet. Nina rolled the marijuana in paper and put a match to it. The smoke swirled through the candlelight.

"Puff a little juju, Preacher. The time has come to talk."

The Spook took the weed in his mouth and sucked hard. Valerie ran her hands over his pant legs.

Nina stroked his fat cheeks with affection. "Where does Dag Rankin keep the opium? We know the black snowballs come in on the train, but where does it go from there? In a warehouse? Into a cave? The Hollyhocks Club?"

The big preacher smoked. Valerie worked a hand under his pant leg.

Nina spoke softly. "Does Roxanne know where it is? Talk to me, Preacher Man. Time is running out. Rankin has cut us all off, and that lunatic St. Sauver is after my hide. He's actually formed a Purity Squad." She leaned into his face. "I've been good to you, Preacher. Didn't I let you spend time with every colored girl that worked for me?"

The Big Holy Spook held the smoke in his lungs and closed his eyes. Valerie caressed his knee.

"What do you owe him?" Nina Clifford asked. "Did he promise to fix your privates? So they work just like his?" Nina laughed. "Dag Rankin is as limp as a wet noodle. Always will be. There is no cure." She turned and snapped her fingers. "Show him, Val."

Valerie stood, stepped back and did a striptease in front of them.

Nina placed a hand on the preacher's thighs. "A white woman," Nina whispered. "Look at those breasts, soft and sumptuous. See how that creamy white skin curves, how it bounces. And her hips, Spook, now those are hips a big strong man can latch onto. Have you ever seen so much white skin in your entire life? There's

more. White northern cunt from the land of sky-blue
waters. Do you want a peek, Preacher Man?" Nina
stuck her hand between his legs. "There's nothing happening here, but you're sweating, Preacher." She
winked at Valerie. "Go slow, dearie. Let's see if we
can get the pastor to stand."

Valerie turned her back to them and inched her
panties down her legs.

Nina Clifford rubbed the Big Holy Spook, rubbed
him the wrong way.

"It is sin!" he exploded. "It is sin! It is sin!" He
bounced Nina off the couch and picked Valerie up from
behind by her tits. "It is sin!"

The old madam was furious. "You big, stupid ape.
I'll teach you. Nina Clifford is going out of this world
in style. I am sick and tired of living off what that
dickless boss of yours doles out. I will build a new house,
I will buy new girls, and St. Paul will be the wonderful
city it once was, and I will be the queen."

While Nina Clifford was giving her "back to the good
old days" speech, Valerie was having the life squeezed
out of her tits.

"It is a sin! It is a sin!" Marijuana smoke was spewing
out his mouth.

"Big nigger," Nina raged on, "isn't afraid of anybody, huh?" She passed through the curtain and
stomped up the basement stairs. "You will talk to me.
You will tell me everything."

Valerie passed out in the Spook's arms. He dropped
her to the floor.

A moment later the boots of St. Paul's finest hit the
stairs. Nina Clifford wagged behind, cackling with cer-
titude. "You will talk to me."

When the curtain parted again there stood the only
man in St. Paul bigger than the Big Holy Spook: Patrolman Emil Gunderson, in full uniform, nightstick in
hand. He was an inch taller than the preacher, and
where the Spook showed signs of fat the big cop was

mean muscle. He was twitching with anticipation. "Ask him one more time, Miss Clifford."

"Pardon me, Pastor," Nina said sweetly, "where does Dag Rankin stash the opium?"

"Sinners!" screamed the Spook.

"Beat it out of him," Nina ordered.

Emil Gunderson raised his nightstick high and brought the long arm of the law down upon the head of the Big Holy Spook.

Saint Jude

Grover Mudd sat inside the Union Depot, gazing out at the train yard. A convention of bugs gathered under the lights. Again the night was hot and muggy. Other reporters and cameramen were milling about the area. Franklin Roosevelt was coming.

There was no crowd. The President was returning from the West, passing through St. Paul on his way to a physical examination at the Mayo Clinic in Rochester. But surely he would stop and make some kind of statement to the press. It was an election year and St. Paul was a Democratic stronghold. Yes, the reporters believed, he would stop and say something.

It was getting late. The train was past due. Grover lit a cigarette. A pair of prostitutes were seated across the way.

Even with Roxanne Schultz working into his life, the long summer days seemed awful lonely. He missed working with Fuzzy Byron. He missed Stormy Day. And what of Roxanne? How much of Rankin's business did she really know about? Did Rankin have Stormy killed? Was Rankin following him now? Did Roxanne know the answers? She did not talk from the heart the way Stormy did. Roxanne Schultz shared nothing but her body and her drugs. Would she really leave Rankin? What was she waiting for? Grover's reporter mind was working overtime. For every answer he gave he came up with three more questions.

"Got a light, handsome?"

Grover looked up. One of the prostitutes was dangling a cigarette between her fingers. He struck a match.

She was a skinny girl. She took his hands in hers and put the flame to her mouth. "Where you headed?"

"Probably hell," Grover answered.

The girl giggled. "I have friends there. Give them my best." She returned to her seat and crossed her legs.

"We've cleared the yard," an official announced. "He's coming. Track one."

They poured into the boarding area, pencils in hand, cameras on shoulders. Depot workers dropped what they were doing and filtered out to the platform. Even the wayward girls took positions in the window. All was silent but for the rush of the train. Anticipation was high. Would the President talk about the gangsters who were dropping like flies? Would he defend his attorney general's attacks on St. Paul? Would he mention the cleanup campaign?

Grover Mudd grew knots in his stomach as he saw the sharp beam of light bearing down on him like a page out of his nightmare. But, as in the nightmare, the tracks were clear, the lights were green, and the presidential express roared by without so much as a wink. The disappointed huddle watched the speedy train curve to the right beneath the sandstone cliffs and disappear around the bend in the river where Pig's Eye Parrant once sold whiskey to the Indians.

"I think he was in the last car," somebody said.

"It's a shame."

"I'll never vote for him again."

The humidity was murder. Grover Mudd went back inside and collapsed on a wood bench. The ladies of the evening were gone. Payday was two days away, but it didn't matter. Nina Clifford said the town was dry.

"Who's in St. Paul?" the President asked.

"A handful of local reporters, two prostitutes, and one dope-head," his aide told him.

Grover grinned at the thought. Then he had another

thought. Franklin Roosevelt, the man who brought back beer and whiskey, the man bringing an end to the gangster era, an end to the depression, could he be the man to put an end to organized crime forever?

"You can't write something like that," Grover told himself. "They'll crucify you."

He remembered the words of Walt Howard: *"I print everything you write. That will be your undoing."*

"Ah, what the hell," Grover said, "we'll do this one for Saint Jude, patron saint of lost causes." He sat up and fished through his pockets for a pencil. He flipped open his notebook and began writing.

And true to his word, Walt Howard printed every single letter.

SAME OLD MONKEY BUSINESS
by Grover Mudd

There is a unique advantage to being a columnist for a dying newspaper. Complete, total, and unequivocal honesty.

I have spent the past several years writing much about the crime problem here in St. Paul. So it is with a touch of irony that I now find myself involved in criminal activity.

In the cover of night I steal down a lonely street and knock on a basement door. I hand over some money and then spend a few hours breaking the law. I smoke opium. I offer no excuses for my behavior, it simply makes me feel better. If people drank as little as I smoked opium, alcoholism in America would become a thing of the past.

Rampaging crime in America began in 1919 with the passage of the Volstead Act. Prohibition was dynamite that exploded. But I believe an even slower fuse was ignited five years earlier— Saint Valentine's Day, 1914. That was the day President Woodrow Wilson signed into law the Harrison Act, the day opiates disappeared from the corner drugstore and the dope-peddler appeared on the corner. Opium, cocaine, morphine, and later heroin could no longer be sold legally.

Did we learn the lessons of Prohibition? Will narcotics become the next moonshine?

There is mounting evidence right here in St. Paul that this has already begun.

Do you remember Casey, the monster gorilla from Omaha, and Dag, the wet noodle of a gangster from Chicago I made famous in my "Monkey Business" column last autumn? Well, this past spring Casey got Tanya in a family way, recorded for posterity on the front page of the other paper. But Dag's luck has gone limp. He first tried to spread the ridiculous rumor that he was cured. This fell flat. As told in a Chinese proverb I picked up in my opium den: "Man without cannonballs can never shoot cannon." Next, our new public safety commissioner began dropping in on Dag's nightclub, deflating his business. So to regain erect status Dag turned to narcotics. Somewhere in our city he hoards a mountain of the stuff.

I hope we soon come to the same solution with narcotics we came to with alcohol: Legalize it, inspect it, regulate it, and tax the living hell out of it. And let's do it before this gangster's resolve stiffens.

After reading "Grover's Corner" Homer Van Meter was livid. His disease was spreading fast. The dog days of August were upon him and the crippling heat wave was taking its toll. Saliva kept drooling out of his mouth.

He was standing on a corner surrounded by the big brick warehouses of Lowertown. In the noon heat it was like standing between brick ovens, boiling his temper along with his skin. Dag Rankin was a liar, but Homer Van Meter had been a fool. He pulled up his untucked shirt to reveal the .38 stuffed in his pants. He slid the newspaper in front of it and dropped his shirt over them both.

Homer Van Meter marched up Fourth Street, past the *Frontier News* and the *North Star Press*. The local chapter of Moral Rearmament was picketing both sides of the street. On the *Frontier News* side of the street they were demanding the ouster of dope fiend Grover Mudd. On the *North Star* side of the street they de-

manded the closing of the *Frontier News*. Van Meter
stopped and wiped his mouth. Which window, he wondered, was Grover's Corner? Kill him? He wanted to
kiss the son of a bitch.

Nobody was more surprised by "Grover's Corner" than
Roxanne Schultz.

Nobody was more angry or more humiliated than Dag
Rankin. On the dance floor of the Hollyhocks Club
ballroom he took his humiliation out on Roxanne.
"How did he know about the dope?"

"Everybody in town knows about the dope," Roxanne told him.

"Yeah, they do now." He slapped her again and she
crashed into the bar.

"How did he know about the cure?"

Roxanne laughed in his face. "He could tell by the
way I fucked him."

Rankin rolled the newspaper tight and beat her to
the floor with it. "What else did you tell him?"

Roxanne kept laughing as the *Frontier News* was repeatedly slammed across her head. She had been a fool.
Grover Mudd had used her. He had used her for her
opium. He had used her for information on Rankin.
But worst of all, he'd used her lonely cunt. She had
been a fool. Rankin grabbed her hair and jerked her
face from the floor. "Grover's Corner" ripped across
her nose. The newspaper would leave her face bloody
and bruised but it would never scratch her heart. This,
she swore, was her last beating. If she survived she
would be free.

Dag Rankin backed off. Roxanne lay still on the floor.
She heard a bottle break. Was this the part where he
cut her up? Then across the dance floor she saw a pair
of worn shoes and ill-fitting pants.

"Is that how the dickless treat their women?" It was
Homer Van Meter. He leveled his .38 at Rankin's head.

"What are you doing here?" Rankin demanded to know. "Don't you know the cops are watching this place?"

"Your cops or St. Sauver's?"

"Put that thing away and get the hell out of here."

"I've come for the cure."

"You're not ready for it."

"There ain't no cure," screamed Van Meter, foaming from the mouth. "You limpy liar." He pulled the newspaper from his pants. "I can read."

"I suppose you're going to believe that Grover Mudd," Rankin argued. "A dying dope-head writing for a dying newspaper. Don't make me laugh."

Roxanne stirred on the floor. Van Meter put the question to her. "Who's telling the truth, him or the newspaper?"

She climbed to the bar and poured herself a drink. It stung going down.

"Answer me," Van Meter ordered.

"Slim," she said with a painful smile, "that newspaper in your hand is stiffer than he'll ever be."

Van Meter turned on Rankin. "There ain't no cure, you dickless liar. You owe me ten grand."

"Ten grand? Now how do you figure that?"

"That's my fee for services rendered."

"Who do you think you are? A dirty rat like you making those kind of demands. In two years I'll be king of Chicago." Homer Van Meter fired a shot over his head. Rankin ducked. A bottle above him exploded.

Roxanne didn't flinch.

"I'm the man with the gun," Van Meter barked out. "And in two minutes you're going to be dead. Is ten grand worth dying for?"

Roxanne, bloody and bruised, was smirking in her drink.

Dag Rankin thought it over. "I haven't got that kind of cash around."

Again Van Meter turned to Roxanne. "Is he bull-shitting me?"

The skinny bastard might kill her, too, Roxanne thought. "No bullshit, Slim. This dope puts all his cash in dope. But he can get cash for you. Can't you, sweetie?"

"Give me a call tomorrow," Rankin told him. "I'll tell you where you can pick up the money."

"I want it by tomorrow night, Rankin. If not, I'm coming for you."

Roxanne grabbed a bottle from behind the bar. "How about a lift, Slim?"

"Okay," said Van Meter, surprised by the request, "but I don't do nothing."

That was the funniest thing Roxanne Schultz had ever heard, and she was hysterical as she left the Hollyhocks Club behind.

Nina Clifford escaped the afternoon heat by sinking into a bathtub filled with scented water. She was old. The summers were too hot, the winters too cold. The spring rains caused her arthritis to flare up. It was only the cool, colorful autumns she enjoyed now.

The Big Holy Spook had told them nothing and Patrolman Gunderson had dumped the half-dead preacher near the tracks.

She folded the newspaper, sipped white wine from a chilled glass and read "Grover's Corner" one more time. Grover Mudd was smart. There would be no blackmailing him.

Now the whole world knew about the dope. Nina's mind raced over the chase. Rankin had it. The crooked cops wanted it. St. Sauver was after it. The G-men were hot on the trail. The newspapers had picked up the scent. Chicago's mob would pay handsomely just for a whiff of the stuff. So where was it? Even if the Spook knew, he was a lunatic, and what kind of information could be extracted from a lunatic? That left Dag Rankin, and maybe . . .

Someone was knocking on her front door. The madam had given the help the afternoon off. She pulled her weary bones from the cold water and slipped into her Oriental robe.

The house was dark. The shades were drawn and the curtains were closed to keep out the sun. When Nina inched open the front door the daylight stung her eyes. She could see the outline of a woman's troubled face, the glow of golden hair, and when the caller moved her cracked lips to speak Nina Clifford wanted to cry.

"I've left Dag for good. I need a place to stay."

Saint Trinity

The three intrepid saints parked on University Avenue, just west of the State Capitol. The sun died behind them and the street lamps popped on. Floodlights outlined the halls of government. A ribbon of used-car lots lit up like a cheap carnival. Traffic was heavy but moving along.

Gil St. Sauver was behind the wheel. He balanced a shotgun against his leg, leaned his head out the window, and took a deep breath. "Feel that breeze," he said. "There's a storm coming. I can smell it. By this time tomorrow it'll feel like autumn. Count on it."

Steff Koslowski was seated across from him, his short-sleeved shirt sticking to the leather. "I hope so. One more day in that oven of a police station and I'll explode." He rested a submachine gun across his lap.

"How much longer?" St. Sauver asked.

"Maybe another month," Steff told him. "A lot of the recordings are redundant, the same evidence against the same people over and over again. But even if we don't get the chief on record the circumstantial evidence against him is mounting every day. Most of his assistants we could nail tomorrow if we had to." A shiny new motor bus stopped at the corner in front of them and shot exhaust fumes over the car. Steff winced. "Where did that thing come from?"

St. Sauver rubbed his irritated nose. "The city bought a dozen of them. They're going to try them on University Avenue to see if buses are more efficient than the streetcars. You can bet somebody got paid off."

The bus pulled away. "They stink like hell," Steff said for the record.

A wretched cough tore up the backseat. Steff Koslowski pretended not to notice. Gil St. Sauver wasn't so kind. "Still a little warm for a coat, isn't it, Mudd?"

"Summer cold," Grover told the commissioner, bundling up.

"Where did you get the piece?" St. Sauver wanted to know.

"What piece?"

"The one bulging under your coat like a cannon?"

"That's my typewriter."

St. Sauver looked over his shoulder. "You just keep that typewriter in your pants tonight. That's all I need, is you blowing your toes off. Why don't you go home? This is probably a wild goose chase, anyway."

"A deal is a deal," Grover reminded him.

The commissioner scoffed. "If I thought Walt Howard was going to send you I never would have called him."

"And I thought you were starting to like me."

"You know, Mudd, every time I think there may be an ounce of responsibility in that thick head of yours you go and pull something that drives me right up a wall. Smoking that shit and telling the world. I ought to bust your ass. And don't give me any of that wounded soldier crap."

Steff Koslowski could feel the tension rising. They were all three in an awkward situation—the city, the feds, and the press on a joint stakeout. Six months earlier they wouldn't have given each other the time of day. "That's a beautiful sculpture up there on the dome—that gold chariot and those four horses," he said, trying to make conversation.

"The quadriga," St. Sauver told the G-man. "It represents the triumph of government, or so we've been told. The thing is all carved up. Every little bastard that ever toured the capitol engraved his initials on a horse's ass."

"Still," Steff said, "it's an impressive capitol."

"There's a whole master plan by Cass Gilbert, the guy who designed it. That cesspool of a neighborhood out front is supposed to come down and be made into a capitol approach park with a sweeping view of the city. Nothing in front of the capitol for three blocks except parkland. Then they want to run a highway from downtown St. Paul to downtown Minneapolis. Do away with Rondo Avenue. Between the park and highway everything on Wabasha and St. Peter above Tenth Street would be wiped out. Wouldn't that be a shame?" said St. Sauver with a chuckle.

Grover cleared his throat and interrupted. "What makes you so cocksure he's going to be here tonight?"

"I just told you," said St. Sauver uneasily, "it's probably a wild goose chase. Go home."

"Wild goose, my ass," Grover quipped. "You dragged the feds along to show them you mean business. You called Walt Howard to ensure press coverage. For a wild goose chase? Hah."

Steff glanced over at St. Sauver. "I've been wondering about that myself."

St. Sauver took a deep breath. "I got it from two different sources. I trust them both. He's supposed to pick up some money here tonight."

"So this is no bum tip?" Steff volunteered.

Gil St. Sauver conceded. "No bum tip." He checked his shotgun one more time. "Speaking of bums, Mudd, we've found three of them in the last week dead as a doornail. Doc Bjorkland says they all drank denatured alcohol. Looks like somebody put a batch of poison moonshine on the street."

"This is the first I've heard about it."

"Well nobody's drinking that stuff but bums. Who cares?"

"A lot of people might care."

"Don't get the city in a panic, Mudd. They're just bums, okay?"

"Your sympathy for the plight of the poor is well documented."

St. Sauver, clearly upset, leaned over the back seat. "I'm cleaning up this town, Mudd, and nobody's getting in my way. Understand? That goes for you too. I catch you dirty, I'll bust your ass."

Steff Koslowski wiped the sweat from his brow. "Will you two knock it off?"

Lightning broke over the capitol dome. Thunder rumbled in the distance. A good breeze whipped through the heat. Traffic abated. The trio of saints truced in silence. An hour passed.

He came out of the north on Rice Street, stood on the corner, and waited for the traffic light to change.

The G-man spotted him first. "That's him. That's Homer Van Meter."

"He looks like a clown," Grover remarked.

Gil St. Sauver shouldered the shotgun and grabbed the door handle. "Stay here, Mudd."

Steff Koslowski was already out of the car.

Grover Mudd came out of the backseat, service revolver in hand.

Homer Van Meter started across University Avenue.

"Homer Van Meter," the commissioner shouted. "St. Paul police!"

Van Meter didn't blink. He drew the .38 from his belt and fired twice. The shots pinged off the car, and one of the most wanted men in the country was off and running.

He ran south toward the cathedral, and then made the same mistake as his pal John Dillinger had. He turned into a blind alley. By the time he realized the error of his path he was a trapped gnome.

St. Paul's trinity of saints sealed the exit and used the alley for a shooting gallery.

Homer Van Meter raised his gun in defense but never got off a shot. So many shotgun slugs tore into his arm that his trigger hand was severed from his body. Machine-gun bullets riddled his chest and sent him flying against a wall, where his malignant heart burst. His mouth dropped open in shock, but pistol shots ruptured his perverted smile and blew out the back of his head, splattering his brains against the bricks. His smoking clothes and fleshy remains slithered onto the tar, and, in plain sight of the gilded quadriga on the State Capitol, Homer Van Meter got his final wish.

He'd been thrown to the wolves.

Saint Chester

The September night was cool and wet. After the long, hot summer the steady rain falling on the city seemed like a celestial gift.

Grover Mudd stopped by Granny Walker's to check on Fuzzy Byron. He had not seen his friend in weeks and so much had happened. For Grover there was no escaping controversy. The news of a reporter helping police gun down a gangster was no less disturbing to many than a columnist breaking the law and then boasting about it in print. But what stuck in Grover's mind was the pride in Gil St. Sauver's voice when he shouted "St. Paul Police!"

Granny told him Fuzzy had not been there in days. She promised not to refuse him shelter if he showed up.

Up at the capitol, lights were burning in the governor's office. Next door, the Historical Society was dark. Grover Mudd started down St. Peter Street. Fuzzy Byron was a bum, but a bum with a pattern. When he had a job he showed up and worked. He avoided the roughhouses, and he made sure there would be a roof over his head come night. Grover was worried, but where to look along the endless row of joints? The puddles reflected deserted sidewalks. Cars sloshed along the patched street. Up on the hill the illuminated domes of Saint Paul's Cathedral blessed the drizzle with color. The rain came down harder, and Grover jumped into the doorway of a cheap hotel.

At the top of the rickety stairs a blue-eagle sticker was pasted to the door's glass. A woman's face appeared in the window. The door opened and Grover's senses were struck by the warm redolence of a whorehouse, sweet and sinfully inviting.

"Coming in?" she asked. She was a handsome woman, full-figured, her bathrobe slit up to her thigh.

"No," Grover said, "just getting out of the rain."

"That's too bad. You're a pretty man. If you change your mind—" She portrayed a Mona Lisa smile and the door brushed closed again.

Grover Mudd turned his collar to the damp night, folded his arms and squeezed away a touch of regret.

He had not heard from Roxanne since the opium column. Did she feel betrayed? Had she left Rankin? He could smell her perfume, and just thinking about the taste of her skin got his heart pounding fast. Too fast. He coughed into his hands, and specks of blood wiped out his fantasy.

Headlights cruising down St. Peter spotlighted the rain and revealed an alley across the street, and with every passing car Grover caught the spark of a reflection, a glimmer of curiosity; more a sixth sense than anything he could discern with his eyes. Grover stepped to the curb and when the traffic cleared made his way across the street and down the dark passage that ran between the tenements. Wet cinders stuck like paste to the soles of his shoes. Trash cans spilled their guts along the walls. Rainwater swirled in circles and rushed down a manhole. Grover Mudd did not have to go far to discover his sixth sense rang true. There was Fuzzy Byron.

He was sitting in a basement window-well against the rusty cage that protected the glass, only half out of the weather. The rain poured off the bricks and ran down the side of his face. His glasses were missing, his skin was paint white, and the eyes that were so useless to him were washed closed. Grover knelt down and took

his hand. For the first time he noticed what delicate
hands they were, thin hands with long lissome fingers,
like those of a fine lady, marred only by age. The rainwater in the window-well was up to Fuzzy's lap, and
floating in it were empty bottles of beer—Hamm's,
Schmidt, cave-aged Yoerg—as if Fuzzy had tried and
rejected them all; and cradled in his arms, reflecting
the headlights, was an empty bottle of Stearns County
13. He was as content as a drunkard gets, as peaceful
as an old wino can be. He was dead.

In the September rain that warns of winter, Grover
Mudd pressed the cold skin to his lips, and unbeknownst
to him at the time he was kissing the hand of a master
whose genius would never die.

On the night Grover Mudd was grieving over his friend
Fuzzy Byron, Special Agent Steff Koslowski was grieving over fallen comrades.

BABY FACE NELSON DEAD
Last of Dillinger Gang Killed in Fox River Shootout
Two G-Men Die in Running Gun Battle

They had worked out of the Chicago office. Steff had
known them both. He removed his headphones, turned
away from the stenographer to hide his sorrow, and
folded the newspaper in half.

His investigation was almost complete. Evidence of
corruption among St. Paul's top police officials was
overwhelming. But, ironically, with the exception of a
few bad apples, the average cop on the beat was clean.
It was certainly something for St. Sauver to build on.

Steff Koslowski made his way to the window. The
cool, misty breeze splashing through the screen felt
good against his face. He watched the rain wash down
Steep Street past the county morgue, where a week
before people had stood in line to view the mutilated

body of Homer Van Meter, much as people in St. Paul had lined up fifty years earlier to see the holes in James Gang member Charlie Pitts.

The gangster era was coming to an end. The nation's police had finally joined the twentieth century. Law enforcement would never be the same. Every day the headlines told of another gangster dead, another case solved, including the biggest case of all: Police in New Jersey had arrested a man named Bruno Hauptmann and charged him with the kidnap-murder of the Lindbergh baby.

The lights were on down at Nina Clifford's place, and Steff found himself wondering about life inside a whorehouse. He often resented the Boy Scout ways his career committed him to.

"Mr. Koslowski?"

The stenographer's voice brought him back to the task at hand and he sat down at the table and adjusted the headphones to his ears.

"Hitler? Crumbs here."

"It's late. What are you calling me at home for?"

"I found a mike in my office."

"Why you whispering? I can't hear you."

"I knocked the lamp off my desk. It broke open and there was a goddamn microphone in it."

"You're joking."

"I tell you my office is wired."

"Jesus."

"Can they record that stuff?"

"I don't know, but we better check the chief's office in the morning."

"What if he's behind it?"

"No. More likely St. Sauver. Better warn the others tonight."

"How?"

"Call them up."

"Do you think that's safe?"

*"They can't hear a telephone conversation. Don't be
ridiculous. Just talk soft."*
"We gotta find where that mike leads to."

Steff Koslowski pulled his gun from the holster and
laid it on the table. The stenographer got up and
checked the bolt on the door. Thunder broke over the
river and they both jumped.

"He was buried at Oakland Cemetery," Grover Mudd
told the stonecutter.

"Oakland. How did old Fuzzy swing that?"

"When will the marker be ready?" Grover asked.

"Depends on what you want on it."

Grover bowed his head. "Just put 'Chester D. Byron.
He could paint the wind.' "

Earlier that day Grover had hiked down to Lowertown. It was cloudy and cool. He cut through Smith
Park to the warehouse district and found the building
he was looking for, on the corner of Fifth where Wacouta Street crossed and ran down to the tracks. It was
a hexagonal fortress and like most of the warehouses
it had been built of red brick during the railroad boom
of the 1890s.

Inside, it was cavernous, with high ceilings and thick
cobwebs that snaked down to the floor. The lighting
was poor. Years of dirt were ground into the planks.
Sawdust was scattered at the foot of huge crates that
could only be lifted by machine. The windows were
filthy and covered with iron masks, much like the window Fuzzy Byron chose to die in.

"Whatcha want?"

"Do you work here?"

"This is my job, whatcha want?" He was a colored
man, tall and ungainly, dressed in gray, something like
a custodian's uniform.

"Did you know a man named Chester Byron?" Grover asked.

"Chester Byron? Never heard of a Chester Byron."

"He was known around town as Fuzzy."

"Oh, yeah, Fuzzy. Little blind man, can't see a wall right in front of his face. Yup, he gots a cage up on three."

Grover reached into his pocket. "Fuzzy died the other day. I had him buried at Oakland Cemetery."

"Fuzzy died and went to Oakland. Ain't that a laugh."

"He didn't own anything of value, but I found this key on him." Grover displayed a rusty key. "A locksmith up on Wabasha told me this series is registered to this warehouse."

"Yup, sure, that's his cage key."

"Can we have a look?"

"You some kinda policeman?"

"No, I'm just an old friend and reporter doing a story."

"Newspaper story about Fuzzy. Ain't that a laugh."

They stepped into a freight elevator. The warehouse keeper pulled a rope, and the heavy lumber doors closed from the top and bottom like a big jaw. On the third floor they walked the length of the warehouse. Against the wall was a row of cages fastened to the bricks, a zoo for cartons and crates, a prison for junk.

"He wanted up here 'cause he says his stuff gots to stay dry. See if it fits," the keeper told him, pointing at a cage.

Grover put the key into the lock and turned. It clicked and opened.

Stacked neatly against the wall according to height were flat packages wrapped in thick brown paper, so neatly stacked Grover counted twelve with just a glance.

"Old Fuzzy'd come down here on the first of the month and pay his rent just like clockwork," the warehouse keeper told Grover. "Then he'd come up here and sit in this cage for hours. I let him sit here, he weren't hurting nothing. He never drank here. Except once. I come up here on a stormy day and he had his arms around one of those packages and he was crying like a baby. He musta been drunk that time."

"Can you leave me alone?"

"Yup, sure. Fuzzy dead, you gots the key. I guess you pay the rent, it's your stuff now."

Grover knelt down and examined the goods. Each one was addressed to Chester D. Byron and postmarked New York, May 1929. Not long after Fuzzy said he fell off the train. Grover lifted a package from the tallest stack. He laid it flat, address side down, and peeled it open, being careful not to tear the paper. Underneath was a sturdy canvas framed with simple wooden strips. Grover lifted the painting with his fingertips and turned it over.

"Landscapes so gorgeous city slickers would cry at the sight of them."

That's what Fuzzy said. Fuzzy had not lied.

Floating before Grover's eyes were the majestic Adirondack Mountains of New York. The dim yellow light spilling in from the hallway cast a vicarious sunset across Byron's work and gave it a noble melancholy. The scenery was wild and spacious but void of needless detail. The colors were undefinable, almost eccentric for a landscape painting.

Grover opened another, a smaller one.

It was a forest brook flowing musically into a pond, less panoramic, more intimate, with an artist's instinct for the essential. Grover carefully placed the tumbling brook next to the mountains and reached for another.

A single tree stood above the ocean shore, stripped of its leaves in the dead of autumn. Flicks of sunshine made the sky twinkle. Soft seaside colors sailed away from the tree to the unembellished edge. The work of a true loner.

Grover's grief grew with the unveiling of every painting. The theater of landscapes before him transcended
any hint of the ordinary, and in the corner of each
beautiful piece the calligraphy read, "Chester D.
Byron."

And in his mind Grover Mudd painted a picture of
his own, of a diminutive blind man sitting on a warehouse floor smelling of whiskey and rain, fighting off
the chills, hugging a masterpiece and drowning in his
watercolored memories.

Saint Jordan

"I only regret that I have but one life to lose for my country."

Pretty words, but the little fool got caught and hanged. Big Emil Gunderson turned away from the sappy green statue of Nathan Hale and marched across Summit Avenue into a small park where the avenue of the rich curved away from the cathedral and began its long run along the river bluffs. It was a patriotic little intersection. An American flag was blowing in the wind over the University Club. A trolley clanged its bell, tripped over Ramsey Street and began jerking its way down the steep hill that dropped off Summit into downtown. Gunderson stood in the last rays of sunshine, behind a park railing, slapping his nightstick against his leg. Victorian mansions lined up behind him. The great dome of the church hovered over his left shoulder. He fingered the Saint Christopher medal around his neck. Murder was on his mind.

Summer was over and the weather was changing faster than St. Paul. The city in front of Gunderson was bathing in sunshine. The city behind him was dark and chilly. Then the sun slipped behind a line of ugly clouds. The wind went from warm to cold. It was almost dark. Pellets of white ice rained down from the sky, rolled over the streets, and melted on the grass. Suddenly it was winter. The huge Norwegian found the change refreshing. He turned his back to the nasty weather and wiped his nose. When that didn't work he plugged a nostril with his thumb and blew snot. A slimy green booger wrapped around the railing, hung there like Nathan Hale and gathered sleet.

The giant cop remembered how much money he'd made selling narcotics to prisoners while stationed at the jail. But now St. Sauver had him confined to desk duty—and, as he'd recently learned, it was a desk with a microphone hidden in it. Did they have something on him? If he was going to get a piece of this new drug trade, he had to move fast. That meant one of three people had to die—Dag Rankin, Roxanne Schultz, or . . .

Nina Clifford breezed out of the University Club, sporting the ugliest blond wig Emil Gunderson had ever seen. She turned her yellow head to the attacking sky, then popped open her umbrella. "What is this stuff?" she asked, crossing to her favorite patrolman.

"Sleet," he told her. "In Norway it's when God can't make up his mind what to dump on you." Ramsey Hill was the only place in town where they could look down at the High Bridge that stretched across the sylvan cliffs; the High Bridge, where so many leaped to their muddy deaths into the Mississippi River. Through the combination of snow and rain they could still see the rooftops of Irvine Park, and the penis-head columns erected over Nina's house. Even in the inclement weather they could see steam rising from the roof of the police station.

"The station house is wired," Gunderson said. "We've been finding mikes for a week."

"It's that St. Sauver and his Purity Squad," Nina insisted.

"No, it's the feds. Town's crawling with 'em. Is the blonde still with you?"

"Yes, she's in my care."

"Time for Blondie to go for a ride. I'll take her across the river and slap her around."

"And if she doesn't tell you any more than the Spook did?"

"I'll dick the bitch till she dies."

Nina Clifford hauled off and socked him, a good right uppercut.

Gunderson was stunned. He looked over his shoulders at traffic, choking in his embarrassment. He thought he heard giggling coming from the statue of Nathan Hale.

"Don't you ever talk like that in the presence of a lady! Where in God's name do you think you are?"

"Sorry, Miss Clifford," he offered as meekly as he could. "Me and the boys are under lots of pressure. Nobody knows what they got on who. Nobody trusts nobody."

"I'll deal with Angel Face in my own way. And when I need the devil's help, I'll call you." The sleet stopped almost as suddenly as it began. The sun slipped back into the sky. The wind subsided and warmed again. Nina Clifford closed her umbrella and looked down the hill. "What are they doing to my city, Emil?"

The seventh-grade class at Mound Park Elementary School gave Grover Mudd a standing ovation. He was surprised, a bit embarrassed, and proud. He made his way to the back of the room and squeezed into a school desk. Grover took out his notebook and pencil. The sun was shining, and the easy October wind that wisped through the open windows whisked him back to his own school days. What he'd give to be innocent and healthy again.

It was Walt Howard's idea—a follow-up story on the boy whose father was machine-gunned to death in Como Park. Jory Ricci's teacher this year was a man named Grahm. Before class he explained to Grover some of the boy's problems—his being older than his classmates, his recalcitrance, his difficulty with reading. But Mr. Grahm was a disciplinarian and he was making progress with Jory Ricci. He confessed he liked the boy.

"Your biographies are due today," Mr. Grahm said with a booming voice that intimidated even Grover. He was a big man. There was no fooling around in his classroom. "Jeffrey Bradhoff, is your paper finished?"

The boy stood at the side of his desk. "Not yet. But I'm working on it."

Jory Ricci was keeping a low profile in the desk behind him.

"What famous person are you writing about?"

"Dan Patch," the Bradhoff boy told his teacher.

"Dan Patch was a horse."

"I know. But he was a famous Minnesota horse."

"Okay, Cowboy, we'll come back to you," Mr. Grahm said. "Did anybody write about a human being?" A multitude of hands shot up in the air. He called on a skinny boy up front. "Who's your paper on, Bobby?"

"Joe Rolette," Bobby Irving told him, jumping to his feet.

"You people were supposed to write about *famous* Minnesotans," Mr. Grahm reminded them.

"He was the most important man in St. Paul's history," Bobby Irving argued.

Mr. Grahm looked skeptical. "This better be good."

Bobby Irving cleared his throat and read with authority. "In 1856 the territory of Minnesota was on the verge of statehood, but the borders for the new state were in hot dispute. The people in southern Minnesota wanted a narrow east–west farming state running from the St. Croix River to the Missouri River, and the new state capital would be the town of St. Peter. St. Paul would then be in the northeastern corner, without much to do. But people from St. Paul up to Canada wanted a north–south state that would include the farming of the south, the forests of the north, the iron of the northeast, and the headship of the Great Lakes. St. Paul, the territorial capital and new state capital, would be a major railroad center smack dab in the middle."

While Bobby Irving was explaining how St. Paul schemed to become the state's capital, Grover watched Jory Ricci whack Jeffrey Bradhoff on the shoulder. The Bradhoff boy pulled an essay from his folder and passed it back. Jory looked over his shoulders and caught Grover's eyes. They both harnessed a laugh.

Bobby Irving continued. "In 1857, with the southern faction in power, the territorial legislature passed a bill moving the capital from St. Paul to St. Peter. But a funny thing happened to the bill on the way to the governor's office for his signature. Enter the famous Joe Rolette. He was a legislator from the north. He stole the bill and hid in an attic and played poker with his cronies until the legislature adjourned, with the bill unsigned. And in 1858, St. Paul, the city founded by a bootlegger named Pig's Eye, and now the poison spot of the nation, a haven for criminals, and a citadel of crime, became the capital of the north–south state of Minnesota." The boy took his seat, grinning ear to ear.

"Famous Minnesotans," Mr. Grahm said, shaking his head. "So far we've heard about a horse and a poker-playing thief."

The classroom filled with laughter. Grover made a note of the teacher's sense of humor.

"Celia," Mr. Grahm called out. "Will you read your paper, please."

Grover had spotted her the minute he walked in the room. They must have been the only family of their kind on the East Side. When she rose to speak the class seemed more uncomfortable than she did. Grover found her difficult to watch and focused on the sky outside as he listened to her sweet voice.

Celia tossed her pigtails over her shoulders. "One of the first group of negroes to reach Minnesota was led by Pastor Robert T. Hickman," she read. "A steamboat found them adrift on the Mississippi River near Jefferson, Missouri, in 1863. There were seventy-six of them—men, women, and children—crowded on a raft.

The steamboat towed them to St. Paul, where they got harassed by Irish dockworkers. Then they were towed up to Fort Snelling. Some of them found work at the fort, but Pastor Hickman led others back to St. Paul, where they settled. In 1866 Pastor Hickman founded the Pilgrim Baptist Church, and in 1870 they built a church of their very own on Cedar Street."

Mr. Grahm thanked her. "Jory Ricci," he called. "Paper done?"

"Yes, sir." Jory stood at the side of his desk.

Grover smiled. There was one in every class. His hair was moppy. His clothes were tattered. He was tough as nails. The kid had pride.

"I'm almost afraid to ask," Mr. Grahm said. "Who did you write about?"

"John Carver."

"Jonathan Carver," Jeffrey Bradhoff mumbled.

"Jonathan Carver," Jory said, correcting himself.

"Did you do this paper by yourself?"

The teacher's question seemed to take the boy by surprise. He gave it a moment's thought, then answered. "No, sir. Jeffrey Bradhoff helped."

"Good boy. Give credit where credit is due. Let's hear what you came up with."

Jory Ricci concentrated on the paper until Grover thought the kid's eyes were going to fall out. He read better than expected.

"Jonathan Carver was born in Massachusetts and served as a British officer in the French and Indian War. Then he became a explorer. In 1766 he came up the Mississippi River to St. Paul and found Carver's Cave. He held a council there with the Indians. Carver kept a diary and later wrote a famous book about his travels. It was the first book about Minnesota by a English writer. In his book he wrote down about the cave in St. Paul. He said, 'It is a remarkable cave of an amazing depth. Indians call it "Dwelling of the Great Spirit." The entrance into it is about ten feet wide, the height of it, five feet. The arch within is near twenty feet high and about thirty feet broad. About twenty feet from the entrance begins a lake, the water of which is clear, and extends an unsearchable distance.' Carver says, 'I threw a small pebble. I could hear that it fell into the water and caused an astonishing noise that reverberated through all those gloomy regions.' Carver says, 'I found in the cave many Indian . . .' " Jory stopped, puzzled. He held the paper in front of Jeffrey Bradhoff. "What's that word?"

"Hieroglyphics. Means scribbling on the walls."

"Like in our lavatories?" A round of giggling broke the reading. Jory stuck his nose back in the paper. "Indian scribbling 'which appeared very ancient. They were cut in a rude manner upon the inside of the walls. The floor of the cave consists of the finest, white sand I have ever seen. The cave is only accessible by ascending a narrow passage that lies near the brink of the river.' Jonathan Carver's cave was destroyed to build railroad tracks," Jory Ricci said summing up, "but his book about our Minnesota long ago will live forever."

"The finest, white sand I have ever seen."

Grover Mudd went cold. The railroad tracks. The Kendrigan twins. St. Sauver and his unsolved sand. But, if the cave is gone . . .

Gil St. Sauver and Steff Koslowski waited in the mayor's office on the third floor of City Hall. The view out the window was spectacular. The autumn rains had turned the bluffs over the river lush green again. In the theater of seasons the leaves on the trees were opening the closing act.

"What are you going to tell the mayor when he comes in?" Steff asked.

St. Sauver turned away from the window. "That our police department reeks with corruption. That everything the goddamn newspapers have been saying is true.

I'll ask him to call a second grand jury as soon as we're ready. Have you got everything out of the station house?"

"We cleared the last of it out yesterday. They know we're on to them."

"Don't worry about it. Those bums aren't going anywhere. Not yet, anyway. How much longer?"

Steff was seated in front of the mayor's desk. "We've got over four hundred phonographic records," he said. "That works out to more than three thousand typewritten pages. It's going to take us another week to organize it all. As soon as that's complete we can start feeding it to the *Frontier News*. Brace yourself then, because it's all coming down."

"What's the final toll?" the commissioner asked.

The G-man peeled open his thick notebook and rattled it off. "One police chief, four ex–police chiefs, one son of an ex–police chief, three inspectors of detectives, two detective lieutenants, seven detectives, and three patrolmen working as detectives." Steff Koslowski shook his head in disbelief. "Your police department has more ranks than our combined armed forces."

"That's going to change. What else?"

Steff flipped the pages as he talked. "Just on St. Peter Street and Wabasha Street alone there are no less than twenty-seven 'hotels,' also known as bawdyhouses. Twelve 'cigar stores,' 'barbershops,' and 'sundries shops,' also known as numbers rackets. And last, but not least, eleven 'nightclubs' and 'strip joints,' also known as gambling casinos. You'll also find several dozen of your good citizens are walking around town with police courtesy cards, which is a euphemism for criminal I.D. cards that offer immunity from arrest."

"And the dope?"

"We've got more than enough to bring Dag Rankin in."

"But no idea where the dope is?"

"No, nothing," Steff told him.

"Let's hold off on Rankin."

"Did you mean that stuff about busting Grover Mudd?"

St. Sauver paced the office. "No, of course not. But I'm bringing that old lady down and God help anybody that gets in my way."

"She's clean as far as the recordings go."

"That figures," said the commissioner with frustration.

"I heard about what happened to your father. This is going to mean a lot to your family."

"It's going to mean a lot to the whole city. The mayor is proposing a new public safety building. I've got those new squad cars ordered, each equipped with powerful radios. Be a whole new broadcasting system. New, modern weapons too, and a police training school. All we need is the funding, and those recordings of yours are going to get it for us."

"Our prestige has never been higher," said Steff proudly. "J. Edgar Hoover is getting almost limitless funding. We'll be opening permanent offices in nine more cities, including St. Paul."

St. Sauver let loose an ironic chuckle. "I guess we've earned it."

"I don't think you'll be needing us anymore."

"What about you, Steff?"

"My transfer came through. Chicago. I'm going home."

"This wiretapping operation of yours is going to change police work, isn't it?"

"Yes. I'm sure there will be new methods, and new laws to deal with them. The potential for abuse is great."

Gil St. Sauver strolled back to the window. The fact that he had helped usher in a new era in crime fighting pleased him. The afternoon sun was warm. He followed the skyline over to the bluffs of the East Side, where he could see two tiny figures scaling the cliffs below

Indian Mound Park. Kids, the commissioner thought, forever playing along the tracks, forever climbing the cliffs. And just for a moment he was back on homicide and troubled by one of the few incomplete marks on his record. The grisly, unsolved murders of the Kendrigan twins.

———————

Jory Ricci led Grover Mudd down the cliff to the railroad tracks. Grover collapsed at the bottom. He rested against the sandstone and cleared his throat. The sun reflected off the river.

"Are you sick?" Jory asked.

Grover smiled up at the boy, the picture of health. "No. I just didn't think it would be this tough getting down here."

"Didn't you ever play in the caves when you were a kid?"

"Yes, but upriver more. This wasn't our territory."

The boy looked toward the water. "This is where we have to watch out for Old Man Fabio."

"Who's that?" Grover asked, getting to his feet.

"The harbor patrolman. He cruises up and down the river in his boat looking for bodies in the water and kids in the caves."

"We'll show him our press pass. We'll be okay."

The boy stepped back and pointed up the bluff. "There it is. See that shack?"

It was up a small hill. More climbing. "It doesn't look like a cave at all," Grover said. "More like a shelf under the rock."

"It goes back farther. Looks like someone's living there."

A sandy path ran along the cliff. Two men of doubtful character were perched on a bench out front, a matched pair who abruptly ended their conversation and watched warily as Grover and Jory climbed toward them. They wore dirty suits with no ties. Their shoes had walked a thousand miles. One was carving up an apple with a hunting knife while the other kept his shadowy face to the ground like a guilty dog.

"Is this Carver's Cave?" Grover asked out of breath.

"Yeah," the bum with the apple answered, "but Carver ain't lived here in a long time." His friend spit out a snickering laugh.

It was a wood shack nailed together with slats. The address above the door was 1934. Stovepiping ran out the tar-paper roof and bent up the cliff. Nearby, on a pile of odd-size boards, was a coffee pot. Alongside were the cold ashes of a campfire, and a roasting pot.

"We're looking for the entrance to the main cavern," Grover informed them, brushing sand from his hands.

"Caved in."

"Mind if we look?"

"This is my home, not a tourist attraction."

"This is public property," Jory snarled.

The bum squeezed his knife and gave the boy a killer's eye. He looked up at Grover. "You a flatfoot?"

"No. I'm a reporter working on a story."

"Will you put my name in the paper?"

"Sure. What's your name?"

"Hoover," the bum said. "Herbert Hoover."

Grover and Jory walked to the back of the cave. A pool of clear water was carved into the rock floor and was fed by a stream trickling out the foot of the wall. Stone stairs wound down to the pool's bottom.

"The cave is behind that wall, Grover. The water comes out of the big lake inside."

"Excuse the pun, but that wall is solid as a rock."

"So?"

"So it doesn't look like a cave-in. Nothing around here looks like a cave-in." Grover stooped down and picked up a handful of sand. He squeezed it between his fingers. It was soggy and coarse. He showed it to Jory. "You're a kid. In your expert opinion is there anything special about this sand?"

"Nope. Sand is sand."

"Hate to cold-water you, kid, but I've been told different."

"You mean like that white sand Carver wrote about?"

"That's what we're looking for."

"It's inside the cave."

"So how do we get in?"

"Must be a back door."

They moved back to the shack, out of the damp shade and into the warm sun. Grover noticed a stack of newspapers beside a stained pot. His newspaper. He tried to start an amiable conversation. "I see you men read the *Frontier News.*"

"Don't matter to us what we wipe with."

Grover Mudd shook his head. "I know this is a stupid question, but is there any other way to get inside that cave?"

The talkative bum spit. "Stupid question."

The silent bum mumbled his first words. "We should have been reporters, Herbert." They both laughed.

"Do boys ever come around here playing?" Grover asked.

The bum with the knife looked at Jory long and hard. He cut a slice of his apple and poked it in his mouth. "Yeah," he answered, "they do. But if we catch 'em, we eat 'em."

Grover and Jory started down the path to the tracks. "Does it bother you that those bums wipe their butts with your newspaper?"

"You should be a reporter, kid. Your questions go right to the gut. Let me see that article again."

Jory fished the crumpled paper out of his pocket. "Jeffrey Bradhoff copied it from the one at the Historical Society." He handed it to Grover.

JONATHAN CARVER AND THE ST. PAUL CAVE
by Armand Smith

"This article was written twenty years ago," Grover told the boy.

"So? The facts haven't changed."

"You're right, they haven't. I'll check with the Historical Society and see if Mr. Smith is still around."

Roxanne Schultz was still around, but for her the future was in California. St. Paul's Union Depot was bustling. The big iron clocks were ticking off her final days in the city. Never in her life had she felt so optimistic, so free.

"When do you leave?" Nina Clifford asked.

"Next week," Roxanne told her, tucking the ticket to Los Angeles into her purse. "I have a few loose ends to tie up."

They made their way down the long marble hall toward the exit.

"When you got to that ticket window, Angel Face, I thought for sure you'd catch the first train out of here. I can't accept the thought of losing you." The old lady was tired. "Can we sit for a minute?" she asked.

Roxanne helped Nina onto a wood bench and they watched the people come and go.

"Many of my girls I found at the train depot," said the madam, reminiscing. "Oh, not this depot, but the old one. It was next door. A massive Victorian structure. Beautiful piece of architecture. I'd go down there and they would be sitting on a bench, much like this one, with that starving look in their eyes. And I would take them home and I would feed them. So many girls I helped through the years. Yes, I remember the old Union Depot. I remember the great debates at the old State Capitol. And the old City Hall. I even remember soldiers at the old fort. I used to have military specials at the house."

"All you can eat?" Roxanne asked.

Nina laughed. "I'll miss you, Angel Face."

Roxanne sighed. "I won't miss St. Paul."

"There are worse places in the world."

"Name one."

"Minneapolis."

Now it was Roxanne's turn to laugh. A colored family strolled by and she remembered something she wanted to ask Nina. "What happened to the Spook?"

"He quit," Nina said, a bit miffed. "I haven't seen him in weeks. Why do you ask?"

"I saw him up on St. Peter Street. He looked like he'd been run over by a train."

"And what of Grover Mudd?" Nina asked, quickly changing the subject.

Roxanne gazed into the sky lights. The sun was shining through. No more winters, she thought. "A Grover Mudd is no different than a Dag Rankin."

"You shouldn't hate him."

"I don't hate him. I all but suggested he write the piece. He freed me. I can see that now. I just keep thinking that a man who bathes in that much self-righteous water must get awful lonely. I can't help but feel sorry for the son of a bitch." With train tickets in her purse and dreams of Hollywood flickering in her head, the gangster's moll helped St. Paul's golden-aged whore to her feet.

"I'm glad you'll be here another week, Angel Face. We've so much to talk about."

Outside, Roxanne hailed a taxi.

Nina climbed in the backseat and slid over to the window. A squad car was parked across the street, and behind the wheel sat big Emil Gunderson. Nina Clifford flashed him a smile.

"You have profaned the Dwelling of the Great Spirit. His ill shade will follow you the rest of your life. Or so goes the Indian legend."

"You've been in Carver's Cave?" Grover asked.

Armand Smith wheeled his chair around. "When I was a boy it was the old swimming hole. You'll find my initials in there along with the others. Should be a year next to it, but I can't tell you what year that would be."

"They say it caved in when they blasted for the railroad."

"Oh, hogwash. If that hole ever crumbled half the East Side would end up in the river. Carver's Cave still exists in its entirety."

"You're sure of that?"

"I was the county surveyor of Ramsey County. Youngest they ever had. Proud of that. I made the survey for the Burlington Road when they cut down part of the bluff for their right of way in 1885. Was it fifty years ago? I've still got the records." Mr. Smith lifted a box filled with papers from the dresser and plopped it on the bed.

Grover looked around this home for the aged. It was a room much like his own, maybe smaller. "Is there sand in the cave?"

"Oh, yes," the old man said, his crinkled hands fingering through the papers. "Prettiest white beach you'd ever want to see. There were rocks of white sandstone, so pure I'd bring them home to my mother. She swore they were better than Old Dutch Cleanser."

"I was down there the other day," Grover told him. "Behind a hobo shack is a small pond from a stream flowing out of the rock. But the rock around it is solid, not stacked or crushed. It's hard to believe it was ever an entrance."

Mr. Smith stopped. He removed his glasses and pointed them at Grover with the grin of a sage. "And this small pond is perfectly rounded, with circular stone steps leading to its depth, like some kind of Greek swimming pool?"

"That's the cave."

"Not Carver's Cave. You were in Dayton's Cave."

"Dayton's Cave?"

The retired county worker nodded his head. "Everybody makes that mistake." He put his glasses on and went back to his digging. "For years Dayton's Cave was used as a vegetable cellar, then as a bottling vault for ale and ginger pop. Carver's Cave is downriver more. It's a shame. One of the great historical finds in this state's history, and nobody even knows where it's at."

"I'm impressed," Grover said. And he was. For a man in his eighties the old surveyor seemed sharp as a telescope and as accurate as a compass.

"I read your column in the paper, Grover. I don't always like what you write, but I read it."

"I appreciate that."

"Your days are numbered, huh?"

"You mean the paper?"

"Of course. What did you think I meant?"

"Yes, our days are numbered."

"Got it." Armand Smith fished a tattered map out of the box and wheeled his chair back around. "Today the best way to get to the cave would be to take the Rondo–Maria trolley eastbound. Hop off at Maria Avenue and Plum Street and walk to the right two blocks. Then down the bluff you go to the tracks." He shared the map with Grover. "There's a spot right between the rails. You may have to dig some dirt away. Should be an old stone marker. Now you run your line from the stone to the bluff. Burlington cut back twenty-two feet, destroying the natural entrance. So your marking should land between two trees up the bluff." He tapped the map with an arthritic finger. "That's where the cave is."

"How big is this cave?"

"Hard to say. Could be miles. We didn't have the powerful lights you have today. Did our exploring with torches. There's no telling how many caverns are in there, but it's a natural warehouse. Great for storing things. Over the years beer was stored in there, butter, cheese, even wine. If Prohibition weren't over it would be a natural for bootleggers, being right there by the tracks. If you find it, are you going in?"

"If it can be found."

"What I'd give to come with you."

"I wish I could take you with me, Mr. Smith. You're probably the only man left in this world who knows where the damn thing is."

"Yes, sir, maybe so. Me and the Spook."

"Who?"

"Big colored preacher, haunts St. Peter Street now. He worked for the county just before I retired. Used to carry my equipment."

Saint Carver

The flashlights cut through the dark, like swords through water. Grover Mudd rested against the soft stone. He spit out a hacking cough and the sound of it tore through Carver's Cave a thousand times, then returned to haunt him. "Switch on the lanterns," he told the boy.

"Are you okay?"

"I'll be fine. Let's get some light in here."

Jory Ricci lifted one of the heavy electric lanterns from the light wooden skiff they had pulled through the entrance tunnel on a long rope. He searched the wet ground for a dry spot and set it down. Then he threw the switch and the capacious dome with its found-again wonder came to light.

The beach was like sugar rolling down to the lake. White sandstone walls rose straight out of the shimmery water to a beautifully arched ceiling twenty feet above their heads. The walls were dry and stained with smoke from explorations of centuries past. The water in the lake was over ten feet deep and so remarkably clear a simple flashlight beam illuminated the bottom. It was too black to see the extreme end, but Grover was told it bent to the left and ran into a second cavern. Beyond that was no-man's-land.

Jory threw a rock into the lake and listened to it reverberate through all those gloomy regions, just like Jonathan Carver said it would. He walked through the sand to the edge of the water. Grover watched him.

Staring into the darkness, the boy put his hands to his mouth and yelled as loud as he could.

"Long live 'Grover's Corner'!"

The cheer for Grover Mudd ripped through the cave at unbelievable decibels. The walls began to rumble. The water rippled. The boy fell on his back. Grover covered his ears as echoes of his own column tried to tear his head off. He scrambled down the beach to shield the boy from the rock that was sure to fall. But no rock fell—only a dusting of sand. "Grover's Corner" did indeed have a long life, but the echo finally bounced off its last stone wall and faded away down the cavern.

Grover put his hand to his chest. This time it was fright that robbed his breath. The boy's face was as white as the sand. Grover gently touched Jory's shoulder. "I think it would be better if we kept our voices down."

The temperature inside the cave was a cool 50°. Armand Smith told Grover it stayed that way winter and summer.

In the stream that flowed from the lake Jory Ricci found a confused crayfish. He picked it up with his fingers and held it in front of his flashlight. It was slightly smaller than most crayfish, and it struggled helplessly in the light. The boy could not believe his eyes. The crayfish had none. "Grover," he called, "come look at this."

"What is it?"

"This crayfish ain't got any eyes."

Grover held his light on it. "I'll be damned."

"There's another one. Hold it up."

Grover picked the small crayfish out of the stream by its tail and examined it. There were no indications of eyes where eyes should be. "I can only guess, if they've lived in here for a million years they wouldn't need eyes."

"Boy," Jory exclaimed, "I'll get an A in science for sure if I bring back one of these."

"Grab a few and put them in the jar along with that sand."

While the boy scooped up crayfish and sand, Grover Mudd explored the edges. A pair of beer barrels were half buried nearby. On the wall were the ancient Indian hieroglyphics Carver wrote about. Not so ancient, but more fascinating to Grover, were the initials of old-timers carved in stone. All the dates were from the nineteenth century. Between the initials and the hiero-glyphics there was etched a serpent three feet long. Whether it was left by the Indians or drawn by the white man, it was clearly a symbol of evil.

The boy spoke up and startled Grover. "You've never really said what we're doing in here, or why you want this sand."

Grover turned. "Do you remember the murder of the Kendrigan twins last year?"

"Sure. They went to our school."

"I think this is where they bought it."

"You think they were killed in this cave?" the boy asked, getting to his feet with the jar.

"I think they were killed right where you're standing. How's that grab you?"

Jory swallowed hard. "Right by the throat," he said. And the boy moved to the edge of the sand as if he'd been standing on a grave. "Who killed them?"

"I'm not sure yet, but I'll bet the answer is in here somewhere."

"Is it true what your paper said this morning? You got the cops dirty?"

"It's true, Jory. You might say we got them on record."

"The *Frontier News* strikes again."

"Our last hurrah."

"What do you mean?"

"We've scooped the *North Star* for the last time. They're closing us down."

"That's too bad," Jory said. "Now we'll only have one newspaper."

Grover was touched. "With a world filled with radios," he told the boy, "I don't know how much longer any newspaper will survive. Today, people want a man with a nice voice reading the news to them. Tomorrow they'll want a pretty girl singing it."

They dragged the skiff to the water. One lantern was placed on the bow, the other at the stern. "Is this thing going to hold us?" Jory asked, not so sure.

"The man at the store said it holds two comfortably, but I didn't have time to test it. Can you swim?"

Jory Ricci rolled his eyes. "I can swim." He stepped gingerly into the boat and wobbled up to the bow where he took a precarious seat.

"Are you in?"

"Yeah," Jory said, "but I'm not very comfortable."

"Take a drink of water."

The boy scooped a handful of the lake into his mouth and moaned with delight. "We should have brought some pop bottles, Grover."

Grover pushed off, eased into the back, and settled in. For a moment they just sat in stony silence, getting their balance and staring into the blackness ahead. Then they dropped paddles into the water. The splashing sound twirled over their heads and took off down the cavern like an announcement. And Grover Mudd and Jory Ricci floated out upon the surface.

"Here we come, Great Spirit."

Roxanne Schultz sat in the crusty parlor of Nina Clifford's house. There, she and the madam perused the newspapers stacked on the ornate coffee table. The dust-stained curtains were drawn tight as if to block out the cleanup campaign. Roxanne held up the front page of the *Frontier News*.

POLICE HIT BY ST. SAUVER IN
"FRONTIER NEWS" INQUIRY
8 Cops with Underworld Ties Fired or Suspended
Scientific Equipment Used to Record Conversations

"It's never been like this, has it?"

Nina Clifford did not answer. St. Paul's day of reckoning had arrived. The jaundiced skin on the face of the ancient whore was turning ash white. Her feeble hands were shaking. Her blue-veiny nose was buried in the *North Star Press*, and her failing eyes tried to capture every letter of the fall.

POLICE GRAFT ON RECORD
St. Sauver Suspends Police Chief
Mayor to Take Scandal Before Grand Jury

In a bitter voice the old lady read off the list of cops she knew so well. "This is atrocious," she said. "I've been supporting that police department for years. These men have families."

"They're crooks, Miss Clifford. They got caught."

"Crooks? What's wrong with earning a little money on the side? If it weren't for the financial imagination of good civil servants this town would have been dead fifty years ago. What does the *Frontier* say?"

Roxanne read her the news. " 'At least eighty percent of the conversations recorded were damaging. Specifically, a startling connection was found between certain police officials and a ring of gamblers conducting a racehorse lottery on a large scale. In addition there is surprising evidence of police ownership of slot machines, a tip-off system on raids, police connection with prostitution, police political activities, police efforts to block proper management of the department, a sensational and illicit connection between police and criminal lawyers, and many other activities. Other dismissals and suspensions will undoubtedly follow.' " Roxanne scanned the rest of the page. "There's no mention of Dag."

"Don't be naïve, girl. He's through. This list of cops reads like Dag Rankin's telephone book. What's important now is the opium. We must get it before St. Sauver. Where does Dag store it?"

"I don't know."

"Angel, this is no time for games. I am not going to die in prison."

"I really do not know. He never talked about it and I never asked."

Nina Clifford tossed off an evil laugh. "Do you really think your little fanny is clean?"

"What are you talking about?"

"By the time St. Sauver is done with your pretty ass they'll lock you up in Shakopee and throw away the key."

"For what?"

"Gambling, dope running, prostitution, and probably an accessory to a murder or two."

Roxanne jumped to her feet in protest. "I never did most of those things."

"You're a gangster's moll," Nina scolded. "In the eyes of the law you did all those things and more."

"I'm going to California."

"You're going to jail, Angel Face, unless you let me help you."

"How?"

"Do you have any idea what that opium is worth?"

There was a pounding on the front door, the kind of knock that sends shivers up the spine. It came again, louder and harder.

Nina Clifford walked to the window and parted the curtain an inch. "It's the police," she said matter-of-factly. "Roxanne, this may be your last chance. Where's the dope?"

"How do you know they're coming for me?"

Nina Clifford walked to the front door and flung it

open. Roxanne listened from the parlor. She heard the old lady say in her sternest voice, "What is it, Officer?"

"Give me the blonde, Grandma, and I'll go on my merry way."

"Don't you dare knock on my door unless you have a warrant."

"Here's the warrant, Grandma. Step aside."

Roxanne heard the boots stomp over the rugs. He took up the whole doorway, a giant in a green tailored uniform, buttons polished, badge shining. But as sparkling as Emil Gunderson appeared, Roxanne sensed he was dirty.

"Let's go for a ride, Blondie."

More hieroglyphics, dates, and initials highlighted the smoke-stained walls along the way. Five feet above the lake were faint waterlines. On the left, about halfway up the cavern, was a small grotto that sucked water from the cave.

"I'll bet that water runs down and out Dayton's Cave," Grover said.

"I didn't think caves got this big."

They came to the end of the cavern and, just as Armand Smith had claimed, the sandstone in the ancient Indian courthouse veered considerably to the left where the passageway narrowed, then opened into a second, much smaller cavern. The ceiling was only ten feet high, the lake more shallow. The walls rolled in and out. Indian hieroglyphics were more sparse and scattered. Signatures scrawled by the old pioneers got left behind.

The dampness was eating Grover's lungs. He tried to muffle his coughing but all those gloomy regions soaked it up and threw it back in his face—toyed with his illness.

"Are you okay, Grover? We can go back."

"I'll be fine. Let's rest here a minute."

"Over there looks like a landing."

It was a natural rock dock. They pulled the skiff alongside and climbed out. Grover collapsed on his back, the stony environs seemingly closing in on him. The boy looked worried.

"It's my cigarettes, kid. I think I'll switch brands."

"Some kids in school say you're a junkie."

Grover laughed a sad laugh that echoed through the cave. "Kids can be awful cruel. No, I'm not a junkie. I'm just a guy with some problems."

"My dad liked you. He thought you had the answer to everything."

"I'll bet I would have liked your dad."

While Grover rested, Jory searched the crevasses with his flashlight. In the corner where the dock met the wall were chunks of wood, burned wood in the shape of a campfire, a fire the boy guessed had gone out centuries ago. Jutting out of the sand he found a long sack made of woven rushes. Jory dragged it back to Grover and sat down, folding his legs beneath him like an Indian brave at council.

"What did you find?" Grover asked.

"Don't know." Jory stuck his light in the sack and was taken aback by what he saw. He dumped the contents in front of him.

Grover came to life, his hair almost on end. "Jesus Christ, those are scalps!"

"Wow," exclaimed Jory, holding one in the air.

"Put that down," Grover ordered.

Among the scalps were three strings of beads, a necklace of buffalo claws, three arrowheads, two arrow shafts, a scalping knife, and a tomahawk. Jory Ricci was fascinated. "This is better than the stuff in museums."

"Put it back in the sack."

"Are you kidding, Grover? If I bring back a scalp I'll get an A for sure."

"If you bring a scalp to school Mr. Grahm will scalp you."

"I never got an A, Grover."

Grover Mudd could see how bad the kid wanted the Indian treasure he'd found. He tried to remember his own childhood and what a find like this would have meant. "Things don't get you an A, Jory. When we get out of here I'll help you write a paper on our adventure. We'll see if that gets you an A."

"I really can't keep it?"

"I just think the Indian stuff should be left here. It was something Mr. Smith said about ill will following us around the rest of our lives if we take things out of here. I've got all the ill will I can handle now."

"The tomahawk. Let me keep the tomahawk."

"Leave the rest of it?"

"Still help me write my paper?"

"It's a deal."

Back on the water, they paddled to the end of the cavern, where the soft white walls were blank.

"Looks like the end of the road, Grover."

"No, there must be more. Everything I've read, everything I've heard says there's more." The skiff hugged the stone and slowly followed its curve until an opening appeared, a huge crack in the rock. "Looks like an alley, doesn't it, kid?"

"Yeah, a dead-end alley."

"Only one way to find out."

"We're going down there?"

"You scared?"

"No."

"Liar."

A nervous Jory chuckled. "Well, if I was the Great Spirit that's where I'd hide."

"My thinking exactly."

The blind passage was only eight feet wide, the ceiling not much higher. The bottom of the lake was coming up fast. After a minute the boat ride was over. The only water was above them now, a small stream trickling over the rocks. They beached the skiff on the sandy shore and scanned the pristine walls. The stone was rough and jagged and filled with nooks and crannies that climbed up and away.

Grover's breathing grew heavy. The cave was closing in on him. The boy helped him over the rocks to a resting spot. "Switch off those lanterns," he told Jory. "We're losing power."

"We should start back, Grover. We got the sand and the crayfish. We know about the scalps, and I got the tomahawk."

"Not yet. I'm sure there's more," Grover said, wrestling his breathing under control.

"No, Grover. I think this is the end."

Grover turned his light on the tumbling stream. "Then where is that water coming from?"

The two spelunkers let their flashlights do the climbing over the subterranean cliffs.

"That corner up there," Grover said, pointing. "I want you to crawl up there and have a look. Then we'll start back."

Grover rested his aching bones. His head was congesting. The hot coals in his chest were beginning to stir. In the beam of light he watched the boy scale the rock with the simple joy of childhood. Jory stumbled.

"Are you all right?"

The boy was up and climbing again. "There's a big hole up here, Grover. Looks like a tunnel."

"Big enough to crawl through?"

"Yeah, real big."

Grover fought to his feet and made his way up the cliff. He shined light down the hole. "I'm going in." The thought of crawling on his belly through another tunnel was no more appealing than crawling through the entrance had been. The ache in his back warned him he'd been this way before. The ex-marine felt old and feeble and couldn't remember the last time he had been so exhausted.

"Do you want me to do it?" Jory asked.

"Stay here and keep your ears open."

"We should have brought a gun."

The path through the blackness was smooth and void of obstacles. Grover stopped once to shake off the fear. After twenty feet the inky sky opened up.

"You there, Grover?" the boy called from behind.

"It's another cavern," Grover answered. "Push one of the lanterns through when you come."

A minute later Grover pulled Jory out of the tunnel.

The boy tucked the tomahawk under his shirt and switched on the lantern. The most incredible cavern of all lit up like an ice castle at the winter carnival. It was a long winding affair, with a ceiling fifty feet high. The roots of trees from the cliff above lined the top. Water dripped down the outer walls like an aquatic symphony. A tumbling brook ran along the floor. But the most remarkable feature was the multicolored sand, striking golds and browns running through radiant reds and sparkling shades of white.

"Oh, Fuzzy," Grover whispered, "if I'd known, I would have buried you in here."

The cliffs were like stairs and Grover and Jory hopped down to the floor and made their way along the flowing water, which was clear as glass.

For the moment Grover forgot every ache and pain in his body. The wonder of it all made him boyish again.

They scaled rock formations around a bend until the terrain flattened out and widened.

"Look over there, Grover."

Wood boxes. They were stacked neatly on a rock platform and covered with a yellow canvas. The tarp had a musty military smell. Grover threw it aside and found chests of mango wood, five high. He ran the light over his head. Then he returned his attention to the crates. "Have you ever heard of the St. Paul Fruit Company?"

"No," Jory answered.

"Me neither. Let's see what kind of fruit they sell." Grover forced open the lid and knew the smell in an instant. They were shaped like grapefruits and smothered in green paper. He took one in his hand like a crystal ball and tossed away the wrapping. "Looks like the St. Paul Fruit Company is in the poppy business," he said, cracking open the hard skin.

"What is it, Grover?"

"Nightmares, kid. Spectacular nightmares."

"It's that stuff you wrote about, isn't it? Opium."

Before Grover could give the boy an answer, a roaring, hollow cackle shot through the cavern like a sick hyena and shook the walls to the breaking point. Grover dropped the booty and drew away. The boy grabbed on to Grover's belt. When the rumbling stopped the unholy laugh came again out of the black regions above, even louder and more petrifying than before. The echo was maddening.

"That must be the Great Spirit," Jory choked in a trembling whisper.

"Great Spirit, my ass," said Grover. "I'd know that voice anywhere."

"The police station is across the street," Roxanne protested.

"Shut up and get in the car," the big cop told her.

She got pushed into the front seat of the rusty squad car. Nina Clifford stood at the curb arguing the arrest, but somehow her voice had a gutless ring to it.

Emil Gunderson dropped the car into first gear and spun off Washington Street and away from the law. "What do you know about telephone conversations?"

"How would I know about those?"

"The *Frontier News* was behind it. That's how."

They swung by the mansion of fabled governor Alexander Ramsey, then climbed West Seventh Street to Smith Avenue, which led across the High Bridge.

"Where are you taking me?" Roxanne demanded.

The lanes were narrow and he slowed, crossing the iron bridge that linked the bluffs. The trees were flecked with colors. The sun was shining. Roxanne saw an eagle sail over a cliff. It seemed much too beautiful a day to be murdered.

"Where's Rankin got the dope?"

The magic words. Now she knew. Nina Clifford had sold her down the river.

Roxanne flung open the door and rolled onto the pavement. The squad car squealed to a halt. She got to her feet and dodged an oncoming car as she crossed to the sidewalk side of the bridge and started running back toward the city. But she didn't run far.

Gunderson slammed her into the wrought-iron railing that ran along the walk. He had comic-book strength, and once again Roxanne Schultz was helpless in the wanton arms of a man. First he pushed her head down and she saw the dark river running fast and mean under the bridge. Then he jerked her face skyward, just in time for her to see the bright sun slip behind a cloud. He lifted her by the neck. Her feet were off the ground. She was being strangled. A passing car sounded its horn. The big cop eased up and her feet hit the sidewalk. It was all the time she needed. She poured every ounce of strength she had left into her leg and brought her knee into his groin. He released her in an instant and doubled over in agony. Roxanne fell. She looked up to see him staggering down the sidewalk, one hand on the railing, one hand on his crotch, his mouth muttering every filthy word imaginable. She pulled herself up and searched the St. Paul skyline. There was nowhere to run. She was furious. The crippled patrolman was straightening himself, leaning out over the water. Roxanne charged him, and just as he turned and looked into her eyes she planted both her hands on his chest.

Gunderson's own weight carried him up and over the railing. His giant fist made one desperate grab at the wrought iron. But his muscular grip wasn't enough to support the rest of his hulk and, with an ear-piercing scream, he made the big drop to the water below and, with a whacking splash, disappeared beneath the murky Mississippi.

Roxanne collapsed on the sidewalk. Cars stopped at the curb. Sirens grew in the distance. On the tracks that followed the river under the High Bridge she saw a train chugging west. She couldn't stop the tears.

The crowd around her was asking senseless questions. The sirens screeched to a stop. Police boots surrounded her.

"Get her on her feet."

"Say, Commissioner, this is Rankin's moll," a cop said, hoisting her up.

"I thought she looked familiar." The commissioner stuck a finger under her chin and lifted her pretty eyes to his face. "Was that my old friend Gunderson I just saw fall in the drink?"

"He was trying to kill me," she cried.

"Well, Blondie, now it's your turn to swim. Up the river. Book her."

Roxanne Schultz was taken away.

The crowd broke up. Traffic moved across the tall span once again. The last of the squad cars pulled out. But one man stayed behind.

Just a couple more nails in the coffin, he thought, a couple more nails. Out of a sense of duty Gil St. Sauver peered hopelessly at the muddy water far below. "Damn shame. I wanted to jail him."

The commissioner of public safety folded his hands behind his back and looked out over his city. The sun escaped the clouds. A sweet autumn wind hummed through the bluffs. The air had never smelled better. The visible currents in the mighty river that stretched before him were shaped like lightning; they broke downstream, where the cliffs climbed to Mound Park and children played among the Indian legends.

————————

When the sacrilegious laughter died and the last echo got lost in a faraway cavern, Grover Mudd and Jory Ricci trained their lights on the dark regions above. On a sandstone cliff that hung over them like a balcony they spotted two evil faces. One white. One black.

"There's your charred spirits, Jory. Dag Rankin and the Big Holy Spook."

"You're very good, Mudd," Rankin said from his perch. "But we heard you coming. Hell, Jonathan Carver probably heard you coming."

"I always knew you'd crawled out of a hole, Rankin."

The cliff wound down like a spiral staircase, and Dag Rankin worked his way to the floor of the cave, gun in hand, the Spook behind him. "Great little hiding place, huh, Mudd? The Spook here found it. How in the devil's name you got in here is beyond me. Hand over the lights."

They surrendered their flashlights. Grover kept the boy behind him. "Why here?"

"Besides the fact that nobody knows it exists," Rankin explained, "it's the perfect distribution spot. Rail. River. An airfield across the way. Chicago to the east, St. Louis to the south. Bootlegging was never so easy. I can carry this stuff in my pocket." He lifted a ball of opium from the open crate and tossed it in the air like a baseball. "I hear you like this stuff, Mudd. Roxanne loves it. Quite a dish, isn't she?"

"And the two kids that came in here last year?" Grover wanted to know.

Rankin leaned in to him and lowered his voice to a whisper. "The Spook got them. I wasn't here. What can I say? I was sick about it for hours."

"You can crawl out of this hole one more time,"

Grover warned him, "but outside you'll find some changes."

"Yeah. Neat little trick with the telephones. Was that your idea, or the feds'? No matter, my lawyers will chew it to bits. Loudmouth saints like you come and go, Mudd, but gangsters like me and the Spook will always be around."

"Gangsters?" Grover laughed. "I heard there ain't a pair of balls between the two of you."

The game was over. "Step aside, kid," Rankin ordered.

"Go wait over there, Jory." Grover pushed the boy away.

Rankin backed off, pointing the gun at Grover's chest. "I would," he said, "but I promised the Spook first dibs. You see, he reads your column every day."

"Sinner!" cried the preacher.

Grover grabbed a handful of the white sand and threw it in his big black face. It got in the Spook's eyes and gave Grover enough time to throw a cross-body block and knock him to the ground. But it was the only play the old Golden Gopher had left in him. His lungs collapsed, his throat constricted; he got to his knees, totally exhausted.

The Spook helped him to his feet by the scruff of the neck. "Sinner! The time has come!" He chopped Grover Mudd across the head and sent him sprawling to the stone.

Grover wanted to spit up, but he didn't have the strength. He swallowed his blood and prayed for the boy. The blind fear that ached in his back was gone, left in the cave to swim with the sightless crayfish. Now it was only helplessness he felt, what he had been running scared from since the end of the war. A short lifetime spent fighting for the right, and in the end he couldn't muster enough will to stand up for a child. The time had come. Grover Mudd resigned himself to his pathetic fate. Another blow crossed his head. And then another.

"He's a sick man. Leave him alone," Jory cried, tearing at Rankin's arm.

"Back off, chubs." Dag Rankin brought the butt of the gun across the boy's face and sent him spinning to the ground behind him. "He's sick all right. And I always thought heroes went down fighting." The gangster watched with glee as the giant preacher beat on the crumpled newspaperman with his fists. A corner of Rankin's mouth curved upward. He broke into a sick grin. And Dag Rankin was smiling his last wicked smile when the tomahawk split his skull open just behind the ear. The gun fired into the stone as it dropped from his hand. Cannon fire roared through Carver's Cave. Rankin clasped the back of his neck. He turned to the scrappy boy, his mouth wide and long, and in delayed shock the impotent gangster vented a shivering shriek of death that was deafening. His final earsplitting scream ran rampant, and he stumbled down the rock and landed in the brook.

The earth shook beneath the boy's feet. Sand snowed from the ceiling. The wall was losing its grip. The balcony cliff over his head was crumbling. Jory jumped for safety.

The Big Holy Spook stepped back and looked heavenward. With hate in his heart, Rankin's deathly wail ringing in his ears, and the words of God spewing from his mouth, he extended his arms to the Lord above and caught the brunt of the cliff as it toppled over and brought with it a small mountain of pretty sand. The echo of the fall was hellish.

When all was saintly silent again Jory Ricci got to his feet and wiped the sand from his face. The face of the cave had changed. Dag Rankin was dead, his sinister blood defiling the icy clear stream that snaked through the ghostly dwelling. The Great Spirit had claimed another scalp.

The crates of opium were undisturbed, stacked like some great offering to the Junkie God.

Where the cliff had fallen only one black hand was protruding from the stones—huge, fat, and lifeless.

"Grover!" the boy called in fear. "Grover Mudd?"

The boy dove into the colored sand with both hands, tears coating his eyes. Jory dug like a starving dog, but the sand was so fine and there was so much of it, it filled the holes he unearthed in an instant. He looked around for some kind of shovel. Precious seconds were ticking by. The lantern was dying. The flashlights were buried. And, just when he thought all hope was flickering out, a nasty cough cut through the crush, and a rainbow of sand spit in the air.

Show me a hero and I will write you a tragedy.

— F. Scott Fitzgerald

Saint Epilogue

In the autumn the weeds die first. At the house on Washington, at the foot of Steep Street, there was a timid knock on the door. The madam flicked on the porch light and answered.

"I have some newspapers I couldn't sell today. Would you like to buy them, Miss Clifford?"

"How many?" she asked the paperboy, her voice filled with melancholy.

"Three. Two *North Star*s and a *Frontier News*. It's the last copy of the *Frontier*. Gonna be a collector's item."

She handed the boy a dime. "Will you be trick-or-treating tomorrow?"

"Yes, ma'am, I will."

"Behave yourself, and be careful."

"I will, Miss Clifford. Thank you."

Nina Clifford climbed the staircase with a heart so heavy she had to clutch it with one hand. Her arthritis pained her. Tears stained her face. On the top stair she glanced down at the house she loved, and remembered when the rugs were plush and the mahogany shined. She could hear mirth and merriment waltzing below. She saw her girls climbing the stairs with riches on their arms.

Echoes of lovemaking rang in her ears as she shuffled along the dark hallway to the old Presidential Suite. A President of the United States had slept here. Or was that a lie she'd told so often that in her mind it became the truth?

She parted the curtain with the back of her hand and peeked out at the night. The moonlight was fading. Clouds were rolling in. A raindrop hit the window and streaked the glass. The morgue looked deathly, but across the way the police station was full of life. Out front, sparkling white squad cars lined the curb down Steep Street. A newspaper page blew down Washington Street and wrapped itself around the lamppost. Winter was in the wind. The trees along the river bluffs were shedding their leaves. Tugs were pushing downstream. The lights of a train disappeared around Pig's Eye Bend and a whistle bade adieu.

It was here a year ago, she remembered, she had danced to *Swan Lake*. Now it was only her head that was spinning. Spinning with confusion. News was hard to come by. Dag Rankin was dead. The carcass of Emil Gunderson washed ashore at the slaughterhouses in South St. Paul. Jap Gleckman had skipped town, his Pickwick Café closed, his girls held for questioning. Dutch Otto was looking for a new lawyer. His old lawyer was in jail. The Royal Cigar Store was boarded up, and uniformed police stood guard at the door. Hotels along St. Peter Street were being raided nightly. The last of her police contacts was suspended. Nobody returned her calls. Had they tapped her wires, too? Had modern science no scruples? Other madams were being threatened. "Shut your mouths or blow town," they were warned.

And what of Angel Face, still being held up the street at County Jail? What would she tell them to save her pretty skin?

And why was there no mention of the dope, the fruits of the poppy, her livelihood, her social security?

A man came out the front door of the police station and brushed some leaves from the hood of a squad car. He was a sturdy man with a haughty gait and he walked down the hill in her direction. Evening shivers overtook her. He stopped at the corner and gazed up at her window. She stepped back an inch. He crossed the street and stood under the street lamp in front of her house. It was Commissioner St. Sauver. He picked up the waste paper, wadded it like a snowball, and stuffed it in his coat pocket. Then St. Paul's number-one cop leaned against the lamppost, lit a cigarette, and straightened his tie.

She hated him. But for the first time in her life, she was powerless. So many sanctimonious bastards had fallen before him that the spark of his cigarette under his felt hat couldn't match the spark in his eyes.

The commissioner reached into his coat and drew a prize flower, a round package wrapped in green paper, about the size of a grapefruit. He held it up to the light. Then he took the cigarette from his mouth and blew a badge of smoke at her window.

More raindrops streaked the glass. Nina Clifford dropped her hand and let the curtain fall.

Farewell, ballerina.

It was Halloween day, precursor to All Saints' Day. Grover Mudd was forty years old. The afternoon sun streamed through the windshield, and he rolled his window down to enjoy the weather. Football weather. For the moment, in spite of his suffering, he was young again, and he and Scott Fitzgerald were stealing up Summit Avenue in a Model A that didn't belong to them.

The paintings of Chester D. Byron made Grover Mudd a rich man. Rich by his standards, anyway. With cold hard cash he rescued his Studebaker Dictator from his ex-wife. He shared a chunk of his wealth with Jory Ricci, and he sent money to a little boy in St. Louis. He saw a lawyer and drew up a will.

Grover pushed up Ramsey Hill to the University Club

and started down Summit Avenue alone this year, past
the gaudy mansions Fitzgerald had once described as a
museum of American architectural failures. What a day
to be out cruising. It was late autumn in Minnesota—
ten thousand lakes reflecting ten thousand colors. The
trees along the parkway were dazzling and, when
the fiery leaves escaped the branches and floated to the
ground like silent music, Grover believed nothing in
the world could be so resplendent, so tranquil.

The sidewalks along the halls of Saint Thomas College were bustling where famous Summit Avenue came
to an end. Grover swung onto River Drive and followed the woodland along the Mississippi. He slowed,
passing the Hollyhocks Club, and saw a workman
boarding up the windows. Then, less than a mile down
the road, he was forced to stop.

It was a parkside rest overlooking the lush valley
where the Minnesota River joined the Mississippi,
where the two cities parted ways, where a crumbling
fort sat forlorn and forgotten. Grover got out of the
car, staggered over to a retaining wall and coughed his
guts up. He rinsed his mouth at a fountain and, when
his spit was free of blood, he sat on the rocks and waited
for the nausea to pass.

Spread before him on the steep banks was a forest
of the brightest colors imaginable, with church steeples
spiriting out of the trees. In his day Fuzzy would have
captured it all on canvas.

The fall season with its ephemeral beauty always
made Grover sad—the passing of summer, the onslaught of winter—but this year was especially trou-
bling. In the back of his mind was the realization of
summertimes lost and autumns never to come. The fire
inside him was out of control. The sand in his hourglass
was running out. He thought of something he'd read in
the Bible.

*"The harvest is past, the summer is ended, and we are
not saved."*

Across the muddy water lay the decaying buildings of Colonel Josiah Snelling's original stone fort. A new highway ran behind it. The Round Tower, once the defensive strongpoint, with walls six feet thick, was only a collection of vine-coated rocks supporting a pole that hadn't hoisted a flag since the armistice. Swallows nested in the musket slits. Below the north wall a deer chewed at the shrubs until a stone broke away and fell to the water. Grover could not help believing that some-day the old fort would be as lost as Carver's Cave.

"One more thing, Mudd. About the ton of dope we pulled out of the cave? It was all so neatly arranged, meticulously stacked and stored, except for one crate in the middle. A couple pounds were missing. Like they'd been pulled out at random."

"Well, Commissioner, I can only guess. They were probably delivered that day."

"Yeah, that's probably it. It just seemed funny, miss-ing from the middle like that. You don't think the kid took any, do you?"

"Not possible. I was with him the whole time."

"That's right, you were. The entrance to the cave is being plowed over. We appreciated your not printing any details about its location. I suppose kids will go on looking for it."

"I suppose."

"You take care of that cough."

Grover Mudd was back on the road. He followed the railroad tracks that followed the river, returning down-town and up Steep Street to Kellogg Boulevard and into the parking lot that was supposed to be a park. Roxanne Schultz was still in the Ramsey County Jail behind City Hall.

"Is this an interview?" she demanded to know.

"Hardly," Grover said. "I'm out of work."

A tense moment passed. Then the girl from Swede

Hollow surrendered. To Grover it appeared to be a
smile that pained her. The prison garb looked terrible.
Her face was pale. Strands of gilded hair were out of
place. Still, she was as lovely as the autumn day.

"They're dropping everything but the manslaughter
charge," she told him. "If I plead guilty in court tomorrow I'll get three years at Shakopee. With good
behavior I can be out in eighteen months. That's not
such a long time."

Grover could not agree. He stared at her with lovemaking written all over his face.

Roxanne, embarrassed, broke the spell. "So what
does an unemployed reporter do with himself?"

Grover shrugged. "I might write a book about everything that's happened."

"Who'd want to read a book about St. Paul? The
best thing you can do is get out of this weather. Minnesota is for the healthy. When I'm free, I'll be heading
for California."

"California is a place where people go to die."

"You're dying, Grover."

Grover Mudd stood in the sunshine outside City Hall
and waited for the light to change. A church bell was
chiming the hour. He watched traffic work down Wabasha Street and up the hill to the State Capitol. A lily-
white squad car turned onto St. Peter Street and shot
north toward the cathedral. A boy on the corner was
hawking the *North Star Press*.

On October 30, 1934, the last edition of the *Frontier
News* went to press and the heady days of the St. Paul
daily came to an end.

On the night they buried the paper Grover stood,
whiskey in hand, in the doorway of his editor's office.

"I've spoken with my people at the *North Star Press*,"
Walt Howard told him. "We don't have anything for
you right now."

"I wasn't expecting anything."

"I wanted to say your column on Chester Byron was one of the finest I've ever read. Nothing but positive mail."

"All positive? I guess it's time to get out."

"We did something good here, Grover."

The light changed to green, and Grover Mudd crossed the boulevard to the parking lot. Before getting in the car he stole another peek at the aureate bluffs over the river and marveled at the brilliant colors that scaled the sky. Stormy would have said, "It's bea*uuu*tiful!"

Grover tapped his watch. It was losing time. The Indian-summer sun was sinking below the High Bridge. He climbed behind the wheel of his Studebaker and noticed that the view to the east was marred by smoke. Then he remembered. They were burning Swede Hollow.

A wino stumbled by the car and searched the ground for coins. A fate worse than death, Grover thought. At least he would be spared that. But all the cash in the world could not get Roxanne out of jail. Money couldn't douse the flames in his lungs or chase from him the chill gathering in his bones. Money couldn't, but the poppies from the cave could. Grover Mudd tucked a tincture of opium under his tongue and whispered a prayer to a God he'd never had much faith in. Eighteen months. He wanted to live another eighteen months. With a heavenly smile he rested his head and closed his eyes to see how it would be.

It would be in the springtime and everywhere life was starting over again. In the lazy hills above Chief Shakopee's old hunting grounds the apple blossoms were in bloom, and in the valley below, fields of dandelions rolled down to a rejuvenated river that swept away nature's winter debris.

The complex was more like a college campus than a prison. Out front a cleansing wind waved Minnesota's

navy-blue flag at the powder-blue sky, and on that flag
L'Étoile du Nord, the Star of the North, was shining
as proud as the Star of Bethlehem.

He stood at the foot of the stairs in his pressed coat
and his new shoes. His hair was cut and combed. He
shaved that morning. The fresh air stirred by the crisp
breeze settled deep in his chest, then made room for
more of the same.

The prison doors opened. Roxanne stepped to the
top stair. A warm rose kissed her cheeks and a self-
conscious smile crossed her pixie face. The sweet spring
sun colored her hair gold, like the wheat fields that lead
to St. Paul. Her hands were folded in front of her; a
coat draped over her arm. The ivory dress she wore
was frilled with lace. She looked different. Maybe she
had lost the few pounds she wanted to. Perhaps it was
the season. She looked free.

They were happy moments, but uncomfortable in a
romantic sort of way. He saw her in the back of a
courtroom, moving gracefully through a crowd. He saw
her in the editor's office, her gainly legs crossed under
red-and-white flounce, her face flushed by his stare. She
was lying under him, fleshy pink, the warmth of her
naked body pressed against his, holding him tight, putting to rest the fear that ached in the small of his back.

The sensuous memories ran wild.

A gust of wind tousled her hair. The brass doors
slammed closed behind her. Then she was in his arms.
Just like in the movies.

THE END

HISTORICAL NOTES

The following notes are to set the record straight and give credit where credit is due.

The newspaper that launched the front-page cleanup campaign in January of 1934 was called *The St. Paul Daily News*. Ownership of the *Daily News* was transferred to *The St. Paul Dispatch–Pioneer Press* in September of 1933. The *Daily News* ceased publication on April 30, 1938. Some editorials, stories, and announcements that appeared in *The St. Paul Daily News* appear in *Saint Mudd*'s *Frontier News*.

The rediscovery and reexploration of Carver's Cave took place in November of 1913 and were led by John H. Colwell, president of the Mound Park Improvement Association; James Nankivell of the Minnesota Historical Society; and J. D. Armstrong, then county surveyor of Ramsey County. Today a historical marker stands on the bluff above the cave, but the cave itself was long ago sealed, lost, and forgotten. Again.

Nina Clifford died of old age on July 14, 1929. She has been resurrected for *Saint Mudd*. Her infamous house on Washington Street, across from the county morgue and the old police station, was torn down in 1937. A new county morgue was built on the property.

The men who shot it out with John Dillinger and Homer Van Meter at the Lincoln Court Apartments on the same day the first grand jury was handing down its whitewashed results were federal agents Rosser

Knowles and Rufus Coulter, and St. Paul police detective Henry Cummings.

The men who outgunned Homer Van Meter in an alley off University Avenue were St. Paul police chief Frank B. Cullen, former chief Thomas A. Brown, and Detectives Thomas McMahon and Jeff Dittrich.

The man machine-gunned to death in Como Park by fleeing bank robbers was named Oscar Erickson. The man who drove Erickson to a police substation, where he was mistaken for a bank robber and allegedly beaten up, was named Arthur Zachman.

The fictional characters in *Saint Mudd* were inspired by the following people:

Thomas Boyd enlisted in the Marine Corps during World War I at the age of eighteen, emerging with a Croix de Guerre, badly gassed lungs, and numerous wounds from which he never recovered. While engaged as literary editor of *The St. Paul Daily News*, he wrote the critically acclaimed war novel *Through the Wheat*, and became part of a St. Paul literary colony that included F. Scott Fitzgerald and Sinclair Lewis. Thomas Boyd died at the age of thirty-seven.

Howard Kahn was the crusading editor of *The St. Paul Daily News*. He aroused public indignation over St. Paul's crime problem with a series of front-page editorials that demanded reform. For his work he won the national Pulitzer Award for civic achievement. When the *Daily News* ceased publication, Howard Kahn became an associate editor and columnist for *The St. Paul Pioneer Press*.

H. E. Warren was a reform candidate elected commissioner of public safety in 1934. With the backing of the St. Paul newspapers, he launched the cleanup campaign that resulted in a second grand jury and twenty-one indictments.

Gus Barfuss was elected commissioner of public safety in 1936 after serving twenty-five years on the St.

Paul police force. He finished, with a vengeance, the cleanup H. E. Warren started. He held the commissioner's job until 1948. In 1936 the job of police chief was removed from politics in a city election that called for appointment of police chiefs on the basis of merit and set their terms at six years.

Wallace Jamie was the son of Alexander Jamie, head of the famous "Secret Six" who rid Chicago of Al Capone's and other gangs. Trained under his father, Wallace Jamie was convinced by the *St. Paul Daily News* to come to St. Paul. Working with Commissioner Warren and the *Daily News*, he set up an office in the Public Safety Building and, using some of his own inventions, mounted one of the first wiretapping operations. It was these recordings that led to the second grand jury and the twenty-one indictments.

Homer D. Martin was a New York landscape painter who spent his last years living in poverty in St. Paul. When he died of throat cancer he was nearly blind. He was buried at Oakland Cemetery. After his death his formerly unsalable masterpieces became the sensation of the art market. Years later a monument was erected on his grave by people who loved his paintings.

ACKNOWLEDGMENTS

I wrote the first line of *Saint Mudd* in February of 1982. I celebrated the last line on my birthday, March 23, 1986. Special thanks are owed to people who put up with me during that time:

To my sister, Mary Putney, and her husband, Dennis, who took me into their home for four years.

To my friends Curt Petersen and Dianne Purington for their critiques along the way.

To Tino Avaloz, Bonnie Wilson, and Jon Walstrom at the Minnesota Historical Society for their help over the years.

To the Loop Parking Company of Minneapolis for their support, especially Bill Demuth, Jerel Shapiro, and Ed Schultz.

And a special thank-you to author and historian Albert Eisele, Viking Penguin editor Al Silverman, and Washington, D.C., attorney Robert B. Barnett, who made this publication of *Saint Mudd* possible.

S.T.